THE RESISTANCE

Also by Donna Dechen Birdwell

Not Knowing
(2019)
"…an expedition into a magical vision of reality."

EarthCycles, Book One:
Song of All Songs
(2020)
Winner of the SPR Silver Medal
"…an immersive and visceral vision of the future."

EarthCycles, Book Two:
Book of All Time
(2021)

EarthCycles, Book Three:
Beyond the Endless
(2022)

Recall Chronicles

THE RESISTANCE

1
Way of
the Serpent

2
Shadow
of the Hare

Donna Dechen Birdwell

The Resistance: Recall Chronicles 1 & 2
(Incorporating *Way of the Serpent* and *Shadow of the Hare*)

Published by Wide World Home.
8944B Parker Ranch Circle
Austin, TX 78748 USA

donnadechenbirdwell.com

FIRST PRINTING – July 2025.
Way of the Serpent, copyright 2015 by Donna Dechen Birdwell.
Shadow of the Hare, copyright 2016 by Donna Dechen Birdwell.
Both books have been revised and edited for this edition.

Publisher's Note: This is a work of fiction. Names, characters places, and incidents are either the product of the author's imagination or used fictitiously.

Birdwell, Donna Dechen
The Resistance – Recall Chronicles 1 & 2
540 pp.
1. Science Fiction – Fiction 2. American – Fiction
I. Donna Dechen Birdwell II. The Resistance – Recall Chronicles 1 & 2
ISBN: 978-1-7355569-8-7

Library of Congress Control Number: 2025912625

THE RESISTANCE

Way
of the
Serpent

Here's to all the unexpected good fortune that has come my way in this life and in particular to the best of it, namely Brendan and Rebecca.

"She couldn't remember having gone out of her house
that day; she had the feeling that she had made the trip
without a car or a carriage, a trip full of mysterious
shadows, and that she had woken up on a road lined
with trees that smelled like Australian pines where she
had suddenly found herself making nests for birds."

–Silvina Ocampo, "Forgotten Journey" (1937)

Part I
Eternal Youth,
Disrupted

I.

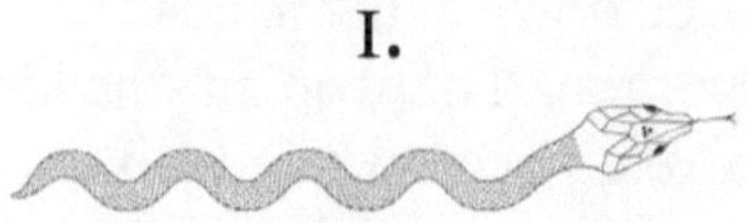

The café was down a couple of side streets, in an area of Dallas Jenda never went to. Without looking at the menu, she ordered a grilled cheese sandwich with fried potatoes and sweet tea. She was halfway through her meal, savoring the anonymity afforded by this out-of-the-way eatery as much as the greasy fare, when she noticed the woman who had turned on her stool at the café's counter to stare.

The woman was old. That in itself was disturbing. Nobody got old anymore, not since Chulel – the drug that prevented aging – had come on the market a hundred years ago. Jenda, at III, was as fresh and vigorous as she had been in 2035 when, at the age of 22, she had received her first annual Chulel treatment. Jenda's grandmother was 165 but appeared no older than she had been when she began taking Chulel in her mid-sixties. What was this old woman doing in Jenda's world?

Jenda turned away, but she could still feel the woman's dark eyes boring into her, probing. Jenda couldn't help herself; she looked again. When the woman saw her looking, she smiled.

"Zujo!" Jenda swore, quickly returning her attention to her unfinished sandwich. It was too late. Taking the look as an invitation, the woman dropped down from her counter stool and shuffled over to Jenda's table.

"You're Jenda Swain," she said, cocking her head to one side and narrowing her eyes. "God, you look the same as you did in high school."

"Excuse me?" Jenda sat up straighter and used her best business voice.

"Of course you don't remember," the woman said, dragging out the chair across from Jenda and sitting down heavily. "Nobody remembers much of anything anymore." She shrugged and looked down at her hands.

Jenda looked, too. The woman's hands were wrinkled, misshapen, and covered in brown and red splotches.

"I remember you, though," the woman continued, looking up into Jenda's face. "My god, you were a firebrand back then. I idolized you and your boyfriend, you know. Such temerity! The things you did..." The woman refused to turn away. "Do you still paint? You always had your mom's gift for art."

"I think you must have made some mistake," Jenda said quietly, fighting to modulate her voice against the tightening in her throat. "You may know my name, but you clearly don't know me. Nothing you are saying makes any sense at all." Jenda felt her cheeks warm as she flashed on an image of herself with an easel and paintbrush. Her last bite of sandwich seemed to have lodged somewhere near the base of her esophagus. "Now, would you please go on your way and leave me alone?" Jenda blinked, shuttering herself away from this intrusive presence.

The woman's face clouded, and she leaned forward, looking Jenda squarely in the eye. "You need to ask more questions." She spoke the words clearly and forcefully. Then she pushed her chair away from the table with a loud scraping noise. As she leaned over to pick up the leather bag she had dropped under the chair, the pendant around her neck clanked on the tabletop. It was an old fashioned timepiece, the kind with a round face with numbers and moving hands. Jenda reflexively reached up to grasp her own necklace, a cluster of plexiform flowers in the latest style from her favorite recyclables boutique. The woman took in a deep breath, as if rising from the chair had taxed her strength. She looked at Jenda again. "You're the one who doesn't know who Jenda Swain is." Her voice was gentle, maybe sad. Then she turned and walked out the front door.

Jenda's impulse to run after the woman and ask her name was unexpected. Holding it in check, she sat rigidly, staring at her cold, greasy food. She swallowed hard, trying to dislodge that last bite of sandwich. Her hands trembled as she finished the last of her dilute, not-so-sweet tea. Looking up and down the street as she exited, she saw no sign of the woman.

Once or twice, Jenda looked back over her shoulder as she made her way back to the main street, back to reality. *What possessed me to go to that café anyway?* she scolded herself, shoving her fists deeper into the pockets of her fashionable jacket.

All afternoon at her desk in the Dallas offices of Your Journal, Jenda's mind paced back and forth across the odd feelings, trying to tamp them down. How did the old woman know Jenda's name? What was that about idolizing her in high school? What boyfriend? Firebrand? Ridiculous. Jenda's personal records with Your Journal clearly indicated that her high school career had been quietly unremarkable. She had been a good enough student with good enough marks who never made trouble. The woman must have gotten Jenda mixed up with someone else. That was it. Old people did that sometimes, didn't they? But Jenda *had* enjoyed painting in high school. And her mother had been a sculptor of some note before the accident.

"Are you okay, Jenda?" It was her office mate, Weldon.

"What?" Jenda started, "No, no, I'm fine," she said. "Maybe something I had at lunch disagreed with me." She gave Weldon a wan smile. It was nearly quitting time.

Jenda's discomfort followed her home. *It's just an attack of cognitive dissonance*, she told herself. There was a pill for that. But when she got home, she didn't take the pill. Instead she poured a glass of wine and pulled up Your Journal on her home screen, accessing her high school years. There wasn't much, but the pictures were all precisely as Jenda remembered them—she had the same golden blond hair, the same flawless fair skin. She stopped for a moment to examine the picture of herself with an easel and paintbrush. Why had she stopped painting? *To make a living*, she reminded herself, *and a contribution.* She had majored in art at Ex University, but her course of study focused on digital design and graphic psychology. With that, she had secured her position at Your Journal. That was ninety years ago.

Jenda loved her job with Your Journal, loved being part of such an important corporate institution. Everybody relied on Your Journal as a secure repository of their personal photos, stories, thoughts and feelings. People interacted with it every day, experiencing pangs of guilt if they failed to respond to the reminders on their digilets. You could also put photos and comments on LifeBook, but those were shared with everyone in your loop. YJ was personal and people often referred to their YJ files as their "exomemories".

Jenda was due for her next sabbatical in a couple of months and she had already booked into a resort in the Republic of California. The social order under Chulel had done away with retirement, moving instead to a system in which every worker received a one-year sabbatical every ten years. Technically, of course, a "sabbatical" should occur every seven years, but the term had a nice feel. Nobody questioned such verbal technicalities.

Jenda pulled up some pictures of the resort, which suddenly struck her as mundane and boring and not somewhere she wanted to spend an entire year of her life. Maybe she should try something different. Maybe she should try painting again. Jenda vaguely recalled a place where her mother had gone a few times, a place that used to be considered something of an artists' colony. Maybe in Mexico. Jenda searched through various mediazones and finally came up with a town in central Mexico called San Miguel de Allende. She wasn't sure that was it, but she decided that was where she would go. She did check to verify that there would be tennis courts. She always said tennis was her favorite activity.

Within a few minutes Jenda had cancelled her reservations for California and made new ones for San Miguel de Allende, Mexico. Then she drafted a memo to her supervisor, asking to begin her sabbatical early. She would lose a few weeks of leave, but she felt an odd exhilaration arising from these rash decisions. It felt good.

2.

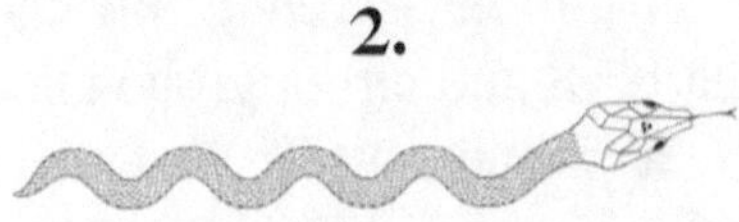

2125 marked the centenary of the entry of the miracle age prophylaxis Chulel into the marketplace. The occasion probably should have been marked by a celebration of some sort, but so few people remembered what life was like before Chulel that it would have seemed rather like commemorating the invention of water or air. So the year would come and go without fanfare.

Two people who did remember life before Chulel were the inventors of the drug, Drs. Max and Emily Feldman, who had lost their only child to Hutchinson-Guilford progeria syndrome (HGPS) back in 1977. "Progeria" referred to a set of diseases that caused premature aging due to a genetic anomaly; HGPS had been its most common (though still extremely rare) form.

The Feldmans had delayed "having a family" as people used to say, until after they both completed medical school. Following their daughter's death, they had devoted their careers to finding a cure for progeria. It had been a long haul. The first significant advance had come from another lab, which announced a promising avenue of research in 2014. Pharmakon Corporation, and specifically the Drs. Feldman, built on this and in 2017 published preliminary results of a drug they named according to its active chemical components. Nobody now remembers that name.

The drug was ready for human trials by early 2018, and a dozen or so families from around the world came forward, traveling to the Pharmakon headquarters in Atlanta to let the Feldmans try out the drug on their afflicted sons and daughters, who had been diagnosed with either HGPS or one of the other, even rarer, forms of progeria.

What nobody knew was that Max Feldman was also testing the drug on himself. Even Emily didn't know. Max Feldman was already 78 and although he checked out healthy enough, he had a family history of heart disease and atherosclerosis and there were certain aspects of the lab tests on the new drug as well as its effects on a small test group of bonobos that had irresistibly piqued his curiosity.

By the time the tests on human progeria patients were declared unequivocally successful in 2021, the people closest to him were beginning to notice something about Max. One of those people was the Feldmans' lab assistant, Winslow Morris.

In the third month of the trials, Winslow noted that there seemed to be a couple of vials of the drug missing. He questioned Dr. Max about it, and was told it must be a mistake. When Winslow re-counted the next day against the numbers in the computer, he found no discrepancy. It happened again a couple of months later and this time Winslow kept his observation to himself. Again, the numbers mysteriously rectified themselves within a matter of hours. Then one day Winslow thought he saw Dr. Max slipping a vial of the medicine into the pocket of his lab coat. That's when it clicked. Winslow started observing Dr. Max more closely. On the day before the results of the progeria field tests were formally announced, Winslow missed work. And then he disappeared altogether.

Winslow hadn't needed to steal any of the medicine. He knew how to make it. His destination was China and within six months a new drug started showing up on the streets. It was called "Fontana" and it was touted as the "fountain of youth". It was outrageously expensive and sold mainly to customer lists Winslow compiled by irrupting into databases of dermatologists specializing in cosmetic surgery. He was an instant millionaire.

Winslow did not know that Dr. Feldman had altered the dosage for his own use. Fontana consumers were overdosing, and before the drug had been on the street for a full year, its reputation went into free fall. People who were self-medicating with this black market miracle potion started to develop strange skin disorders, unexplained neuropathies, and a vulnerability to infection, all of which ended up on the list of warnings regarding possible side effects when the first generation of the real drug went on the market in 2025 under the name "Chulel."

Winslow was sorry about all this. It cut his income stream down to nothing. He took his multi millions and his remaining stocks of Fontana and fled.

3.

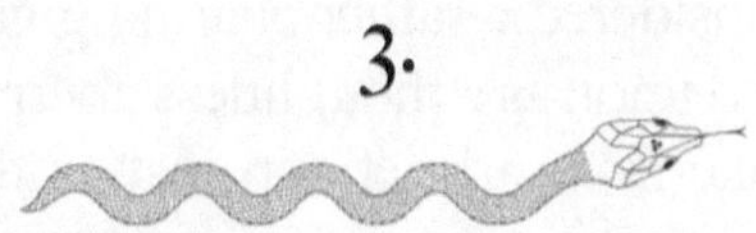

Jenda's spontaneously rescheduled sabbatical began on the first of May 2125. Her grandmother had issued dire warnings about the risks of traveling anywhere other than to the purpose built resort centers, but Jenda was resolute. She was going to the old artist colony of San Miguel de Allende in Mexico.

The nearest airport was in León and it wasn't exactly up to 22nd-century standards, but Jenda found the ambience pleasant and the staff friendly and helpful. She accessed an autocar to navigate the remaining 150 km from León to San Miguel.

The older model autocar bounced uncomfortably over potholes. The attendant at the airport had apologized for these in advance, blaming recent heavy rains. As the car hit an especially large hole, Jenda began to doubt the wisdom of her choice of destination, wondering if San Miguel de Allende might indeed be as unpleasant as Granny El had predicted. A part of Jenda felt excited, thrilled by a sense of impending adventure; but another part of her kept wondering, "Why ever would you want to do anything so silly?" That thought came in her grandmother's voice. *I can always leave and go somewhere else if I don't like it,* Jenda reassured herself.

The road was awful, but Jenda found the views enchanting and, traveling by autocar, she could give the views her full attention. Jenda watched the landscape as it slid by, like a series of pictures on a digiscreen—fields and small lakes, hills and valleys. She passed through a few villages that would have been picturesque if not for the disturbing aspect of dogs and children on the streets. In the primary corporate population hubs, nobody kept pets anymore; they had such short life spans and could carry disease. Efforts to come up with a veterinary form of Chulel had failed. As for the children—through Gen5, they had been considered a rather charming novelty. By Gen7 they were frowned upon as a thoughtless aberration.

Jenda awoke from a brief nap just as the town of San Miguel de Allende was coming into view. She could discern on the near horizon the outline of the iconic old neo-Gothic church. In the distance was a line of mountains. She knew that the town was not nearly as prosperous as it had been in its heyday, but she hoped it still had its charms. These were not apparent on the main artery into town, where the usual corporate recharge stations, quick meal establishments, and roadsteads predominated. But as the autocar slowed into the center of town the streets narrowed and these generic institutions gave way to antique brick and stone facades, adorned with digital skins advertising small cafés, bars, and shops with Spanish names.

Jenda had booked a room at a small hotel near the Jardín Allende. The autocar stopped at the specified location and its service arm hefted her large suitcase out of the trunk, setting it upright on its little wheels on the pavement. The autocar pulled away and Jenda watched with some trepidation as the bulky case navigated the old paving stones that led to the main hotel entrance.

A quarter hour later, as Jenda began unpacking her clothes in a spacious courtyard-view room, she reflected on exactly why she was here. Her distressing encounter with the woman in the café had aroused a yearning to reconnect with art and to try painting again. *I'm here to paint,* Jenda told herself. Then she went through a checklist of her impressions of San Miguel. The roads—it was worth repeating—were awful. The town was attractive enough in a quirky sort of way. The hotel seemed pleasant, despite its limited amenities. The staff were friendly, although their English was eccentric. She'd heard them speaking Spanish with one another. The use of any language other than English or Chinese was discouraged in the major population hubs. On balance, Jenda decided to leave some of her things in the suitcase, which she zipped closed and slid under the bed. *I should try the food,* she decided.

At the recommendation of the receptionist cum concierge at the front desk, Jenda walked a few blocks to a restaurant called La Mazorca Loca, which supposedly had "the best huitlacoche tamales in all of San Miguel." Jenda studied the menu intently and then ordered the huitlacoche tamales with pipian sauce, green chile rice, and a cold beer. Jenda noted that she was one of only a few patrons in the establishment.

While she waited for her food, she unfurled the digilet that she always wore on her left wrist. Granny El called it her "slap bracelet," insisting that there had once been an accessory much like the digilet that had been marketed to children. Of course, it hadn't had a flexible digiscreen or a whole computer with colloidal drive inside.

"Hi, Gran. Just want you to know I arrived safely," Jenda spoke into the digilet as it turned her words into syllabic symbols to pulse to her grandmother's digilet, where they could either be read from the screen or re-formed into speech. "Love the place so far. Exclamation." That was somewhere between a slight exaggeration and a lie—Jenda hadn't decided yet—but there was no point in worrying Granny El. Or, worse, giving her reason to pulse back "I told you so."

After finishing her meal (which Jenda mentally awarded four stars) and a second three-star ice-cold beer, Jenda decided to take a walk through what her NaviGiz claimed was the primary arts district of San Miguel. The street was shaded by ficus trees, most of which looked to Jenda like the fabricated variety, which had become popular after the droughts that devastated much of the planet in the late 21st century. A fabricated ficus only required an occasional shower of water to remove dust, making no demands on dwindling underground water tables. The newest models even had miniaturized 3-D printing devices that produced new leaves according to a convenient timetable, letting fall the old leaves in coordination with the schedule of cleanup crews.

Jenda located the first street of art galleries easily enough and went inside a few. She was not impressed. The work was nice but seemed hardly different from what she could have had printed up in Dallas at 3Dec, the three-dimensional printing company that dominated the interior décor industry.

She was on her way back to her hotel, on the verge of disillusionment, when a building down a side street caught her eye. The storefront, instead of exhibiting the popular digital skin with color-changing geometrics, looked as if it were hand painted with something like a surrealist landscape. The sign read "Galería Kukulcan."

The door to the gallery opened to the tinkling of small bells and Jenda found herself alone and surrounded by paintings that, although clearly recyclable 3-D facsimiles, were a departure from the boring scripted fractals and formulaic abstract landscapes that prevailed in most of the commercial galleries. As Jenda examined each painting first from a distance and then close up, she became aware of someone else entering the room from a rear door.

"These are nice," she said casually, without turning around. "Do you ship internationally?"

"Nice." The answering voice was deep and resonant, but the tone was flat, perhaps sarcastic.

Jenda turned to see who was there. He looked like a native, with his tan skin and dark hair and eyes, but he was taller and more muscular than most of the Mexicans Jenda knew in Dallas. He was clean-shaven, but with longish hair that made him look a little unkempt. What caught Jenda's attention, though, was the streak of blue paint on the side of his white shirt. That and the fact that he was stunningly handsome.

"Yes, we ship to most places," he said, answering the question that Jenda had forgotten she asked. "Where did you have in mind?"

"Oh, I'm from Dallas. Texas. But I may be around for a while. Sabbatical, you know. No rush."

"Hmph." The man folded his arms and leaned against the door frame. "Not many people come here for sabbaticals. What made you choose San Miguel?"

"Well, the art I guess." Jenda paused. "I paint... a little. Or I used to. And I like to be around art. My mother was a sculptor." She was surprised that she had added that last statement.

"Really?"

"She worked in plexiform and plastimold, of course, but also in bronze. Quite a lot in bronze." Jenda was being somewhat reckless in disclosing her mother's penchant for bronze sculpture in an era when making things with intentionally limited lifespans was much preferred, keeping the economy ticking along as it did with recycling and remanufacturing.

"Bronze sculpture is hard to come by these days," the man responded.

"I really do like these paintings," Jenda said. "Who is the artist?"

"That would be me," he replied, with a slight bow. "Luis-Martín Zenobia, à la orden."

"I suspected as much," Jenda chuckled, turning to smile at Luis-Martín Zenobia.

"What gave me away?" he asked, returning Jenda's smile with one of those full-on smiles that crinkled his cheeks and lit up his eyes and made Jenda blush. "Was it my scruffy artist hair?" He ran his hand through his hair, looking like a mischievous schoolboy.

"Well, maybe that. But mainly it was that streak of blue paint on your shirt. Probably Phthalo blue."

"Argh! I thought I'd found one shirt with no paint on it, but it seems I failed." He looked down and scrubbed at the paint stain as if this might make it go away. "How long have you been in our beautiful little city?"

"I've only arrived today."

"And the first thing you did was come to the art galleries? That shows a bit of dedication," he said. "Maybe you would let me show you around to some of my favorite galleries."

Jenda cocked her head to one side, looking at the painting but seeing in her mind the captivating smile of Luis-Martín Zenobia. "That might be nice."

"How about Monday? Eleven o'clock?"

They said goodbye and Jenda went back to the hotel and finished unpacking her suitcase.

It turned out that Luis-Martín was an artist of some note, although his first career had been in anthropology, studying the traditional arts and crafts of the few surviving native populations of Mexico. As people had lost interest in adding to their burden of knowledge about the past, he had abandoned anthropology to devote himself to painting.

Luis-Martín produced a constant stream of novel images in the recyclable materials that society and the economy demanded. Some of his best customers were ready to buy a new piece at least once a month, blithely submitting one of the old pieces for recycling as they hung the new in its place. Luis-Martín had a finely tuned sense of what colors and shapes and patterns were most popular from week to week. He also had a finely tuned sense of how to please a woman, which was something Jenda discovered before she had been in San Miguel for a full week.

Jenda had always found a companion, a lover, on each of her previous eight sabbaticals. The first was the only serious one, leading, as it had, to her marriage to Benjamin Cohen. That marriage had lasted only until Ben's next leave. All of Jenda's subsequent sabbatical relationships had been carefully circumscribed. In light of this experience, Jenda was finding Luis-Martín Zenobia unnerving.

Luis invited Jenda to dinner at a restaurant that he promised would be much better than La Mazorca Loca. "Did you know the receptionist at your hotel is the son-in-law of the owner of Mazorca Loca?" he asked.

Jenda recalled having awarded that meal four stars. The restaurant Luis took her to, however, made her wish she had given Mazorca Loca only three stars, so the five she wanted to give El Piñal would be more meaningful. During dinner, Luis kept her entertained with stories about the history and culture of San Miguel, interspersed with jokes and personal tales of the local populace. Jenda loved listening to his stories. It gave her ample opportunity to study the way his eyes sparkled, the way his hands danced, the way his perfectly formed lips would suddenly part to let her glimpse his perfect teeth. Jenda felt that she had never known such a perfect man. Her mind tried to caution her about letting this potential relationship slip out of her control. But when Luis laid his hand casually over hers she yielded to a shiver of joy that passed all through her body, settling into her belly. When Luis asked if she would like to come up to his apartment to sample some coffee liqueur he had acquired that day, Jenda's only gesture at control came in trying not to sound too eager.

They laughed the next morning as they looked at the unopened bottle of liqueur. Jenda realized she had not taken her usual tablet of Femozem, a pill designed to facilitate and enhance the feminine sexual experience. She hadn't had sex without it in at least forty years and had come to believe it was essential. She didn't recall Luis having taken a pill either. She wondered how she could feel so satisfied, yet so eager for more.

This was not what was supposed to happen. Jenda needed to regain control. She hoped Luis wouldn't notice her sudden withdrawal, her cool silence over breakfast, the flimsiness of her excuse for going back to her hotel, for not being available for lunch. She did concede to let him walk her back to the hotel. She agreed to meet him for dinner.

Jenda lunched on her own. It was only a couple of tacos from a street vendor. They were bland and she ate them while sitting on a broken park bench. Jenda didn't know how to think about what had happened the night before, so she just let it replay. It left her—mind and body—wanting Luis. What she didn't want was this sense of being out of control.

Jenda's eyes settled on a woman near a corner of the park. The woman sat on the ground, trying to attract the attention of passers-by, trying to entice them to purchase what she was selling. Absently, Jenda rose from her bench and walked toward the woman. As Jenda approached, she saw that the woman was selling pieces of white cloth adorned with colorful stitched patterns. *Embroidery.* The word came to Jenda, even though she was uncertain she had ever seen such work before. She picked up one of the pieces and turned it over in her hands. She could see that it was stitched entirely by hand. It was not perfect, but it was beautiful.

"You made this?" Jenda asked. She heard the note of incredulity in her voice.

"Sí, señora," the woman answered. "¿Lo quiere comprar?" She held up her digiscreen to show Jenda the price.

Jenda did want to buy it. She had no idea what she would do with it—it was only a piece of embroidered cloth—but she felt drawn to it. She wanted it. So she bought it and as she walked away, she studied the pattern, trying to discern some kind of meaning. All she saw was a cluster of flowers. Flowers and a little blue bird. But as she folded the cloth and tucked it inside her bag, she felt her mind settling and she began to look forward to dinner with Luis-Martín.

Before the end of another week, Luis invited Jenda to move into his apartment above the gallery and Jenda accepted. Luis' apartment was spacious by contemporary Dallas standards. There was an open living area and a balcony overlooking the tree-lined street. There was a tile-surfaced table with several brightly painted chairs for sit-down dining just like in a restaurant. There was a well equipped kitchen. The bedroom had a large bed and a huge window, which unfortunately opened onto a neighbor's rooftop terrace. Jenda insisted on hanging curtains but contented herself with a diaphanous fabric that obscured the view without blocking the light.

A few days after Jenda settled in, Luis introduced her to what he called his "real art" studio, in the attic above his first floor commercial studio (which, he said, was really more of a factory) and his second floor apartment. Jenda didn't know what to think. The images were no different from the ones in his commercial pieces, since they served as prototypes for the recyclable, 3-D printed replicas. But there was something about the richness of the colors, the subtle detail, the texture and sheen of the surfaces that kept drawing her more deeply into the images. She didn't particularly like the smell of oils and turpentine, but she quickly fell in love with the work. And with Luis-Martín.

Luis was what had become known pejoratively in the commercial art world as a retrogressive, painting in real oil paints on traditional archival canvases that he carefully crafted himself. Of course, the commercial art world in 2125 only knew his 3-D replicas, which fetched premium prices. His originals were known only in an underground art world. The oil paints and rolls of natural canvas and pots of gesso Luis needed for his work were acquired from this underground network of people devoted to preserving the knowledge of how to produce durable fine arts and crafts. In a socioeconomic order in which high consumption was de rigueur, producing anything that was not intended to be readily and willingly recycled was anathema.

Jenda experimented with the oil paints in Luis' clandestine studio and, under his loving tutelage, began to rediscover the joy of painting. She wasn't sure whether her pleasure derived from the rich oil colors or from seeing her mental images take form on canvas. Or perhaps it came from the exhilarating sense of freedom she found spending time with this beautiful man in this secret place.

As Jenda fell into the rhythm of life in San Miguel and her new relationship, she almost forgot about the odd experience that had prompted her decision to come here. *Does it really matter?* she asked herself. The old woman in the café down the side street in Dallas had told her she needed to ask more questions, but when things were going so well, why should she? The only questions she felt like asking were the ones that helped her get to know Luis better.

The man himself was an enchanting enigma. Jenda found his dissident tendencies exciting. He evoked something in her—a frankness, a creative assertiveness—that she found surprising. He invaded her dreams, although in her dream world Luis sometimes seemed darker and a bit shorter than her real world Luis. Once or twice he was accompanied by a lady in blue, a lady hidden in the shadows. Jenda thought she knew the lady. She thought she saw the lady beckoning her, entreating her to look behind the curtains, to find out what lay in those shadowy places. The lady in blue had a kind and tender countenance and Jenda found her terrifying. She wanted to tell Luis about this dream, but when she tried to remember it and put it into words, the images slipped away, and she could think of nothing to say.

"What made you decide to do oil painting?" Jenda asked Luis one afternoon, as she stood back to examine her own small painting on the easel, trying to decide if the central image wanted a trace more Quinacridone magenta somewhere offsetting the shadow to the right.

"It was never a decision," Luis said. "It just happened. When I was at boarding school in the US, one of my art teachers showed me some oils and real cloth canvases one day and I felt it was something I had to do. Some of us were already finding the trend toward recycling everything and only making things that were intended to be recycled quickly, more than a little offensive." He paused and glanced at Jenda, as if anticipating some reaction. Then he continued. "I guess my attitude was a bit ungrateful, given that my education was being paid for by my father's success as an engineer and product designer for one of the major recyclables manufacturers."

"But you make recyclable paintings, too." Jenda wondered how he reconciled this.

Luis frowned. "It supports my real art. And I'm good at it. I can give people what they want. Is it wrong to make them happy?" He paused as the frown softened into a half smile. "My secret aim is to make my consumers feel at least a tiny twinge of regret when they drop off one of my paintings for recycling."

Jenda wasn't entirely sure she understood. Or maybe she didn't want to understand. Luis' motivations were at odds with the dominant culture in which she moved so successfully back in Dallas. The whole economy in 2125 hinged on the motivation to buy lots of things, use them for a short time, surrender them for recycling and buy more. Everybody agreed it was more satisfying to design new things, build new things, and buy new things than it was to deal with a lot of old stuff sitting around needing repairs and maintenance and eventual restoration. Anything worth keeping could be digitized and stored at Your Journal.

"So you did an art degree at university?" Jenda decided there was quite enough Quinacridone magenta on her painting and she picked up a tube of Dioxazine violet.

"No," Luis responded. "I took lots of art classes in secondary school, but by the time I got to university I'd developed an interest in primitive and traditional arts, so I decided to do a degree in anthropology. And then one degree led to another." He stepped back from his own large canvas and turned to look at Jenda's painting.

"What do you think?" Jenda tilted her head side to side as she examined her work. It showed a female figure, her arms flung out, her head tilted skyward, as if dancing to a tune that emanated from the swirl of colors surrounding her.

Luis stepped closer to her easel, closer to Jenda. "I like it," he said. "It has great emotional intensity. Your color choices are excellent. It's a charming self-portrait, Jenda. And I like the slightly metallic quality..."

"Wait. What? Why do you say it's a self-portrait?" But as Jenda looked again at the painting, trying to see it through Luis' eyes, she realized there was a strong resemblance.

"Didn't you intend it as a self-portrait?" Luis asked. "It sure looks like you. Perhaps a more child-like Jenda, but I think this is definitely you."

"Well, it wasn't intentional. But I see what you mean." Jenda stuck her paintbrush between her teeth to adjust the band holding back her hair. "Who knows where these images come from anyway, Luis? You've said yourself that sometimes they seem to well up from nowhere. I'm glad you like it." Jenda dunked her paintbrush into the cleaning solution, deciding she was finished for the day.

"So in anthropology you had to do...what? Fieldwork? Where did you do that?" Jenda picked up the thread of their conversation, settling on the sofa.

Luis sat down next to her. He explained that he had done his doctoral dissertation fieldwork in Guatemala, working in some Mayan communities in the mountains and befriending a few contemporary Mayan artists who were practicing their ancestral arts. "One of them was also a shaman, an artist of ritual as well as a visual artist. He became my primary guide and friend."

"You call them informants, right?" Jenda tried to recall an anthropology text she had read in an introductory class in college.

"Oh god no!" Luis shook his head vigorously. "We stopped using that term long ago. Although, when I was in graduate school, there were still some heated discussions about it. No, that term...I hate it. The way I see things, field studies have to be cooperative. The people have to be full participants in putting together the stories that naturally belong to them." Luis paused, staring at his left hand and stretching out all its fingers, then massaging it with his right hand. "The first day I met Armando—the shaman I mentioned—he was sitting under a ceiba tree with his hand wrapped in a bloody cloth. I thought he looked like he was about to pass out, so I went over to see about him. It turns out he was trancing. I apologized for bothering him, but he laughed and said that he was taking advantage of the opportunity to make an offering to the vision serpent."

"The what?"

"A deity among the southern Maya—southern Mexico, Guatemala, Honduras. In ancient times they made ritual blood offerings. And one of their most important deities was the vision serpent, which connected with the Aztec Quetzalcoatl and Kukulcan among the northern Maya."

"So that's where you got the name of your gallery?"

"Exactly. Kukulcan, by whatever name, is a flying snake. Literal translation is 'feathered serpent.' I've always liked that image. Anyway, Armando had accidentally cut his hand on a machete in the field and decided since he was losing blood anyway, he'd just as well say the prayers of blood sacrifice. He was quite a character. I don't know how I would have gotten through my research without him." Luis paused, looking thoughtful. "Did you know that one of the Mayan words for the life force—which they identified with blood—was Chulel?"

Jenda hadn't known, although she had occasionally wondered how Pharmakon came up with such an odd name for their most profitable drug. Jenda always seemed to be learning something new from (and about) Luis. She liked that. Most of the people she knew were so predictable. They had so few stories of any interest about their past, most of them trivial, although sometimes amusing. But once you had known them for a while you knew all their stories. Of course, Jenda was just getting to know Luis, but there was something about his stories, something about the way they fit together that told her he was different.

Jenda and Luis began going dancing. At first Jenda objected, claiming that she didn't dance. But once Luis got her out on the floor, she wondered whether that was true. "I honestly didn't think I could dance, Luis," she said, after he insisted that she must have taken lessons. "I've always refused to dance, for as long as I can remember. But with you, I have to admit I'm really enjoying it."

She also enjoyed spending time fussing over a painting and trying to comprehend that it was not going to be digitized and tossed into recycling at the end of her sabbatical. Mostly Jenda enjoyed being with Luis. They frequently shared dinner in small cafés and loved going back to El Piñal, where they first ate dinner together. Occasionally they met up with one or more of Luis' friends for drinks. They took long evening walks through the parks. And of course there was their intimate time in bed, although Jenda was developing a predilection for sex on the studio sofa, where the scent of hers and Luis' aroused bodies blended with the odor of oil paints, producing sheer intoxication.

"You know I'm in love with you, don't you?" Luis said one evening, as they lay sprawled on that sofa, savoring the intoxication. He brushed back the strands of dampened hair that clung to Jenda's forehead and cheeks.

"Then I guess," she said, tracing the line of his jaw with her finger, "we're in love with each other." Luis leaned closer, his face almost touching hers. And then they kissed—a gentle, lingering kiss, expecting nothing beyond the moment.

Jenda and Luis spent many hours together in his commercial gallery and work space--Luis' "factory." Sometimes Jenda took the gallery's open hours as her time to wander off on her own. Once a week an art student from the local institute came to mind the studio and Jenda and Luis could take off together. Luis also had talked Jenda into minding the gallery on her own from time to time when he went out to meet with "people," which Jenda assumed meant clients or materials providers, although Luis didn't always say. She liked spending time alone in the gallery and she liked listening to the admiring remarks of the not infrequent visitors. She made some good sales.

"Did I ever tell you why I decided to come to San Miguel?" Jenda asked Luis one afternoon as they sat in the commercial gallery together waiting for customers.

"You said you came for the art."

"Well, yes, that's true. But there's a little more to it." Jenda screened off the book she had been reading and rested her forearms on the worktable. "I'd made reservations to go to a resort center in California. And I was supposed to leave in July, not May."

"You obviously changed your plans."

"Yeah. Because... Well, I was having a sandwich in a little lunchroom. One of those cafés that professionals don't go to, you know? Anyway, this woman—an old woman—started staring at me and then she came and sat down at my table. She knew my name. She said she knew me in high school. She asked if I still painted. And she knew my mother was an artist. But she also said other stuff--crazy stuff—about how she had idolized me and my boyfriend in high school. How we had been such... What was the word she used? Firebrands?" Jenda suddenly felt this might all sound foolish and looked up at Luis to check his reaction. He looked serious.

"Really? And you didn't recognize her at all?"

"No. But she looked so old. How can you tell for sure when someone looks that old? But the upsetting part was when she got right in my face and said 'You need to ask more questions.'" Jenda looked directly at Luis as she said this and the dramatization made her shiver, remembering. "And when I tried to tell her she didn't know who I was, she said that I was the one who didn't know who I am."

"And on the strength of that you changed all your plans?"

"Yeah. I can't explain why the experience affected me the way it did. It just made me want to do something different. To break out of my routines. Anyway, now I'm glad I did."

"Me too, querida."

Jenda was relieved that Luis now knew that little story. She was grateful that he hadn't asked questions because she felt certain she had no answers.

A few days later, Jenda was once again minding the gallery by herself. She looked up from the novel she was reading on her digilet at the sound of the tinkling bells and saw that it was Luis returning from one of his meetings. He was carrying a package that bore the distinctive shape of a bottle of their favorite tequila.

"Celebration time!" he announced. "I've signed a contract with Marvaworld to supply their corporate offices in Texas with a regular rotation of paintings. That should keep us in oils and canvases for quite some time. And, by the way, provide ample excuses for me to travel to Texas."

Although it was still an hour until closing time, he tasked off the "Open" sign and locked the door, grabbing Jenda's hand and giving her a quick kiss as they headed upstairs. It took them a while to get changed to go out for dinner, because Luis had been unable to resist joining Jenda in the shower. Her hair was still damp as they headed out into the early evening to their favorite café, having already shared shots of tequila as they got dressed.

As they lingered over dinner—which entailed a couple of margaritas each—Luis told Jenda the details of his contract and how it would mean taking on a regular employee to replicate the required paintings in the required numbers at the required intervals. Luis seemed excited about the contract, but Jenda also detected an edge of contempt in his voice as he related the frequency with which Marvaworld would want the paintings to be switched out.

"You're sure this won't take you away from your oil painting?" Jenda asked.

"No. Oh, no, not at all!" Luis said. "God, if I thought that, I'd never do it. The only reason to produce these recyclables is the fact that it supports my real work. This is going to make our life better, I'm sure of it." And they gazed at one another, letting the fact that he had said "our life" sink in.

Both Luis and Jenda were slightly drunk as they headed back to the gallery apartment, but they decided to have one more shot of the celebratory tequila Luis had bought for the occasion. Jenda's was more like a half shot and she put it in a glass of orange juice. They went onto the balcony. By resting her head on Luis' shoulder, Jenda found that the world didn't wobble quite so much.

"Tell me more about your mother the sculptor," Luis said. There was a warm breeze and the lights from the street became fireflies amid the dancing leaves. "You told me about her that first day, but... The way you talked about her made me think..."

"My mother is dead," Jenda said. "You remember that spate of autocar accidents back in 2080? When there was that fault in the script update? My mom was one of the fatalities."

"I'm sorry," Luis said. "That must have been awful."

"Don't be sorry." Jenda felt the muscles of her shoulders and neck tense, as if trying to make up for the lack of mental discipline that was letting feelings about the loss of her mother bubble to the surface. "She had gone completely mad, so it was possibly for the best." Jenda heard her words slurring slightly and her voice trailed off. The bubbles of sentiment were coalescing into images, memories. "She was delusional. She would get into these rants, claiming that people she was friends with had disappeared off her LifeBook chapters and Your Journal logs. She accused my father of drugging her and lying to her. Stuff like that." Jenda shook her head, and the world wobbled. "The worst was this story she came up with about how I'd gotten pregnant in high school. We showed her all the YJ records to prove that never happened, but she got crazier and crazier."

Jenda's eyes were having a hard time focusing and she was unclear whether it was the tequila or the pull of resurgent memories drawing her away. Maybe it was her tears that made everything blurry. "Mom was such a good sculptor. A wonderful artist. I wonder sometimes whatever happened to all of her beautiful work. It was so stupid. Her wreck was only two days before the script fix came out. She flipped out on a curve at full speed. She never knew." Jenda began to sob. "Poor Mommy. Why did she get so crazy? She was so good. I wanted her to know how much I loved her."

Jenda surrendered, and Luis held her gently as she wept, whispering quietly that he loved her, that surely her mother knew how much Jenda loved her. "There's nothing wrong about feeling sad," he said.

"I'm sorry, Luis," Jenda said, with one more jerky intake of breath as she wiped her eyes and nose with the back of her hand and searched for a tissue. "I don't know why this suddenly hit me like this." She wondered vaguely why she had never entered anything about it in her Your Journal files. Her files, she knew, contained only a bare mention of the circumstances of the death of Tessa Jenkins Swain and nothing at all about the descent into madness that had preceded it. "It must be the tequila." Jenda forced a smile. "I shouldn't drink so much." But she couldn't help wondering if this was the kind of thing the old woman had meant she should question.

"How about a cup of manzanilla tea before bed?" Luis said, standing up, still holding Jenda's hand.

Jenda looked up at him. "Yes," she said. "Thank you." She hoped he understood she wasn't just talking about the tea.

4.

Amid mounting evidence of the success of their Chulel formula in 2040—the year Max and Emily Feldman both turned 100—the two researchers had decided to retire. It would be another decade before the concept of retirement gave way to the ten-year sabbatical.

The Drs. Feldman watched from afar the unfolding of the new world they had helped to create. When people had started turning 120, it was kind of a big deal. When their offspring started turning 100 it was an even bigger deal. When people were still around to celebrate their grandchildren's century mark, they began to wonder where it would all end. As the Drs. Feldman began to think that they would easily reach their 200th birthdays, they started having second thoughts about the great gift they had bestowed on humankind.

The big question that began to occur to observant and thoughtful people like the Feldmans was whether this present trajectory would end at all. It wasn't that people had become immortal; they were still vulnerable to physical violence and the few remaining infectious diseases that could kill you if not treated in time. But the medical professions were as diligent as ever in defending against all of these potential calamities. If anything, they had become even more adept at keeping people from dying of all kinds of things. Even violence, whether intentional or accidental, rarely resulted in death. Many of the tragically mutilated survivors of the last great wars were still alive, reminders of an incomprehensible time most people preferred to forget. Increasingly, death required deliberate intent. The new normal, the kind with Chulel, was for all the intact cells and organs of the body to continue regenerating in an orderly and reliable fashion, staying perfectly healthy and youthful indefinitely. The decline of cancer had been a pleasant side effect.

Reproduction had declined. As the generations piled up one after another, it seemed unnecessary. It had certainly seemed unnecessary to the plutocrats, who had no desire to relinquish power to a next generation. Fertility was near zero in all the primary corporate hub regions. The few children who were produced were seldom seen, being generally sent away to boarding colonies where they could be raised by professionals.

The pharmaceutical industry had been impacted rather severely by the decline in demand for the lucrative drugs that had addressed the chronic maladies of old age. There was a concomitant uptick in demand for mood drugs, and then after the so-called "War on Drugs" was finally brought to an end with the legalization of almost everything, big pharma found its new calling in the manufacture of all kinds of designer recreational drugs, which merged imperceptibly with the mood enhancers.

The Feldmans closely monitored their own health as well as that of the small colony of bonobos that had been receiving Chulel treatments longer than any humans, even Max. The bonobos occupied a forested reserve near the Pharmakon labs outside Atlanta, where they were cared for by one of the Feldmans' former assistants. The bonobos had been largely forgotten by Pharmakon, but the assistant continued to faithfully cater to all their needs and to provide their annual Chulel infusions and physical checkups. It was in the bonobos that Max and Emily first noted the slight deterioration in the beta chains of hemoglobin. A few years later, they detected the same deterioration in their own blood. The changes were very small, but they bore an odd similarity to sickle cell disease. Max and Emily also noted that the effects were cumulative and that they were most pronounced immediately after an infusion of Chulel.

The health and demographic implications of the new order had been superseded in the Feldmans' minds by concern over an apparent side trip into memory management via cognitive photonic therapy. Max and Emily knew perfectly well that the widely touted memory loss that had come to be associated with Chulel was a fabrication. They had been taking the drug longer than anyone else—entirely self-administered—and they knew exactly what its effects and side effects were. Memory loss was not among them. And yet, in 2045 there had been a worldwide panic as FlixNews and Corporate News Network suddenly began reporting alarming memory loss associated with Chulel, stampeding people into enrolling in a digital media corporation called Your Journal and receiving Chulel exclusively in spa-like clinics that promised memory maintenance and restoration. Max and Emily knew that Chulel maintained the brain in peak health, the same as any other physical organ. Their own memories of both distant events and recent occurrences remained remarkably clear. However, their interactions with people who were availing themselves of the "memory restoration" treatments that were offered at the Chulel spas caused them growing concern. It seemed to be producing some form of collective dementia.

The Feldmans had been more than happy to leave Pharmakon behind. They had felt some solidarity back in the early 2000s with what was originally called the "Occupy" movement, which had briefly tried to rally people against the domination of society, culture, and politics by big corporations and plutocrats. There were rumors that their movement had precipitated a clandestine reaction within the corporate world under the code word "Preoccupied." If it was real, it would indeed have been a clever tag for a project designed to keep people so self-absorbed and emotionally dependent on entertainment, novel material goods, and selected, media-hyped "causes" that they had no interest in real political involvement. They might even be convinced (as indeed they had been) that less government was best government. It was easily recognized by anyone who paid attention to such things that corporations and corporate alliances had become the only meaningful centers of power. Most people complacently accepted the idea that corporations were more reliable than governments in giving them what they wanted and needed for happy lives. As the true elites had become fewer and more powerful, they also had become more brazen. The advent of Chulel and, fortuitously, cognitive photonic therapy had been all they needed to solidify their hold.

There had been a campaign back in the late 21st century: "The best days of your life haven't happened yet. Make room for what's to come!" This had encouraged people to get rid of their last remaining boxes of mementos and artifacts from past eras. It was a cooperative venture between Your Journal and the recyclables manufacturers. The real estate corporations were also on board, as they were squeezing more and smaller residential units into limited urban space. Naturally, these smaller residential units had less and less storage space. The leading home décor company had followed up with their own campaign: "Why live in the past when you can have today's most gorgeous home?" So people had tossed out the last of the Tiffany lamps and the Hepplewhite dining room sets in favor of the latest limited-lifetime items from 3Dec.

The leading 22nd-century economic sectors entailed the manufacture of recyclables, renewable energy (which had been wrested away from the off-grid delusionists and placed safely in the hands of the plutocrats who knew how to make it profitable), entertainment providers of all kinds (a category that included foodstuff producers and pharmaceuticals), and advertising. Of course all of it was done in the context of electronic/ digital/ computerized wizardry, but that had ceased to be considered an industry in itself. It was simply how corporations did business. And really, the less the populace understood about how it worked the better. Digital communications and information sharing had been on a dangerous trajectory around the start of the 21st century, with ordinary workers having access to almost everything across what was called the internet, as well as the ability to communicate with one another in an unregulated manner. They had tried to argue that this was their right. Heroes had risen up, disclosing the ways in which corporations and governments were attempting to manipulate and intrude upon these communications. Fortunately, the corporations had been able to consolidate their control by convincing people it was the governments that were the greatest threat. Before long, governments became practically irrelevant, conceding all authority to the corporations.

Max and Emily Feldman's first stop post-retirement had been Buenos Aires, where they intended to indulge their lifelong love of the tango and other things Argentinian. They had a fondness for old paintings and books and owned a couple of small works by Argentine painters such as Carlos Alonso and Xul Solar as well as books—physical books printed on paper— by Argentine writers including Jorge Luis Borges, Julio Cortázar, and Silvina Ocampo. In Buenos Aires, they discreetly pursued the possibility of acquiring a few more precious books and possibly even a new painting or two. They adored Buenos Aires and, although they lived briefly in many more places over the next seven decades, they kept returning to Argentina. They thought they just might stay this time. They had well and truly fallen in love with the porteños of Buenos Aires.

By the time they settled there for good in 2125, Max and Emily had been witness to many changes in their beautiful city. For one thing, the underground tranvía subterraneo or "subte" had been closed after the devastating floods of 2077, replaced by a solar powered elevated monorail winding its silent, serpentine way through the city. Its exterior was of an alloy that reflected back the colors and forms of its surroundings, but never the glare of the sun. The buses known as colectivos had been done away with. The corporate-owned tranvía alta was much more satisfactory, generating wealth as it did for the corporations and the plutocrats.

Max and Emily were pleased to find that their favorite little Buenos Aires art gallery, the Galería Picaflor, was still in existence, occupying a modest store front on a side street near where the now defunct Contemporary Art Museum had been.

All the public museums had disappeared. As weakened governments found it increasingly difficult to extract revenue from the globally peripatetic corporations that monopolized wealth, public institutions were put on austere budgets. Naturally, the corporations had come to the rescue. National parks went first. In Texas, California, and the USA, park lands had been sold off to corporate interests. Then the artworks of the major public museums, including the once venerated collections of the Musées de France, had been "deaccessioned" at cut rates as even corporate collectors and plutocrats lost interest in the so-called "old masters." The great libraries had been corporatized and subsequently reduced to mere facades for digital collections.

When Max and Emily first encountered the Galería Picaflor in the 2040s, many of the paintings were already being printed in unlimited editions on the increasingly popular recycled and recyclable canvases, but there also had been some traditional oils and even a few bronze sculptures. Now the gallery's inventory of paintings and sculptures appeared to be entirely of the recyclable type. Max and Emily were delighted to find that the woman who had taken over the Galería Picaflor shortly before the Feldmans' last visit to Buenos Aires in 2105 was still there. She was a sprightly woman by the name of Isabel Hernandez.

Isabel's English was as fluent as her Spanish and Emily's conversations with her tended to make use of both languages in about equal measure. "Where did you learn to speak such good English?" Emily asked one day, as she watched Isabel hanging some new pictures for an exhibit.

"Oh, you know," Isabel answered brightly. "Just around."

"No, really, Isabel. Your English syntax is far more sophisticated, your vocabulary much more extensive than what we hear from people who have learned from casual interaction with tourists and sabbaticos. Did you attend university in an English speaking country? You have a bit of a North American accent, you know. Kind of California even," Emily said. Languages and dialects were a hobby of hers.

Isabel's shoulders drooped a bit and she spoke without turning toward Emily. "I honestly don't know," she said quietly. "I guess I've just... forgotten."

"Oh, well," Emily said. "Probably not important. I was only curious."

Isabel finished straightening the painting she had just hung and turned to face Emily. "Actually, it is important. I wish I knew. They say it's the Chulel. I've never been able to get the treatments at the clinic where they give you the memory restoration. Some foreigners seem surprised that I haven't lost my memories altogether."

Isabel took a few steps back to look at the paintings she had hung. She shook her head. "Estas pinturas que se reciclen... ¡Que mierda!" Isabel glanced quickly over her shoulder at Emily, although she was pretty sure Emily would not judge her for this outburst.

Emily was laughing. "You used to have some real paintings, too," she said softly. "¿Que pasó?"

"Oh, I still have some. I'll show you once we get this exhibit over with."

That evening, over their usual restaurant dinner, Emily told Max what she had learned on her visit with Isabel. "The woman has always self-administered Chulel," she told him. "And yet she seems to have some huge memory gaps. What do you think that's about?"

Max looked thoughtful. "You know, there were rumors back in—oh, maybe around 2030 or so?—about some experimentation with photonic memory restructuring going on here in Argentina. Do you think maybe she could have got mixed up with that?"

"Could be," Emily replied. "I think she might be amenable to some assistance in finding out where she lost her memories." Max nodded thoughtfully, and Emily could see that he had already begun plotting a research strategy.

5.

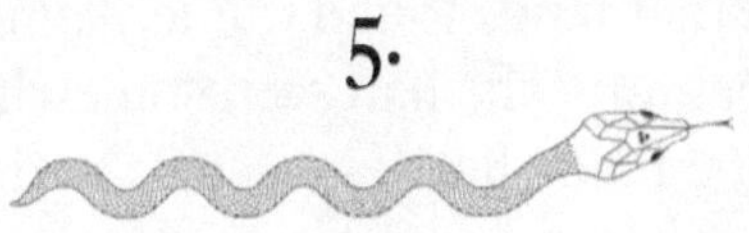

"Do you want to go to a party tomorrow night?" Luis asked Jenda one evening in mid-July.

"Sure! What's the occasion?" Her mind went reflexively to considering what to wear.

"It's just a group of friends. We get together occasionally," Luis replied.

Jenda bought a pair of dark blue form-fitting pants and a sheer, billowing ivory-colored blouse over a lace camisole with a deep neckline. She complemented it with shiny dark blue high-heeled sandals and plexiform pearls. And of course she dropped off some things in the recycling, choosing one of her least sexy outfits.

When they arrived at the party, Jenda realized that she had already met most of the guests, although she had never thought of them as constituting a "group of friends." She didn't know that they knew each other. Luis introduced Jenda to a couple that she hadn't met previously – Tao-Min and Meli.

"Anything to report?" Meli asked, raising her wine glass to clink amiably with Luis' and leaning against Tao-Min's shoulder.

"No, nothing new from me," Luis replied. "What about you, Tao-Min, didn't you just get your annual Chulel? When, last week?"

"Last Tuesday, in fact," Tao-Min replied, her brow furrowing. "So far I'm not finding any discrepancies in my exomemories. Do you think maybe they're onto us and have stopped messing with records of Recall people?" She paused. Her smile was met with concerned looks.

Tao-Min and Meli were a beautiful couple. Tao-Min was taller, with onyx hair, deep brown eyes and creamy skin over a spare, muscular frame. Meli was darker, a little plumper, with a round face and soft, sparkling gray eyes. There was something about Meli's face that Jenda found vaguely familiar—maybe like something in a painting she had seen somewhere. Looking at Tao-Min's and Meli's flawless faces and bodies, Jenda wondered absently what generation they were, or even if they were of the same generation. It was impossible to tell anymore. There were now at least five adult generations of people living together and, with the exception of Gen1 and to a milder extent early Gen2, they all looked much the same. Those first two generations had already been on the downslope toward old age when Chulel became available. The drug only arrested aging. It couldn't reverse it.

They also reminded Jenda of her brief engagement to Sandra and of Sandra's unfortunate disappearance in a mountain climbing accident. Homosexual and heterosexual had ceased being absolute categories some decades ago. It was understood that some people were unequivocally one or the other, but it was widely accepted that there was a broad middle ground as well.

"I still have a few more months of records to compare with what I wrote down in my journal," Tao-Min continued. "And then I'll need to compare the drawings in my sketchbook that I made from some of the original photographs."

Luis produced an exaggerated startle response. "Wait. You mean you've actually been following our advice and keeping handwritten records? And making drawings? Did we finally convince you to take this seriously, Tao-Min?" And he raised his wine glass to touch hers.

"My generation does still know how to write," she laughed. "In longhand script even. And—not meaning to brag—but I even know a good smattering of traditional Chinese characters. Poor Meli, here, on the other hand..." She tousled her partner's hair affectionately.

So Tao-Min could be late Gen2. If so, she was remarkably youthful. *More likely Gen3,* Jenda thought. Meli must be at least Gen3, like Jenda, although she could just as easily be Gen4 like Luis or even Gen5. Nobody remarked on cross-generation partnering anymore, although it had initially seemed a bit scandalous. Age had become insignificant.

Jenda started to say something about her own ability to write in longhand script, a habit rare among Gen3 and almost unknown in Gen4 and beyond. But since she had no explanation for why she had developed this particular skill, she let the thought pass. Written languages, including English, had all evolved into layered forms of digital syllabic symbols. It was easy enough to input to a screen, but hardly anyone tried to replicate it by hand.

As the evening progressed, Jenda drank more wine and conversed with more of Luis' friends, all of whom shared a deep concern about the reliability of their exomemories at Your Journal. She noted that Luis was introducing her simply as an artist from Texas and not mentioning where she was employed. Everybody Jenda met had a story. A woman from Portland, Oregon, claimed that she still remembered being engaged in 2067 to a dissident writer who abruptly disappeared from her life and subsequently from her Your Journal file and LifeBook loop. She had no proof. A man from Mexico City told about a friend who claimed to have quit his job at Your Journal after he was asked to alter some photographic files. He had no proof either. His own YJ files suggested he had never had such a friend. Then there was the man from Montreal who showed Jenda a print photograph that included one more person in the group picture than was shown in the same group photo he showed her in his Your Journal file. He had no memory of who this person was.

As Jenda listened to the stories, she felt flattered by this evidence of Luis' trust. But she began to wish he hadn't trusted her with so much. Luis knew she worked for Your Journal, and yet here he was introducing her to people who appeared to think that YJ was intentionally messing with their memories. Is this what he thought, too? It was true that Jenda had joked with him a couple of times about a work colleague who had her office in the restricted area between the 12th and 34th floors where banks of primary digital termini were housed. Admittedly, she had waxed a bit melodramatic about how this woman was always vague when the conversation turned to specific aspects of her job. But it was just collegial teasing, and even the employee in question participated in the jokes. And then, of course, there were her own mother's chaotic memories that had begun to diverge so drastically from her YJ exomemories in the months before her death. And there was the old woman in the café.

Jenda leaned on Luis-Martín's arm as they walked back to the gallery after the party. Jenda's head was spinning, and she knew it wasn't just the wine.

"I like your friends, Luis," she said. "Of course, I'd met most of them before, but they seem different when you put them all together." She wanted to talk with him about all the stories she had heard from these friends, but she decided that could wait. Maybe tomorrow. Tonight she wanted nothing more than a warm cup of manzanilla tea and to cuddle up in Luis' arms for a long, restorative sleep.

Jenda woke the next morning to a bright sun blasting through her eyelids. She squinted, placed a hand over her eyes and turned lazily to reach for Luis. His side of the bed was empty but still warm. She opened her eyes and looked up to see him offering her a steaming cup of coffee and a smile.

"Come on, sleepy one," he said. "It's a beautiful day and I offer you a cup of real, authentic café." Jenda propped herself up on her elbows. The fragrance emanating from the cup was glorious.

"Why do you always call it 'authentic'?" she asked.

"My friends in the mountains grow coffee beans that are handed down from before Geni," he said. "Their coffee may not have all the added benefits of the redesigned brews, but you have to admit, it tastes wonderful."

Jenda inhaled the heady steam once more and took a cautious sip. She closed her eyes. "Mmm. Delicious." Luis had put in a touch of honey and cinnamon, the way Jenda liked it.

He held out his hand and Jenda took it, letting him lead her out onto the balcony, where the glare of the sun filtered through the shuddering leaves of the ficus and bougainvillea that lined the street. They settled onto the wicker bench and the comfort of brightly printed cushions.

As they sipped coffee, Luis talked about the various trees and flowering plants they could see from their perch and what they were called both in Spanish and English and often in one of the old Mayan languages as well. This was the kind of thing Jenda had always loved about a sabbatical. Nothing to do but revel in small things in the warm company of a new friend. But this particular sabbatical was different, and she still felt uncertain about what might lie ahead.

"So, can we talk about the party?" Jenda asked.

"Cierto, mi amor. What shall we talk about? The wine? A local vintage from..."

"Let me guess: From your friends in the mountains who grow grapes from vines handed down from before Geni."

"Actually, yes," He pulled her closer. "It was good, don't you think?"

"Pukka," she agreed. "And the food was marvelous. And the house was beautifully decorated. And everybody was wearing the most amazing outfits. And..."

"Okay, okay. You want to know how I came up with a whole room full of people who have big questions about the place where you work ¿verdad que sí?"

"Sounds like a good start," Jenda said, sitting up straighter and moving a little bit away from Luis so she could better see his face. "Just start talking." It came out a little harsher than she had intended.

"Am I in trouble?"

"No. Sorry. It's just... I don't even know what questions to ask. Let's try, 'How did you meet these people?'"

"Ah." He took a deep breath, giving her a look that seemed to say he hoped she could handle this next level of trust and wouldn't decide he was a madman. "We're all part of an informal group," he began, explaining that the group was known locally as Trivial Pursuit. They got together usually in small groups, but occasionally in larger gatherings like last night's party. He said that they took their name from an old board game people played back in the 20th century. It made them seem innocuous enough, even a bit ridiculous, and certainly worthy of being ignored. They had found one another in various ways, but all were connected through a zone known as Recall and a communications portal called Interloc, all linking via what Luis called the infranet.

All this was new to Jenda. She was curious about why they did these things. But this wasn't what she most wanted to know about.

"What's your story, Luis? I heard lots of stories last night, some more believable than others. But I haven't heard yours yet. I'm kind of assuming you have one."

"Mine's a little complicated." He paused. "Hard to know where to start."

"The beginning might work."

Luis settled back into the cushions, drained his coffee and set the cup down. He flexed his shoulders as if he were at the gym, about to begin some heavy lifting. "I will tell you the story as close to the truth as I can," he said, "although it may not be exactly the way it's stored with your office."

Luis' story was about his maternal grandmother who, he said, had taught English in Mexico and Spanish in Los Angeles, California, back in the first quarter of the 21st century. "When I was young, my mother used to talk to me from time to time about my grandmother, and the one thing I knew from early on is that my abuela died in Argentina when I was about six or seven. We were living in Merida, Yucatan, at that time. I remember very little about my grandmother, since I was just a little boy when she died. She had lived in California, and my mother was born there. That's where she met my dad, at Meta University."

Jenda shifted impatiently, wondering exactly where this story would link up with the whole matter of what did or did not occur at Your Journal.

"Anyway, when I was about six, as I said, my grandmother and my Uncle Julian—my mother's older brother—went away and my mother told me they'd gone to Argentina. After a while—many months, I think—my mother went, too. She was gone a long time, or so it seemed to me. I remember being unhappy. My father was an engineer and was always at work, leaving me with minders. When Mama finally came back, she took me away and we moved to California. She said my abuela had gone to be with Jesus."

"What does all this have to do with the idea of the unreliability of exomemories at Your Journal?" Jenda asked.

"Right. The thing is that my mother's YJ files have no information about her going to Argentina. Of course Abuela kept no YJ files at all. Yes, yes, I know. I'm not supposed to be able to access someone else's files. Anyway, my mother never liked talking about Argentina and after about 2045 she never spoke of it again. Even when I would ask her about it, she didn't seem to know what I was talking about. Recently, though, I found a little notebook that belonged to my mother, and it had some addresses in it that turned out to be in Argentina, in and around Buenos Aires. When I searched out the exact locations of the addresses from the little book, I learned that they were jails and prisons. So now I have to conclude that is where my grandmother ended up—in prison in Argentina. And I think my mother must have been down there trying to take care of her by bringing her things. There were little lists in the book of things like soap, hand lotion, toothpaste—personal things a woman might need." Luis ran his finger around the smooth lip of his coffee cup.

"And your mother doesn't remember anything more about being there, other than your grandmother's death?"

"And even that isn't in her YJ files."

"Odd." Jenda was trying to come up with an explanation. "Have you talked to your mother recently about this?"

"I can't talk to her, Jenda, because my mother is dead." Luis' gaze wandered off toward the mountains, to the far horizon where the morning mists still lingered.

"Oh, I'm sorry, Luis. I was wondering… from what you said…" She leaned a little closer to him and covered his hand with hers. "How did your mother die?"

"I don't even know." He told Jenda how he had received a notice from his mother's habitat management indicating they had received word of her death and that the unit was passing into the hands of someone whose name he didn't recognize. "Probably a member of the Christian organization she joined. Once I was in high school, she moved off with them and we lost touch." Luis said that first his father and then he himself had made payments on his mother's habitat unit, hoping she might return, but the right of occupancy passed to this stranger rather than to him. There were legally executed papers.

"Didn't that make you angry?"

"A little. But mostly it made me sad. At least I was able to go through her stuff and salvage some things, especially that little notebook about my grandmother."

They sat silently for a while, holding hands.

The sun suddenly glinted off a glass lantern on the balcony and Jenda blinked. "I was in Argentina once," she said.

"Really? When was that?"

"Oh." Jenda dug the heels of her hands into her eyes. "I don't know. Maybe I went. Maybe a long time ago. It doesn't matter. Wasn't there anything else in your mother's little book?" Jenda suddenly felt angry, and she didn't know why. She got up and walked the few steps to the railing, leaning into the breeze that stirred the leaves and scattered the sunlight.

"Her notebook did have some other entries. More like little diary notes. She wrote about being worried that my grandmother was becoming forgetful, even senile. And she thought she was being mistreated in the jails. Poor Mama. All of this must have been distressing to her." Luis paused. "There were also a couple of names with addresses in the little book, and one of them led to an old fellow who remembered a few things about Abuela and her activities there in Argentina."

"Old? How old?" Jenda returned to the settee.

"It's hard to say. I don't think he'd been taking Chulel. Maybe he'd had some treatments earlier on, but he was definitely showing his age when I contacted him in... I guess it must have been three years ago. In 2122."

"So you talked with this man? Where? In Argentina?"

"Well, yes. Querida, once you lose faith in the corporate records and the corporate communication channels, the only thing is to go and see with your own eyes and hear with your own ears."

"So what else did you learn from your old man?"

Luis said that the old Argentine was named Silvestre Ocampo. "His memory was faltering a bit with age, but when I mentioned my grandmother's name—Isabel Hernandez—he started telling stories."

"'La bella Isabela,' he called her. He was only a kid when Abuela Isabel was in Argentina, but he remembered her. Silvestre told me that she liked him because of his aunt, Silvina Ocampo, who she claimed was one of her favorite authors." Luis chuckled softly. "Silvina was more likely Silvestre's great-great-aunt, but who's counting? Or in fact they may have just had the same last name. Makes little difference to the story."

"And that's all you know about your grandmother?"

"I know that she received a degree in languages and literature from the Universidad Nacional Autonoma in Mexico City. I think it was in 1996. That part is—was—still on record. There's still a lot I don't know. I haven't even been able to find a photograph of her. I searched everywhere. And my own memories from early childhood are of course vague."

"There's a bit more that I learned from Silvestre." Luis resumed his story. Silvestre had told about going with Isabel to an estate off in the countryside, behind a tall fence. "He said they never went in through the main gate. There were guards with big guns. They knew a way in through a place where a fallen tree had broken down part of the fence. Silvestre said he would wait near the fence until Isabel returned and that she always came back carrying a little package. And then Silvestre told me that one day Isabel simply disappeared. Later a woman showed up looking for her. That would have been my mother, Juana."

Jenda and Luis sat in silence as Jenda processed what he had told her. Luis watched her face.

"And there's nothing at all in your mother's Your Journal files about being in Argentina?" she asked. This was the part she was having trouble with. Mysterious buildings in the countryside and imprisoned teachers of language and literature couldn't even be entertained as real until she dealt with this question. Jenda's professional life for the past ninety years had centered on writing and producing compelling advertising campaigns about how Your Journal helped you remember, how it protected your privacy, and was "Your Lifeline to Your Life's Story." That one had been her campaign, and she had felt great pride in its success.

"How could that happen?" Jenda continued. "Maybe the old man had her mixed up with somebody else. Maybe she didn't go there." She was feeling irritated again.

"But I remember her going. We used to talk about it."

"Yeah, but you were just a little kid. Maybe..."

Luis inhaled deeply. "What about the book?"

"Okay, I guess that's kind of hard evidence, isn't it." Jenda stared intently at the blossom on the banana tree below the balcony. She wondered how long it might take for the blossom to turn into ripe bananas and if perhaps Luis had some ripe bananas in the kitchen that they could have for breakfast. She watched her mind doing its best to run away from where Luis was trying to take it. She watched herself trying to evade the wave of anger that seemed to be coming from nowhere.

"I talked to Silvestre's wife, too. She remembered Abuela Isabel being there, even though she was only ten or eleven at the time. Silvestre and his wife are still there," he said. "You could go talk to them if you want."

"Really?" Luis' whole story felt somewhat surreal. It was disturbing. Jenda slumped back into the cushions.

"Okay, let's say maybe I believe all this. Most of it." She sounded tentative. "Damn it all, Luis. You're going to have to give me some time. Let me think about it, alright?"

Jenda felt there was something in Luis' story that resonated with something she had forgotten, yet every time she tried to identify what that might be, it slipped away. It was infuriating.

6.

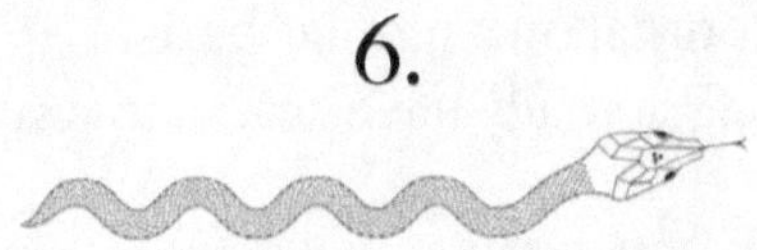

Over the next several months of her sabbatical, Jenda listened to more stories and her mind began to formulate clearer questions. Answers were elusive, and her body reacted to her mental disarray with a whole host of symptoms—headaches, dizzy spells, and loss of appetite.

Luis jokingly accused her of being pregnant. "Isn't that what used to happen to women when they would become pregnant?"

"At the age of III?" Jenda rejoined, with a weak smile. Luis gave her hand a reassuring squeeze.

"Do you need me to get you some more meds?" he asked.

"No. No more meds, I think. Nothing but fresh bananas and some more of that pre-Geni coffee from your friends in the mountains."

"So now you're craving bananas?" He dodged the bed pillow Jenda swung at his head. Maybe she was recovering.

By late that afternoon, Jenda was feeling even better. Good sex always made her feel more centered. As she and Luis snuggled under the damp sheets, she asked one of the questions that had been forming in her mind for several weeks now. "What can I do about all this?" she said softly. "My sabbatical is eventually going to end, and I'll be expected to go back to my job at YJ. If it's as bad as you and your friends say, maybe I should give notice and find some kind of work that's less distasteful."

Luis stroked her cheek and secured a stray strand of her golden hair behind an ear.

"Let's think about that," he said. "Tell me more about what it is you do at Your Journal."

Jenda reminded him that she was in the advertising department, one of several people tasked with coming up with new campaigns to keep people mindful of how important it was to screen in and journal on a regular basis.

"So you don't actually have access to any customer files?" Luis asked.

"Sometimes I do. When I have a particular project in mind, they let me sift through recent files to get a better idea of what's on people's minds, what they're currently interested in. You know," she said. "Research."

"Market research," he countered. "Do they give you some kind of general access phrase that gets you into the files?"

"I guess it's a general access. But I don't enter it myself. Somebody else always gets me in and then I work away until I have what I want."

"This is okay. This could work." Luis lay back on his pillow and stared at the ceiling.

"What do you mean, Luis? Work how? What are you thinking?"

"I'm thinking, " he replied, "that if you're up for it, you might be able to help us get access to some information that would help the Recall network understand more about what goes on at Your Journal."

Jenda raised her eyebrows. She was getting a twinge of that sensation she had felt right before she switched her sabbatical from California to San Miguel de Allende.

"It would be better if you had some kind of access phrase. Of course if they gave you something like that, it would probably be changed the minute you screened off. So never mind. This is okay. There are ways of detecting when files have been altered. I could teach you how to look for those indicators."

Jenda looked away.

"But we can do that tomorrow," he said. "And only if you want to. Today you rest and tonight we'll go to a nice café for some supper. Tomorrow we can work."

Jenda woke the next morning with a sense of dread. She tried to recapture the brief thrill she had felt the day before, but it was gone. Did she want to get into all of this? She felt Luis' arm steal across her torso and pull her closer. "Let's not work today," he said. "Let's close the gallery and go for a walk and let you recover some more. It's a good day for a walk. It's a holiday in some of the old neighborhoods and we can enjoy the fun."

Jenda was relieved. "What holiday? What day is today anyway?" She had lost track.

"It's the second of November—el Día de los Muertos."

"Well, that doesn't sound like much fun. Dead people day?" She pulled the covers back up around her chin and glared at him.

"Sorry, mi amor. I guess it's not a very important holiday in your culture." He shrugged. "Not even very important in mine anymore, but some of the people still enjoy it." And he explained that it was a day when people honored their ancestors, the deceased ones. "Of course, not so long ago, almost all of one's ancestors were deceased."

"Not like today, when you can go visit your grandparents and great-grandparents at their habitat instead of at the cemetery. Even your great-great-grandparents if you happen to be Gen4 or 5. Nobody goes to cemeteries anymore."

"Well, some of these people do. For most of them, though, it's just a day to get together with family and friends and enjoy music and dancing and good food and sweet cakes shaped like little skulls."

"Ewww!" Jenda hid her face in the pillow. "You're trying to make me sick again."

"No, no! I promise you, querida, they're delicious cakes and the skulls don't look realistic at all. They look more like... like little clown faces."

"Luis! You know I hate clowns."

"Oh, come on. Get over yourself and come along and see if you can have some fun doing some of the crazy things your crazy partner's crazy people do."

Luis stood up and held out his hand. His smile was that warm, engaging, big-as-the-world smile that had attracted Jenda to him from the outset. Jenda held back for a moment, then grasped his hand firmly and raised herself slowly from the bed.

"Okay then. Let's go play with your crazy dead people."

The day turned out far better than Jenda anticipated. They strolled at leisure along shaded streets through neighborhoods she had not been to before, neighborhoods where people still lived with their families. Whenever she got tired, they would stop at a sidewalk bar to sip fruity rum punch or they would sit for a while in one of the little parks or plazas along the way. They spent more time sitting than walking.

Luis took her to a few small art galleries, most of which had special displays of Día de los Muertos curios for people to buy and take home with them. Luis knew all the gallerists and shopkeepers. One of the gallerists invited them into the back of his space, to a locked room where he kept what he called his real art—oil paintings and sculptures in stone and bronze. Jenda recognized a few of the paintings as Luis' work. They lingered over a graceful small bronze of a girl reading a book.

"I love this artist's work," Luis remarked. "So sensitive."

"You know this artist?" Jenda also found the piece captivating.

"Not personally. We know her name, though—Setha Tica."

A little further down the street, they entered a small shop selling old paper books, maps, and printed photographs. Jenda picked up a few of the books and found the feel of them in her hands had a curiously comforting effect. She felt the urge to sit down on the floor and open them up one by one and read. One of the books had a warped cover and water stains on its faded binding. When Jenda opened it, she found that many of the pages had stuck together. She felt sad, thinking how whole sections of the story had disappeared into those ruined pages. She wondered why no one had tried to pry the pages apart. She returned the book to the chaotic jumble on the table and picked up another one.

"What are you finding there?" Luis asked.

"Oh..." She looked at the book's cover. "It's something called *The Wonderful Wizard of Oz*. I was wondering if maybe I had seen it somewhere before. Probably not. Look at these strange characters on the front – a little man made of metal and another stitched together out of rags." She ran her fingers over the figures and then laid the book back on the table. Jenda had suddenly thought of her brother Jonathan and wished Luis could meet him. She thought they would probably like each other.

As they made their way toward the door at the front of the shop, Luis stopped abruptly and looked around at all the books and other things on paper. "You know," he said, "Sometimes I feel like we and our things have been evolving in opposite directions—human beings becoming more enduring while the materials we use to record our memories become more temporary, transient." He picked up a tattered paperback in one hand and a well-preserved leather-bound volume in the other. "Of course, nothing lasts forever. It all changes. But I keep thinking, wouldn't it be better to encode our memories on a more human scale? Something more than the momentary digital image but less than the bronze and stone objects we call permanent?" He put the books back on the table, still lost in thought.

"Thank you, Dr. Anthropologist." Jenda hadn't meant to be dismissive of his comments, but the experience of being in the bookshop had made her feel like a kid again and she was having a hard time remembering to behave like an adult.

"So let me tell you more stories about my ancestors," Luis smiled, taking Jenda's hand as they made their way back onto the street. "Día de los Muertos is one of our distinctively Mexican holidays," he said, "a mezcla of old Spanish Catholic customs with even older native ones. Our ancestors believed that crying and mourning would insult the dead ones, and so they celebrated, with lots of good food and drink and music and dancing and entertainments of all kinds."

"I like that part."

"You know, not so long ago, people considered death to be part of life, not so different from birth, childhood, growing up. So on this day, they celebrated as if those who had died were still part of the living community."

"So now that our ancestors are mostly still among the living, I'm not sure I get the point," Jenda said, although she was enjoying this glimpse of the world according to Luis.

"Well, just go along with it at least and let's have fun," he said, as another group marched down the street in their calaveras masks, dancing to the raucous sounds of a mariachi band.

The next morning Jenda was feeling better than she had in weeks. She and Luis lingered over mugs of steaming coffee on the balcony.

"Are you ready for your first lesson?" Luis looked ready.

"Ready as I'll ever be."

They passed through the kitchen to refill their coffee mugs and then settled in front of Luis' large digiscreen.

"What I'll show you first is how to recognize that a photograph has been altered."

"How do you even know about these so-called indicators?" Jenda was becoming more skeptical than she had been before meeting Luis, who didn't mind when she aimed her skepticism at him. He seemed to like questions.

At first, he said, they had used a specialized script to analyze files for evidence of tampering, but since personal digiscreens were kept under surveillance by the corporations, these extraneous scripts had a tendency to disappear overnight. Then one of the Recall geniuses had come up with a way of adapting some standard scripts to the task. They also designed gizmos to masquerade as something else, something harmless and trivial. It made analysis more tedious and time consuming, but it was more secure. Luis screened up some of his own Your Journal files and opened two pictures in PhotoStyle.

"Hey, I didn't know you could do that." Jenda had always understood that Your Journal files could only be opened in Your Journal and not with any other script.

"Some of us can do that," Luis replied, looking smug. One picture showed him with a beautiful woman at one of the more popular restaurants in San Miguel. "That was before I knew you existed, mi amor," he said, grinning at Jenda. "She was only a harmless diversion."

Jenda silently hoped that she wasn't going to be described the same way in another ten years or so, but all she said was "She's very pretty."

The other picture showed Luis by himself in front of an art gallery. It didn't look like San Miguel.

"Where was that taken?" she asked.

"Buenos Aires."

"So now we play 'What's wrong with this picture?' Right?"

"Right." He clicked through a complex sequence of processes for each image, some of which Jenda found familiar, but others she didn't recognize. The way he quickly ran through the sequence suggested that he had done this many times before. He ended up with each image transformed into a screen full of dots. He scrolled through the picture from the local restaurant. "This is how things should look," he said. "See how smoothly the dots align? But now look at this." He pulled up the picture from Argentina and, once Luis pointed it out, Jenda could see some dots that didn't align with the surrounding area. He placed a dark line along these vaguely defined margins and then zoomed out.

"Wayee!" Jenda's eyes widened. What she saw was the ghost outline of another person, apparently a woman. "So I guess your girlfriend must have been in this picture, too."

He shook his head. "No. It was Rosalí. Silvestre's wife."

"Okay, now I'm getting confused. You're saying Your Journal altered your photo but you still remember who was in it before? I thought that memories were reconstructed because of the things you forgot due to the Chulel."

"You know better than that, Jenda. You've heard other people's stories, seen their pictures."

She knew. She knew things she desperately did not want to know. Her mind kept resisting, reverting to her old ways of thinking, shielding some last few tenuous scraps of reassurance that she had not been employed for the last ninety years in convincing people to surrender their minds and life stories to a pack of carefully crafted lies.

"You know," he continued, "that Chulel doesn't actually affect the memory at all."

That was the most difficult piece, the one that threatened the last shred of self-respect that Jenda had been hanging onto.

Luis was relentless. "The forgetting is part of the little show you get that you're told is helping you remember. Anyone who uses off-market Chulel knows this." He reminded her that it was after the big lost memories scare back in 2045 that people had become afraid to take Chulel at home and had eagerly signed up at the new Chulel clinics that offered memory restoration using the customer's own Your Journal records.

"So you self-administer Chulel?" Jenda hadn't known about that. Why did knowing about it annoy her so? "But how do you avoid your appointments. And all those reminders?"

"I self-administer, as you say, and I always have, so I've managed to stay off their appointment calendars. But others go in for their appointments as expected. They smuggle in earplugs and opaque contact lenses so that they're shielded from the photonic memory reconstruction process."

Remembering her own invariably pleasant experiences of Chulel spa days with memory restoration, Jenda felt her defenses and her ire rising. But had they really been so pleasant? She felt sudden sparks, electric pricks throughout her body. Small white explosions. Fear.

"Really, Luis? Come on. That's ridiculous!" Jenda knew her anger was irrational, but it felt real, and it was keeping her focused. "No, really. Now you're making stuff up. No, that can't be. I refuse to believe it!" The questions had been bad enough;

the answers threatened Jenda's mind like a jackhammer. She wanted to get away. She shoved her chair toward Luis.

As he started to speak again, Jenda raised her hands in front of her face. "No!" she shouted. "Enough! Leave me alone. I don't want to hear anymore." She grabbed up her shoulder bag and, shoeless, stomped out of the house, down the stairs, and into the midday sun. Tears were coming, but she refused them. "No," she told herself. "I've let all this get to me too much already. I've had enough. I want my boring, trivial little life back." The graveled walkway was hurting her feet, and it felt good. Her mind was in turmoil.

Jenda stopped next to a fountain in the heart of the little park. The grass under her feet was cool and soft. She stood there, listening to the splashing water. She watched it spurting up, spilling over the first level, the second level, disappearing somewhere beneath the ground to emerge again through the little spout at the top and continue its monotonous cycle. Some of it splashed out onto the ground and disappeared, nourishing the thick carpet of grass. She sat down. The sun was warm on her face and arms. Almost too warm on this sunny November day, but every once in a while a cloud passed overhead and Jenda clung to each deliciously cool shadow. She didn't want to think, she only wanted to feel the sun, the shadows, the cool grass, and listen to the fountain.

By the time the sun approached a more oblique angle, Jenda had given in to her tears. She clasped her arms around her bent knees and put her head down so that no one would see as she wept silently. When her tears finally ran out, she lifted her sweater to wipe her face. *What was it Granny El used to say?* she mused. *You can't put the toothpaste back in the tube.* However much she might want to un-know what Luis had shown her, she knew that was impossible. She might have been able to live with a delusion imposed from outside, but she couldn't—she wouldn't—delude herself. She did want to know. She did want to ask questions and whatever the answers might be, she wanted to know.

She sat a while longer, feeling cleansed by the sound of splashing water. Then she rose, brushed herself off, and began to walk slowly back to Luis' place, keeping to the grassy patches and the smooth paving stones.

She half expected the door next to the outdoor staircase to be locked and her suitcase on the top step. Instead the door was slightly ajar and when she went inside she saw a glass on the table filled with sweet hibiscus tea and some mostly melted ice cubes. The glass sat in a puddle of condensation.

"So you finally decided to come back?" Luis was standing in the shadows by the door that led to the balcony, his arms crossed. His voice was tense.

"What made you think I'd come back at all?" Jenda countered, with a covert sniffle.

"I guess I hoped you would."

"What, so I wouldn't mess up your crazy subversive plot to expose some incredible conspiracy?"

"No, Jenda, I just... I've pushed you. I'm sorry."

"No, Luis. No apologies. Why should you apologize for showing me the truth? I don't understand why I got so angry. There are things I can't explain. But I want to, Luis. I want to know the truth."

She took a couple of steps toward him and stopped. She looked up into his moist eyes. This was her life now, and she was ready to embrace it.

Luis reached his hand toward her, and she took it. They each stepped forward, then leaned together, their arms around one another.

7.

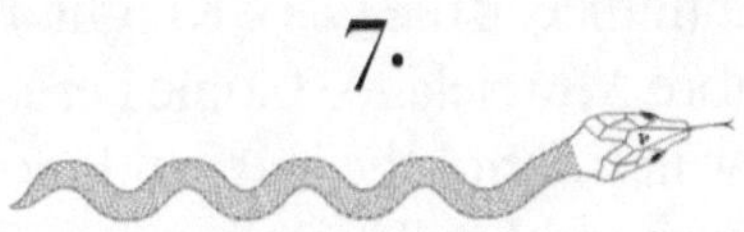

Despite her new resolve, Jenda continued uploading daily posts and photos to Your Journal throughout her sabbatical, largely out of habit, but also due to what she now suspected was an implanted sense of guilt if she failed to give YJ something for the day. Her posts became increasingly cursory, and her photos were now more likely to be pictures of streets or shops or trees in the park rather than of anybody or anything of significance to her personally. She spent long hours in the art studio, painting.

One afternoon, she became a bit stuck with the painting she was working on and began exploring a far corner of the studio that she had not paid much attention to previously.

"What are these?" she asked, picking up a thin but colorful paper book encased in a translucent envelope. There seemed to be a large stack of similar items.

Luis looked over his shoulder to see what had caught her interest. He smiled. "Those," he said, "are my prized possessions."

"Oh." She looked puzzled.

Luis placed his brush in the container of solvent and wiped his hands thoroughly with a clean white cloth. He walked over to where Jenda stood holding the book gingerly as if it were some strange specimen. He took the book from her and lovingly removed it from its envelope.

"This, mi amor, is a Batman comic book." He took Jenda by the hand and led her back to the shelf where she had found the book. "On this shelf, I have an almost complete collection of Batman comics, all carefully preserved in archival sleeves." His face radiated pride.

"What is a batman?" Jenda asked.

"¡Ay, pobrecita! How could you live so long without making the acquaintance of the Dark Knight, the incomparable Batman, el Hombre Murcielago? Come here, querida." He sat down on the floor in front of the shelf and motioned for Jenda to join him. "Sit here and I will introduce you."

First he pointed to the figures on the cover. "This one with the black cloak—this is Batman, the Dark Knight, champion of all that is good, protector of the weak. His real identity is... but we'll get to that later."

"What about that one?" Jenda pulled her knees up close to her chest and pointed to another figure.

"That," Luis said, "is the evil trickster known as The Joker, Batman's nemesis."

"I can see how evil he is. He has a clown face."

Luis opened the book. The first couple of pages were just pictures without words. Jenda followed Luis' finger and the story began. On the next page, there were little white bubbles representing speech, pointing toward the person who was speaking. Luis read aloud, using different voices for Batman and Joker and the other characters. When they came to a page with a woman speaking, he attempted a falsetto to read her words.

Jenda laughed. "No, silly, let me read that one." And she read the woman's words in her best theatric voice. And so they proceeded through the entire story, reading the various voices, alternating between melodrama and laughter. Luis was especially good at reading the sound effects.

When the story finally ended, he closed the book and asked, "So what do you think?" He replaced the book in its protective cover.

"I think that's some pretty scary stuff," Jenda said. "But I like your Batman. I think he's my new hero. Can we read another one?" And so they read another. Reading comic books became their second favorite break activity in the studio.

Jenda would have let her 2025 birth anniversary pass unnoticed if Luis had not become aware of it when he joined her LifeBook loop. It was on November 18. Luis remembered something he had read about Texas birthday traditions and decided he would buy her a cluster of brightly colored helium-filled balloons, a bouquet of real fresh-cut flowers, and a cake with tiny candles. After considerable effort, he had located sources for all of these items. On the morning of her birthday, Luis said nothing to Jenda, having ascertained that an element of surprise was part of the tradition. He was relieved when she announced she was going shopping, as he had not yet settled on a plan to keep her out of the house while he gathered the requisite items from their various sources and arranged them for her.

"No problem," he said, indicating that he would be available to mind the gallery himself all day if necessary. "But on your way home, would you mind stopping by Federico's gallery for me and pick up a pot of gesso? If you do it last thing, you won't have to carry it far." Luis had at least figured out how to determine when she was on her way home; Federico would pulse him.

Jenda agreed. She kissed Luis goodbye and left by the front door, to the sound of tinkling bells. She was looking forward to a shopping excursion. She had been worrying again about her eventual return to Dallas and Your Journal. She hoped shopping would help calm her mind.

It didn't. If anything, the process of sifting through rack after rack of recyclable garments made her feel even more agitated. *It's all so temporary,* she thought angrily. *It's what they want us to do—keep buying more and more things every day and feeding their recycling machine. Bright colors, flashy patterns--it's only to attract our attention. Some of these things are just ugly!* Jenda wondered if the so-called fashion trends weren't somehow included in the memory reconstruction process, herding consumers into buying exactly the things the corporations had already decided to produce. She needed clothes, though, so she bought a few outfits, fully aware that she was selecting what would likely be considered the least fashionable items on the racks.

Her shopping trip didn't take long and Jenda was already on her way back to the gallery apartment when she remembered the gesso. She didn't want to disappoint Luis. Perhaps she didn't want to have to discuss her agitated state of mind with him, which her failure to keep her promise might reveal. Better to backtrack the few blocks to Federico's gallery and get the gesso.

As she finally opened the door to Galería Kukulcan, the sound of the bells gave her a welcome sense of safety. "Luis?" Jenda called. Luis was not at his usual place behind the little desk that gave him a view of the gallery from his factory space. Then she heard him running down the stairs. He looked a bit breathless. "I got your gesso." Jenda held out the package wrapped in brown paper.

"Gracias, querida," he said. "I see you have a few more packages, too. So you had a good morning?" He didn't wait for her to answer but took her hand as he said, "Let's close and go up for some lunch."

"You made lunch?"

As they entered the apartment from the stairwell, Jenda saw the reason for Luis' excitement. The place was filled with balloons and flowers. And there in the middle of the little tile-surfaced table was a sugary cake inscribed "Happy Birthday Jenda." There were tiny candles on the cake.

"Surprise!" Luis said, looking pleased with himself. "Happy birthday, mi amor!"

Jenda was speechless, barraged by a contradictory set of feelings, thoughts, and vague memories. Tears came to her eyes, and she couldn't have said whether they were tears of joy, anger, or sadness. She sat down heavily on an arm of the sofa, facing the table with its disturbing cake, her hand over her mouth, her eyes wide.

"Oh, Luis, you shouldn't have," she said.

"Really?" He looked crestfallen. "I thought it would make you happy."

"No, I mean... it's so sweet. And you went to so much trouble." She got up and threw her arms around Luis, "Thank you. You are a dear, precious man."

Jenda was beginning to understand that if she ever expected to come to terms with memories that might have gotten rearranged in her own mind, she should welcome these ambiguous moments and try to let them move freely through her. It wasn't easy.

Luis pulled out a lighter and began to light the candles.

"Oh, do we have to," Jenda began, her brow furrowing slightly.

"But I thought there was a custom about making a wish," he responded. "You don't want to miss your wish, do you?" He was grinning, apparently enthralled by the whole process, oblivious to her discomfort.

"Okay. Of course." She did seem to remember something about wishes. It all reminded her of her mother, and she felt a strong urge to be held.

Luis lit all the candles—there were ten of them—and stood back. "I think there used to be a song to wish the happy birthday," he said, "but I couldn't find it. So I'll just say 'Happy birthday, Jenda!' And now you wish something and blow out the candles, right?"

Jenda paused, watching the candles burn, trying to decide what to wish. "I wish..."

"No, no! I don't think you're supposed to say it out loud. Your own private wish." Luis took her hand. Jenda looked up at him then and felt what he was wishing for; she silently wished the same thing. Then she blew out the candles.

"And now," she said with a laugh, "I'm pretty sure we're supposed to eat a piece of cake before we have lunch."

The next day Jenda told Luis she needed to go look for some new shoes to match the outfits she had bought. Truthfully, she just wanted to get away on her own. She didn't understand why the odd candle-bedecked cake had upset her and she needed some time to reflect.

Without thinking, she found herself following the route that Luis had shown her on Día de los Muertos and within a short while she was deep into the neighborhood that belonged to the native Mexican inhabitants of San Miguel. She found a sidewalk café that she remembered visiting with Luis. She sat down at one of the tables and picked up the plastiflex menu screen. She was a little hungry, so when the waiter came to see to her needs, she ordered a taco de nopalitos and a glass of rum punch. This was exactly what she had ordered when she had come here with Luis. She sipped the cool citrusy punch and watched the passers-by, letting her mind wander.

There was a park across the street with lots of open space where the grass was worn thin. On one of the thinnest patches of grass there was a little seat attached by long ropes to a tall frame and a child was sitting on the seat as it moved forward and back like a pendulum. As Jenda watched, she felt the child's sense of the ground rushing closer, the feeling of flying up into the sky, falling back to earth. Jenda realized she was smiling. Had she ever been on one of these devices herself as a child? A woman who had been sitting on a bench near the device got up to give the child a push. "¡Mas alto! ¡Mas!" the child shouted, laughing. There was something odd about the woman's appearance. She had a slender frame, but her body seemed strangely round. Jenda realized the woman was pregnant and her hand went involuntarily to her own flat belly. How odd it must feel, she thought, to have something alive inside your body. She ordered another punch when the waiter brought her taco. The day was warm, and she was thirsty.

She looked across the street again and saw that the child had left the swinging contraption and was walking alongside the woman, holding her hand. Another woman rose slowly to her feet to join them. This second woman had a body that was frail and bent. She was old. How old? *Without Chulel, she's likely not even as old as I am. How can it be that there are still people living like this? Living without Chulel, having babies, growing old? We should do something to help them.* Jenda scowled. Then her expression softened as she watched the two women walking arm in arm, the little boy holding his mother's hand.

8.

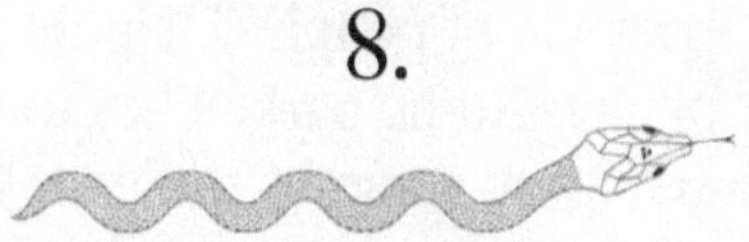

"What do people around here do for winter holidays, for Christmas or New Year's?" Jenda asked one morning as she and Luis sat on the balcony enjoying the December sunshine.

"Ah. I guess that will be coming up soon," he replied. "Well, there used to be elaborate celebrations, but now we have only a couple of days of Posadas. And a few decorated trees, I guess."

"Posadas?"

"Commemorating Mary and Joseph's search for lodging. There are processions leading from one church to another. There used to be a lot of churches. Now there are only three. The rest have been turned into shops and restaurants and hotels. More profitable, you know."

"We used to decorate a tree, I think." Jenda tried to remember. "Maybe with lights. And sparkly things. And gifts are always nice."

"We could do a tree. Shall we? And gifts?"

Jenda smiled. She already knew what she would give to Luis.

The next afternoon they went in search of a tree, which they purchased from a temporary street vendor in an old neighborhood. It was an asymmetrical and ungainly thing, but they liked it. They found some strings of tiny, lighted tin lanterns shaped like stars and some glittery paper flowers for decoration. They set the tree into a bucket with rocks and a little water and placed it next to the doors that led onto the balcony, laughing at its insistence on remaining just off vertical. Once it was decorated, they switched off the lights and sat on the sofa, admiring their glowing handiwork.

In the week before the twenty-fifth, they studiously avoided questioning one another too closely about the intent of their various errands. They watched the Posada processions and enjoyed the spectacle of people (including a few children) swatting away at piñatas in the park. They took evening walks to enjoy the various lights some of the people had put up to adorn their houses and gardens. Jenda found the entire spectacle familiar and was pleased that, for once, something that seemed to awaken old memories wasn't distressing.

The final Posada terminated in front of the temple of San Juan de Dios. "Do you want to go inside?" Luis asked, as the crowd began to disperse.

"Sure." Jenda was curious. She had never been a churchgoer, as far as she knew. These buildings looked so wise. She expected the stone interior to be cold, but instead it felt warm with the glow of fragrant candles and incense, the press of bodies. Individual candles flickered and danced, but the glow was steady, unmoving. Jenda reached for Luis' hand.

As one group of pilgrims parted, revealing the object of their devotion, Jenda caught her breath. It was a lady in blue, like the one she dreamed about. She tugged at Luis' arm and gestured toward the statue.

"Who is she?"

"Her?" He looked in the direction Jenda indicated. "Ah. The Virgin of Guadalupe," he said, pulling Jenda forward for a closer look.

Jenda held back. "She frightens me. I think I used to have dreams about her. I can never quite remember."

Luis placed a comforting arm around Jenda's shoulders and, as they left the church, he explained how important the Virgin of Guadalupe was in the history of the Mexican people.

On Christmas morning, Jenda woke early, but tried to keep quiet and still so as not to disturb Luis, who was still snoring softly. Carefully, she turned to face him. Just as she was closing her eyes to settle into her pillow, Luis let out a huge snort. "You goof!" Jenda laughed. "You're not asleep at all. God, you almost scared me to death." They smothered their laughter in a Christmas kiss.

"No gifts without coffee," Jenda commanded. They went to the kitchen to make coffee, then placed their steaming mugs on the little table in front of the sofa. Each one disappeared to retrieve a carefully hidden gift.

"Now what?" Luis asked, looking at Jenda for guidance. "Do we go have breakfast and come back later?" He grinned.

"No, no," Jenda instructed. "We definitely open gifts before breakfast. You go first." She handed Luis her present, using both hands. "Merry Christmas, Luis!"

"It's heavy," he observed. "But I think you should go first, querida."

"Okay, I'll tell you what we'll do. First, we'll take turns removing the ribbons. Then the paper. Then...you know, whatever comes next."

Luis handed Jenda her gift. "¡Feliz Navidad!"

So they each removed the ribbons, savoring the anticipation.

"This paper is so pretty. I don't want to tear it," Luis said. He folded the paper and then set his unopened box in his lap and looked expectantly at Jenda.

She could tell her gift was a book. As she removed the paper and turned the book over to reveal its cover, a smile lit up first her eyes and then her whole face.

"Oh, Luis," she said quietly. "I remember this. We saw it at the old bookshop. You know, I think I do remember it from when I was a child. It's about a little girl, isn't it? And she has a dog. And they fly through the air to a magical place." She leaned over to give Luis a kiss. "Thank you," she said, stroking the cover of the book.

"I thought you might have some connection with it."

"Time for you to open your box now," Jenda said, hugging her book to her chest.

Luis lifted the cover of the box and reached inside, giving Jenda a puzzled look. He pushed the box aside and set a tissue-swathed object in front of him. Then he carefully removed the layers of paper.

"¡Ay! querida," he whispered, and then fell silent, mesmerized by the sculpture that sat before him. It was the small bronze of a little girl reading a book.

Jenda saw that his eyes were moist. "I noticed how you admired it when we went to your friend's gallery that day—the day of the dead people. Do you remember?"

"Oh, I've admired this little piece even before that," he confessed. "I can't believe you got it for me. ¡Qué milagro!"

He lifted the figure up to admire it at eye level. He looked at Jenda and then back at the sculpture. "You know, she's sitting exactly the way you sit when we're reading Batman comics in the studio," he said. Then he set the figure under the tree and reached to embrace Jenda. "Mil gracias, mi amor." And they followed up with another Christmas kiss.

"Now breakfast," Jenda said. But she made no move to extract herself from their embrace.

During the final months of Jenda's sabbatical, her days became more balanced between painting, learning useful digital skills, and enjoying spending time with the man she knew she was going to miss more than she had missed anyone in a very long time. She noticed that Luis was absent more and more frequently, leaving her to mind the gallery on her own.

On an unusually rainy afternoon in late March, Luis returned from one of his unexplained errands soaking wet and out of sorts.

"Why did you have to go out on a day like this anyway?" Jenda admonished, helping him out of his wet jacket and shirt.

"I had to go, Jen."

Jenda stood back, holding his wet things. "Because..." she prompted.

"Okay. Sorry. I guess I owe you more of an explanation of why I've been out so much lately. Let's close up and go upstairs. I could use some hot cocoa."

Dry clothes and a mug of steaming sweetness put Luis in a better state of mind.

"I've been meeting with various Recall people," he explained. "There are plans afoot."

"Plans?"

"Mmm." He took a big gulp of hot chocolate. "They're not telling us any details yet, but they've been asking us to make some test posts on various mediazones and then monitor how they're dealt with. Honestly, Jenda, I don't fully understand what it's all about. At first I figured you'd be better off not knowing anything about it. Now I think that was probably unfair. I trust you, querida, and I also have confidence in your intelligence and discretion. Why shouldn't I tell you everything I know? Even though, as I said, that's not a lot."

Jenda smiled at him and then kissed his cheek. "Thanks, Luis. I'm glad to know you've been attending to important matters. And I'm glad to learn that, as you say, there are plans afoot. Maybe we should get you some kind of costume to put on when you take on your Recall identity and go out to save the world." They spent the next ten minutes imagining elaborate superhero costumes and identities for one another, laughing as they became increasingly ridiculous.

As the time neared for Jenda to return to her job at Your Journal in Dallas, she and Luis worked out a project for her. It was a loose plan whereby she would devise an advertising campaign for Your Journal that would require her to get access to a wide range of files. Luis supplied her with a tiny wireless device she could use to draw down these files for subsequent analysis off site. It was a rather open-ended assignment.

"You'll have to come up with a great proposal to convince them, I think," Luis said.

"Not a problem," Jenda sniffed. "You are looking at the queen of Your Journal advertising campaigns. Well, not officially. But still, definitely not a problem."

Jenda felt comfortable and happy in San Miguel. She had even resigned herself to the idea that the company she worked for engaged in activities she found objectionable. But when she thought about the fact that she would be returning to work there soon, her serenity faltered. She worried about the fact that she would be due for her Chulel spa day upon her return to Dallas. Sabbaticals and Chulel days were generally synchronized such that the spa treatment was perceived as a welcome re-entry into working life.

"Is there any way to avoid it?" she asked Luis one day. "I've always looked forward to my Chulel spa days in the past, but now, after what I've learned...Luis, I don't want to forget even one moment of the time we've spent together."

"Well, if you worked for anyone other than YJ, I'd suggest you start self-administering," he answered. "But in your case, your employers would notice, and it could put your job in jeopardy."

"You told me that some people have found ways of protecting themselves from the memory reconstruction. Could you help me do that?"

"Of course, mi amor. They tell me it's not that hard, since they leave you alone in the room during the photonic treatment. They can't monitor it on camera because of the photon bursts. And I guess it would be dangerous for anyone else to be in there. They might come out thinking they were you." He laughed. Jenda didn't.

In the past, whenever she had approached the end of a sabbatical, Jenda would begin to distance herself from whatever lover had been her companion for the duration. This time was different. Missing Luis would be painful, she knew, but she also knew they would be together again. A lot. For a long time. They had a joint project and an immediate plan to meet in Houston in just over a month. Jenda already had made plans to attend a tennis tournament there, so her travel would require no explanation. Luis would try to arrange a Marvaworld trip to coincide.

When they finally said their farewells at the León airport, they agreed to say only "hasta luego"--"until later". But Jenda cried a little, and Luis held her as if he would never let her go.

Part II
Questions

90

9.

"Increase speed!" Jenda commanded, addressing the control panel of the autocar. A red light flashed, and the voice admonished: "The speed limit in this zone is...fifty-five...kph. You may not exceed...fifty-five...kph." Jenda glared at the panel's clock. It was her first morning back in Dallas and she was running late for her appointment at the Chulel spa. Also, she didn't like the voice's prissy tone. She fiddled with a hangnail and finally bit it off.

"Zujo!" Jenda swore, as a tiny spot of blood rose up on her cuticle. Jenda was more nervous than she had been before her first Chulel treatment back in 2035. That one had been a celebration of her college graduation.

"Pull yourself together, Jen," she said, which didn't help at all because she hated taking orders, even from herself. She felt once again for the earplugs and opaque contact lenses she had stashed in the pocket of her trousers. They formed what she hoped was an undetectable bulge hidden under her loose shirt. She removed the band holding back her long hair and shook the hair down over her ears. She didn't think the earplugs would be noticeable, but she thought this would help. It was one less thing to worry about, anyway.

Arriving at the spa, Jenda passed her digilet in front of the registration point and took a seat. She searched for something to read, even though she didn't feel like reading. When her digilet chimed, Jenda went into the next room and entered the first unoccupied cubicle. She arranged her body in the exam chair, settling her arms and legs into the supports that would read her vital signs and analyze her blood composition. A few minutes later, the results came up on her digilet. Jenda thought her blood pressure looked a little high. She was instructed to report to room 217 in the spa wing. A medical attendant arrived, holding a digiscreen containing all of Jenda's medical records. She asked a few questions about the state of Jenda's health.

"And your medications? Is everything satisfactory, or do you wish to schedule a consultation?"

"No, everything's fine," Jenda said. She hadn't been taking most of her allotted medications, but she didn't want to be burdened with an appointment for a consultation and all the questions that would entail. The attendant ticked off each medication on the screen.

"Room 217 is all set up for you," she chirped. "Right this way."

As they walked through the soft lights and soothing music that filled the walkway, Jenda felt her blood pressure rise another few points. She wondered if any of the other clients they passed in the walkway were carrying earplugs and opaque lenses.

"Here we are," the smiling attendant said. Jenda was struck by how much her voice resembled the synthetic voice in the autocar.

Jenda placed her right hand on the entry pad and the door opened. Jenda knew what to do. The attendant helped her adjust the recliner to the position she found most comfortable and gave her two quick and painless infusions. The first was the Chulel and the second was a drug designed to make the memory restoration process maximally effective.

As soon as Jenda was sure she was on her own in the room, she inserted the earplugs and contact lenses. She was glad she had tested them out at home, because the loss of sensory input was unnerving. Luis had suggested she use the time trying to recreate the plot of a favorite novel or flick or remembering the lyrics of some of her favorite songs—anything to keep her mind focused and diverted away from what was happening around her. As the second infusion began to take effect, Jenda found it was becoming difficult to concentrate on anything at all. Her mind kept popping from one image to another and she was only able to drag it back to her selected storyline by force of will. She had to remember to keep her eyes open, too, so that if for any reason the attendant popped in, she would not be caught napping. The process would last three hours, and Jenda had set her digilet to vibrate and remind her to remove her protective gear.

She removed the lenses first, and was immediately inundated with images from the past year being shown on the 360-degree floor to ceiling screen. She closed her eyes as she removed the earplugs. The sound was white noise, but Jenda knew from her conversations with Luis' friends that it supposedly contained abundant subliminal messages. *Or maybe not,* she thought. She was exhausted from the effort of maintaining her focus during the treatment, but, recalling that in the past she had always felt relaxed and exhilarated, she did her best to appear that way when the attendant entered to take her to the snack room, which clients simply called "re-entry." Jenda was glad it was over. She hoped her efforts had protected her memories of San Miguel, her memories of Luis.

Jenda had the rest of the day free. She decided to take the monorail home instead of an autocar. She had time and submitting herself to the efficient confinement of an autocar was not appealing.

The rail station was not particularly crowded, and she had only a brief wait before a stage going her direction glided in. She found a seat near the middle of the stage and unfurled her digilet. She didn't want to engage with her fellow passengers, although she found their physical presence somehow comforting. Rails were used primarily by lower level workers. Jenda thought about the backstreet lunchroom. She looked up from her digilet to scan the faces in the stage, to see if the old woman might be there. She wasn't. But there was one woman who seemed to have been staring at Jenda. She had turned her attention quickly to her digilet as soon as Jenda looked toward her. Her perfect hair and erect posture made Jenda vaguely uncomfortable. Everyone seemed thoroughly engrossed in their own digilets, with the exception of one young man—an adolescent, by the look of his soft face and slender build—who was reading a paper book.

Jenda disembarked at the station nearest her habitation complex and emerged into the April warmth. She noticed the woman with perfect hair get off, too. Then, as Jenda headed toward her habitat, the woman went back inside the station. Jenda's endurb was built for autocars rather than pedestrians, and she had to choose whether to walk in the edge of the roadway or on the manicured lawns. She chose the lawns.

Back inside her own habitat, Jenda set about rearranging things. She felt different and she wanted her surroundings to reflect that. She moved a few small pieces of furniture. She placed the book that was her Christmas gift from Luis on the table next to the sofa and hung one of the small oil paintings she had made in San Miguel on the wall next to her home screen. She might seem like the same old Jenda when she was at work or meeting friends somewhere, but at home she wanted to be able to be herself, whoever that might turn out to be.

The next day Jenda went back to work at Your Journal as if nothing of any consequence had transpired over the past eleven months. She joked with her friends about the sexy Latino she had met, but she refused to give him a name. Jenda knew it was for her own and Luis' protection, but she let her colleagues believe it was because he was nothing more than a sabbatical flirtation, someone she had no intention of seeing again or remembering much about, other than the fun they had had. And the sex.

Coming back from sabbatical was always a delicate transition and companies had learned to reserve a simple assignment for returnees to let them slip into routines again without becoming overwhelmed. Jenda busied herself with her assignment as she also began working on the plan she and Luis had devised.

In her free hours at home, Jenda spent time on the Recall zone. She had learned how to access the inner depths of Recall, where she screened in to Interloc under a persona Luis had created for her. The messaging system was decidedly old fashioned and cumbersome, but since it took up far less bandwidth than visual or live audio communication, it was easier to blend in unnoticed. On one of her first tentative forays into Recall, Jenda found this item:

> *Time was when memory existed solely in the minds of men and women, and the elders of the society were its treasury. As humankind evolved, art became the handmaiden of memory, encoding in images and in stories that were recited or sung or danced, the episodes and values that defined a people. Writing was the next revolution of memory. The printing press was another. Digital electronic storage took memory to the next level but also put it at risk as never before. In every age, people believed their encoded memories to be somehow infallible, unassailable, invulnerable. They were always wrong, but the notion was pervasive and reassuring. It still is.*

The item was written by someone calling himself "HombreMurcielago"—Batman. It had to be Luis. Although this was an old item, Jenda responded: "Sometimes the short-term memories, shared only with one other, are the best." It wasn't profound, but she knew Luis would understand. She didn't care what other readers might think.

Jenda quickly developed favorites to follow on Recall. Number one, of course, was HombreMurcielago. Then she added Crone-1 and HillBill. Crone-1 was a woman who, after some forty years of Chulel treatments, had finally given it up. She was now experiencing aging and reporting on it in eloquent detail. Jenda found her accounts a bit frightening, but she liked the wise insights that Crone-1 often put forward. HillBill was the most entertaining. He had a way of cleverly ridiculing almost everything about the current cultural ethos, and especially the penchant for recycling everything, which he termed "destroy and reinvent." He exhorted people to resist the mindless submission of all their old books and printed photos for recycling.

Jenda found some of the items posted in Recall confusing or disturbing, prompting her to screen up a game or a flick or go to the kitchen for a dram. Increasingly, though, she found herself picking up a bound journal of paper pages and writing. At first she only wrote brief notes such as the ID tags of particular entries or pictures that caught her eye. Gradually, her handwritten journal entries became longer and more rambling. Jenda wasn't sure what some of the things she wrote meant. She wasn't even convinced they made any sense at all. Maybe they didn't need to. She only knew it felt good to write things down on paper.

By the weekend, Jenda was more than ready to get away from Your Journal. On Friday (the first day of the weekend) she had a tennis date with her grandmother. As usual, Jenda was running late. Granny El was ready and waiting and, as she slid into the leftside seat of the autocar, Jenda reached across to give her a quick hug. Then she pressed the "resume" button on the car's control panel. "Sorry I'm late, Gran, but..."

The autocar voice interrupted. "Proceeding to next destination. Lakeland Sports Complex. Time to destination...12...minutes." Their reservation slot began in eight minutes.

Jenda sighed audibly. "I'm sorry, Gran. I know we've been looking forward to getting back to our weekly tennis dates."

"Never mind," Jenda's grandmother said. "I wasn't nearly as interested in the tennis as I was in finally getting to spend a little time with you. Why don't we just go to the Food Strip and get a glass of tea and catch up. You've been way too busy since you got back from sabbatical. You've been back... what? Almost two weeks now?"

"Almost," Jenda said. "Gosh, it's good to see you Gran. I've missed you."

"Redirect." Jenda addressed the autocar. "New destination Hydra Delect at M Court."

Although she had put off their reunion longer than she should have, Jenda was deeply fond of Granny El, her mother's mother, who was her only family in Dallas, the only family she still had regular contact with anywhere.

"So tell me all about the sabbatical, Jen. Your pulses have been awfully brief, so I really have no idea. How was it?" Granny El began, as they settled into a courtyard table with their icy drams.

"Sabbatical was good, Gran."

"So, what was his name this time?" Granny El gave Jenda a sly look.

Jenda pursed her lips and stared into the distance as she struggled unsuccessfully to suppress the smile that seemed to surface whenever she thought of Luis. "Let's just say he was Latin and beautiful," Jenda said, taking a long draught of her NutriQuaff.

"So your inexplicable choice of San Miguel de Allende was not a total disaster?"

"Not a disaster at all, Gran. I made some new paintings." Jenda was unsure how much to share with her grandmother. "The weather was lovely," she said.

On Saturday, Jenda met up with her friends Eldred and Yeshe to visit a new experiential museum that had recently opened. As people had lost interest in the past, museums for all ages followed in the footsteps of early children's museums, providing engaging interactive exhibits and activities. A couple of times, Jenda thought she saw the same woman she had caught staring at her on the monorail her first day back in Dallas. She had the same perfect hair and erect posture. It was that posture Jenda found slightly unnerving. The woman carried herself like a member of the corporate police.

As Jenda and her friends sat in the museum snack shop enjoying cold drams after an exhausting romp through the exhibits, Jenda broached a question that had begun to nag at her during the visit.

"You know," she said, "museums used to provide people with information about the past—about history, evolution. Do you think it's important for us to know about things like that?"

"I seem to remember some of those," Eldred responded. "I always found them kind of boring. These new interactive museums that focus on vanguard culture are a lot more fun."

Yeshe frowned. "Past, future—not important. The Buddha taught us to always live fully in the present moment." Smiling, she added, "And these activities sure do keep me in the present moment!"

Jenda stared into her dram, stirring it thoughtfully. She was trying to recall a conversation she had had with her brother Jonathan shortly after he came back from Tibet. "Didn't the Buddha also teach about...What is it called? Dependent origination? You know - cause and effect. How can we understand where we are if we don't know anything about the causes? And causes have to be in the past."

"I don't know about that," Yeshe said. "But I do know that the Buddha taught that reality is only a construction of the mind. So I like to engage in activities that help me construct a happy mind."

Eldred leaned back in his chair, studying the colorful kinetic sculpture above their heads. "You know I'm a fan of the Buddha. But I also think sometimes we might be missing something by never looking back at the past or thinking where our present actions might be leading. What do you think Jenda?"

"If I knew what I thought I probably wouldn't have asked the question." Jenda knew she was being evasive. "I guess I get a little weary of just running around creating happy mind. No offense, Yeshe."

Jenda was troubled. There was undeniable appeal in living in the moment with no thought for the past or future. And if the neo-Buddhists were right about all reality being a construction of the mind, where did that leave Luis and his Recall crowd?

On her way home, Jenda sent a pulse to the last contact phrase she had for Jonathan, her brother who had left home at the age of fourteen to follow a Buddhist guru and who eventually ended up spending years at a monastery in Tibet. One of his gurus had pronounced him a reincarnation of a 20th-century monk known as Kentsy Norbu, who had been a modestly successful producer and director of flicks. It was because of him that Jonathan had become a flick maker.

"Been thinking about you lately." Jenda spoke into her digilet. "How are things? Are you still in Denver?" Jenda had seen a brief flurry of advertising hype while she was in Mexico over the release of Jonathan's latest flick. When she later searched for it to draw it down from the atmosphere, she couldn't find it. Jenda also was shocked to see that Jonathan had somehow disappeared from her LifeBook loop. She was certain she had not erased him herself. Jenda was worried. The last few times she had spoken with Jonathan, he had tried to talk to her about things that happened when they were kids, things Jenda couldn't remember. Now she thought she might want him to tell her more. She checked her digilet. There was no immediate response to her pulse.

Jenda felt restless. She missed Luis and the world they had inhabited in San Miguel. She needed a new activity. Maybe a dance class. But not couples dancing; she knew she wouldn't enjoy that without Luis. She did a mediazone search and found several dance classes at convenient locations. She decided on a class in a building she knew, which also housed an odd little boutique where she had shopped a few times. The boutique, of course, had clothing in many of the popular recyclable fabrics and materials, but it also had some unusual accessories, including neck pendants with old watches and lockets.

The dance studio, it turned out, was on the floor above the boutique and was run by the same owner, a woman by the name of Leticia Poole. Leticia didn't have the dancer's body Jenda anticipated, but as Jenda watched her move about the shop, she had to admit there was a certain grace and strength in her short, roundish body. She sold Jenda a form-fitting outfit with a wispy skirt, assuring her that it would be perfect for the class she was signing up for. Shoes would not be needed, Leticia said.

At the start of her first class, Jenda felt awkward and self-conscious, but as she followed the instruction to stop thinking and to let her body reflect Leticia's movements, she began to relax. When they reached the end of the class and Leticia put on a solo cello piece and told the students to move in their own way to the music, Jenda felt transported. She wondered why she had never tried this before. Or had she? There was something about the free movement to music that felt so familiar, that seemed to be stirring some forgotten feelings.

After class, Jenda chatted pleasantly with Leticia as they changed into their street clothes. As Jenda picked up her shoulder bag to leave, Leticia turned to her and laid her hand gently on Jenda's arm. "A word of advice: If you want to get the most out of this class, don't mention it on LifeBook or in Your Journal." Then she turned and went inside the shop.

Jenda walked back to her habitat, thinking of Leticia, thinking of how the dancing had made her feel, and thinking that whatever was hiding in those forgotten recesses of her mind, not all of it was bad. Her heart ached for the good friends she might have forgotten, and she wondered if Leticia might be one of them.

She came to look forward to her weekly dance classes. Her favorite moments, however, came when she was alone in her habitat, chatting with Luis on Interloc.

"How long do you expect to live?" Jenda pulsed Luis one day, when they were both on Interloc, where Luis was identified simply as "Murcielago." Jenda was "Polilla." Luis had tried to select "Mariposa" for her, in honor of her butterfly-like qualities, but too many people already had claimed some form of that, so he chose "Polilla"—clothes moth—in honor of her constantly morphing wardrobe of fashionable clothes.

"I don't know," Luis replied. "What about you?"

POLILLA: Not fair. I asked first.

MURCIELAGO: Okay. Let me think.

There was a long pause. Jenda liked that Luis took her questions seriously. Unlike herself. She would probably have made some clever or sarcastic comeback and hoped the question would go away. Or at least, she used to do that. She knew Luis would give her a thoughtful response.

MURCIELAGO: We're in a strange place, mi amor. Nobody I know from Gen1 or Gen2 ever expected to live nearly as long as they have. But it's happening. The scientists are not reporting any deterioration in our bodies' ability to continue regenerating themselves indefinitely under the Chulel regime. It's only the memory thing that gives most people doubts, and you and I and a few others know that is a false fear. Of course we are all subject to being killed in accidents or dying from some lethal disease. But as our futures seem more and more unlimited, you can see how people shy away from risky behaviors. When people figured they were going to die relatively soon anyway, why not risk your neck for the pleasures of fast driving, rock climbing, scuba diving, traveling to foreign places with strange diseases? "Nobody lives forever," right? Well - now maybe we do. And maybe we find that disturbing.

Jenda didn't respond. She was thinking.

MURCIELAGO: You still there?

POLILLA: Still here.

POLILLA: You haven't answered my question
yet.

MURCIELAGO: Okay. I'll try harder.
...
MURCIELAGO: I expect to live to be a very
old man.

POLILLA: That's it? What's that supposed
to mean? Nobody gets old anymore!

MURCIELAGO: Exactly. What I mean is, I
think humankind may have pushed it too
far. Living forever is not natural. And
it's not some eternal bliss of heaven-on-
earth as some of the Sanguinists would
have it. The demographics are already
getting unmanageable and potentially
disastrous.

POLILLA: I think I only wanted to know
how long YOU expected to live. You know,
so I can make plans to live that long.

MURCELAGO: Then you'll have to accept the
answer I gave you. And the fact that I
love you. Unto death.

POLILLA: I love you, too. But let's not
get morbid about it.

MURCIELAGO: How's the research going?

Jenda was grateful that he recognized her cue that
she wasn't in the mood for further philosophical and social
scientific analysis of the current state of the world, even
though she knew her question had clearly invited it.

POLILLA: Pretty good. I can send you a
full report by the end of the week.

Jenda's research had, in fact, been proceeding nicely. Three weeks after her return from sabbatical, she had proposed an exciting new idea for an advertising campaign featuring a series of photos from customers' files. It was part of the contract that personal photos could be used for advertising purposes, but without identifying the persons in the photo, which of course would be an invasion of privacy and YJ deeply respected people's privacy. So Jenda had been sifting through people's YJ personal files for several weeks and surreptitiously drawing down large segments of the files to the wireless device Luis had given her, carefully timing her work to blend in with high activity to avoid detection.

Once Jenda received access to these private files, she couldn't resist examining them in the evenings on her home screen. She intended to look through only a few of them, but she found herself staying up late in order to go through just a few more. She was noticing a lot of empty walls behind people. Or finding the same boring prints of the same popular commercial artists of the day. She painstakingly applied the transformation process Luis executed so expertly and found telltale signs of alteration. She made notes.

On the fourth night, as she was flipping through photos, barely aware of what she was doing, she suddenly startled awake. *Wait, what was that?* It wasn't the picture currently on the screen that had caught her attention. She backed up. Not that one either. One more back. There. What was it about this picture that seemed so odd? She looked at the people. She looked at the wall. There was nothing strange there. Then she looked at what the young person on the left was wearing. She zoomed in. What were those big stitch marks on his shirt and pants? And how had she noticed something so small when she was half asleep? Fully awake now, Jenda put the photo through the steps for analysis. The only thing she found that had been changed was the young person's hair—not the shape, so possibly the color. And maybe something had been hanging around his neck. What color had his (or it could be her) hair been before it became the rather unremarkable chestnut brown it appeared to be in the YJ photo? And what kind of objectionable jewelry had they been wearing? Jenda wished that the analysis could restore what was originally there, but unfortunately all it could do was reveal that something had been changed. She stared at the photo for another couple of minutes. Finally, she shook herself and, after noting in her book a few details about the picture, she screened out.

Luis cautioned her that sleep deprivation might attract undue attention. He reminded her that she needed to give her creative attention to making her project a successful one. Besides, Luis was going to be coming to Houston soon and they could meet there and analyze things together. Jenda tried to be patient.

The next Friday afternoon as Jenda and her grandmother were sipping drams after tennis and swapping stories about their latest fashion finds, Granny El told Jenda about a friend who had recently returned from a sabbatical that had included a wonderful voyage aboard a brand new vessel called Oceans Celestial.

"She's come back all refreshed and happy to be part of the corporate world again. Especially after that wonderful Chulel memory refresher."

"Yeah," Jenda ventured. "You know some people think they do more than just refresh and restore memories, Gran."

"Oh, I know about that," Granny El responded, with a laugh and a wink.

"You know... what?"

"I know what you people do," she replied, stirring her drink vigorously. "Hell, girl, when you reach my age and have an additional fifty years or more of memories to deal with, you'll be grateful for clever folks like your YJ people to help you keep things, you know, kind of pruned back into something manageable."

Jenda was unable to swallow her mouthful of NutriQuaff and it dribbled back into her straw. She stared at her grandmother.

Granny El took a more serious tone. "Gosh, Jenda, if your YJ didn't help us get shed of some of the old memories, we'd be like... like a bunch of reptiles trying to live out our lives always in the same old skin. You have to move on and not be always living in the past. Especially these days, when we have no idea how much past we might still have to look forward to."

Jenda was surprised, but not exactly shocked. She knew that Granny El had always been one of the "technology-can-solve-everything" types. She had scoffed at the nay-sayers when Chulel first became available. She was quite a beauty in her youth and in 2025 when the earliest Chulel was offered, she had been nearly sixty-five, although a well-cared-for sixty-five, having benefitted from good nutrition and exercise, as well as the best dermatological treatments available. She admitted to having been tempted to try Fontana when she received that suspicious pulse about it, but a bad experience with a street drug when she was a teenager back in the 1970s had made her cautious. She was glad she had waited.

This was a new insight into Granny El, Jenda thought. It was also a new perspective on YJ.

10.

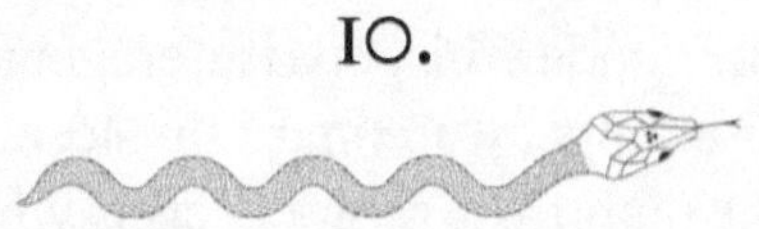

Jenda grew giddy with anticipation as the date approached for her long weekend in Houston with Luis. She was careful to make everyone think it was the big tennis tournament that was making her eyes sparkle. Keeping her relationship with Luis secret might have been unnecessary, but Jenda was unwilling to give him substance in a world she increasingly rejected.

Jenda wanted them to stay at her favorite boutique hotel, but Marvaworld was paying for Luis' room at one of the big corporate hotels and Jenda conceded the point. She didn't care so much where they were, as long as they were together. Although, she mused, the surprises of the ever-changing décor in her favorite hotel, and the constantly novel menu in the restaurant, and the elegantly presented room service—all of that had contributed to her frequent daydreams over the past weeks. Magnum Hotel would have to do.

Jenda checked in several hours before Luis was expected. Time enough to unpack and enjoy a shower and put on one of her new outfits bought for the occasion—a pair of loose trousers in a deep red and a flowered top with a provocatively draped neckline. She wished vaguely that she still had one of the outfits Luis had admired in San Miguel, but those had all long since hit the recycling bins.

When Luis finally pushed open the unlatched door, Jenda almost tackled him, pushing the door closed behind him, knocking over his suitcase, and locking him in a fully reciprocated deep kiss. They murmured some unintelligible greetings to one another. Jenda knew Luis would be tired out from travel, so she had figured sex would wait until later. But as

Luis' hands gently moved from her face to her neck to her shoulders to her breasts, she decided now was good, too.

"I was right," Jenda whispered later, gently stroking Luis' new beard at close range, watching him sleep. "The poor dear is exhausted. But damn you're good even when you're tired." She could have sworn she saw a faint smile cross Luis' face.

Jenda dutifully attended what she calculated to be a respectable minimum of her tennis events, trying to appear enthusiastic while also trying to avoid her old tennis friends. She didn't want to be constantly making excuses about why she couldn't meet them for dinner and drinks. The first morning at the tennis venue, Jenda thought she saw the woman from the monorail stage again, the one with the military posture. She decided maybe it was time to mention these encounters to Luis.

"What do you think, Luis? Am I being followed?" Jenda asked, after she had told him about all three sightings of the mysterious woman.

"Are you sure it's the same woman?"

"Pretty sure. But I think the most disturbing thing is that every time I've seen her, I had some sense I was being watched and then I look up...and there she is. And then she disappears."

Luis looked troubled. "Well, if it's the corporate police, you know they can get pretty ugly. Let's stop drawing down files for a while. And if you see her when we're together, please let me know. It's probably nothing to worry about."

Jenda could tell Luis didn't believe that, but she nodded and smiled. "Right," she said. "Now can I show you what I've found?"

She screened up the photos she had identified as altered during her first sleepless week of spy work. Luis hypothesized that the missing or altered backgrounds probably contained either photographs showing someone best forgotten or else paintings or prints that were the work of dissident artists or any artist no longer in favor.

"How can art be that big a deal?" Jenda asked. "Sorry," she backtracked. "Don't mean to imply artists are insignificant."

Luis nudged her with his shoulder, almost pushing her off the chair. "I know most people today think art is just for entertainment or personal therapy, but not so long ago there were some artists using it more politically."

Jenda's attempted "Hmmm..." as an expression of mild interest somehow came out more of a "Hmph!"

"No, really," he said. "One of our early heroes was a fellow called Ai Weiwei, an artist working during the declining years of Chinese state capitalism. There are photos of some of his work on Recall. You should check it out sometime."

They looked at a few more of Jenda's selected pictures. "Good work, Jenda," Luis said, with a note of finality. She could tell he was impatient to get on with his own expert analysis.

"Let me show you one more," Jenda said, checking her notebook for a number. She reached over Luis' arm and entered the number on the keypad. The photo of the family with the youth in the oddly mended clothing popped up.

"So what did you find on this one?" Luis asked, placing his hand on Jenda's thigh and massaging gently.

"You tell me," she said. "I want to know what you see." His pressure on her thigh lightened.

Luis sat back in his chair and squinted at the picture. His mouth curled into a smile, and he began running through the transformation steps, zeroing in precisely on the youth's hair, then moving to his/her neck area.

"Good eye, Jenda." This time he seemed genuinely pleased. "What did you notice first about this one that made you decide to analyze it?"

"It was the odd stitching on the kid's clothes. And I have no idea how I noticed it, since I was half asleep at the time. What do you think was altered about the hair, Luis?"

"I can tell you exactly what was altered: The color. This guy—or it could be a girl, it's often hard to tell with these youngsters—was a 'Vintie.' This is a particularly sloppy alteration. YJ is usually more thorough."

"A what?" Jenda rejoined. "Like a twenty-something? That doesn't help." She looked disappointed.

"No," Luis laughed. "Not 'vente' – 'Vintie.' They were part of a political movement that called themselves Vintagonists. They were opposed to the destruction of anything old. That was a big trend during the late 2020s or so. Surely you knew some of them. This would've been when you were in high school or early college."

"But I don't remember anything about them. Maybe there weren't any Vinties in my school. Probably not in my circle anyway."

"They were pretty much everywhere, although not always in large numbers. You don't remember them at all? Do you have some old high school photos we could look at?"

"Sure. Although not a lot. Screen up YJ." Luis did and Jenda reached over and put in her access phrase.

"Let's try 2028," Luis suggested.

As Luis began flipping through the photographs, Jenda muttered, "That seems an odd cause for a group of young people to get behind."

As Luis scrolled through the pictures, he began to frown. He leaned toward the screen with his chin in his hand.

"Not finding anything?"

"Al contrario, querida. I'm seeing at least some evidence of Vinties in almost all of your pictures."

"What?"

"Let me show you." Luis deftly processed a photo and showed Jenda the results. "You see there?" he said. "The hair color has been changed. And see these little marks on the clothing? Evidence of mending has been removed. And in the neck area—these Vinties always wore some kind of pendant, usually old-fashioned things like timepieces or lockets. Also, on this one, some makeup has been added to the face."

"I don't remember ever having even heard of these Vinties." Jenda looked troubled. "Tell me more, Luis."

So as the two of them stared at the screen full of tell-tale misaligned dots, Luis explained that it had been a time when recycling everything was the message coming from the great corporations and their media affiliates. In opposition to this, the Vintagonists advocated the preservation of printed books and photographs, physical works of art, and any clothing, decorative items, and furniture that they termed "vintage."

"Much of what they were preserving was of dubious merit, but they didn't care. Vinties were considered to be dangerously conservative, even retrogressive." Luis explained further that Vintagonists dyed their hair in pale shades of sepia and wore old clothing salvaged from recycling bins. They repaired these items with crude hand stitching and the more an item could call attention to inferior materials and shoddy workmanship, the more they liked it. Every once in a while, however, someone would come up with a trove of items from earlier generations, items made with quality natural cloth like silk, linen, cotton, or wool, and carefully tailored or even embroidered in fine stitching. Many of these garments had holes where the moths had eaten through the fabric, but these were considered a garment's badge of authenticity, and no effort was made to repair or hide such damage. Their philosophy was one of continuing connection with physical objects in the face of constant novelty, impermanence, and change.

"I sort of remember some people called 'Menders'," Jenda mused. "Were the Vinties like that?"

"No, the Menders were different. They were nto repairing, reusing, repurposing, rebuilding everything. They had a lot in common with Vinties, but where Vintagonists wanted to preserve and protect old things for their own sake, Menders wanted to fix things or find some way to make them useful again. They criticized Vintagonists for being overly attached to material things."

Jenda frowned, looking confused. "So who is this person in the photo, Luis? Zoom back out and let me see if it's anyone I can remember."

Luis placed his arm around Jenda's shoulders as he clicked the enlarge symbol several times in rapid succession and a face gradually formed on the screen.

Jenda's eyes widened, and her hand came to her mouth. She glanced uncertainly from the photo to Luis and back again. There was no doubt. The face in the picture was her own.

Jenda grabbed Luis' arm with both hands. She couldn't breathe. Everything stopped stone still. Her tear-filled eyes stared fixedly at the photograph that claimed to be Jenda at the age of fifteen, a Jenda who looked like a normal teenager with short golden hair and too much makeup. But that was not her. She had been someone else, someone obscured by this very image, someone she couldn't remember. Jenda's body began to shake as everything broke into pieces.

Luis killed the offending picture and turned to hold Jenda as she began to sob. He led Jenda to the sofa. She whimpered like a lost puppy as he held her, gently stroking her hair, her shoulders, the nape of her neck. There was nothing left to talk about.

Luis insisted that Jenda take a few tabs of Duermata. "It's late. You need some rest, querida," he said. Jenda took it and slept.

She woke suddenly, just before dawn. Although Duermata usually blocked out dreams, Jenda had been dreaming. She struggled to retrieve the images. There had been a dark-skinned young man and laughter. It felt like a group of friends. The lady in blue was there, hidden in the shadows, filling Jenda with terror. In the dream, Jenda closed her eyes tight shut and willed herself to follow this woman, to break through whatever obscured her. It was no use. When Jenda opened her eyes, the dream was gone.

It was exasperating. Why couldn't she make herself recall these things? Where were they hidden? She rose quietly and went into the bathroom where she splashed cold water on her swollen eyes. She stared at her reflection in the mirror, trying to imagine herself as a Vintie with sepia hair. She felt her anger resolving into a fierce determination. "I will find you, Jenda," she said to the woman in the mirror.

"Jenda?" Luis stood in the doorway. "Are you okay?"

"Yeah. Yeah, I think I am," she said. "When can we order breakfast? I'm starving."

"How do you know so much about these Vinties?" Jenda asked, as they ate their omelets and toast. "If the corporate memory reconstructionists wanted us all to forget about them, how is it that you know so much?"

"I've never been subjected to memory restructuring," Luis reminded her. "That's probably the most important thing. But add to that the fact that I was one of them back in my youth. Yes, they were still active in the early 2040s when I was a teen. If anything, we'd become more radical by then, although we were probably a somewhat smaller group."

"You never told me about that," Jenda said.

"Well, it never came up. Look, Jenda, at our ages we both have a lot of history behind us. And, no offense, but even though you may have a few more years, I have a lot more history, since my memories haven't been disrupted by photonic treatments. I'm not pretending I remember everything, nor can I claim to remember things exactly as they were. But at least nobody has been messing with my memories for their own ends. So, yes, there are probably still a lot more things you don't know about me. And probably a good deal of things I don't know about you, too."

"Considering there seem to be quite a lot of things I don't know about myself... Do we know where any of these Vinties have ended up today? Well, besides you, my love—you with the definitely non-sepia hair."

"Actually, yes. A lot of the people you find in Recall are old Vintagonists. Some Menders, too. And a fair number of Minimalists who were advocating overall reduced consumption of material goods." Luis chuckled softly. "They're usually called 'Simpletons' because they were always going on about simplicity. And then they kind of embraced the term, claiming that 'any fool can see the wisdom of simplicity.'" He grinned at Jenda. "You don't remember them either, I guess. I think the corporations hated them most of all. Most people who were once in one of these movements have had their memories and records redacted and rearranged to the extent that they don't identify with the movement anymore, nor even remember much about it. But yours is the most extreme case I've seen."

Jenda probed her broken mind for traces of memories about Vintagonists and Menders and Simpletons. A few vague images seemed to drift just below the surface, just beyond the blank white screens that filled such a large part of her thinking mind whenever she tried to remember her youth. "This is going to take time, Luis," she said finally. "Can we talk about our project?"

Luis picked up her hand and gave it a quick kiss. "Of course we can. We'll have plenty of time ahead of us to investigate all kinds of things." So they spent the rest of the day looking at other people's files and discussing potential plans for their project. Since drawing down additional files was on hold for a while, Jenda offered to select a series of photos from among those she had already seen and propose them for her new YJ campaign. She would select photos that were absolutely perfect, except for some small detail that unfortunately marred the image. Then she would suggest that these be photographically altered. After that, they would see what happened.

II.

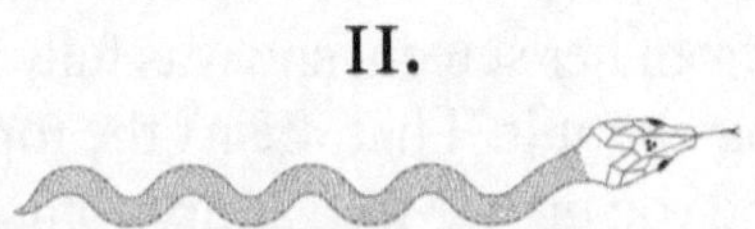

A week after her meeting with Luis in Houston, Jenda went to her supervisor with the set of photos she had selected for her campaign.

"Unfortunately," Jenda pointed out to him, "as you can see, a few of the photos contain elements that... Well, this picture would be absolutely perfect if we could get rid of that grumpy-looking child in the front here. Or block out that recycling barrel next to the table in this one. I tried cropping them out," Jenda continued, "but on some of them it's not enough. I know this is against everything we stand for as a company, but since this is for advertising and the pictures in people's files won't be changed, do you think... maybe... just this once?"

Jenda was wheedling. Her supervisor frowned. "It's nice that you understand you shouldn't even be asking to do this, Jenda." He studied the pictures. "But I see what you mean. And I love everything else about your proposed campaign. Let me take it up with my super. I know she's probably going to say 'no' but she's been pretty enthusiastic about your concept. So I guess we can try." He told Jenda he would get back to her.

"By the way," he added as Jenda turned to leave. "Your screen may be off for a while sometime this week. There have been some unusual usage patterns picked up, so they're doing a sweep of all the screens to make sure nothing has been irrupted—no infections or anything. Tech talk, I know. I'm sure it's nothing. I just didn't want you to worry."

Jenda thanked him and returned to her desk, grateful that she and Luis had decided to postpone further drawdowns of personal data.

Two days later, Jenda's supervisor called her into the office. She steeled herself for the possibility they had detected the drawdowns from her screen; she was fully resolved to deny knowing anything about it. That wasn't the topic.

"I'm sending you up to Ms. Landry's office to discuss your request about the photos. She's in suite G4 on the twenty-fifth floor." Jenda tried not to look startled. That was one of the restricted floors. She was being called to one of the restricted floors. Her appointment was in twenty minutes.

She reviewed her proposal materials and then returned to her supervisor's office, where an escort was waiting for her.

The escort entered the elevator with her and quickly keyed in an access phrase. Then he exited, leaving her alone on the elevator as it ascended to the twenty-fifth floor. The elevator doors opened, sounding the same as they did on any other floor.

Jenda stepped out and looked around. It didn't look so strange. The signs letting you know which way to go for which suites were a different color but otherwise looked the same as on other floors. *So what was I expecting?* Jenda asked herself. *A portal into a separate reality?* She took a deep breath, adjusted her grip on her portable screen, and headed off in the direction that the signs indicated for suites D1 through G7. There was no plexi around any of the rooms, so Jenda couldn't see what lay behind the closed doors. A man in a suit came out of suite D5. He acknowledged Jenda with a nod, while also giving her a look that made her feel like an intruder.

Other than that single encounter, the hallway was quiet and empty. Jenda hesitated at the door marked G4. Should she knock or just walk in? She knocked.

The door opened, and a smiling gentleman in casual attire motioned for her to enter. "You're Ms. Swain?" he asked.

"Yes. Jenda Swain." She tried to keep her curiosity reined in, resisting the temptation to stare at everything in the office. There seemed to be more machines than people. *Keep focused,* she told herself.

"Ms. Landry is expecting you," the man said, as he led Jenda through a maze of equipment and opened a large plexi door at the far corner of the space.

Ms. Landry shook Jenda's hand. "Please. Have a seat."

Jenda sat. She could see that it had been unnecessary for her to bring her own digiscreen with the proposal materials, as Ms. Landry had the whole thing spread out on her desktop screen. She enlarged a couple of the photos, rearranging them and studying them closely. Then she looked sternly over her glasses and directly into Jenda's eyes.

"You know this request goes against everything we stand for here at YJ," she said, reiterating the point Jenda's supervisor had made. "You of all people—the originator of 'Your lifeline to your life's story.' You should understand this."

Perhaps she had been sent upstairs to be scolded. And maybe fired. She and Luis hadn't considered that possibility.

Ms. Landry continued. "We're taking something of a risk here. But we're impressed with your campaign concept and we're hoping the people whose pictures are used will be so flattered that they won't even notice the alterations. Everybody always likes their pictures to look good, and these... Well, I have to say I think they will look fantastic." She gave Jenda a reassuring smile. Jenda thought she could almost guarantee that the subjects would be thrilled—after their next Chulel spa day, anyway.

Jenda was relieved. They were going to alter the photos. She was confused, however, by the genuine discomfort she sensed in Ms. Landry. If there was a sector at YJ that was engaged in systematic altering of files and memories, Ms. Landry didn't seem to be part of it. Was it possible that there was nothing going on within the restricted floors of the YJ building in Dallas other than diligent minding of the termini that guarded people's precious memories?

"It will take a few days to get the processing done and we'd like to send you to our office in Abilene where this will be handled. That way you can give them immediate feedback on the pictures and guarantee that they meet your standards." Jenda wanted to shout "Aha!" but instead tried to look compliant and grateful. "Your supervisor will give you some time off, but we'll make the arrangements from here and let you know the details by tomorrow afternoon."

Ms. Landry bid Jenda farewell with a smiling but still ominous sounding, "Let's hope this will all be worth it."

The remaining two hours of Jenda's workday dragged on intolerably. As soon as she was in the autocar for the drive home, she unfurled her digilet and pulsed Luis. "Good day at work. Check with you later." She hoped Luis would be waiting for her on Interloc by the time she got home.

Jenda flew through the doorway and grabbed a glass of Prosecco as she dashed through the kitchen to her home screen. She felt celebratory. She quickly screened up Recall and made her way to Interloc. There was a message waiting.

```
MURCIELAGO: Good day??

POLILLA: Pukka day!
```

Becoming "Polilla" always made Jenda smile; it meant she was talking with Luis. She quickly recounted all that had occurred—her visit to the restricted floor, her conversation with Ms. Landry, and most importantly, her impending business trip to Abilene.

```
POLILLA: I don't think Landry knows
anything. She seemed genuinely concerned
about my request somehow pushing the
envelope. I'm thinking I may learn more
in Abilene.

MURCIELAGO: You may be right. Let's hope!

POLILLA: By the way, you remember my ex-
husband?
```

MURCIELAGO: Wait. What? You were married?

POLILLA: Oh. I'm sorry, Luis—I've been divorced from him for more than seventy-five years. I sometimes forget about it myself.

MURCIELAGO: Okay. What about him?

Jenda told him that Ben had been working for YJ in the Abilene office in 2045 when they met. She added a few details about how they had married after a brief courtship when Jenda was on sabbatical in Barcelona.

POLILLA: Sorry I never mentioned Ben before. It never seemed important.

MURCIELAGO: No problem. I know you had a life before me. Most of it, in fact.

POLILLA: As did you yourself, Señor. We've talked about this. Anyway. I think the ex may still be in my LifeBook loop. Do you think I should pulse him that I'm coming to Abilene?

MURCIELAGO: You think he may still be in your loop? And you're asking your partner if you should pulse your ex-husband. Pukka. Is he the only one?

POLILLA: Only one, my love. I swear. So what do you think?

Jenda figured the story of her unfortunately brief engagement to Sandra could wait for a more appropriate time.

MURCIELAGO: It probably makes sense. What department was he in?

POLILLA: That's the thing. He was never
clear about that.

MURCIELAGO: Ah. Well then, maybe it's
time to find out.

After Jenda and Luis had both signed out of Recall (after some ambiguous exchanges that may or may not have been loaded with sexual innuendo) Jenda screened up her LifeBook loop. There he was: Benjamin Cohen. She wasn't sure what to say. Finally she pulsed, "Hi there, old man! It's been a long time. I've got a business trip to Abilene soon—probably next week. Think maybe we can get together? If you're still around."

Jenda checked LifeBook before heading to work the next day, thinking there might be a message from Ben. There was nothing. *Oh, well,* she told herself. *It was worth a try.*

When Jenda arrived at work, all the details for her trip to Abilene were already there on her desktop. The trip wasn't going to be next week; it was tomorrow. There were monorail and hotel reservations and the name and office number of the person she would be meeting with. All of this was in a digital folder marked "Private" and keyed to her access phrase. She went to her supervisor's office to let him know about her assignment.

"I know, I know," he said with a wave of his hand as she appeared in the doorway. "No explanation necessary. Have a good trip and I'll see you next week. Feel free to leave early if you need time to pack."

Jenda left early. She stopped by a couple of shops on her way home to buy some new outfits for the trip. She felt guilty about not having anything for the recycles box but promised herself she would bring extra next time. Shopping was feeling like a chore until she ran across a dress in that lovely bright blue that matched her eyes. Jenda bought it, along with a coordinating scarf. But then she seemed to vaguely remember that this particular color had been Ben's favorite on her. *What am I trying to do? Seduce my ex-husband? What craick!* She had a sudden desire to share the joke with Luis, and that amused her even more.

As soon as she got home she screened up Interloc to tell Luis about her plans, leaving a lengthy message. She didn't mention the blue dress. Before screening off, she thought she would check LifeBook again.

There was a message from Ben: "Well, hi, doll! It's been a while, hasn't it? Would love to get together with you when you hit town. Are you still with YJ? Let me know if you might be available for dinner next Tuesday. Ciao!"

"How about this Thursday instead?" Jenda responded. "Turns out I'm coming this week instead of next. Arriving tomorrow for meeting at YJ." Then she screened out and started packing. She'd share this development with Luis later.

Jenda did not own a small suitcase. She did own several large ones. Even for short trips, she habitually took more outfits than the number of days she would be away, with each outfit fully accessorized. Satisfied that she had packed clothes suitable for whatever occasions might arise on her brief business trip, and having laid out the outfit she intended to wear for the journey, Jenda prepared a quick supper, poured a glass of wine, and settled into her nook next to the home screen. She had a message from Luis on Interloc.

```
MURCIELAGO: That all sounds great. Just
take it easy with those folks - don't
want to arouse any suspicions. You won't
be able to communicate with me on any of
the local screens out there, only on the
digilet. And watch what you say while
you're in unfamiliar zones. If I don't
catch you onscreen before you go - GOOD
LUCK! I LOVE YOU!
```

Luis was still onscreen.

```
POLILLA: Looks like you caught me!
```

```
MURCIELAGO: Pukka! So... did you hear
anything back from your ex?

POLILLA: I got a message this evening. I
offered to meet him for dinner. No
response yet.

MURCIELAGO: That would be good.
MURCIELAGO: You see how much I trust you?

POLILLA: I'm fully worthy of your trust,
you know. Don't know if he's still with
YJ, although he did ask if I was. Why
else would he still be in Abilene?

MURCIELAGO: I guess it's fortunate you
guys are still on good terms.
MURCIELAGO: I'd love to see your pretty
face.
```

So Jenda pulled up the visual communication facility called Chat², and they enjoyed a half hour of banter that cheerfully avoided even oblique references to their project.

Jenda's monorail journey to Abilene the next morning was uneventful. By noon she was checking in at a hotel near the Your Journal building. Her appointment was for 2:30 p.m., so she unpacked her outfits and went out to find lunch. She wasn't particularly keen on going anywhere that would remind her of the places she and Ben had frequented during their long-distance marriage (the distance between Dallas and Abilene being longer than most people think). The names and décor of the restaurants had changed, of course, but Abilene's options hadn't improved much over the years. Jenda ended up in a salad and juice bar similar to the one she had always loved, and Ben had hated.

As she settled into a window seat with her salad, Jenda caught an image reflected in the window that made her catch her breath: It was the woman from the monorail—the one she and Luis agreed must be corporate police. This woman was definitely following her. Jenda controlled her inclination to look at the woman directly, since that always seemed to trigger her disappearance. *If this is about YJ,* Jenda thought, *why would she follow me here? YJ knows what I'm doing here. Don't they trust me? Who does she work for?* She knew she couldn't talk to Luis about this latest sighting until she returned to the more secure communication available from her habitat in Dallas. The next time Jenda glanced at the reflection in the window, the woman was gone.

After lunch and a quick shower and change of outfits, Jenda walked the two blocks to Your Journal, feeling vulnerable as she scanned the faces on the street for the suspicious policewoman. She noticed that the modular façade of YJ had been altered again and now incorporated panels of digital colloids showing episodes from YJ's latest advertising campaign. The YJ building was easily the tallest building in the city and to emphasize the point YJ had installed an awe-inspiring photonic 3-D image generator at the apex of the structure.

Jenda's meeting with her primary collaborator—a slightly pudgy man named George Putnam—was not as interesting as Jenda had hoped. She described exactly what she was going for with her campaign and pointed out what needed to be done with the pictures. George acted bored and asked hardly any questions. Jenda felt irritated, despite the fact that George seemed to grasp precisely what she wanted.

"I should have something for you to look at by 9:30 tomorrow morning," he said, screening off the images in a way that clearly indicated they were finished. The meeting had lasted barely half an hour.

Jenda thanked him for his time and walked out of the conference room, wondering what she was going to do for the rest of the afternoon. Then she noticed the name on the door of the big office at the end of the hall: "Benjamin Cohen. Vice President for Customer Relations."

Without hesitation, she walked down the hall and through the doorway. The executive assistant was sitting at a desk that was easily twice as large as Jenda's desk in Dallas. He looked at Jenda blankly. "May I help you?"

"Is Mr. Cohen in?"

"Do you have an appointment?" The assistant looked doubtful.

"No. No I don't, but I just wanted to pop in and say hello. I'm in town from the Dallas office and I thought…"

"Oh, are you Ms. Swain? Mr. Cohen said you might come by. Let me check and see if he has a minute." The assistant disappeared into the inner office momentarily, then the big frosted plexi door slid open again. The assistant was smiling. "Please come in, Ms. Swain."

Jenda returned the smile and walked into the office, taking in at a glance the fact that Ben had definitely reached the upper echelons of the YJ hierarchy. Ben himself, of course, looked much the same as he had when they married in 2045.

"Jenda!" Ben's face broke into a broad grin as he rose from behind his immense desk to give her a quick hug. "How have you been? It's been a while, hasn't it!"

"A while, yes," Jenda said, responding to the apparently sincere warmth of Ben's smile. "And here we are, both still working for the same company."

They chatted about nothing in particular for a few minutes, standing in the center of the office. "I wish I had more time right now, but I've got a meeting coming up. Can we have dinner this evening?" It was quickly settled. He would pick her up at the hotel at seven.

Jenda was wearing the new bright blue outfit as she settled into the rightside seat of Ben's top of the line personal autocar. She knew the top of the line models weren't that different from the others, but they did have better advertising. Ben had made reservations at a steakhouse similar to the one that had been their go-to place for date nights. Jenda wasn't much into steaks these days, but she figured she could make an exception. It wasn't like steaks came from actual cows anymore.

Jenda was surprised that Ben remembered her favorite wine—a Spanish Tempranacha with a delightfully tangy cherry note. Jenda herself had forgotten about this particular wine, but the taste seemed familiar, so she said she remembered.

Keep your head, Jenda, she told herself. The wine was beginning to make her respond to Ben's attempts at humor with more laughter than they deserved. She excused herself between the salad and steak to go to the ladies' room and give herself a talking-to.

With squared shoulders and freshly applied lipstick, Jenda was ready to take the conversation in a potentially more interesting direction.

"By the way," she said, as she settled back into her chair, "I have a message to your people from my grandmother. She wants to thank you—and these are her words, mind you—for 'pruning her memories' and making them more manageable for a 165-year-old lady." She watched to see Ben's reaction.

Ben was watching her, too, and Jenda tried to appear as open and ingenuous as possible. He hesitated for a moment, looking down at his steak. Then he looked up at Jenda. "Well, at least some people appreciate what we do, right?"

Jenda was uncertain where to go with this new opening. Then she said, "Well, you know, some of us in YJ have been a bit naïve about all this. But I guess I can understand how important it is." It seemed like the right thing to say.

Maybe it was the Tempranacha or maybe it was the way Jenda's blue eyes picked up the blue of her outfit, but Ben opened up.

"There's no point in people having to be forever burdened with remembering things that are best forgotten," he told her. "When we know, for example, that a certain person has moved out of someone's LifeBook loop, we remove the memories as well. That person just won't be in the picture, anymore." He winked at Jenda. "It's a good thing we're still connected on

LifeBook, right? Otherwise we probably wouldn't be sharing this excellent dinner." Jenda laughed politely, wondering how Ben would explain the disappearance of her brother from her LifeBook loop. Ben continued. "And then there are those genuinely unpleasant things that can happen through nobody's fault, and we know what those are and we can make them go away. Or at least carve away a lot of the messy details. And of course managing demand to conform to what we know is going to be available in the market—well, that's just efficiency, right?" He smiled and nodded, agreeing with his own assertion. He paused then, as if debating whether to go on. "And sometimes people make unfortunate decisions—poor choices in companions, that sort of thing—and we can help them manage that, too."

His face took on a stern look, as if he was afraid he might have said too much. "It's important for all of us at YJ to understand that everything we do is for the good of our customers. Some employees, especially lower level ones, might not fully grasp the critical need we're filling by aiding our customers with memory management. I'm glad you get it, Jenda. And I know I can trust you to be discreet."

Jenda said something that she hoped sounded appropriate. It occurred to her that maybe the mysterious policewoman did in fact work for YJ and that all of this was a way of testing her. She should be careful. Ben offered to top up her wine glass but Jenda demurred. He poured a little anyway.

"God, you look beautiful tonight, Jenda! Thank you for wearing my favorite color. You know I always loved you in that color."

Jenda was jolted back into the moment, wary about where Ben might be heading. She was reassured by his next statement: "You know I'm married again." Then she reminded herself that marriage had never deterred him before.

"Carol and I are very solid," he said.

Jenda relaxed. She listened distractedly as Ben recounted the mundane activities in which he engaged with the beautiful

Carol and the child they had produced back in 2062. Apparently they had been married a long time.

"Of course, part of what has kept us together this long is the fact that we sort of give one another the freedom we each need to move outside the relationship from time to time." Ben reached over and took Jenda's hand, gazing deeply into her eyes.

Oh, Lord, here we go, Jenda thought. *You're such a cliché, Ben Cohen.* But in the last ten minutes, while Ben had been droning on about his life with Carol, Jenda had figured out how she would have evaded his advances if it had become necessary.

"Oh, Ben," she said, doing her best to look pained. "I'm flattered, of course, but... well... I've finally come to terms with the fact that I'm really more attracted to women than to men. You understand, don't you?"

Ben released his grip on her hand and patted it with suddenly fraternal affection.

"So." he said. "I guess maybe... maybe I had wondered about that."

Jenda restrained her desire to laugh. She knew that if Ben checked into her Your Journal files—and he certainly could—he would find that the last person she had written about being seriously involved with was Sandra. After Sandra's death, which of course was not mentioned in YJ, Jenda had been so distraught that she had vowed never to enter names of any of her lovers in YJ again, refusing to give them personal power over her story. Now she was grateful for what she had often considered to be a childish impulse.

After a nice crème brulée and a decaf with coffee liqueur, Ben took Jenda back to her hotel. He explained politely that he would be busy all the next day in meetings and she said that if the photos came up to her liking, she would be headed back to Dallas on the midday monorail. They gave each other a peck on the cheek and said their fond, platonic farewells.

Jenda walked into the hotel lobby with a distinct sense of relief. Hers and Luis' suspicions about YJ were confirmed. But what about the policewoman? Jenda was eager to get back to Dallas and her own home screen with all of its maze-like capabilities that would connect her with Luis.

12.

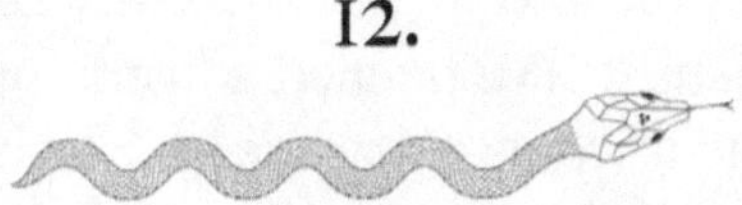

Max and Emily Feldman attended the big opening at Galería Picaflor for the collection of recyclable decorative paintings that Isabel Hernandez considered to be shit. There was an enthusiastic crowd, and Isabel made a lot of sales. The gallery was busy for the next two weeks of the exhibit, as May's pleasant autumn weather gave way to the southern hemisphere's more wintry early June temperatures. Isabel took scores of orders for the unlimited copies the featured artist was willing to print. She had learned to put digital counters next to each piece indicating how many copies had been sold, since the more popular a piece appeared to be, the more likely the next consumer was to want their own copy.

Emily Feldman pulsed Isabel, congratulating her on her success and inviting her out to lunch for the Sunday after the show's official closing reception on Saturday evening. Isabel pulsed back: "That sounds wonderful, but why don't you pick up something to bring over? Then we can have a quiet lunch here at the gallery. I have some things I want to show you."

Shortly after noon on Sunday, Max and Emily went to their favorite Pakistani restaurant to pick up food to take for their luncheon. When they arrived at the gallery, Isabel was at her desk. She rose to welcome them, tasking her digilet to lock the door and darken the windows. "That smells delicious," she remarked. "Come this way."

Down a side hall at the back of the gallery, Isabel unlocked what looked like the door to a janitor's closet. The door opened to reveal a second gallery space, beautifully if artificially lit, with a table set up in the center, laid with real china and silver and crystal and table linens. The walls were lined with real oil paintings. The table and chairs looked like authentic Art Deco. Max and Emily were speechless.

"Hand me those containers before you drop them," Isabel chuckled, looking pleased at the effect her secret gallery was having on her friends. "I've opened a bottle of wine. I think it should complement your curry nicely." Isabel set the food containers on a small side table and poured wine.

"So this is where you're keeping the real art." Max's face glowed with evident delight. "Look, Emily, she still has the Xul Solar."

"Ah, I remember how much you liked his Ña Diáfana," Isabel said as she poured some of her best Argentine Malbec into the crystal wine glasses and handed one each to Max and Emily. "It's an exquisite piece. I was fortunate to acquire it when they sold off the inventory of his museum." Max and Emily murmured excitedly as they identified the work of one after another of their favorite artists.

"I don't recognize this one," Max said, standing in front of a vibrant retro-Expressionist oil.

"That one is by an artist currently working in Mexico," Isabel said.

"You mean there are still people painting like this?" Emily said. "I'm stunned. Who is the artist?"

"He's known as Charro Negro. In Mexico, that means something like 'black cowboy'. He always paints a tiny bat somewhere in his paintings - you see right here?" Isabel was pointing to a dark area where the silhouette of a bat was barely visible. "We don't know much about this Charro Negro, but his work is getting some attention in the underground art world. I was pleased to be able to acquire one of his paintings. These kinds of acquisitions are always a bit risky for both collector and artist."

"I can well imagine," Emily responded. There was more to see—more paintings, as well as some sculptures in stone and bronze. Emily noticed a few shelves of books inside a polished wood cabinet with glass doors. "I see you collect books, too," she ventured.

"I guess I do," Isabel said. "To tell the truth, I can't remember where I got most of my books. But I do know that it's a rather good collection. Many of the best Latin American novelists and poets are there." She opened the doors to the cabinet.

"My goodness, this is a fine collection," Max remarked, as he scanned the titles on the spines.

"There are only a few that I remember acquiring," Isabel said, running a finger along one row of books. "They are the ones I got from what used to be the Bartolomé Mitre archives. However..." Isabel reached for a slim paperback with a light blue cover and pulled it out. "I've always felt this one holds some special significance for me."

"Ah, Silvina Ocampo." Max held the book in his hands like a delicate flower as Emily peered over his shoulder. "*Viaje Olvidado.* Her first publication, I believe."

"That's right," Isabel affirmed. "That's not an original edition, of course. But look inside."

There was an inscription in pencil: "Feliz cumpleaños a mi querida mami – ¡besos y abrazos! Juanita."

"You have a daughter?" Emily asked.

"So it would appear," Isabel replied. "That's one of those things I don't seem to remember. And perhaps that's the one that hurts my heart the most." She took the book from Max's hands and replaced it lovingly in its slot on the shelf. She ran her fingers along the line of books until she came to a pair of books in glossy dustcovers. She took one of them out and held it up. "This is another book that mystifies me," she said. "All the rest of my books are in Spanish and are by Latin American authors, but this one—there are two of them, actually—is in English and is by an American author by the name of Martin Jameson. As best I can tell, he was a highly successful novelist back around the turn of the 21st century. My books are signed first editions, and I have no idea where I got them." Isabel replaced the book and closed the glass doors. "Well. Shall we let that yummy smelling food sit there or shall we eat it?"

Lunch conversation was animated, revolving around art and artists and authors. As Isabel poured out the last of the second bottle of wine, Max decided it was time to broach a new subject.

"Isabel, would you be interested in trying to find your lost memories? Emily and I might be able to help."

"¿Será? How could you help with something like that? It's hard to find something when you don't even know where or when you lost it. Anyway, it's just the Chulel and it's my punishment for having been vain enough to continue taking the stuff."

"Chulel has not done this to you, Isabel," Emily said gently. "Max and I have been taking it even longer than you have, and our memories are remarkably intact."

"Ah, but you come from North America, and you've had access to the memory restoration process," Isabel rejoined.

"No, Isabel. We've never used that procedure. Not even once," Emily said.

"I don't understand. What are you telling me? Isn't it true that Chulel after many years of use destroys the memory?"

"No, Isabel." Max's voice was soft but forceful. "It is not true. It's a lie. A useful one for some people, but an absolute lie."

"Why have I forgotten so much, then?" Isabel looked perplexed.

Gently, carefully, Max and Emily explained to her about photonic memory restructuring, a process that could both remove old memories and implant new ones. They had recently uncovered information in some old scientific journals that referenced research conducted in the late 2020s and early 2030s at an institute somewhere right here in Argentina. The cited sources were no longer available, but the work appeared to focus on exactly this photonic process, the same one that was now being used in the Chulel clinics and called "memory restoration." They were having difficulty ascertaining exactly where the institute might have been located, but they thought it might be near Buenos Aires.

"What we know about the process, though," Max said, "is that it can leave latent memories that can resurge. At first memories may come back spontaneously, as a vague sort of familiarity. With patience and a little help, these memories can sometimes be restored in more detail."

Isabel's expression was drawn and tense as she fought to retain her composure. "Like a sense of déjà vu? That thing that some Sanguinista people say is a memory of a past life?"

"Past life!" Max snorted. "Like last year?"

That made Isabel smile. She took a deep breath. "So, what would you propose to do to go about this search?"

Speaking in turns, Emily and Max suggested that they would first put together as complete a life history as they could in order to see exactly where Isabel's memory gaps occurred. Then, she would need to tell them about anything that ever caused her to have that sense of familiarity, of déjà vu.

"We don't want to get your hopes up too much, Isabel," Emily said. "This may not work. And of course, we're assuming that the cause of your memory loss is in fact the photonic process, which we don't know for sure yet."

"I understand. As long as you won't be giving me drugs or anything that will make me forget even more." Isabel paused. "Just one more thing: Why? Why would you want to help an old woman like me with something like this?"

"Max and I have become increasingly distressed about the way our... the way Chulel is being used in conjunction with memory restructuring. That was not the intention of the drug's makers," Emily said, giving Max a sidelong glance.

"Oh, tell her, Em." Max slapped the table with his open hand. "Tell her we're the culprits who came up with this devilish Chulel thing in the first place."

"So you are those Feldmans," Isabel said. "You know I often check out people who start coming to the gallery and inquiring about, you know, real paintings. And the only Max and Emily Feldman I could find in the LifeBook directory had been scientists at Pharmakon. I didn't know if that was you or not. And now you tell me this Chulel was your own invention? Well, then I guess I need to believe what you tell me about what it does and doesn't do. Yes. Yes I will work with you in whatever way you recommend, to see if I can find what I have lost." Isabel's face was glowing. "When do we start?"

13.

When Jenda arrived home from Abilene and tried to screen up Interloc, she found herself locked out. *Well, zujo!* she thought. She screened up LifeBook instead and found a brief personal pulse from Luis: "Looking forward to seeing you next weekend. Until then."

Jenda didn't remember any plans to meet so soon. Their next meeting was supposed to be in El Paso in early July. Had Jenda missed something on Interloc? *Well, I can't check now,* she told herself. Then she noticed some new pictures in her current LifeBook chapter. One was a photo of her and Luis in San Miguel – a very bad photo. You couldn't see either of their faces. *Oh,* Jenda thought. *The Dark Knight is sending me a message.* She examined the rest of the photographs more carefully. One of them was of a hotel, its name clearly visible. Jenda searched and found that there were several hotels with that name, but the one that matched this photograph was in San Antonio. In fact, this was the same photograph, drawn directly from the hotel mediazone. As she looked at the other photos again, she realized that they all seemed to be from San Antonio.

"So. I guess I'm going to San Antonio this weekend," Jenda said aloud, quickly glancing around as if looking for some kind of surveillance. The worries that had nagged her in Abilene after her latest sighting of the policewoman were now compounded by concerns about Luis.

Jenda reserved a room for Friday and Saturday nights at the hotel in the picture and bought a ticket for the hyperloop for Friday morning. Then she deleted all the photos Luis had posted.

Jenda's project at work was moving at hyperloop speed now that she had the photos she needed. Nevertheless, with no communication from Luis, the week seemed to drag on. She went to a couple of entertainments with friends. She went shopping for some outfits for the weekend. She even called up Granny El and took her to a new restaurant that had recently opened. It wasn't really a new restaurant, but it had been thoroughly rearranged and redecorated and had a revised menu. Wherever she went, she kept an anxious eye out for the corporate policewoman. Even when she didn't spot her, Jenda had the distinct feeling she was being watched.

Friday morning finally came and Jenda settled into her seat for the 40-minute hyperloop journey to San Antonio. She checked her digilet for messages and found a reply to the pulse she had sent weeks earlier to her brother. "Hi, Jen. I'm okay, although I'm not sure I'm someone you want to know at present. Here's an alt contact phrase in case you ever need it. Be well!" He had appended the phrase. She wondered what he meant and why it had taken so long for this message to come through.

Jenda considered taking a tab of Duermata and sleeping for half the journey, taking advantage of Duermata's guarantee of precisely twenty minutes of restful sleep per tablet. She decided against it, occupying herself instead with conjuring up explanations for why she was going to San Antonio to meet Luis, pondering what might be happening to her brother, and trying to fathom the motives of the mysterious policewoman.

Although she knew he wouldn't be there, Jenda scanned the crowd in the hyperloop station, hoping to glimpse Luis' familiar form and face. She didn't see the policewoman, either. She went to the autocar dock and selected a shiny blue vehicle. She tapped the trunk; it opened, and the grabber snapped up her suitcase. Inside the car, she passed her digilet across the blinking blue light that both started the car and tasked her account. Then she spoke the address of the hotel and the autocar moved onto the street.

Jenda glanced into the rearview mirror just as a dark green autocar pulled onto the street behind her. The car had only one occupant: It was the policewoman. Jenda's mind went into overdrive. She couldn't lead the woman to the hotel where she and Luis would be staying. But where could she go? She didn't know San Antonio. Only one idea presented itself. "Redirect." Her voice was tense as she gave new instructions to the autocar. "San Antonio Art Museum." The car confirmed and set in a course for the museum. All Jenda knew about the museum was that it was on the river walk. She thought if she could lose the policewoman somewhere in or around the museum, she would be able to walk the rest of the way to the hotel.

When the autocar pulled up in front of the museum, Jenda got out quickly and sent the car to park itself, unconcerned about the fate of her suitcase. Inside, Jenda paid her entry fee with her digilet and glanced at the map of exhibits that popped up. Her heart thumped wildly as she headed for a darkened gallery featuring holographic sculptures. It was a good place to hide but offered no vantage point from which to see whether the policewoman had followed her into the museum. Through the gallery, she found stairs leading up to the next level. Obscured by some hanging textiles, she peered over the balcony. The policewoman had entered and was heading for the main staircase.

Zujo! What now? Jenda looked around the second floor. All the galleries seemed to open onto the main balcony. Desperate, she ducked into the bathrooms and locked herself inside a stall. *God, Jenda, is this all you can think of? You know she'll come look for you here!* Just then the bathroom door opened and through the slit at the edge of the stall door, Jenda saw the policewoman. She sat on the toilet and pulled her feet up on the seat. She would have to remain perfectly still so as not to trigger the automatic flush, but she was shivering from the chill air of the museum, and her mounting fear only made it worse. It was just a matter of time now and Jenda wished desperately that she had chosen to take self-defense classes instead of dancing.

The bathroom door opened again and Jenda saw that the person entering was a man. He stood with his back against the closed door, facing the policewoman. "You need to let this go, Selena," he said.

"What are you doing here?" the policewoman replied testily. "You know this is my assignment. I've been tasked to find him and by god I'm going to find the comemierda, even if I have to follow this bitch all over Texas and back! What business do you have interfering?"

"Let it go. You're on the wrong side here. Come with me and I'll explain."

"What the zujo? Are you fucking crazy? What's got into you, Nick? They've got to you, haven't they? You're on report, amigo, and right now."

Jenda saw the woman remove her digilet and then she heard the high-pitched zing of a laser shot, followed by a thud as Selena collapsed onto the floor. Jenda's eyes went tight shut. She heard the door to the bathrooms open and close. Then silence.

She opened her eyes and waited.

I can't wait too long, she thought. *Someone else might come in.* She got down cautiously from her perch and jumped as the automatic flush engaged. She opened the stall door and saw the woman—Selena—lying motionless. She was still breathing. On impulse, Jenda picked up Selena's digilet from where it had fallen on the floor and tucked it into her bag.

With the aid of her museum map, Jenda quickly located a back exit that opened onto the river walk. The sunshine and warm air began to calm her shivering. As she approached the cover of an overhead bridge, she took Selena's digilet out of her bag. Leaning against a support post, out of sight, she touched the screen, and a photo of her own face emerged. She gasped as she recognized the emblem of Marvaworld in the corner of the screen. Was Selena searching for Luis? She touched the screen again and Jenda's picture was replaced by another—her brother's.

Jenda stared for a moment, not comprehending. *Is that what this is about?* She didn't understand, but she knew that as soon as Marvaworld knew something was amiss, they would be tracing Selena's digilet. She needed to get rid of it. She dropped the digilet onto a rock and stomped on it with the heel of her shoe, pleased at the crunching sound it made. Then she kicked the digilet out into the current, watching as it floated for a moment and then went under. She glanced around, desperately hoping no one had observed her action. There was no one in sight. Clutching her bag under her arm, she hurried away. The hotel she had booked—the one Luis had selected—should be less than two kilometers downriver.

Arriving at the hotel at last, Jenda checked in and made her way empty-handed to her room. It had a big window overlooking the hotel's main entrance and she stationed herself there to watch for Luis. She wondered if one of the people she saw might be Nick, the man who had lasered Selena. She hadn't seen his face. The people she saw were uniformly youthful and energetic and appeared fully engrossed in their devices or one another, happily going about their own lives, oblivious to the fact that a corporate policewoman lay unconscious in the bathroom of the art museum.

Then she saw Luis. He had shaved off most of his beard, maintaining a small goatee and mustache. It made Jenda smile. She thought she would recognize him anywhere, no matter how his facial hair changed. She pulsed him the room number and waited, her need for his reassuring presence growing more intense with each passing second.

Finally there was a soft knock on the door. Jenda opened it and there he was, smiling broadly. He closed and latched the door behind him and Jenda flung herself into his arms. After a long kiss, Luis said, "God, I'm so glad you understood what to do. I was so afraid I might have been too cryptic. Why are you trembling, querida? It's not that bad."

"Yes it is, Luis. It's worse than you know."

As Jenda recounted her experiences of the day, Luis grew increasingly agitated. When she got to the part about the Marvaworld emblem on Selena's digilet, he was dumbfounded.

"Marvaworld? Good god, why would they be looking for you. Or your brother?"

"I think my brother worked with Marvaworld on his last flick. You knew he was a flickmaker, right? Of course, he used his Buddhist name, as well as our mother's maiden name. So professionally he was Jampel Jenkins."

"Wait. Jampel Jenkins is your brother Jonathan?" Luis placed both hands on his forehead, his eyes wide as he stared at Jenda. "And you told me his last flick had been withdrawn. What was the title of that flick?"

"I told you that, too, Luis— *The Nagas and the Garuda.*"

"Zujo! Why am I just now putting all of this together? That film was a huge hit in the Recall community. Why didn't I realize it was a Marvaworld production? Or know that your brother directed it? Damn Marvaworld! Is there no one a decent man can work for anymore?" Luis paced angrily. "Why did I convince myself that my contract with them was okay? 'They just do entertainment,' I thought. No, what they do is propaganda. That's it! I'm done with them. This can't go on. You know there's a plan in the works to bring an end to all this. I don't know the details, but I know it exists and the word going around Recall is that it will be happening soon. I'm glad you don't know where your brother is. My bet is that he's found a safe place and he's protecting you by not telling you where it is. It's obvious Marvaworld doesn't know where he is."

Jenda watched Luis' tirade in thoughtful silence, trying to make sense out of everything. "What about Selena?"

"Well, if she's still alive... Yes, she's probably still alive, but from your account, I'd say the setting on that laser pistol was likely high enough to have wiped a fair few neurotransmitters. She probably won't remember much about that encounter, which is lucky for—what did she call him? Nick? Lucky for

Nick, who is probably working with Recall. You didn't think you were the only spy in the corporate ranks did you Jenda?"

"Won't Marvaworld assign another officer to finish Selena's task?"

"They might. Or they might be so concerned about what happened to her that they'll let it drop for a while."

Jenda wasn't sure whether Luis truly believed that or was merely trying to placate her fears.

"In any event, you should be careful, Jenda. And we probably need to get your suitcase back, don't we? Hand me your digilet and I'll call in the autocar you were using."

Jenda handed him the digilet, relieved that he seemed to consider this a simple task. "So why were you being so secretive about this trip, Luis? I'm assuming it didn't have anything to do with my brother's flicks or Marvaworld."

"Recall's been irrupted. As soon as I knew about the irruption, I deleted your persona. We'll have to set you up again, once we're sure the zone is secure."

"Irrupted? Who…?"

"We're not sure yet," Luis replied. "Our people are still analyzing. But I've been dying to hear about your exciting trip to Abilene. Well, I guess not so exciting compared to today." He held up a hand as he picked up his digilet. "But wait just a minute while I order us some drinks. I think we could use drinks."

A short while later, as they settled onto the boxy sofa with glasses of Cuban rum with lots of ice, Jenda began her story, telling Luis about George, the photo specialist she had worked with and how bored he seemed to be with her project.

"But he was proficient," Jenda said. "He obviously had a lot of experience. It all seemed so simple and straightforward at the Abilene office. I don't understand why they wanted me to go there instead of doing it all through the atmo. It wasn't that complicated."

"Well, if you truly want something to be secure," Luis said, "it's best to keep it in-house. You know the history of the 'nets:

Something gets irrupted, new security protocols are initiated, then that gets irrupted, prompting more new security systems. And on it goes. There's no such thing as absolute security outside the supranet and maybe even there... Anyway. It's a challenge. But the thing is, if everybody working on a project is kept denned up together and disconnected from the digital world—well, that's pretty secure. Then you only have to worry about your location and your people."

"Yeah, I guess I get that. The most interesting information came from the Vice President for Customer Services."

"You got to meet with a vice president?"

"Yeah. Ben. My ex."

"Your ex is a vice president at YJ? Oh, please, tell me all about this." He took Jenda's hand and cradled it against his chest, relaxing into the uncomfortable little sofa as best he could. Jenda told him about her first encounter with Ben in his office, followed by their dinner date.

"Ben ended up telling me about their guidelines for revising people's memory files. Basically, we each have a set amount of file space on YJ and when we reach our limits, they have algorithms that start deleting files." Jenda described in detail his revelations about how this is done. "Anyway, Ben seems convinced that the file revisions are an important service, helping people feel happier with their lives, helping them adapt to change and especially to new technology. He kept emphasizing that this wasn't that different from the memory loss the elderly used to experience anyway, just more organized and beneficial."

"What a convenient misunderstanding. Yes, of course people have always had memory loss with old age, but mostly they'd lose their short-term memory. Long term memories—the very things that YJ is taking away—would be retained in often amazing detail right up to the day someone died. Old people's memories were the continuity of the whole culture and society. That used to make them special."

Jenda was thinking, formulating a question. "So, if Granny El hadn't been going in for Chulel all these years—well, for the memory restructuring—she'd have a lot more information about what her life was like back in, say, the 1970s and 1980s? More information about my mother's life? More information about me?"

"Without a doubt," Luis said. "Now, exactly what she'd remember and how she'd tell the stories... Well, that would be somewhat unpredictable. Human memory is hardly infallible. But at least they'd be her memories and her stories and not some set of memories deemed socially or economically beneficial to the plutocrats and cobbled together by algorithms at Your Journal."

Jenda continued her story. "After Ben and I finished dinner, he started telling me about his wife. Yes, he's been married to her for the past seventy-five years and counting. He talked about how important it has been to their relationship that each one has had the freedom to experience other relationships along the way." Jenda watched Luis to see his reaction.

"No! So he tried to seduce you?"

"Yes." Jenda said calmly. "So I told him I had finally come to terms with being lesbian."

Luis laughed and pulled Jenda closer to him on the sofa. "You'll never get away with it. You don't seem like a lesbian to me," he said.

"I guess I never told you about Sandra." So Jenda told him, and for the first time she understood how important Sandra's vibrant femininity had been to her after Ben's arrogant alpha male displays had left her lonely and desolate. As this understanding dawned, it reinforced another feeling that had been emerging into her awareness over the past several months—the conviction that she did know what true love is and that she had experienced it somewhere, sometime, maybe even more than once, before Luis.

The next morning as Jenda lay on her side, facing away from Luis, he started stroking the small of her back, seeming to trace a pattern over and over.

"When are you going to tell me about this tattoo?" he asked.

"What? I don't have any tattoos." Jenda turned to face him. "You old Joker!"

"No, really, Jen. There used to be a tattoo here." He gently turned her back on her side and traced the pattern again.

"How can you tell? It's probably... maybe where I was lying on the crumpled up sheets."

"I noticed it a long time ago. In San Miguel in fact, one day when we'd been to the pool and you were a little sunburned. I could see where the ink was removed. Those areas never quite blend in with the surrounding skin when it changes color."

"Okay," Jenda said. "If there's something there, show me."

Luis got up, pulled on his undershorts, retrieved his digilet, and took a photograph.

"You just wanted to take some nude photographs of my backside," Jenda grumbled as she got up and pulled on the hotel robe, which was skimpy but adequate.

Luis had already linked his digilet to Jenda's traveling digiscreen and was processing the photograph, enhancing the contrast.

"Wayee, it does look like ... something," she conceded. "Can you get any more detail?"

"Not without a better equipped screen," he said. "But at least you know I wasn't making this up. Does the shape or anything look familiar at all?" Luis zoomed out to show the entire figure. It was about twelve centimeters high by eight centimeters across, narrowing at the top.

"No, I don't think so," she said, then suddenly added, "Can you make it blue?"

"What? Blue? Why?"

"I don't know. Just do it. Blue."

Luis complied.

"No, not my whole back," she complained. "Just the image. Or maybe only part of it."

He did his best. It still didn't look like anything, but Jenda continued staring.

"It reminds me of something," she murmured, her brow knitted into a frown.

"Well, let's wait and see what a better giz can do," Luis said. "You know, you're not the only one who had a tattoo. Can you see mine?" He raised his left shoulder toward Jenda.

"You, too?" she said, examining the shoulder he presented. "Hmmm. I don't see anything. Maybe you need some sun. What was it?"

"Nothing interesting. Just Batman." He grinned.

"You're craicking me. You had a tattoo of Batman?"

"Well, I got it when I was eighteen and I thought it was terrific. Maybe yours is something like that, too."

"Why did you have your tattoo removed, Luis?"

He leaned back in the chair and folded his arms, glancing again at the shoulder where the tattoo had been. "Not my choice," he said. "I got picked up at a protest back when I was... oh, maybe twenty-two? And that had become standard procedure. Tattoos weren't against any law, but if you passed through the hands of the corporate police you were going to come out the other side with no tattoo. I've thought about having it redone, but there are so few good tattoo artists anymore. And they mostly make those temp-tats that can be erased whenever you want or that fade away on their own after a year or so."

"Why do you think I would've gotten a tattoo? Why did you get yours?"

"I think Vintagonists were drawn to anything that felt permanent. Making images in ink on your own skin felt like a statement, regardless of what the image was."

Jenda walked over to the window and stared out at the street, wondering if anybody out there also had tattoos, old or otherwise. "Do you think we could risk a walk by the river, Luis?

I need to do something with all this nervous energy. We could get lunch."

They left questions of tattoos and corporate intrigue behind, then, and went for a stroll along the river. It was one of those summer days when the cool moist air along the stone-lined banks of the river gave way only grudgingly to the heat of the sun. They watched the ducks and the grackles and listened to the cooing of doves, all of which had escaped Jenda's notice as she fled her morning encounter with Selena. They admired the new sculptures, the ones with digital skins that beamed back versions of whatever the oscillating hidden camera was perceiving. They even laughed a bit as their own faces showed up on the faces of one sculpture.

Suddenly Jenda stopped. "Oh, look, Luis!" She pointed to the edge of the pathway. "Poor thing." She was looking at a young dove. A dead young dove.

Luis stared at the bird for a moment. "This reminds me of something, something I haven't thought about in years. There was a flick I watched back in graduate school. It was an old flick, in fact one of the first ethnographic flicks ever made. Can't remember the guy who made it, but it was about a group of people on a Pacific island. They had this legend about how at the origins of humanity there had been a contest between a bird and a snake, to determine whether human beings would be like snakes, shedding their skins and living forever, or like birds, who have to die. They say the bird won. I wonder if maybe they were wrong."

Jenda was feeling more fragile than she wished to admit and the dead bird brought her close to tears. Luis took her hand and pulled her away onto a little bridge so they could cross over to the other side of the river.

After stopping for enormous ice cream sundaes that they figured would hold them until dinner, they made their way back to the hotel.

"What's next?" Jenda asked, settling down on the sofa next to Luis.

"Well, there will be dinner. Maybe some heterosexual sex," he responded.

"That's good." She nestled closer. "But you know what I mean. What's next for our project? And can we talk about exactly what that project is now?"

A major part of the project, Luis acknowledged, had been accomplished in that they had solid information on where and how YJ managed people's files. Much that had only been suspected was now confirmed.

"Personally, I'd like to find out more about what happened to my grandmother in Argentina," he said. "And of course I want to help you find more of the missing pieces of your own past." There was bitterness in his voice as he added, "Now that I'm finished with Marvaworld, I should have plenty of time." He folded his arms across his chest. "I'm sure higher level plans will be on hold until they figure out who irrupted Recall and recreate a secure means of operation. So why don't we take the opportunity to concentrate on our personal concerns— finding out what happened to my abuela and finding out why you don't remember having been a crazy Vintagonist?"

"Pukka," Jenda said. "I've been kind of wanting to see if Granny El can remember anything that might help me piece things together. Her memories may be full of holes, but at least she has some. It would be great if she had something like the little book you found in your mother's things, but you should see how vanguard Gran's habitat is. I can't imagine she would've kept anything old. But she might remember something."

"That would definitely be worth a shot," Luis said. "And as for me, I've been thinking maybe I should take another trip to Argentina."

Realizing that it might be difficult to communicate for a while, they made a date to meet again at this same hotel in two weeks. Most of Sunday they spent in bed.

14.

Back in Dallas, Jenda sorted through the oldest photos she could find in her personal YJ files. She was dismayed at how few there were. She indexed some of them to ask Granny El about. One of them was the altered photo she and Luis had examined from her Vintie days. Another showed her as a child with what appeared to be a white cat in the background. A third showed her as a serious looking teenager in front of an easel, with a paintbrush in her hand. This one also had been altered to obscure her Vintagonist traits. Now all Jenda had to do was convince Granny El that instead of tennis this Friday, they should get together at Jenda's place for dinner and a flick.

"Why don't we go out to that new dinner theater?" Granny El countered.

"I'd rather you come to my place, Gran." Jenda hesitated. "Sometimes it seems so empty, and I like having people over." There was no response, so she tried a new tack. "I redecorated my front room, and I want to know what you think of it."

"Ah, well then. Okay, we'll do it. Shall I bring the dinner or are you cooking?"

Jenda thought she heard Granny El snicker. She knew Jenda didn't cook. Most people didn't cook these days. Kitchens were designed strictly for entertaining and convenient preparation of pre-cooked meals.

"You can bring the dinner. I'll pick out a flick," Jenda responded, quickly calculating when she'd have time to go to 3Dec and buy some new items to redo her front room. She wouldn't have time to order anything custom made on the 3-D printers they were known for. She'd have to settle for something pre-scripted.

On Friday, Granny El showed up three minutes early at Jenda's door, bearing containers filled with barbequed beef product, mashed potatoes, fried okra, and coleslaw. "You are so old-fashioned," Jenda chided her, but she had to admit the spicy fragrance of the sauce was making her mouth water.

Jenda modestly accepted Granny El's effusive praise for her redecorating job. In fact, Jenda hated the bright oranges and yellows in the floral patterned window treatments and sofa pillows, but she knew her grandmother favored this color range, and she was trying to put her in a good mood. She had also selected one of Granny El's favorite musical comedies for their entertainment.

"I love that show," Granny El sighed, after the final big number left her once more with happy tears.

"So do I!" Jenda tried to sound enthusiastic, despite the fact that she had found the story thin and meaningless this time around. Why had she never noticed that the song lyrics were one long sequence of clichés?

She served up ice cream with chocolate mint syrup, and as she and her grandmother scraped the bottom of their dishes, Jenda said, "How about looking at some old pictures?" as if the thought had just occurred to her.

"Oh, Jen, why would you want to do that?" Granny El demurred.

"No, no, I think it will be fun," Jenda said, hastily opening her YJ folder on the home screen. "Let's see what I can find." She pulled up the indexed photos. They had a good laugh over a picture of Jenda as a young child wearing what they agreed was a ridiculous swimsuit. Jenda moved on to the picture with the cat.

"Do you see that little white cat in the back of this one? Do you suppose I ever had any pets, Gran?"

"Pets. Such a foolish indulgence, only designed to make you cry or make you sick," Granny El replied. Then she squinted at the screen, studying the photograph. "Maybe you did have a pet. That little cat does look... familiar." Jenda could see that her grandmother's mind was taking a detour. Her head tilted to one side as she murmured something that sounded like, "Sweet

Milly..." Then she turned abruptly to Jenda and said, "No, I don't remember any pets."

Jenda moved on through another few pictures and then to the one of herself as an altered teenager. "Do you know how old I was in this picture, Gran?" Jenda asked. "The tag says it's from 2028, but I look... I don't know, older than fifteen, don't you think?"

Granny El studied the screen. "If the YJ tag says 2028, then 2028 must be right."

"Do you remember my crazy friends from back then?" Jenda laughed, trying to imply that she herself remembered them only too well.

"Oh, yes. I don't know how you ever fell in with that crowd, but I'm so glad that gap year trip got you over it."

"Yeah..." Jenda's mind was racing. "Gosh, where all did I go that year?"

"Oh, I don't remember. South America, I think. Yes, maybe South America, but I don't know exactly where. The important thing, of course, is that you came back refreshed and ready to tackle your coursework at Ex University." She sounded almost like she was quoting from a brochure for gap year trips. "You made some beautiful paintings that summer," she continued softly. "I put them in the closet after your mother died. My beautiful Tessa..." Granny El suddenly looked sad and old, in spite of her good skin and hair.

"What closet?" Jenda almost whispered.

"Closet?" Granny El came out of her reverie abruptly. "Oh, there are several closets at my place that I don't use anymore. Who knows what's in there? Feel free to use them if you want, if you need to store anything for a while."

After Granny El left, Jenda wished she could talk to Luis. Instead, she picked up one of her little paper books and wrote her thoughts there:

> *Your Journal thinks they're doing such a fine job of pruning and reorganizing people's memories, when what they're doing is condemning people to live with broken*

memories and lives that don't make sense anymore, fragmented memories that don't fit together, lives that don't link up with the lives of the people they love.

Part III
Pieces of
the Puzzle

15.

Dr. Emily Feldman took on the task of piecing together Isabel Hernandez' life story while Max continued his search for more information about the clandestine institute that had engaged in photonic memory experimentation back in the 2020s and 2030s.

Emily preferred interviewing Isabel inside her secret gallery, hoping the proximity of the artworks and books would be conducive to remembering. It quickly became evident that most of Isabel's life before about 2080 was a grab bag of scraps and fragments. Whatever had scrambled her memories had done a thorough job.

Isabel did remember a small apartment where she used to live in Buenos Aires, and Max had examined residential records and determined that she had moved into that apartment in November of 2080. Isabel had lived there for about ten years. She didn't remember moving in. One of her earliest memories of that apartment was of a man arriving at her door with several large boxes with her name on them. He claimed to be someone she knew. They had gone out to dinner that day and he had come back to visit a few more times. The boxes were filled with books and small works of art.

"Who was this man?" Emily asked. "How did he know you?"

"He said his name was Silvestre Ocampo. He claimed that I'd worked for a while in his home village, near one of the old estancias up-river," Isabel said.

"What kind of work?" Emily prompted.

Isabel laughed quietly and looked away. "Well, it sounds kind of crazy, but he seemed to be implying that I'd been involved in some kind of... I don't know, spying activity? He would never say much about it. And once he realized that I had no memory of him or his village, he didn't come back anymore. He seemed a simple fellow. Not like someone who'd know much about spies. Maybe it was just a made-up story."

"Did he say how he'd ended up with the boxes?"

"He claimed I'd left them with his family and made them promise to find me and return them to me afterward," Isabel said, looking thoughtful.

"After what?"

"I don't know. He never said. But I must have been expecting to go away somewhere for quite a while. Otherwise, why would I have packed up my precious books and paintings so carefully? They were all wrapped in paper and then the boxes were wrapped in Defense-Coat to protect them from moisture. It was quite well done. That's why my books are in such good condition."

They sat in silence for a few moments as Emily scribbled some notes in her paper notebook.

"I have so enjoyed reading—or I guess re-reading—all of those books," Isabel continued, glancing toward the corner where the books were shelved behind their glass doors. "Some of the passages seem so familiar and the characters feel like old friends."

Guided by her books and artworks, Isabel said, she had constructed a life for herself in Buenos Aires. She had found a job working at a commercial gallery, where she met a couple of people in the underground art network who seemed to appreciate her apparently intuitive knowledge of literature and art. Through them she had secured a position at Galería Picaflor, which she eventually took over.

"And you were taking Chulel all the time?" Emily wanted to know.

"I can't say about the time before 2080. But when Sr. Ocampo delivered the boxes, he also gave me a small packet containing several doses of Chulel." Isabel paused. "It took me a while to figure out what it was, but it seemed like it wasn't going to do me any harm, so I learned what the proper dosage and time interval was, and I went ahead and took it. And by the time that ran out, I'd found out how to get it for myself." Isabel gave Emily a sly look. "Are you trying to figure out how old I am? I've done some work on that, too. Not that it seems to matter so much anymore, thanks to you and Max. But a person does want to know how old she is."

Emily agreed.

"Some of my books seem like they were used as textbooks for university classes and the latest publication date on one of those is 1996. So I figure if I was in college in the late 1990s I would have been maybe twenty? So maybe I was born in the late 1970s. Unless, of course, those books were from a post-graduate course, in which case I could be a little older. But not much."

Emily nodded appreciatively. "Good sleuthing. If you weren't a spy, maybe you should've been. What about the publication date on the book that's signed by your daughter, the book by Silvina Ocampo?"

"The date on that one—it's a reprint, of course--is 2010. And the handwriting looks like a younger child. I have only a few books with publication dates past 2000."

"I also noticed that the Ocampo book is from a California publisher: Meta University Press."

"True. Most of my earlier books are from Mexican presses. The few I have after 2004 are all California. So maybe I was in California, like you thought based on my accent. The two Jameson volumes are from a California press, too. I think the publication dates on them are 2002 and 2006. Did you see how they were signed?" Isabel went over to the polished wood bookcase and opened one of the glass doors. She retrieved the volumes in question and returned to the table, placing the books in front of Emily.

Emily opened the first one. The inscription read, "To the keeper of my treasure. Fondly, Martin." This was the one from 2002. The second book was inscribed simply, "With undying gratitude," and signed. "These look very personal, Isabel," Emily said, closing the second book and stacking the two books neatly. "This Martin Jameson must have been someone you knew well. Yes, I think you must have spent quite some time in the Republic of California."

Emily glanced back through her notes. "So, did this Mr. Ocampo... That's interesting that he has the same surname as the author. Do you think you remembered that correctly?"

"I've asked myself that question. But I'm sure that's what he said his name was. It didn't mean anything to me at the time, only after I started re-reading my books."

"Hmm. So did he tell you the name of his village, or of the old estancia you said it was near?"

Isabel closed her eyes to think. "It was... San... San something." She opened her eyes and grinned at Emily. "That doesn't help much, does it? Everything is named after some saint or another." Isabel put her hand over her eyes. "San... San Román? That could be it. San Román."

They ended their session with a couple of glasses of Malbec and a free ranging discussion of art. Emily made only a few additional notes.

Later that evening Emily told Max about her visit with Isabel. "I get the distinct feeling that her mental state must be something like the visual field of someone with macular degeneration. You know, where you see things in your peripheral vision, but as soon as you turn to look directly at them, they go all out of focus, and you lose them."

"But of course that's only when she's trying to look at things from the distant past, right? Her more recent past—since about 2080—seems remarkably clear. Her case is far worse than what occurs in patrons of the Chulel spas. My god, if this was the work of that research institute, I wonder how many people they did this to?"

Emily nodded in sympathy. "I asked her about the name of the village where the man came from with the boxes of her things, and she said it might have been San Román. She didn't seem entirely convinced."

"San Román? Well, let's see what a map can tell us." He screened up a map of the Buenos Aires region and searched.

"By the way," Max remarked as he scanned the map. "Have you seen some of the reports coming out of East China about a blood disease they're calling 'idiopathic hemolytic anemia'?"

"Idiopathic?" Emily snorted. "That just means they don't know what causes it. I'll look for the reports, Max; it sounds interesting. Do you think it might be related to the changes in the beta chains of hemoglobin we've been monitoring?"

Max reached up and patted Emily's hand, which was resting on his shoulder. "Exactly what I've been wondering myself, my dear. In fact, you can help me finish a message I've been drafting up to send to a couple of our colleagues, suggesting that they look into it."

"Max, you know I think Isabel must have had more or less continuous access to Chulel from an early point. As best I can figure, she must be at least 145 or so and...well, you know what she looks like."

"At least those scoundrels who were experimenting with her mind were offering her something of modest benefit as well. At least I suppose it's a benefit."

Max pointed to a spot on the digiscreen he had spread out on the desk. "There's a locality fairly near here called San Román. But it's to the south and near the coast. Didn't she say the village and estancia were 'up river'?"

"She did," Emily replied. "And she seemed pretty sure of herself when she said it."

"So let's loosen up our search parameters."

Max and Emily watched as several new tags popped up on the map. One of them was alongside the name "San Ramon." This locality was up river.

"Would you like to take a little trip tomorrow?" Max asked.

16.

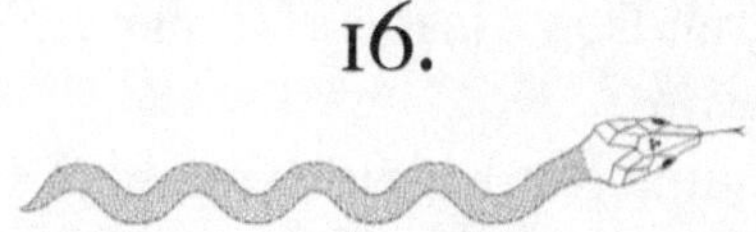

On the plane to Argentina, Luis reviewed his plan. His main goal was to meet again with Silvestre Ocampo and possibly talk with some of the other people in the village of San Ramon where Silvestre lived. Maybe he could find out more about this mysterious estate his grandmother visited. Luis' first journey had been hurried, and he had only gone to San Ramon at the end of it. This time he planned to spend a full week in the village, which would leave him a few days in Buenos Aires at the end of his journey before flying back to Texas to meet Jenda in San Antonio.

Luis was impatient to get to the village and stayed only one night in Buenos Aires before accessing an autocar for the short journey. He used a device supplied by one of his friends in the underground that would effectively scramble the data on the autocar's navigation recorder so that there would be no accurate records of where he went. Luis wasn't sure why he wanted to do this, but on this particular day he enjoyed doing it simply because he could.

He left the autocar near what passed for the San Ramon town plaza and walked the few hundred meters to Silvestre Ocampo's house. The weather was cool and clear, a perfect late June winter day. The door opened, and Silvestre's wife Rosalí, after a moment's pause, gave him a smile of recognition and a hug.

"And your husband?" Luis inquired.

"Yes, he's here," Rosalí said. "But he's ill, more so than the last time you came. I can't promise he'll remember you. Please, come in." She gestured toward the doorway of Silvestre's room.

Silvestre was propped up in the bed. Luis thought he looked fragile, perishable.

"Do you remember this man?" Rosalí said in a loud voice. "He's Isabel's grandson. Isabel Hernandez' grandson. He visited us once before."

Silvestre squinted at Luis for a moment and then held out a trembling hand in greeting. "Oh, yes, I remember him," he said. His voice was thin, but his eyes glowed with genuine recognition.

Luis was surprised by Silvestre's rapid decline into old age. He chided himself for not having been prepared for this. But when was the last time he had seen an old person?

Luis let Silvestre talk about whatever he wanted to, listening as he again told about the many flowers and birds and insects he and Isabel had enjoyed viewing together. "Did I show you our flower book?" he asked. He told Luis that he and Isabel had made a book of pressed flowers. Rosalí pulled it down from a shelf and dusted it off. Luis watched while Silvestre told him about each of the flowers, many of which were now disintegrating in the pages of the album. Silvestre's impaired vision still perceived each blossom to be as fresh and colorful as the day he had picked it.

"I should have given this to her with the other things," he mused.

"Other things? What things did you give her?" Luis asked.

"Her boxes. The ones she left with us. She made us promise to get them back to her after she was released." Silvestre was still holding the book of flowers.

"Released?" Luis didn't wish to interrupt Silvestre's thoughts, but he did want to direct them.

"Oh yes, they put her in prison, you know," Silvestre murmured. "Those hijos de puta put pretty Isabela in prison." Luis knew that Isabel had been in prison, but Silvestre had not talked about it before.

"And you gave her some boxes?" Luis spoke softly. "After she was released?"

"Her things. We'd promised her. And I kept the promise. I found her in the city, and I gave her the boxes. But she didn't remember." Silvestre started to cough. Rosalí coaxed him to drink a little bit of water through a straw. He lay back on the pillows.

"That's probably enough for now," Rosalí told Luis as she gently stroked Silvestre's forehead.

"I understand." Luis took Silvestre's hand and told him how happy he was to see him again. Silvestre thanked Luis for visiting, but his eyes had lost the spark of recognition.

Rosalí invited Luis to stay for supper, and he readily accepted. "Do you remember when or where Silvestre delivered those boxes he talked about?" Luis wanted to know. He had always believed his grandmother had died in prison, but this sounded like she may have been released. Perhaps Silvestre had been one of the last to see her alive.

"You know, I had forgotten that those boxes were Isabel's," Rosalí said. "They were here for so long, they became like part of the furniture. Let me think. I believe Silvestre took the boxes away about the same time that the old estancia was razed, and that was in about 2080."

Luis was stunned. How could this be? According to the story he knew, Isabel had died in the early 2030s, when Luis himself was only six or seven years old. "Are you sure?" Luis asked.

"Well, it could have been a little earlier or later, but about 2080. I'm sure of that," she said.

Luis struggled to grasp this new information that called into question the one solid fact he had always had about his grandmother. Was it possible that she had been alive for fifty years or more after his mother was told of her supposed death?

"Do you think you might still have the address where Silvestre delivered my abuela's boxes?"

"I think so. I still have a lot of old record books stored in the back room. I can look for it this evening. Will you come back tomorrow?"

"That would be great," Luis said. "Yes, I'll come back tomorrow."

"For breakfast?" Rosalí asked.

"I could be persuaded to do that." Luis smiled. "Also, do you remember Silvestre talking about an old estate that he used to frequent with Isabel? Do you know where it was?"

"Yes, of course," Rosalí replied. "That's the one I was talking about that they destroyed back in 2080. Would you like me to take you there tomorrow?" Luis' eager expression indicated that he would indeed like that. "You know, it's kind of odd, you showing up like this. There were some other people here earlier this week asking about the old estate and I took them out there, too."

17.

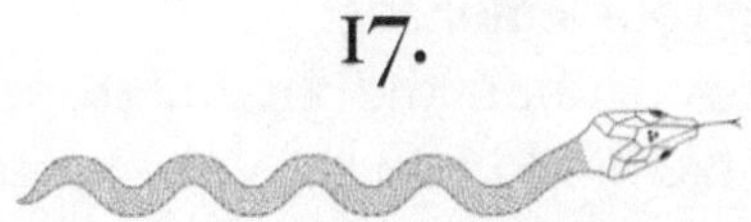

Jenda packed up a box with bedroom curtains, a bedspread, and a couple of throw pillows to take to Granny El's. "I only took these down last week, but I'm not sure I like the new ones, Gran. Can I put the box in one of your closets until I make up my mind?" That's what she told Granny El as an excuse to look inside her closets and see what was already stored there.

"Seems kind of silly, Jenda," Granny El scolded. "Just take them to recycle and if you decide you don't like the new stuff, recycle that too. Recycling makes the world go 'round, sweetie." But she invited Jenda in and pointed her to a hall closet. "There may be room in there, but if not you can check the closet in the spare bedroom. I don't know why I still have such a big place." Granny El busied herself opening some bottles of lemonade and a packet of ginger cookies.

Jenda opened the door to the hall closet. It was stacked to the ceiling with boxes and things wrapped in brown paper. Then she checked the bedroom closet. It was full, too. There were a few out-of-season clothes hanging to one side and Jenda quickly realized they were also long out of style. Both closets looked like they hadn't been opened in years.

"Gran!" Jenda called out. "These closets are both pretty much at capacity. Why don't you let me help you clear them?"

Granny El appeared in the doorway to the spare bedroom and peered into the open closet. "Oh, Jen, it seems like such a waste of time. I don't need the space and I'm sure you have better things to do."

"No, really, I wouldn't mind. I'd even volunteer to take some of this away for recycling. I bet we could get some great credits at the shops for some of this. Think what fun we'd have spending those credits."

"You're sure you wouldn't mind? You want to start with this one? I'll bring your lemonade."

Jenda pulled out one of the boxes and opened it. What she found was a jumble of old papers, greeting cards, brochures, gift bags, notebooks, and something wrapped in an old, badly mended shirt. She knew she would take this one home with her, so she set it aside and pulled down another.

Granny El sat on the edge of the bed, sipping lemonade as she watched Jenda opening box after box. "Look at all that junk!" she laughed. "Why did I ever hang onto such trash?"

"Gran." Jenda looked at her sternly but spoke quietly. "Gran, were these my mother's things?"

Granny El looked confused. Then her eyes fell on the object wrapped in the old shirt that Jenda had found in the first box. "Let me see that," she said.

"This?" Jenda asked. Granny El nodded. Jenda picked up the object and removed the wrappings. What she held in her hands was a graceful bronze sculpture of a child dancing. Jenda recognized the posture; it was almost identical to the painting she had made in San Miguel.

"Oh, Jenda... I... why?" Granny El closed her eyes tightly. "I can't... I don't remember." And then she let go a huge sob that seemed to overwhelm her like a tidal wave. Her eyes opened wide, as if fixed on something in the distance. "I do remember. I remember you, Tessa. My beautiful Tessa." Jenda reached to take Granny El's lemonade, which was teetering precariously in her trembling hand. She set it on the floor and took both of Granny El's hands in hers and knelt as she laid her head in her grandmother's lap.

"I'm sorry, Gran," Jenda whispered. She stroked Granny El's hand and wiped her own tears away on the sleeve of her blouse. "Has all this been here ever since... ever since Mom died?"

"I guess so," Granny El replied. "I never use this closet. Never even use this room. I should move to a smaller place."

"Look, Gran. If you won't mind, I'd like to take most of this stuff back to my place to sort out. It's going to take some time, but I'm beginning to think I need to remember Mom, to remember my own childhood, you know? I think this could help me."

"Please. Take it all if you like. I may not remember everything, but I remember enough. Sometimes I think I remember too much. But yes, take whatever you want." Granny El's tears had stopped. Her hands were steady and her voice firm.

It required three trips with a tiny autocar packed full for Jenda to transfer all of the boxes and wrapped items to her apartment. At both ends, the neighbors looked at her like she was some kind of sociopathic hoarder, but Jenda didn't care.

By evening the task was done and Jenda was physically exhausted from the unaccustomed exertion of carrying all those heavy boxes in the summer heat. Her curious mind, however, was still crackling with energy. "One box," she told herself. "I'll pilfer through one box. And I'll unwrap a couple of the packages, just to see what's inside. And then I'll take some Duermata and get some sleep."

She opened a pack of Nutrichips, poured a glass of wine, and reached for the nearest box. This was a heavy one. She opened it and found it was full of books. She took them out one by one, leafing through pages, looking for something, though she didn't know what. They were mostly books on art. A few of them she knew were her own college textbooks. Others clearly had been her mother's. Near the bottom were some children's books, including a few by authors Jenda thought she might remember—Beatrix Potter, James Herriot, Nikki Loftin, Ty Weaver. And there was *The Wonderful Wizard of Oz*. These were good memories, gentle memories. Jenda thought she might be able to get some sleep after all, even without the meds.

She reached for the nearest of the wrapped items. The encircling tape was resistant, and she had to use scissors. Finally the corner of a painted canvas emerged. The opposite corner revealed the artist's signature: Jenda Swain.

Half an hour later, Jenda sat in the center of the floor, surrounded by fourteen paintings, each one produced by someone calling herself Jenda Swain. She held her head in her hands and wept. Her memories were all around her and they made no sense at all.

Jenda fell asleep on the floor, curled in a fetal position. She awoke after only a brief sleep, feeling stiff and old. Her hip and shoulder hurt. The sight of the paintings was less of a shock now, and she sat up to look at them. Each one evoked a wave of emotion from some forgotten place. She got up and found her digilet and carefully photographed each painting, as if she were afraid they might disappear again if she had no digital record.

One painting, dated April 2031, kept drawing her back for another look. It showed a crowned female figure draped in billowing embroidered blue robes, surrounded by spikes of light.

Jenda was sure it was the lady in blue, the one that hid in the shadows of her dreams. Seeing her face-to-face like this frightened Jenda, grabbing at her belly and throwing up a dense cloud in her mind. She took another photo and turned the painting around to face the wall.

After an early breakfast, Jenda called her office and told them she was not feeling well and would be working from home today. By noon, her front room looked like an old fashioned yard sale. She had devised a sorting process for the materials. Her mother's things were assembled on one side of the room, her own on the other. Shared things were kept on Jenda's side.

Her mother's side included books, sketchbooks, assorted papers, and a couple of small sculptures. There was one more sculpture to unwrap. Even before Jenda had finished unwinding the tattered cloth that had protected it, she knew what it was. It was the bronze of the little girl reading a book, the same one she had bought for Luis in San Miguel as a Christmas present. She turned it over to look at the base, and there was the artist's signature: Setha Tica. Tessa Jenkins Swain and Setha Tica were one and the same. Jenda didn't know whether to laugh or cry. She and Luis both loved her mother's work.

The collection of things on Jenda's side of the room was more diverse, including pieces of clothing from her childhood and youth, a neck chain with a small clock pendant, mementos from various events, some school papers. There were printed photographs on both sides. One pile on Jenda's side kept getting larger and was rapidly reaching critical mass in terms of her ability to resist delving into it. This was the pile of little paper journals that apparently she had kept ever since she learned to write. The earliest ones were all dated in her mother's clear hand. Jenda tried to put them in order.

She spent much of the afternoon reading these notebooks, alternately laughing and crying as she read. She found out that she had indeed had a pet, a white cat named Milly, who had been a close companion and was the subject of many of Jenda's childhood journal entries. The notes she wrote shortly after her tenth birthday told of Milly's death.

My dear, dear Milly is no more. They wouldn't let me see her at first, but I cried so hard they finally let me.

She had her eyes closed. She didn't look comfortable with her paws the way they were. I tried to move them, but she was so stiff. And cold. Not warm and soft like always. Well, her fur was still soft. Her fur was always the softest! It was so strange seeing her dead. Daddy and Paloma dug a hole in the ground in the back garden and put her inside and covered her up with the dirt. I've been saying some of Mommy's prayers to the Buddha, because she says the Buddha can bring people and animals back again for another life. Paloma says she's in heaven with Jesus. I want Milly to come back. I miss her so much. OM MANY PEMMY HUM.

The cat in the photograph was Milly, Jenda thought, as she wiped away a stray tear for her long forgotten pet. She had even forgotten Paloma, the woman who had been her nanny from infancy until she was a teenager, although by that time she was more of a combination personal maid and best friend.

Jenda found a gap in the sequence of notebooks between the start of 2030 and the summer of 2031, just before she began her studies at Ex University in Austin. Some of the other books had pages missing. Even so, Jenda found a few references to friends who must have been Vintagonists, and remarks that clearly showed her own sympathy with the Vinties. In a 2031 book, she found remarks such as "when Paloma and I were in Chile" and "after Paloma took me to visit the museum in Cuzco."

As she rummaged through one final box, she found, at the very bottom, an old paper passport. Her passport. And it showed clearly her travels from May 2030 through March 2031 through Ecuador, Bolivia, Peru, Chile and Argentina.

Luis had notified Jenda that Recall was partially restored, although the burdensome encryption this required meant that real time messaging was still impossible. Jenda decided it was time to post a message to Luis:

POLILLA: I can't handle this on my own. I
need you.

Jenda went to the kitchen to pour a glass of tea. She
checked Recall's Interloc again. There was nothing from Luis.
But Jenda knew what she was going to do.

POLILLA: Fuck YJ. I'm coming to you.

Then Jenda screened out of Recall and closed down her
screen. Taking the tools she had been using to assist in opening
boxes, she broke through the back cover of the screen's housing
and began prying apart everything she could lay a hand on. She
was amazed at the array of intricate, tiny pieces. Leaving it all in
a pile on the table, she hurriedly packed a suitcase, spending
almost no time selecting clothing and taking great care in
choosing notebooks, photos, and papers from the recently
opened boxes. She tucked her current plastiflex digital passport
into her handbag. Then she secured a couple of small
notebooks and the old paper passport in an inner pocket,
snapped her digilet around her wrist, and headed for the
airport. She would find a flight once she got there.

18.

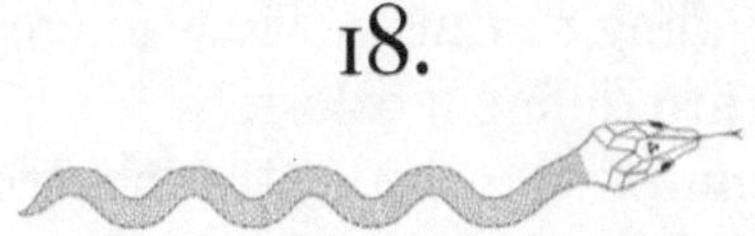

Luis spent a sleepless night at the San Ramon inn. The bed was uncomfortable, and his mind was bedeviled by the idea that Abuela Isabel had still been alive for fifty years after they had given her up as dead. He was grateful for the steaming mug of coffee Rosalí offered him as she prepared a breakfast of eggs, ham, and rolls. As they were finishing their meal, a neighbor arrived who would keep an eye on Silvestre while Rosalí and Luis went out to the old estancia.

The drive didn't take long. "We could've walked, I guess," Rosalí said. "There used to be a path on the back side of the village that led out here. The workers used to take it. Nobody had a vehicle back then, much less an autocar."

They got as far as they could inside the property with the car. Luis parked where the road became a path, and they continued on foot. The weather had grown colder overnight but the sun kept playing with the edges of the clouds, promising a warmer afternoon.

"Tell me about the couple who came to visit. Earlier this week you said?"

"They were a delightful couple, probably Genı. A little bit old, you know?"

"Why did they want to come here?" Luis asked.

"They said they were scientists and that this might have been an important research institute of some kind. They found something under the rubble in one of the rooms and took it with them. I'm not sure what it was." Rosalí motioned to Luis, and they stopped next to the remains of what once must have been an impressive gateway. "This was the main entrance to the grounds. And up there was the entrance to the central building. Such a beautiful place. It's a shame they destroyed it."

"The entries were decorated with those tiles," Rosalí continued, responding to Luis' obvious interest. "They all had the same design, just different colors."

Luis recognized the medical professions emblem, the Rod of Asclepius, but this particular rendition was distinctive with its little fan-shaped leaf at the crest of the staff. Luis took a couple of photographs of one of the unbroken tiles before placing it in his pocket.

"So this place was a medical research institute?"

"We always thought it was a clinic," Rosalí said, kicking some rubble out of her path. "But for rich people only. Patients used to come and go by air shuttle. People say the villagers who got jobs here were well paid."

"What do they tell about their experiences here?"

"That's a funny thing," she replied, shading her eyes and looking toward the trees on the periphery of the grounds. "Nobody seems to remember much about working here. They all say it was a wonderful place to work and that they were treated well."

Luis asked Rosalí to show him where the previous visitors had found the item they took away. He poked around through the rubble there but found nothing remarkable. In fact, he found the whole place to be a rather unexceptional knocked-down building. Nothing but stones and broken concrete. It must have been cleaned out long before the wrecking equipment arrived. He wondered if even an experienced archaeologist would be able to learn much from the jumble.

"What about that little house over there?" Luis asked, as they headed back to the autocar. He gestured toward a cottage off near the crumbling fence. "Why was it left standing?"

"I don't know," Rosalí responded. "It wasn't part of the clinic. Just the caretaker's house. Maybe they ran out of time."

"Why would anyone want to destroy this place anyway?"

Rosalí shook her head and shrugged her shoulders. "I can't even guess. By the time they came, there was nothing going on here at all. It had been empty for years. But they came one day with all these big machines and by the time they finished, this was all that was left."

Over the next couple of days, Luis spoke with at least a dozen people who had once worked at the old clinic or research institute or whatever it was. They all said the same thing, "It was a wonderful place to work, and we were treated well." And they all said it in exactly the same words. None of them remembered anyone named Isabel Hernandez. No one remembered the names of anyone who had worked at the clinic other than their closest kin or neighbors. One man did show Luis where the path used to be that they would take to go to work. Luis had thought he might try going back to the estancia the way the workers had gone—the way his grandmother and Silvestre Ocampo would have gone—but the path was so overgrown now, he felt it would be pointless.

On his way back to Rosalí and Silvestre's house, Luis stopped by the village church, the chapel of San Ramon No Nacido. It was cold inside and dark, except for the patterns of afternoon light slanting through the colored window glass and the flickering of a few candles. The stone floor was worn smooth from the footsteps of generations of worshipers. At one side there was a niche with a statue of San Ramon and on the other side a similar niche for Nuestra Señora de Lujan, once honored as the patron saint of Argentina. Luis sat on one of the wooden benches to review his situation.

It was clear there was little more to learn in San Ramon. Luis was still trying to comprehend the possibility that his grandmother had been alive so long after his mother was told she had died. Could she still be alive? That seemed unlikely. He should go back to Buenos Aires. Rosalí had given him the address where Silvestre delivered the boxes. He would try to find that apartment and see if anyone was still around who might remember Isabel Hernandez, anyone who might know what happened to her in those missing fifty years. As he rose to leave the chapel and continue on to Silvestre and Rosalí's house, he found his feet nearly numb from the cold stone floor. He walked toward the niche dedicated to Nuestra Señora de Lujan, drawn by the warm glow of the candles. He looked at the lady with her crown and her billowing embroidered blue robe, surrounded by beams of golden light, her potencias. The candles emitted more glow than warmth. As Luis turned to go, he instinctively crossed himself. *God*, he thought, *I haven't done that in ages.*

Luis left his contact phrase with Rosalí, with the request that she let him know how Silvestre was doing. Also, he wanted to be notified if, by chance, she or Silvestre or anyone else might remember any additional information about Isabel Hernandez.

When Luis went in to bid Silvestre farewell, the old man insisted that he take the book of pressed flowers. "When you see your grandmother, you can give it to her," he said. Luis didn't know how to refuse, so he reluctantly accepted the fragile book.

"Thank you. I'll do that," he said.

Luis had one last question for Rosalí. "Those people you took to the estancia last week—what were their names?"

"I believe they said their name was Field," Rosalí said. "Something like that. I know the woman's name was Emily, but I don't remember his. I never expected to see them again, so I guess I wasn't bothering to remember."

As Luis packed up his small suitcase to check out of the San Ramon inn, he wrapped the book of pressed flowers carefully inside one of his shirts. He had the fleeting thought that maybe Silvestre had just given him a talisman that would lead him to new information about his grandmother.

Back in Buenos Aires, Luis felt less optimistic. The next morning he left his hotel early, thinking he would let the various aromas of fresh coffee and pastries and fried foods help him choose where to have breakfast. He was also remembering that there was an underground gallery somewhere in Buenos Aires that had acquired one of his paintings. Maybe he would seek out that gallery. The quest for information about his grandmother could wait one more day. He needed time to formulate a plan.

As he drank his café cortado and devoured his simple tostada de jamón y queso, Luis searched through data files on his digilet for some reminder that might help him locate the gallery that had his painting. Connecting underground transactions with real world people and places was intentionally difficult, even for those on the inside. It was supposed to be impossible for those on the outside, and Luis now found himself mostly on the outside. He finally found what he was looking for—the address where he had shipped the painting. He was surprised to see also the name of his contact: Elena Troika. He figured the address would probably lead him to a place that didn't exist, but he thought it was worth a try.

Luis' NaviGiz placed the address on the Plaza Wanxiang, about three kilometers away from the café where he was sitting. Plazas in Buenos Aires, as in so much of the world, had come to be known only by the name of their corporate sponsors and old commemorative statues had been replaced by vanguard sculptures in plastimold that could be switched out every few months like old-time billboards. The Plaza Wanxiang appeared to be in the old San Telmo neighborhood, once famous for its art and antiques.

The route to Plaza Wanxiang led through a couple of other plazas and a small park. Down a narrow alley, Luis noticed a shop with a display of what looked to be real silk scarves printed with watercolor flowers. He selected one of these scarves for Jenda. Beside the shop was a small café, where he ate a piping hot empanada and drank a mug of sweet mate. Warmed and reinvigorated, he continued his trek.

At last Luis found his destination, and was surprised to see that it was indeed an art gallery, with a sign reading "Galería Picaflor". He pushed open the door and found himself surrounded by the usual inventory of commercially viable recyclable paintings and small sculptures in plexiform and plastimold, the same kinds of things sold in most of the galleries in San Miguel.

"May I help you?" the woman behind the small desk asked as she rose to her feet. "They are lovely paintings, don't you think? Which one would you like to take home today?" She smiled engagingly as she delivered her sales pitch.

"Oh, yes, lovely," Luis responded, with an obvious lack of fervor. "Actually, I'm looking for someone. Her name is Elena Troika. Is she by any chance someone you know?" Luis was examining the paintings, trying to discern which of the successful commercial artists of the day had produced them. Everything looked so similar. The woman who had spoken to him was silent. He looked over at her and saw that she was studying him intently.

"The name sounds maybe a little familiar," she said. "Why do you ask?" Now it was Luis' turn to engage in that intense visual scanning that attempts to ascertain how far to trust a stranger you have just encountered with sensitive information.

"Well..." Luis decided to be cautious, despite an almost overwhelming urge to fully disclose his intent. "A friend of mine... I think he may have sold her a painting once." He paused. "An oil painting."

"Ah," the woman said. "We don't have any of those in this gallery."

They were studying each other again. Luis looked away and took a deep breath. "Of course," he said. "I didn't mean..."

The woman interrupted. "What is your friend's name?" she asked.

"He calls himself..." Luis took a deep breath. *Here we go,* he thought. "He calls himself Charro Negro."

The woman seemed to stand a bit taller. Her eyes narrowed and her brow furrowed; then she appeared to reach a decision. She passed her digilet over a pad on the desk and Luis heard the front door lock click. "Follow me," she said.

He felt uneasy, but the small woman hardly seemed threatening, so he followed her down the hallway. She unlocked a door that looked like the door to a janitor's closet. She swung the door open and tasked on the lights. In front of him, Luis saw a second gallery and this one was full of real paintings and real sculptures. And there in the center of one wall was his own painting.

"So," the woman said, crossing her arms and giving him a mischievous look. "You say you know this Charro Negro fellow?"

Luis was overwhelmed. Without consciously deciding to do so he said simply, "That would be me. I am el Charro Negro. But my real name is Luis-Martín Zenobia."

"And I am Elena Troika," the woman said, holding out her hand and grasping Luis' proffered hand. "But my real name is Isabel Hernandez."

Luis felt the room suddenly flooded with bright light and the ground slipping out from under his feet.

"My hand," the woman was saying. "You're hurting me."

Luis released his grip on Isabel's hand, his thoughts still incapable of forming sentences.

"Would you like to sit down?" Isabel said kindly. "I'll get you a glass of water. You don't look well." Isabel led Luis to one of the chairs next to the table and went to fetch some water. She glanced toward the door anxiously, as if wondering how she would get this strange and rather large man out of her secret gallery if he passed out and required medical attention.

When Isabel returned with the water, Luis was still staring at her, but now his face was contorted into a crazy grin and tears overflowed from his eyes. She set the glass down and backed away. Luis reached out and caught her hand again, more gently this time.

"You don't know me, do you?" he said softly.

"Should I?"

"I'm your grandson. I'm Juanita's son."

Isabel pulled her hand back. There was fear and confusion in her eyes. It struck Luis that maybe this was only someone who happened to have the same name as his grandmother. The room became solid again.

"I'm sorry," he said. "Perhaps I've made a mistake. My grandmother's name is Isabel Hernandez, like you. I lost her a long time ago, after she was in prison here in Argentina. I thought..."

"Your grandmother was in prison? Here in Argentina? How do you know?" Isabel asked, a bit less fearfully.

"My mother Juanita kept a little book when she came here to look after my grandmother. And there are people in San Ramon who remember, too."

Isabel's eyes widened. "That was it. San Ramon," she whispered to herself. "What people?" she asked Luis.

"Well, there is an old man there named Silvestre Ocampo. I just came from visiting with him, and he told me he brought my grandmother some boxes here in Buenos Aires after she was released from prison."

Isabel's eyes were closed. Tears were forming, and one ran down her cheek.

"I believe," she said, sitting down in the chair across from Luis and leaning slightly toward him, "I believe I may be that same Isabel Hernandez. I believe I may be your grandmother."

Luis reached over and took Isabel's hand in his.

19.

The first flight to Buenos Aires from the Dallas airport wasn't until early the following morning, but Jenda bought a ticket anyway and checked her suitcase, paying extra to have it stored until flight time. She hoped it and its precious contents would travel safely. She purchased a full eight hours in a sleep pod, not caring whether she slept or not but craving the privacy. After a couple of hours looking over the two notebooks and old passport she had hidden in the inner pocket of her handbag as well as the photos of the paintings on her digilet, her anticipated sense of privacy felt more like claustrophobia. She took a dozen tabs of Duermata and accessed the sleep pod's audio options, selecting the lakeside sounds of lapping water and gentle breezes...

Exactly four hours later, she was awake and hungry. She decided to sacrifice her last two hours of prepaid sleep pod claustrophobia in favor of food and exercise. The transit way of the airport seemed vast after her stay in the pod. She made a quick mental inventory of the cuisine on offer, finally selecting the Americana Café. Finding a seat in a secluded corner, she ordered the burger with fried broccoli and a NutriQuaff shake. She finished off the meal and then dawdled over the last of the shake, mentally trying to organize what she had learned from her recently un-closeted artifacts.

She now knew that almost a full year between the summer of 2030 and spring of 2031 was missing from her records. She knew the names of a few of her friends from the period in question. One of them was Leticia Poole, the woman she had been taking dancing lessons from, the woman who sold pendants with watches and lockets in her boutique. Of course Jenda hadn't remembered her at all.

Jenda also knew she had traveled to various South American countries, including Argentina, during her missing year. She had been accompanied by her old nanny, Paloma. Jenda still found that part a bit odd and wondered whether in fact her companion might have been a school friend who happened to have the same first name. She had not been able to find Paloma's last name in any of the notebooks or records. *I should've asked Granny El about that,* she thought. Jenda also suspected that there was a lot to be deciphered from her paintings, with their oddly juxtaposed figures and objects. And then there was that one haunting image of the lady in blue.

She hoped Luis had received her message before his intended departure for their rendezvous in San Antonio, Texas. They were supposed to be meeting there—Jenda checked the calendar on her digilet—day after tomorrow. She let out a slight groan. What if he didn't get her message in time? Maybe she should cancel the Buenos Aires ticket and go to San Antonio on the hyperloop instead.

Shut up! Jenda told herself. *There you go, second-guessing yourself again. This time go with it, Jenda, okay?* But she did allow herself to take a moment to send off a quick pulse to her supervisor at YJ: "Family emergency. I am requesting a week off. Please task this against my next scheduled sabbatical." Then she went back and made it "two weeks" and transmitted. She screened up LifeBook to see if she might have a message from Luis. There was nothing. Checking Recall was still impossible. She waved her digilet at the pay point and left the café, heading for her departure area. She stopped briefly at a kiosk to draw down a trashy novel into her digilet. She was tired of thinking.

The novel lasted until two hours before the plane was due to arrive in Buenos Aires. Jenda shut off her digilet and curled it around her wrist as she settled down, hoping she could manage a short nap. But as soon as she started to think about her situation again, she panicked. How was she going to locate

Luis? What if he hadn't gotten her message and had already left for Texas?

She unwrapped her digilet again and tapped the LifeBook symbol. There were a few entries from friends. And then she saw the photo of a hotel. In Buenos Aires. Jenda felt a wave of relief. She made a note of the name and address of the hotel. It was going to be okay. Luis knew she was coming. He would be waiting for her at the hotel.

And there he was. Feeling no need for discretion, they embraced right there in the lobby, and in that imbricating kind of not-quite-conversation told each other, "I'm so glad you're here" and "I have so much to tell you." Then they stole a quick kiss and, leaning heavily on one another, headed for the elevator.

"Have you found out anything useful?" Jenda asked Luis.

"Yes, quite a lot. But you go first. You're the one fleeing Your Journal to come here to Argentina."

She hardly knew where to begin. "Well, it turns out Granny El did keep things after all—a lot of things. I'd forgotten about all the little notebooks I kept as a child. Some of my mother's sculptures, too. Her art name was Setha Tica, Luis. She made the bronze I gave you. And there were photos. Not so many as I might have hoped, but still...real printed photos. And my paintings. Luis, Granny El kept more than a dozen of the paintings I made in high school and college. I couldn't bring those, of course, but I took pictures. God, Luis, I'm babbling!" She had flung her suitcase into the middle of the bed and was opening it to show Luis her collection.

"Take it easy, querida. Come sit here next to me and tell me one thing at a time."

So Jenda sat on the edge of the bed beside Luis, leaning lightly against his solid frame, her folded hands between her knees, and told him about the things she had found and about what she thought some of it might mean.

"One of the best things," she said, grabbing for her handbag, which had fallen to the floor, "is this." She pulled out her old passport and handed it to Luis. "I may not remember what I was doing, but now we know where I was."

He leafed through the passport. "So do you think we should take a trip and try to track you down?"

"Oh, do you think we could? When?" Jenda's mind was already on board with its seat belt fastened. "But first, you have some things to tell me, too, I think."

"Mmm," he responded, still holding Jenda's passport as if it were a signed first edition. "Yes. Well, the most important is: I found my grandmother."

"Oh my god, Luis!" Jenda felt as if her chest would burst open. "She's alive? Where? Here? Oh, tell me." She huddled up closer to Luis to listen to his story, savoring every syllable as he told about his visit to San Ramon and then finding the Galería Picaflor.

"So you'd sold one of your paintings to your grandmother?"

"Another thing I've found... Wait, let me show you." He led Jenda to the desk where his packable digiscreen was laid out, attached to a couple of odd-looking devices. He pulled up Recall and then an advert within its deeper recesses:

ARE YOUR ANNUAL ADJUSTMENTS NOT DOING
JUSTICE TO YOUR CHERISHED MEMORIES?
WE HAVE UNIQUE ACCESS TO NON-YJ RECORDS OF
PEOPLE WHO SPENT TIME IN ARGENTINA ROUGHLY
2025-2035.

There was a contact phrase listed.

"What do you think? Is it worth a try?" he asked.

"Sure, why not? This person might know something about me and maybe even about your grandmother. But of course, now you can ask her about things."

"Not really. She has bigger memory gaps than you do. But I'm glad you agree we should talk to the person who's running this ad, because I've already contacted him and made an appointment for tomorrow morning. And then in the afternoon we're meeting up with my grandmother. I can't wait for you two to meet. She's also invited her friends, who turn out to be the couple that visited San Ramon the week before I did."

"Pukka!" Jenda's eyes grew large with excitement. "Oh, Luis, this is all so amazing. Scary, but amazing!" Jenda felt she had left much of the scariness back in Dallas. If not for her nagging concern over her brother, she would have been more than ready to celebrate. She hugged Luis and planted a big kiss on his cheek, which was again becoming shrouded in a beard. "Shall I show you the pictures of my paintings?"

Jenda took off her digilet and transferred the pictures to Luis' screen. As the pictures came up, Luis remarked, "Wayee, Jen. You painted these in high school? They're beautiful."

"Tell me what you think of this one. It seems to be the first one I painted after I got back home from my South American travels," Jenda said, as she screened up the image of the lady in blue.

"You painted Our Lady of Lujan?"

"Is that what it is? It's like the statue in the chapel in San Miguel, right?"

"Well, that was the Virgin of Guadalupe. They're both the Holy Virgin Mary, but the one in your painting is definitely Our Lady of Lujan. Your image is odd, though. You see what she's holding there? Most paintings of Nuestra Señora de Lujan show her with hands joined in prayer." He zoomed in on the center of Jenda's image. "Very odd."

"What is it?" Jenda was examining the picture more closely. What she saw the beautiful lady holding looked like a tall thin tree with a snake curled around it.

"Basically, it's the Staff of Asclepius, the symbol of the medical professions," Luis said. "But usually it doesn't have that little tree-top, or gingko leaf or whatever it is. However..." He screened up a photo from his own files.

"It's the same symbol," Jenda said. "Where did you find that?"

"At the old estancia, or rather clinic or maybe research institute. The whole place was decorated with this symbol. I've never seen it represented exactly like this anywhere else. Also..." He screened up one more photo from his files. "I think the Virgin of Lujan may be the image that was tattooed on your back."

The next morning, Jenda and Luis met with the man from the Recall advertisement, who handed them a business card, introducing himself as Dr. Maurice Winfield. He told them he was once employed at a research institute north of Buenos Aires that had been doing some early experimentation with what had become known as photonic memory reconstruction. Their early methods had been crude, he claimed, and many people had lost significant portions of their memories. But apparently Dr. Winfield, whose business card touted a Ph.D. in clinical psychology, had, out of his deep humanitarian compassion for the unfortunate patients, salvaged most of the institute's old records. He had also, he claimed, developed methods that over time would assist people in restoring their memories.

He seemed a bit shady, but Jenda and Luis agreed Dr. Winfield might very well have some legitimate information. They were interested to learn more and invited him to join them later in the afternoon at Isabel's. They hoped they might entice him into giving them a discount on the information he was offering to reveal to them in exchange for a shockingly large sum of money. Dr. Winfield agreed to the meeting, assuring them that they were lucky he had that time slot open, as his calendar was generally kept quite full attending to so many satisfied clients

Jenda was eager to meet Isabel, this woman who Luis barely remembered and who apparently remembered him not at all. Luis reminded Jenda that he had been only six years old when his mother Juana left him with his father in Merida and went to Argentina to care for Isabel. Luis said his mother had never been quite the same after her return, apparently blaming herself or maybe her husband as somehow culpable for Isabel's presumed death.

After a light lunch at a café, Luis and Jenda walked to Galería Picaflor. Luis held the door for Jenda to enter.

"Here we are, Abuelita," he announced. "Here is my lovely Jenda, come to meet you."

Isabel was smaller than Jenda had imagined, but as she rose from the desk, her smile seemed to give her a presence much grander than her diminutive body. She was dressed in a simple dark skirt, golden yellow blouse, and sensible shoes. Her dark hair with its gray streaks was drawn up in a twist and fastened with a gold ornament.

She greeted Jenda, embracing her warmly and offering the little pecks on the cheeks that people of her generation still occasionally practiced. Then Isabel hugged Luis, clinging to the big man with shy affection. "Come," she said. "Let's go into the private gallery where we can be together, just us three." She tasked the front door to lock and a sign lit up, informing subsequent arrivals about ringing for attention.

Jenda was breathless in her admiration of Isabel's private gallery, heading immediately for Luis' painting. She looked at Luis and said simply, "It looks so right here, so at home." Isabel gave Jenda a quick tour, ending at the polished wood bookcase with the glass doors. She offered tea and they went upstairs to her apartment, leaving further exploration of the secret gallery for another day. As they sipped tea, they exchanged disjointed vignettes about their lives. Watching Luis and Isabel, Jenda thought how odd it must feel to be with someone who, by all rights, ought to know so much about your life but who in fact knew almost nothing. At least Granny El had a few selected memories about Jenda.

The bell rang and Isabel excused herself to go admit her callers, Max and Emily Feldman. "I haven't seen them since they got back from visiting San Ramon," Isabel said.

"She's so different from my own grandmother, Luis. You know, they both have lost memories in one way or another, but

Granny El doesn't even seem to mind about that. She never tries to remember anything. Your abuela, on the other hand—such a passion for life, in spite of all that's happened to her. I like her, Luis." She gave his hand a squeeze.

As Isabel and the Feldmans came back up the stairs, Jenda could tell by their easy banter that these were people who trusted one another. When they entered the room, Jenda was surprised at how old the Feldmans looked. She would have been even more surprised to know that Luis, who knew from Isabel that the Feldmans were early Genı, was thinking how young they looked compared to Silvestre Ocampo in his sickbed in San Ramon.

After the requisite introductions and greetings and congratulatory remarks about Isabel and Luis' reunion and Jenda's unexpected arrival, the conversation quickly turned to their shared research interest.

"I understand you were in San Ramon just a week before I went there," Luis said to Max. "And you met Silvestre Ocampo and his wife Rosalí?"

"All roads seem to lead to San Ramon on this quest," Max replied. "Yes, we met Silvestre and Rosalí, but she didn't seem to have a lot of information, and he was so ill he wasn't able to tell us much. But Rosalí took us out to the old institute grounds. Interesting place."

"Rosalí said you found something."

Max accepted a cup of tea from Isabel. "Nothing of great importance," he said. "That place was rumored back in the 21st century to be conducting experiments with photonic memory restructuring. Well, under some of the rubble I found some broken goggles that looked like the kind that were used by laboratory workers to try and shield themselves from photon bursts. Turns out that is indeed what they are. That's not a lot of evidence, but it does lend credence to the rumors."

"We may be able to help you on that," Luis said, and he told Max and Emily about meeting with Dr. Winfield. "We hope you don't mind, but we invited him to come over later this afternoon. If you'd rather not talk to him, we can leave him at the front door and Jenda and I can explain to him later."

Max waved his hand. "No, no. We'd be interested to meet with this fellow. Winfield you said his name is? Nothing to lose, you know." Then the Feldmans began telling Luis and Jenda about their mounting concerns over reports of a deadly blood disorder that was attacking Chulel users, with recent users apparently most vulnerable. It had originally been confined to eastern China but was now cropping up in Indonesia and the Philippines, with reports beginning to come in from other countries as well. It produced acute anemia and was not responding to treatment. An alarming number of people had died.

The buzzer indicating the arrival of another visitor interrupted their conversation and they all turned to look at Isabel. "Yes, go let him in," she said. Luis volunteered to go down and fetch the expected guest.

Luis let Dr. Winfield in, switched off the sign about bell ringing, and locked the door. He led Dr. Winfield down the hallway, past the little door that looked like the entrance to a janitor's closet, and up the stairs to Isabel's apartment. They went inside and Luis closed the door behind them.

"I would like to introduce..." Luis began, then stopped as he looked toward Maurice Winfield.

The man's face was drained of color, frozen into a look of stunned terror. He cast a desperate glance back toward the door and saw Luis standing directly in front of it. Max Feldman had risen to his feet and Emily's eyes flashed daggers.

"Winslow... Morris..!" Max spat out the words like a mouthful of poison.

20.

Winslow Morris had encountered more trouble than he'd anticipated getting his millions in Fontana profits out of China. As he bided his time in Mexico waiting for things to work out, most of his stash of Fontana was stolen. When your inventory is all black market anyway, you can't just go to the authorities and report a theft, so Winslow had taken it into his own hands to track down the culprits.

He had finally found them in Argentina and, because he was still short on cash and because there were more of them than there were of him, he joined up with their thieving and smuggling ring. They weren't a big operation nor were they terribly sophisticated, so Winslow had also put together a convincing résumé and secured a job as a research assistant at a private institute outside Buenos Aires.

Winslow, who was always quick to suspect the worst of almost everyone, readily ascertained that the institute was in fact engaging in some pretty nefarious business. Seeing an opportunity for profit, he began copying and smuggling out records from the institute. He did not share these with his pharmaceutical thieving colleagues. This was something he wanted for himself. He thought of it as an investment in his future.

Now, face to face with the very people from whom he had stolen the original formula for Chulel back in 2021, Winslow found himself questioning some of his career choices. He guessed he was probably not going to make a lot of money from Luis-Martín Zenobia or his partner and grandmother.

Winslow Morris held up both hands in a gesture of surrender. He looked at Isabel, almost as if he were appealing to her for help, but Isabel didn't seem to notice.

Luis stood dumbfounded as Max explained who this man he and Jenda knew as Maurice Winfield really was and exactly how he and Emily knew him. Luis' effort to restrain his laughter out of respect for the Feldmans' justifiable outrage was only partially successful. Jenda was saying something about karma.

"My god, man!" Max said, now that it was clear Winslow was not going anywhere. "How did a scoundrel like you get involved in this institute's work?"

Luis was less interested in hearing about Winslow's circuitous career track than he was in ascertaining what the man might know about Jenda or Isabel. He got the distinct feeling that this would be their one and only opportunity to interrogate Winslow Morris.

Here is what Winslow told them: For one thing, most of the institute's experimental subjects were being recruited under the auspices of an international cult deprogramming business. For another, the clinic end of the operations purported to provide abortion services but instead ran a brisk business providing babies to plutocrats around the world. And, yes, he had records. It was obvious that he had brought his packable digiscreen with him and his interrogators insisted that he show them records immediately. Winslow feebly agreed to do as they demanded.

With a pitiful sigh and a defeated look, Winslow unfolded his digiscreen. Luis stationed himself at Winslow's elbow so he could monitor his every keystroke. "What am I looking for exactly?" he asked.

"Search 'Isabel Hernandez'," Luis said.

No one noticed when Winslow glanced toward Isabel again, looking as though he were about to say something. Then he turned toward his screen and entered the query. "Nothing," Winslow said after a few seconds. "She's not mentioned in any of the records." He seemed relieved and perhaps slightly defiant.

Luis had another idea. "Can you check to see if there are any records of dealings with the Argentine criminal justice system, penitentiaries in particular?"

Winslow paused for a moment, and then tapped some syllables into the screen. "Oh," he said, looking surprised. "Actually, yes. They had a standing contract as medical consultants with several prison facilities."

Luis glanced at Isabel. She was wide-eyed. Emily Feldman was holding her hand. So this was where Isabel had lost her memories. He had hoped for some evidence regarding why she ended up in jail in the first place, but at least this was something.

"Now search, 'Jenda Swain'," Luis instructed, spelling the name out for Winslow. Luis turned and sent Jenda a reassuring look. Isabel rose from where she had been sitting and went to stand next to Jenda.

"Hmm." Winslow stared at the screen. "Yes... Jenda... Jenda Swain. Entered the clinic on 31 May of 2030 for both deprogramming and abortion. I guess she got the package deal," he joked. But as he looked at Luis looking at Jenda, his smile vanished.

"What?" Jenda cried. "No! My mother... Oh my god..." She covered her face with her hands and turned away. Luis saw Isabel put an arm around Jenda's shoulders.

"It's okay, hija," Isabel said. "Tienes tu gente aquí contigo." There were tears on Jenda's face.

"Stay here, Max," Luis said. He strode across the room to take Jenda in his arms. Jenda clung to him for a moment and then said, "Go, Luis. Go find out more. I'll be here with Abuela Isabel. Make him tell you what happened to me." Her face was a prayer and a plea and Luis did as she asked.

"Hers is an odd case." Winslow turned toward Luis and explained what he meant without looking back at the screen. "I have the admission record, and a few months of treatment records. And then nothing. No release record." Once more he glanced toward Isabel, then looked back at the screen and shrugged.

Luis pulled out a storage device like the one Jenda had used at Your Journal. "Give us what you have," he said. "In fact, let's draw down all of your data on the institute." Luis and the Feldmans gathered around Winslow, examining records and interrogating him for some minutes more. By the time they finally agreed to let him go, all of his stolen data were duplicated in Luis' storage unit. Just before Winslow screened out, Luis reached over and entered a few syllables of his own. Winslow stared at the screen as if he expected to see all of his data disintegrate before his eyes. When nothing happened he looked puzzled. Luis patted him on the shoulder.

Luis walked him back down the stairs and out through the gallery to the front door without speaking. As the door closed behind Winslow, Luis headed back upstairs. *What a stroke of luck for us,* he thought. *Although not so lucky for that poor rascal.* He took the stairs two at a time returning to his grandmother's apartment. More than anything, he wanted to hold Jenda in his arms and tell her everything was going to be okay. He hoped that would be the truth.

21.

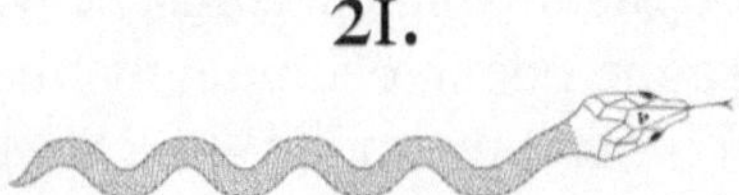

Jenda was still clinging to Isabel. As Luis put his arms around the two of them, she felt momentarily reassured and safe. She wanted desperately to hang onto that. The news that she had in fact been pregnant as her mother had said ricocheted through her mind, finding no lodging place. The entire contents of her heart were spilled. Jenda gave Isabel a kiss on the cheek as Luis said their farewells. They walked downstairs in silence. Luis offered to summon an autocar.

"I think I need to walk," she said. "It might help clear my head."

They walked in silence, Jenda clutching tightly to Luis' arm. Halfway back to the hotel, they passed through a tiny park, and she insisted they stop. They sat down on a bench, which felt almost warm from the late afternoon sun.

"This has got to be pretty overwhelming," Luis said, folding her left hand gently between both of his strong hands.

"You might say that." Jenda stared absently at a small child dipping his fingers into the icy waters of a fountain a short distance away. The fountain was clogged with dead leaves and the child seemed to be trying to retrieve something. "I keep thinking I should remember this or at least remember something about it. But there's nothing there. I find nothing but a big aching hole where the memories should be. My poor mother. Why didn't we believe her? And don't ask what I feel about all this, Luis. I don't even know. Shocked. Angry. Sad. I think mostly angry. How could they have done this to me?" Jenda's palms went to her temples and her fingers cradled the top of her head. "How can someone just decide they're going to alter your life and obliterate your memories without your permission? Without you even knowing what's happening?" As soon as she said this, she heard an annoying inner voice saying,

Isn't that what you've been doing for a living? She looked at Luis, but if he thought anything like this, he wasn't saying it.

"Well, you're the one in charge now," he said. "What do you want to do? This is your story. Where we go with it is your call."

They sat in silence for a while as Jenda battled for control of her jumbled thoughts and feelings. *I have no time for tears,* she thought. *I've lost too much time already.*

Finally she spoke. "We should compare the dates on the clinic records with the dates on my passport," she said. "And I think I'd like to go see this San Ramon place and meet your old man and his wife." Jenda shivered in the evening twilight. She got up from the bench and held out her hand for Luis.

By the time they reached the hotel, Jenda was cold and tired. She welcomed that coldness and tiredness; it was something she could name, something normal. She handed her passport to Luis. "Here," she said. "If you don't mind, you can check on those dates while I go take a hot soak in the tub."

Emerging from the bath with wet hair and no makeup, Jenda felt revived but still disoriented. She thought she wasn't going to have a headache after all, and she didn't mention to Luis that she had thrown up. She rubbed her hair with one of the soft white hotel towels, remembering how she had always loved hotel towels in foreign countries where they were still made of cotton and meant to last.

"Did you find anything?" Jenda asked.

"Yes," Luis said. "Look at this." She peered over his shoulder at the screen while he explained what she was seeing. The dates did not match up at all. According to clinic records, she was admitted on a date when her passport said she was in Ecuador and receiving daily treatments while her passport tracked her through Bolivia and Peru. Her passport put her in Argentina only after the clinic records abruptly ended.

"So what do you think? Is it possible someone else used my name at the clinic while I was traveling elsewhere?" Jenda knew she was grasping at straws.

Luis flipped through the pages of her passport again. "That's odd," he said, looking at a page near the front of the book. He held the book in front of the digiscreen camera and snapped two photos.

"What are you looking at?" Jenda asked, as the photos came up on the screen. All she saw was the page showing traveler's contact information at home and address of destination abroad. It had her parents' contact and the address of a hotel in Ecuador. The second photo was the back of that page, which contained general information about travel protocols. Luis put the second photo through some changes and then pulled it up side-by-side with the contact page. "You see that?" he said.

"I see what looks like a bunch of backwards writing."

"Oh, sorry. I can fix that." He flipped the page horizontally.

"Wait. These are not the same. Something different was written on the contact page first."

"Exactly," Luis said. "What we see on the second page—with enhancement, of course—is the original information. Look what it says."

The contact information was the same, but the destination address read: "Instituto Nueva Vida, San Ramon, Buenos Aires, Argentina."

"So the clinic records are probably right. I must have gone there first. And my famous gap year traveling around South America was an utter fiction." Jenda was standing behind Luis and she put her arms around him. He felt like the most real and solid thing she had in her confused life.

On their drive out to San Ramon the following morning, Jenda was pensive. "Luis," she said finally, "since I was apparently at the clinic for nearly three months, and since there's no record of an abortion... do you think? Do I have a child out there somewhere?" Then, with an ironic smile, she added, "Of course he wouldn't be a child would he? He'd be ...what?

Ninety-five years old now. That's insane. What if he didn't get Chulel? He'd be older than me!"

"We can paint all sorts of possible scenarios, querida. But let's not do that. Let's just wait and see where this takes us, okay? There's still so much we don't know." He put his arm around Jenda and, when she turned to look at him, he gave her a long reassuring kiss. It was still a long drive before the turn for San Ramon. They would let the autocar navigate on its own.

By the time they reached San Ramon, they agreed it would probably be a good idea to go ahead and check in at the inn before going to visit Silvestre and Rosalí. They didn't emerge from their room until mid-afternoon.

Rosalí met them at the door. "This must be your partner," she said, releasing Luis from her warm abrazo and turning to embrace Jenda. "Silvestre is having a pretty good day," she said. "I think he'll be happy to see you."

He was. "Ah, Luis-Martín!" His voice was fragile, but his eyes sparkled behind their drooping lids. "Did you give the flower book to your abuela?"

"Oh, yes," Luis said. "She said to tell you 'thank you'." Jenda sent him a questioning look and he quickly gestured her into silence.

"I knew she'd be pleased," Silvestre said, stroking the bedcovers with his gnarled hands. "Who is this pretty señorita with you?"

"This is Jenda Swain," Luis said. "She visited San Ramon a very long time ago."

"Jenda? Swain you said?" Silvestre was thoughtful. "No, I don't remember that name."

"Maybe you remember my friend," Jenda said. "Her name was Paloma."

"Oh, yes. Paloma. The sweet dove," Silvestre replied. "She was so kind. She was Isabel's friend." He was getting that distant look.

Jenda's eyes widened as she looked first at Luis and then back at Silvestre.

"Do you know Paloma's last name?" Luis asked.

"No. No, I don't recall. Just Paloma, the sweet dove." Silvestre was drifting. Then suddenly he looked at Rosalí. "But I think we were sending her the medicine. After she left. Wasn't she on our list, Rosalí?"

Rosalí looked embarrassed and muttered something into Silvestre's ear in Spanish that made him laugh. "Oh, they won't mind about that." Turning to Luis, he said, "Rosalí doesn't want you to know that our families used to be Chulel thieves." He was grinning like a schoolboy. "I'm pretty sure we sent it to Paloma for a while."

Luis was looking at Rosalí now. "Do you remember Paloma, Rosalí?" he asked.

"I'm not sure," she said, looking chagrined. "It must have been a long time ago. But I may have a record of the address where we sent her the... the medicine. Come with me." She motioned to Luis and Jenda. Silvestre's eyes had closed, and his jaw had gone slack, but there was a faint smile at the corners of his mouth. His hands continued gently stroking the bedcovers.

"So, did you really find your grandmother, Luis?" Rosalí wanted to know. "Or were you humoring the old man?"

"Oh, yes, I found my grandmother. Strong and well. She's been running a little art gallery in Buenos Aires for decades now. I lied about the book, though. I promise I'll remember it next time I go to visit her."

"Well, that is exciting news," Rosalí responded. "Tell me about it while we look for the address."

Luis began his story as he and Jenda followed Rosalí down the hallway to a back room. The room held only a bed, a small table, and a couple of old wooden cupboards against a wall.

Jenda found the room suffocating, as if it were filled with a dense fog. She looked at Luis, but he and Rosalí didn't seem to notice anything. The fog was oppressive and frightening. She sat down on the end of the bed to catch her breath. As she looked up at the wall, at the painting on the wall, she gasped. She inhaled the fog, and the room began to clear.

Rosalí opened one of the cupboards and took down a cardboard box. It was filled with old paper notebooks. "Do you know what years we're looking for?" she looked at Luis for guidance, interrupting his tale just as he was getting to the part about seeing his own painting in Isabel's gallery.

"Let's try 2030," he said. "No, try maybe 2031 or even 32."

Luis glanced over his shoulder at Jenda. She was sitting on the end of the bed.

"Jenda?" Luis called to her.

Jenda was motionless. Tears streamed down her cheeks. She was staring at a wall on which someone had painted an image of Nuestra Señora de Lujan. The painting was old and faded, but it was identical to the one in Jenda's own painting, except that the hands of this lady held only a prayer.

Luis walked over and sat down next to Jenda. He reached for her hand, but she pulled away. She was trembling.

"Jenda?" Luis said again. "You remember this picture, don't you? Do you think you remember this room?" His voice was gentle, and he looked as if his heart would burst with wanting to care for this woman he loved.

"I don't know," Jenda whispered. She heard her own voice coming from somewhere far away. There was a quiet hum of other voices. She closed her eyes to listen. "Milly, Milly," she murmured, rocking slightly as she drew her knees up and grasped them in front of her.

"What did she say?" Rosalí asked, looking suddenly pale. "Milly?"

Rosalí went to a different cupboard and opened another box, pulling out an old and tattered stuffed animal. It looked like a cat and had probably once been white. She brought it over and held it out to Jenda. "Is this Milly?" she asked.

Jenda opened her eyes. She saw her precious cat. She saw her friend Rosalí. "Gracias, hermanita," she said. Then suddenly she doubled over, screaming in pain. She fell back onto the bed, clutching her belly, her eyes wide. *What's happening to me?* she thought. She looked desperately around the room, searching for someone who could make this stop. The only one she saw was Rosalí, who knelt beside her, placing the stuffed cat onto Jenda's stomach.

Rosalí looked at Luis. Through her own tears, she said, "I know this woman. I know your Paloma. And I know Jenda's child."

Luis lifted Jenda from the bed. "We need to get her out of here," he said. Rosalí led them to the sitting room where he placed Jenda on the sofa. She continued trembling, moaning, and convulsing painfully every few minutes. Luis sat on the floor next to her, stroking her arm and talking to her softly. Gradually, the intensity subsided.

"Rosalí grows beautiful flowers, doesn't she?" Luis remarked, as Jenda's blank stare came to rest for a moment on a small pot of purple chrysanthemums. Jenda turned her face toward him and gave him a faint smile.

"I'm thirsty," she whispered hoarsely.

An instant later Rosalí was offering her a glass of cool water. Jenda struggled to sit up. She took a small sip and then a huge mouthful, which made her cough and spit water all over herself and Luis. She began to laugh. "Oh, I'm sorry, Luis," she said, setting the glass on the table and brushing Luis' shirt with her hand.

"It's okay, querida," Luis said. "It's all okay." He handed the glass of water back to her and this time she sipped it slowly and carefully.

"How about some cookies?" Rosalí said. "Have I shown you our little garden? The sun has come out. Let's take a walk in the garden and then have some cookies and tea."

Luis helped Jenda put on her coat.

The garden was exactly what Jenda needed to settle her disturbed mind. It was spacious and open at the center, with a clear view of the bright blue sky with small clouds scudding across. The garden was surrounded reassuringly with a hedge of what Jenda knew was fuchsia and flowering jacarandas, along with a few fruit trees. She remembered the taste of fresh plums.

"This was Silvestre's pride and joy," Rosalí said. "He and his father planted everything here and looked after all the plants with such love. They even built the little stone wall with the fountain there at the end of the path. It used to work, but the pipes rusted through some years ago and nobody fixed it."

They went back indoors and sat around the table in Rosalí's warm kitchen. They drank hot spiced tea and ate cookies, complimenting Rosalí on her baking skills. They could see the garden through a big window and Jenda wanted to know about the plants. She knew the names of many of them, although Rosalí had to remind her. There weren't any flowers at this time of year other than the carefully tended pots of chrysanthemums by the back steps, but Jenda could see the garden overrun with a riot of colorful blossoms.

"What is the blue butterfly, the one that loves the little yellow amancay flowers?" Jenda asked, gesturing toward an insect only she could see in the brown winter garden. Rosalí named it and told Jenda a bit about its habits.

Jenda reached across the table and placed her hand over Rosalí's. "You said you remember me. Can you tell me about that?"

Luis intervened. "Jenda, we don't have to go there today. We can wait. We can give you a little more time. You've been through so much already."

"No, Luis," she said. "I don't think I can deal with these strange fragments of memory until I know what they mean." She didn't know how to explain to him that the memories seemed to be arising from deep within her body rather than from her mind and that her mind was longing to link up with them.

"Well, here is what I remember," Rosalí began. "I was only a little girl back then, so my memories won't be the whole story. You know Silvestre and I were childhood friends, so I used to come over here to play. I remember when Paloma brought you here to the house. Your hair was a different color then, kind of a grayish tan. I think you didn't wear makeup. You looked so different from the way you look now. And they never told us your name. We called you 'hermana,' 'older sister.' You seemed so sad. I kept wanting to bring you my toys to play with. You know, to cheer you up. I probably came over more while you were here than I had before. Maybe that's when Silvestre and I became so close. Isabel was here, too, now that I think of it. She seemed to be friends with Paloma and both of them were looking after you."

"How long was I here?" Jenda asked.

"A long while. It seemed like that to me, anyway. You kept getting fatter and they told me you were going to have a baby. You never talked about it. Not with me. Then one day they told me you had become ill, and I was not to go into your room. I heard you screaming, so I sneaked in and brought you my stuffed cat, the one I showed you earlier. You took it and you were stroking it and calling it Milly." Rosalí stopped and looked out the window, brushing some cookie crumbs from the tablecloth. "I'd forgotten why I named it that. Anyway, the stuffed toy seemed to calm you, so they let you keep it, but they shooed me out of the room, and I went to play out in the yard with Silvestre. A while later, we heard a baby crying."

Luis was watching Jenda carefully; she was fully absorbed in Rosalí's story.

"You and the baby—it was a little girl—stayed here with us for a while longer. Then you and Paloma went away and left the baby with Isabel. I think it was with Isabel. And that... that is all I know. I'm sorry I can't tell you more."

"Thank you, Rosalí." Jenda's voice was quiet, calm. "You've told me a lot, and I'm grateful for your memories. I think you were a good friend."

"Would you like me to take you out to the old estancia?" Rosalí asked, looking at Luis.

Jenda answered. "No. Maybe another time, Rosalí. I don't think I have anything more to learn right now from going there. Were you able to find Paloma's address?"

"Maybe so. I think I found the right book. Let me go get it. Would you like to move back into the sitting room? It's so warm and sunny this time of day." Jenda and Luis got up from the table and went back to the sitting room, settling onto the sofa while Rosalí went into the room with the Holy Virgin on the wall. She returned with two notebooks. She lay the books in her lap and opened the first one, scanning its pages carefully.

"Here it is," she said finally. "Paloma Suarez. There's an address in Costa Rica. Shall I record it for you?" Luis unfurled his digilet and handed it to Rosalí to enter the address.

"You know," Rosalí said as she tapped the syllables into the screen, "they came around a couple of years ago collecting up old paper for the recycling and I almost gave them all these boxes. Now I'm glad I kept them." She handed the digilet back to Luis and he coiled it around his wrist, giving it a pat as if instructing it to guard this information.

Jenda thanked Rosalí again and then looked over at Luis. "One more thing," she said. "Is it okay if Luis takes some pictures of the room, especially of the painting?"

"Of course," Rosalí said. While Luis went into the little room to photograph the Holy Virgin, Jenda and Rosalí sat by the window in the sunshine like two old friends. Rosalí was in the easy chair and Jenda sat with her feet drawn up under her on the end of the sofa. Between them was the little table with the pot of purple mums.

Luis and Jenda said their farewells and went back to the hotel to collect their belongings. Although they hadn't stayed the night, they felt they had made good use of the room.

Luis guided the vehicle back to the main road. Then he put the car on auto and turned in his seat to face Jenda.

She was looking out the window, but she knew she had his attention. "You know," she said, "at first I thought I just wanted to know what happened during my missing year." She turned and reached for Luis' hand. "Talk about your gap year..." She chuckled softly and began again.

"At first I only wanted the story, you know? The sequence of events. But now I'm finding that the story itself seems to be about a different person. And yet, that person was me. Is me. Was I really such a committed Vintie, Luis? Was I foolish enough to get pregnant in high school? I thought I was just an ordinary, sensible, reasonably successful mid-level professional and obedient 22nd-century consumer. Now I find someone completely different claiming to be me—a crazy girl with sepia-colored hair, a baby born in a back room in an Argentine village, and a tattoo of the Virgin Mary on her backside." Jenda looked out the window again and sighed. "Maybe we can track me down in Costa Rica, Luis. Is that where we go next?"

22.

Jenda and Luis awoke the next morning to a tentative winter sun shining through lace curtains in Isabel's spare bedroom, which she had insisted they occupy. As they snuggled under the mound of quilts, Luis stroked Jenda's tousled hair. "Maybe you should go sepia again, querida," he said.

"Only if you will. And we both have to get our tattoos restored." Jenda caught a sudden fragment of memory: She was peering over her shoulder into a mirror at a colorful tattoo on her back of the Virgin of Lujan. The image stung.

After a quick shower, they got dressed to join Isabel for breakfast, trying not to trip over one another as they sidestepped their bags. It was a small room, but a pleasing one, with real wood furniture and what looked like a handmade wool rug.

"How are you feeling this morning, mi amor?"

Jenda thought for a minute. "You know, I think I'm feeling okay. It's like I've stopped looking away every time I almost remember something. Yesterday shook loose some things in my mind, Luis, and it will take time to figure out what it all is, how things fit in. I don't know what I'd do without you, my love."

Luis looked at her, standing there only half dressed. Jenda felt his gaze. She had such desire for this man, but without urgency. She knew her desire would not go unfulfilled.

"This is my last outfit," Jenda said, pulling a soft purple knit top over her head. "I'll have to go shopping today." The prospect was not pleasing. She arranged the colorful silk scarf Luis had bought for her around her neck.

"You could try washing some things," Luis said. "I think it used to be called 'doing laundry.'" It had become customary to buy new things and almost never bother with washing clothes. It kept the recycling process moving along at a nice clip.

"Hmm. Maybe I'll try that." Jenda picked up a couple of items from her jumbled suitcase and shook out the wrinkles. "I think the old Jenda probably did laundry."

By the time they entered the kitchen, Isabel was adding the last pancake to a delicious looking stack.

"Wayee." Jenda inhaled the sweet aroma. "You made those yourself? They smell wonderful." She was also noting the fragrance of freshly brewed coffee. It smelled as good as the stuff Luis made for her in San Miguel.

As they sat around the table, exchanging pleasantries, Jenda thought about how different this felt from her breakfasts at the beverage shop in Dallas with Granny El. Dallas felt very far away.

They finished the pancakes along with some fresh oranges and grapes. Isabel poured them each a second cup of coffee. "So how did it go yesterday?" she asked.

"Amazing," Jenda answered. "Rosalí remembered me. And my companion Paloma. She gave us the last address they had for Paloma, in Costa Rica. Rosalí also said that you and Paloma were friends. Do you remember her at all? Her last name is Suarez. She even said you kept my baby while Paloma took me back home to Texas."

"Your what? So it's true then. But you had the baby? And they didn't..."

"Oh, I'm sorry, Isabel. All of this is still such a jumble. Yes, Rosalí said I had the baby there at their little house in San Ramon, in the room with the Virgin of Lujan on the wall. Like my tattoo."

"Your what?" Isabel said again.

"Oh, Luis, I'm going to make a muddle of this," Jenda groaned. "You tell her." She knew her own telling would be filled with feelings she couldn't name and images that kept slipping away even as she sought to describe them. So Luis took over, telling what they had learned as best he could.

"I wish I could recall something that would help." Isabel looked at Jenda. "It seems like I may have as much shared history with you as I do with my own grandson." She reached across the table, placing one hand over Jenda's and the other over Luis'.

"I have something to give you," Luis said suddenly. "Wait a moment." He went back to the bedroom and came back with the flower album.

He laid the book on the table, opened it, and pushed it over in front of Isabel. "Silvestre wanted you to have this. He told me you and he made it together, back when he was a child and you were in San Ramon."

Isabel stared at the book. "Oh," she said. As she began carefully turning the pages, her eyes took on a faraway look. "From the garden..." She turned another page. "And from the meadow behind..." She looked up at Luis. "Maybe I do remember, just a little bit. Or maybe I know these flowers. It's a beautiful album, but some of the flowers have almost turned to dust. We shouldn't be handling it. I know someone who might be able to encase what remains in polyplex to preserve it. Thank you for bringing this, Luis. One day soon, I think I need to go visit this Silvestre and his wife."

Luis got up and started collecting the dishes to take to the kitchen. "We had something we wanted to ask you," he said, pointing his chin at Jenda, "about doing laundry."

"Oh, yes, I still have one of those old-fashioned laundering devices," Isabel said. "It was here when I moved in, and it still works. I use it myself from time to time." They collected up some of their used clothing and, with Isabel's advice, put it into the machine.

Jenda suggested that, in light of the new information they now had, it might be a good idea to take another look at the things she had brought from the boxes at Granny El's. Jenda's suitcase was nearly full of the stuff, which accounted for her clothing shortage. They pulled the case into the middle of the floor in Isabel's sitting room and sat next to it. The items were in a jumble. Luis went for the bundles of photographs and papers.

"Luis," Jenda said, staring at the chaos in her suitcase, "if Silvestre and Rosalí are the same generation, why does he look so much older?"

"Rosalí told me that whenever Chulel was in short supply—and given the way they were accessing it, that happened a lot—whenever there wasn't enough for both of them, he insisted that she take it and he would do without. And then after a while he stopped taking it altogether. I think she's stopped taking it now, too, although I'm not sure Silvestre knows."

Jenda turned her attention to her digilet. "Here's something I wanted you to see, Luis. I couldn't bring it with me; all I have is a photo." She handed the digilet to Luis.

"Wayee," he said. "Is this what I think it is?" He looked at Jenda and then back at the photo.

"It's one of my mother's sculptures. And, yes, it's the same figure I put in the painting I did at your studio in San Miguel, the one you said was a self-portrait. And of course this picture is the same sculpture I gave you for Christmas in San Miguel. You know I thought I'd forgotten what my mother's work looked like. This tells me I still remembered it somewhere, somehow." Jenda paused, looking over Luis' shoulder at the photo of the little dancer. "Did I tell you I was taking a dance class?"

Luis and Jenda started at a sudden loud buzzing noise.

Isabel laughed, "Calm down, it's only the washing device telling us it's finished its job. You keep on with what you're doing. I'll go put your things in the dryer."

Jenda looked relieved. "So you have a drying machine, too. I was wondering what we were going to do with all those wet clothes. Thank you, Isabel." If devices such as washers and dryers had ever been part of Jenda's experience, she had no recollection of it. Paloma might remember, Jenda thought. She hoped Paloma might remember a lot.

"By the way," Isabel said as she moved toward the closet that housed the washing and drying machines, "I've invited the Feldmans over for supper. I hope you don't mind."

"Oh, no," Jenda said. "We'd love to see them again before we go to Costa Rica."

Luis had collected several of Jenda's printed photographs and arrayed them in a line. "Look at these," he said to Jenda. She scooted over next to him and peered at the pictures, trying to see what had caught his interest. The photographs showed groups of obviously Vintie young people, one of whom was Jenda. Some other individuals seemed to repeat in the various pictures, too. In particular, a number of the photos showed a well-built young man with dark hair and a dark complexion, and in all of them he and Jenda were hand-in-hand or had their arms around one another.

"Do you think that was my boyfriend?" Jenda asked, realizing at once that this was not a particularly insightful inference.

"What I find interesting is who your boyfriend is."

"You know him?"

"Well, unless I'm seriously mistaken, your boyfriend is Montagne Williams, who is still a committed political activist. He got his start as a leader in the Vintagonist movement. And given the time frame of the photographs here and what we know about your trip to San Ramon, he could very well be the father of your child." Luis looked up from the photos to see Jenda's face.

Jenda stared at the images. The Jenda in the photos looked so happy. Her boyfriend—Montagne? He looked happy, too. Jenda's heart warmed as her observation morphed into a fragment of memory. "Why hadn't I even thought about the fact that the baby—my daughter—would have had to have a father?" she said softly. "My mind is such a mess. So you know this Montagne?"

"Not well. We've worked together on some things. But everybody in Recall knows who Montagne Williams is. You may have run across some of his writings," Luis continued. "He goes by the name of HillBill."

"Zujo! Are you craicking me?" Jenda rocked backward, her hands on her knees. "I've been following him ever since San Miguel. He makes a lot of sense. A bit extreme sometimes." She was trying to comprehend that the faceless scribe she had been following might be the father of her child, the ninety-five-year-old child she had not been sure even existed until yesterday.

As Luis went to reclaim their freshly washed and dried clothing, he found himself wondering if Jenda could be the girlfriend Montagne had told him about, the one he had adored for her fierce loyalty to Vintagonist principles and her whimsical creativity in devising acts of rebellion and disobedience. Could she be the girl who had created that incredible web-like installation of broken chairs, old clocks, discarded books, and ropes plaited from torn clothing that had mysteriously appeared on the steps of 3Dec headquarters one morning? Montagne said it was his girlfriend who made it. The installation itself was legendary.

The Feldmans arrived right on time and Jenda went downstairs to let them in. After a glass of the wonderful Malbec that Isabel favored, they sat down to a home cooked meal. *I could get used to this,* Jenda thought, looking around the table at the group of friends and family.

"We've bought the old estancia, the old institute property out by San Ramon," Max Feldman announced, as they were finishing the soup and moving on to the main course. "While we were checking into the records, we found out that it was available for a ridiculously low price, so we bought it."

"And what exactly do you propose to do with such a ruin?" Luis wanted to know. "It would cost much more than you paid, I'm sure, to set it up as a research institute again."

"Oh, no," Max said, "our research days are over. We've done all the damage we intend to do on that front. No. We're going to turn it into an old folks' home. And we have people coming out next week to clean up the old caretaker's cottage and repair it so we can move out there right away." He gave Emily a triumphant look. They raised their wine glasses and tapped them together with a musical clink.

"An old folks' home?" Luis laughed. "And where do you expect to find the old people to populate it?"

Max raised his eyebrows and then looked suddenly serious. "I guess I shouldn't joke about it," he said. "You remember that blood disorder we were telling you about that was breaking out in several different parts of the world? Well, it's now clear that it's caused by a virus that affects only people who are Chulel users. It's most dangerous to those who've used the drug most recently. It's continued to spread and although the doctors are scrambling to figure out how to deal with it, their best line of attack so far is to tell people to lay off Chulel. So, you see? An old folks' home may not be so far-fetched. Besides," he added, "Emily and I will be there and we're both finished with Chulel." He reached for Emily's hand.

After the Feldmans left, Luis went back to the digiscreen to confirm his and Jenda's tickets to Costa Rica and select a return schedule.

"How long can we stay in Costa Rica, Jenda?" Luis asked. "Are you planning to go back to YJ?"

"I don't see how I can. But maybe we should get one-way tickets. Who knows where we might want to go if we don't find Paloma at the address Rosalí gave us."

Jenda had told her work supervisor she would be gone for two weeks. One week of that was already gone. They would have to move quickly if they hoped to find Paloma.

23.

It rained a little that evening, and then shortly before midnight the sky exploded in a spectacular thunderstorm. Isabel hated thunderstorms. She found something deeply disturbing about the flashes of lightning. She had learned to pull the extra set of darkening curtains over the only window in her room and to put on her sleep mask whenever storms were threatening. This one caught her by surprise.

By the time she awoke to an unusually loud clap of thunder, she was in a cold sweat. She had been dreaming. In her dream, she was packing up boxes of books. A young man was helping her, and he called her Mama. They were frightened. And then she was in a little garden. The garden was beautifully planted. It was spacious and open at the center, and surrounded by a hedge of fuchsia, a few fruit trees, and flowering jacarandas. Isabel found the spaciousness threatening. She was cowering behind a little stone wall at one end of the garden, clutching an infant and quaking with fear that the baby would awaken and reveal their hiding place.

Isabel got up and, with trembling hands, closed the extra curtains. She found her sleep mask, but she didn't put it on. For a while she just lay there on her damp pillow, letting her tears flow as she remembered that little garden, remembered the beautiful brown baby, and tried to remember what it was that terrified her so.

24.

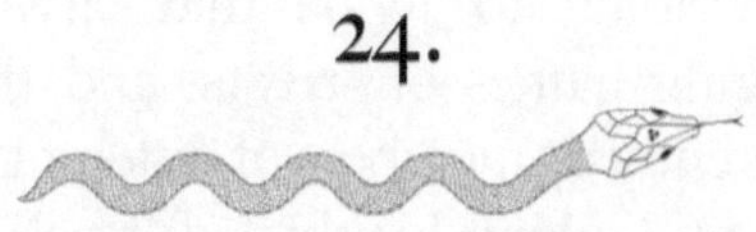

Parts of Costa Rica were fully as vanguard as Dallas or Buenos Aires. The part that Jenda and Luis found themselves in was not one of those. The address Rosalí had given them led from an international airport near Liberia, Guanacaste, to a small town near an old sugar plantation on the Tempisque River.

The town itself was pleasant enough, with an immaculate plaza surrounded by small shops and an old church, but the address Rosalí had given them seemed to confuse their NaviGiz. Most of the intersections had no street signs. They parked the autocar and went into a shop to ask for directions.

The apparently Geni shop assistant made it sound like their destination should be within walking distance, so they left the car where it was. Twenty minutes later, they were questioning this decision. They went inside another shop to get out of the sun and to see if they could figure out where they had gone wrong.

"Traveler's tip, Luis," Jenda said, rolling the sleeves of her blouse down to protect her arms, "when you're in a new place, always ask at least two people for directions before you set out."

"Now you tell me. But who would have thought we could get lost in a small town like this?"

Luis told the youthful shopkeeper the address they were looking for and waited. "I'm pretty sure that place was knocked down maybe eighty years ago," she said at last. "I think it was where the technical college is now. They renamed the street after the college was built."

Luis and Jenda exchanged a defeated look. They were afraid this might happen, but they had been hopeful, nonetheless. What now? They bought a couple of bottles of fortified water.

"Gosh, you'd think we were still in Buenos Aires," Luis complained, describing to Jenda that city's reputation for constantly changing names of streets, and thereafter having them called differently by members of different generations.

"Why are you looking for this address?" the shopkeeper asked. "Do you know someone who lived there?"

"Yes," Luis responded. "We're looking for an old friend. Her name is Paloma Suarez."

The shopkeeper looked down, shuffling some papers behind the desk. "Paloma?" she asked. "Suarez you say?"

"That's right," Jenda replied. "I knew her back in Texas. And in Argentina." The shopkeeper was giving Jenda a hard look, as if trying to decide if it was worth spending any more time on these strangers.

"Well, I will tell you where you can ask. Where they might know something." She drew a little map on a slip of paper. "This place is across the street from the college," she said, explaining how to get to the renamed street. "Good luck," she added, as Luis and Jenda left the shop.

"Well, this looks promising," Luis said, showing Jenda the address written in block letters on the slip of paper. It read: "NO. 27, AVE SUAREZ".

This time they found the address with no trouble, although they began to wonder how they would remember their way back to the car. As they walked up to the door, checking the number on the paper one more time, they looked at each other and Luis said, "Well, here goes." He knocked firmly on the wooden door.

Jenda clung nervously to Luis' arm while they waited, squinting at each other in the bright sunlight reflecting off the brilliantly blue door. Luis knocked a second time, and at last the door opened.

"Yes? May I help you?" asked the woman peering from the shadow of the half-opened door. Then the door opened fully. "Luis? Luis-Martín?"

"Meli?" Luis responded, as he recognized the woman in the shadow as one of his friends from San Miguel.

"¡Adelante!" she said. "Please come in."

They entered the cool breezeway. "Whatever brings you here to Costa Rica?" Meli laughed, closing the door behind them.

"I might ask you the same question," Luis responded. "This is surprising, to say the least."

"Well, I'm here because this is my home," Meli replied. "Please, come let me introduce you." Luis and Jenda followed Meli into the patio, where a dark-skinned man sat talking with an old woman with wrinkled fair skin.

"No introduction necessary for us," Luis said, as the man rose from his seat and strode forward to grasp his hand. "Meli," Luis said, "Why did I never know that you were kin to Montagne Williams?" Luis abruptly turned to look at Jenda, who still stood at the edge of the patio, staring. He quickly moved back toward her.

"Well," Meli said, in answer to Luis' question, "I've only known it myself for the past few months. It turns out he's my father."

Luis reached Jenda just in time. She had taken a step back as her knees weakened. She stared first at Montagne and then at Meli. Montagne had taken a few steps in her direction, his hand extended for an introduction. Then he stopped, looking suddenly serious. "No," he said. "It can't be. Jenda?"

Luis grabbed Jenda as she swayed uncertainly. "Okay, can we all back off a minute?" he said sternly, taking Jenda in his arms and leading her to the sofa.

Jenda sat silently, looking from one to the other of the people in the room. She felt all of their eyes on her and heard them speaking to one another, although she could not make out what they were saying. She was caught somewhere between abject tears, hysterical laughter, and an impulse to bid all of these people a polite farewell and run away. And yet, she could almost feel a clarity dawning. Wasn't this what she'd come to

Costa Rica to find? She was pretty sure she was looking at her own daughter, the man who had impregnated her at the age of seventeen, and the dear old nanny who had accompanied her during her missing year in Argentina.

25.

The little group spent the next several hours arranging and rearranging the pieces of a story that involved all of them in one way or another, but which none of them had fully known until now. Paloma's pieces were the most encompassing and Jenda hung on every syllable she uttered. Despite her visibly advanced age and quavering voice, Paloma's memories painted a vivid picture of Jenda's infamous gap year.

Shortly before her sixty-fifth birthday in 2029, Paloma Suarez had retired from her many years of service, first as nanny and then as more of a personal maid to Tessa and James Swain's daughter Jenda and younger son Jonathan. As a parting gift, she had received her first Chulel treatment and a generous amount of cash and investments, which the Swains thought would provide her with a nice pension.

"I was grateful, of course," Paloma said, "and happy to be back in Costa Rica with my husband. But I was lonely for Jenda and Jonathan. I was never able to have children of my own." Less than a year later, the Swains contacted Paloma, pleading with her to come back to Texas to accompany Jenda on a trip to South America. They made it sound like Jenda was in trouble and so Paloma said goodbye once again to her husband and set out to care for the girl she had loved for so many years as her own.

Jenda was pregnant and threatening to run away with her Vintagonist friends, which included Montagne Williams, the father of her child. Tessa and Jim were beside themselves. Their son, Jonathan, had left home the previous year to follow a Buddhist guru of questionable lineage. They couldn't bear to lose their daughter as well. Besides, Jenda had earned a prestigious art scholarship to Ex University in Austin and was due to start college the next fall.

The family was torn by the issue of an abortion. They were perfectly legal and readily available in Texas. "But you know your mother was a sensitive Buddhist and your dad was a bit of an old-fashioned Catholic, so this distressed them terribly," Paloma said. Then they had found out about a clinic in Argentina that offered both abortion and a new form of cult deprogramming. They were eager to get Jenda over what they saw as her ridiculous Vintagonist ideas before she started college, and so finally agreed to send her to Argentina. "They knew you would never go willingly," Paloma said, "so they told you it was going to be a wonderful vacation for the summer between high school and university. You didn't want to go and leave your friends, but you finally agreed, thinking you'd only be gone for a couple of weeks. It was still rather early in your pregnancy."

Paloma said she remembered arriving at the clinic and seeing Jenda's horror as it dawned on her what was happening. She screamed for Paloma to take her away, but Paloma turned her back.

"I think that is the most painful memory of my entire life," Paloma said. "I let my loyalty to Tessa and Jim override my love for you, Jenda. I had no idea what that place intended to do to you. How can you ever forgive me?"

"It wasn't your fault, Paloma." Jenda was fighting back tears. "You weren't the one who sent me there."

For the next several weeks, Paloma said, she was barred from the clinic and told varying stories about complications with Jenda's abortion and treatment. When they finally agreed to let her see Jenda, they put her in a room where they told her she must wait. Paloma remembered that there was a strange flick that seemed to be on all the walls at once. And there were bright flashing lights and a loud monotonous noise. Paloma became upset and, convinced she was still not going to be allowed to see Jenda anyway, she sneaked out of the room and fled.

"The next part I don't remember myself, but I trust I've been told truthfully what happened," Paloma said. A kind woman had found Paloma, wandering distressed and disoriented along one of the side streets in San Ramon. The woman was Isabel Hernandez. Paloma could not explain why she was in San Ramon or even how she came to be in Argentina. Isabel took her in. Going through the items in Paloma's bag, they found a small notebook that included contact information for the clinic. There were also two passports--Paloma's and Jenda's. Isabel knew about the clinic and its activities, so she and Paloma began making a plan to rescue Jenda.

"Isabel knew someone inside the clinic, and he helped us get you out. I know now that he was part of a ring that was stealing medicine to give to the poor, but I was unaware at the time."

"I don't suppose you remember that person's name, Doña Paloma," Luis said.

Paloma paused to reflect, staring at the melting ice in her drink. "Winston? Something like that. I think that's what Isabel called him. I never met him myself." Luis looked at Jenda, who was staring at him wide-eyed. They both knew she was talking about Winslow Morris. Perhaps he was not the total thug and scoundrel they had thought him to be.

By the time they got Jenda away from the clinic, Paloma said, her pregnancy was well advanced, and they knew abortion was out of the question. Furthermore, she had been extracted from the clinic in the middle of the deprogramming treatments.

"Experiments, more likely," Luis interrupted. "Those people had no idea what they were doing. I'm sorry, go ahead, Doña Paloma."

Paloma described how Jenda had been left in a daze and could not even comprehend that she was pregnant. They cared for her as best they could. She took walks in the garden with the little boy who lived in the house where they stayed. His best friend was a little girl who came by frequently and spent time with Jenda, bringing her toys and paper and colored pencils.

Jenda had become like a child herself and seemed to enjoy the company of this young friend.

It was in this house that Jenda gave birth. It was hard to watch, Paloma said. Jenda did not understand what was happening but was comforted by the little girl's plush cat toy, which reminded her of the pet she had when she was small.

After the baby came, Paloma and Isabel were left with looking after not only a still confused and needy Jenda, but a newborn infant as well. They needed a name for the baby girl, and Isabel suggested Ermelinda. Paloma agreed, but insisted on calling her Meli for short, as a nod to her mother's beloved pet.

"You said Isabel is your grandmother, Luis? I'm so glad to know she's well." Paloma picked up her iced tea glass from the table and took another sip. "When I met her, she was in Argentina with her son, Julian, who was not one of the Vinties, like Montagne and Jenda, but also a dissident. Many of their friends were Menders, but the political group Julian sided with often went by the name of 'Unpreoccupied'--'Despreocupado'. I never knew exactly what that meant until Montagne explained it to me recently. They talked a lot about how critical medicines were being kept in short supply by corporations like Pharmakon. They used to say they were liberating supplies of medicines to be used in treating the poor. Isabel was sympathetic, I guess. I suppose that's why she had gone with her son to Argentina."

"I didn't know at first what they were doing," Paloma continued, "so I didn't understand the risk I was taking in leaving little Meli with Isabel while I took Jenda back to her parents in Texas. Jenda was still in a confused state, so we took a little time going back. You know, to give her some fresh memories and stories to tell when she got back home. Her parents had been okay with extending Jenda's trip on into the new year, since I wrote and told them she was doing well and that we were in this country or that one. Julian's friends knew how to fix up our passports so that her parents would never know."

The Swains had been distressed by Jenda's state of mind upon her return, but deeply grateful for Paloma's service. They had given her the gift of additional doses of Chulel and another generous payment and investments.

"After getting you safely back home, Jenda. I went back to collect your baby daughter from Isabel. I was horrified to find Isabel was in hiding and it took me a while to track her and Meli down. Isabel told me the corporate police were after her and her son because of the stolen medicine, so she was happy to hand Meli back over to me. I brought Meli here to Costa Rica and this is where I raised her, here in Ortega, here in my hometown. I took the Chulel the Swains gave me and then what I received later from the Ocampo family in Argentina," Paloma continued. "I didn't want to look too old to have a daughter Meli's age. But after she was an adult and gone away, and after my husband died... Well, as you can see I stopped taking it."

"Please understand," Paloma said, looking at Jenda, "I never told Meli your name. I was trying to protect both of you."

"That's true," Meli said. "I begged her for years to tell me my mother's name. At first she told me she didn't know, and I believed her. Then she told me..."

Paloma interrupted. "What I told her was that the names of people with whom we have no shared stories are not so important. Only the stories we share are important. Meli and I shared stories. Jenda and I also shared many stories. But for Meli, Jenda was such a minor character in her story, the name was not important and would only make her mother seem more real than she was." Paloma paused for a moment, her eyes on a tiny yellow butterfly that had alighted on the edge of her tea glass. "Memories are as short-lived as butterflies, you know, unless they form stories. And stories must be shared."

"How did you and Montagne find each other?" Luis asked Meli.

"He's the one who found me." Meli replied.

Montagne scowled at the empty glass in his hands. "I can't believe it took me so long," he said, sounding apologetic. "I had always assumed that Jenda had the abortion. She didn't remember me at all after she got back, so we parted ways. I always wondered what had happened to her in South America. I had no idea." He paused and looked over at Meli. "But I never forgot. And then several months ago I ran across this advertisement on Recall from a guy who claimed he had access to records from a clinic in Argentina."

Luis stifled a laugh and even Jenda was smiling. "What?" Montagne said. "You know Dr. Winfield?"

"Oh, you might say that," Luis replied. "He's out of business now, you know. But that's for later. Please continue."

Maurice Winfield told Montagne about Jenda's abrupt disappearance from the clinic, with no record of an abortion being performed. "That's when I knew I needed to try and track you down, Jenda, you and our child. I thought maybe Paloma could help me, since she never seemed to dislike me nearly as much as your parents did."

"How did you find Paloma?" Jenda asked.

"It took a while. I knew her last name and I was pretty sure she was from Costa Rica. So I searched every area of the medianets and the infranet and finally found a small reference on Recall to a Paloma Suarez who had founded a technical college in rural Costa Rica in 2045. It turned out to be her and...well, here I am," he said. "Of course, it did take a while for me to convince Paloma to let me tell Meli who I am. She had never told her my name either, Jenda."

"So the college is yours, Doña Paloma?" Luis asked.

"Well, I built it, yes, but it belongs to the people. Jenda's parents had been so generous to me, and I wanted to do something useful with their gifts."

"Some of the best trained 'net scripters in the world are coming out of this little college," Montagne added. "And not a one of them is owned by a corporation. They're doing great work for Recall."

Luis had one more question for Paloma. "Do you know what happened to Isabel?"

"I was told," Paloma said. "That the corporate police finally caught her and put her in jail. I believe her son Julian was killed."

Meli and Paloma insisted that Luis and Jenda stay at their house. It was a big house by 22nd century standards and a vanguard one for rural Costa Rica. After receiving directions from Montagne, Luis headed back to the plaza to fetch the autocar containing their bags, leaving Jenda with Meli and Paloma and Montagne.

As Luis walked back toward the plaza, he chided himself for the twinges of jealousy he was feeling. *She and Montagne were lovers, yes,* he told himself, *but that was nearly a century ago. Why should I not feel only joy for them to find each other again, and especially to find their daughter?* But he knew that Jenda was finally reconnecting with some pieces of her past and that Meli and Montagne were easily the most important of those pieces.

Despite these vague trepidations, Luis was pleased to see Montagne again. Montagne had been aligned with the branch of Vintagonists that had persistently called for direct political action. As the movement evolved over time, his commitment and dedication had never wavered. The fact that he had managed to pursue a successful career as a hydrologic engineer and to evade the corporate police was a tribute to his ingenuity. Luis himself had always been more inclined toward symbolic resistance.

After dinner that evening, Luis and Montagne discussed recent developments in the Recall community. The zone on the infranet had finally been restored and re-secured after the irrupting incident, which had galvanized the more radical participants into putting into motion a plan they had been working on for many years, a plan designed to bring down all the medianets and with them the supranet.

"Zujo!" Luis said. "That would have disastrous consequences for everything. It would disrupt food supplies, banking, the energy grid—everything."

"Well, that's kind of the point. But you know there is a widespread network of sufficiency communities that are equipped to survive whatever happens. The ones we call Simpletons led the charge on that, thank goodness. And we should have a new and independent 'net up and running to unite those communities within a few weeks of the takedown."

Luis looked doubtful. "Can you share any details with me? I've been aching to know exactly what's in the works."

"It's a new and fiendishly clever type of digital infection, one that should remain undetected for just long enough to become unstoppable. But it requires that we introduce it simultaneously in all of the key sectors. We have recruits ready within the energy distribution network, in the transportation net, media—pretty much every major sector. The only thing we're missing is someone to introduce the infection into screens at one of the LifeBook or Your Journal centers." Luis guessed that Montagne didn't know yet where Jenda worked, and he quickly decided it was not his place to offer up this information.

While the men talked, Jenda was left with Meli and Paloma and after a few minutes, Paloma excused herself. "I'm an old woman and I need my rest," she said, offering each of the younger women a peck on the cheek as she retired to her bedroom.

Jenda and Meli—mother and daughter—sat looking at one another in awkward silence.

"When I first met you in San Miguel, I felt there was something familiar about you," Jenda offered at last, thinking how much Meli looked like Montagne.

"I wish I could say the same," Meli replied. "But I'd never seen a picture of you and of course I'd never known your name. Paloma always said I looked like my mother."

"I'm not sure how we're supposed to do this, Meli. I never knew my own mother that well. She was always so troubled. And I've never been around children. But of course," she added, "you're hardly a child."

"This has kind of taken both of us by surprise."

"I guess I just don't know how to be your mother."

"Paloma was my mother," Meli said softly. "She is my mother. And since she was kind of like your mother too... Maybe you and I are really more like sisters. Do you have sisters or brothers?"

"I have a brother. We were always close as children."

"Well, then maybe we could start with that."

Jenda smiled and nodded. She reached over and took Meli's hand in hers, their fingers intertwining. By the time Luis and Montagne rejoined them, they were engaged in lively conversation. The topics may not have been as portentous as the ones that had occupied the men, but the simple exchange of small facts about their lives felt monumental to Jenda.

They all said goodnight reluctantly and Jenda and Luis retreated behind the closed door of their little bedroom off the main courtyard. When Luis returned from showering in the shared facility across the yard, Jenda was sitting cross-legged in the middle of the bed, staring at the calendar on her digilet.

"You know, YJ is expecting me to report for work on Monday. To make that, I'd have to start back day after tomorrow." She laid the digilet on the bedside cabinet and leaned back on the pillows. "I can't go back, Luis. I'm so sick of what YJ does. I don't see how I can continue to be part of that." She turned to face Luis and folded her arms. "If I went back, I'd probably end up planting a bomb in the building or something."

Luis studied her face. "Maybe you should talk with Montagne."

"What? So now Meli's daddy knows about bombs? You know I'm just kidding about that. You know I'm not a violent person, Luis."

"Well, Montagne isn't a violent person either. But he knows much more than I do about the plans being formulated in the Recall community, and part of that may involve bringing down YJ. More or less peacefully."

"More or less? What are you talking about, Luis?"

"It's not for me to say. Talk to Montagne." Luis lay down and Jenda rolled over toward him. She wanted to feel the strength of his body next to hers. Luis reached over and pulled her closer.

After breakfast the next day, Jenda and Luis and Montagne gathered under the banana trees in the courtyard.

"One of our old Vintie friends from high school got in touch with me a year or so back to say she had run into you in a café in Dallas," Montagne said.

Jenda's eyes grew big, and she exchanged a quick glance with Luis. "Who was she anyway?" Jenda asked.

"Her name is Malia Poole. She was a couple of years behind us in school, but she idolized you. As I recall, you thought she was a pest." Montagne laughed. "She had a twin sister Sophia. I think they must have been in your brother's year. Their older sister, Leticia, was in our year. Surely you remember her."

"No. I don't," Jenda said, "or at least I didn't until I saw her name in one of my old journals." She still felt angry, knowing that the woman she'd been taking dance classes from was an old high school friend and that she hadn't remembered her at all. Her bitterness toward Your Journal intensified.

"Luis says you know about a plan. Something to do with putting an end to what Your Journal has been doing with memory restructuring. Is that true, Montagne?" Jenda asked.

"Well, yeah I've heard... Why do you ask?" Montagne hesitated, looking toward Luis, who seemed suddenly engrossed in studying the design printed on the throw pillows.

Jenda laughed. "So Luis didn't tell you? YJ is where I work, Montagne. I've been there for ninety years now. And over this past year I've become, let's say, disenchanted with our work."

"Ah," Montagne said. "In that case." And he explained as succinctly as he could exactly what the plan was.

"So what would someone at YJ need to do?" Jenda was intrigued.

"It's simple, really. We'd give this person..." Montagne paused and glanced from Jenda to Luis and back to Jenda. "Whoever this person might be, we would give them a digital reservoir—an ordinary looking 2XV insert—containing the infection, which they would introduce into one of the work screens connected to their corporate medianet."

"Why can't this be done atmospherically?" Jenda asked. "Why does it have to be done on site?"

"There are too many layers of anti-infection when you come in through the atmo. And with a corporation like YJ, there's the problem of supranet protection as well. We're pretty confident our infection is unique enough to slide through most of these things undetected, but even a minor drag could prevent the whole scheme from unfolding according to plan. It needs to be done internally, on schedule, by all of our operatives at once."

"What if I got caught?" Jenda asked, dropping all pretense.

"It won't be detectable—we hope, anyway—for at least six hours after it's introduced. And it won't be traceable to the point of introduction at all, because by that time everything will be falling apart."

"You hope?"

"I'm only being honest. You can never be one hundred percent on these things, Jenda, but we're confident enough to be ready to go ahead as soon as we have this one additional person in place. And if that person were to be you... Well, it can be done in such a way that by the time things start coming apart, you'd be safely back here in Costa Rica with us."

Jenda knew she wanted to do this. All the confusion and shifting realities had left her with a burning need to take charge of her life, to do something that mattered. The more she remembered, the more she knew she couldn't go back. Doing this would be an unequivocal, irrevocable commitment to her newly claimed reality, a pledge of faith between the girl with the sepia hair and the woman Jenda intended to be going forward, the woman she might have been if not for Argentina.

Jenda leaned closer to Luis and slipped her hand inside the crook of his elbow. "Okay, then," she said. "I'll do it."

Part IV
Coming Together,
Falling Apart

26.

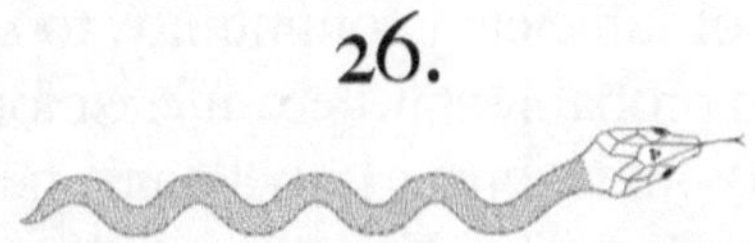

They found Jenda a flight back to Dallas departing Liberia airport shortly after noon on the following day, which was Sunday. They also booked a return flight for Monday evening under the name given on a passport Montagne provided. Jenda borrowed a small suitcase from Meli, knowing she wouldn't really need anything, but figuring she shouldn't travel without some kind of luggage. Montagne spent the afternoon notifying all of the project operatives that they were a go for 4:50 p.m. Texas time on Monday. He gave the data insert containing the infection to Jenda, who stored it in her bag along with her other 2XV camera inserts. It was the one with the diagonal scratch across it.

Despite the early hour of their departure from Paloma's house, everyone was up to bid Jenda farewell and wish her good luck with her mission. Montagne treated her like some kind of superhero. Paloma was more subdued, not fully understanding what was happening, but sensing that Jenda was about to put herself in serious danger. Hugs were exchanged all around.

Jenda lingered as she embraced Meli. Both women had tears in their eyes. As they released one another, Meli reached up to give Jenda a kiss. "Make sure you come back," she said. "We have so much more to talk about."

"Don't worry, hija," Jenda reassured her. "I'm only leaving for a couple of days." And she returned the kiss.

On the drive to the airport, Jenda and Luis talked mostly about what they were going to do when Jenda returned. "We could stay here in Costa Rica," Luis said. "Montagne has collected all the materials to set up a sufficiency community here and life should go on pretty smoothly. Or we could go to Argentina and live with Isabel in Max and Emily's old folks' home at the old estancia. It sounded like they were going to set that up as a kind of sufficiency community, too."

"We should probably stay here at least for a while and see how things go. Would Abuela Isabel come here? Can you get in touch with her and the Feldmans to tell them what to expect? And what about Granny El? What can I tell her? Could we bring her here, too?"

"We'll figure this out. I wish we could tell all of them exactly what's happening, but we can't jeopardize the project. Isabel is the only one on Recall so far and I did send her a message, but you know she doesn't check very often. And I was pretty cryptic. I should have set Max and Emily up on Recall before we left. As for your grandmother...as soon as we know all the operations have been completed we can send information to her. I'll talk to Montagne about it as soon as I get back and let you know."

Jenda inhaled deeply. "I hope we're doing the right thing." She knew she had to do something, and she fervently hoped this was the thing.

"Well, we both know we can't go on forever as if it's all okay," Luis reassured her. "We've tried for years—decades—to fight off the plutocrats, and they keep getting stronger, richer, and more controlling. It has to stop."

She leaned closer and lay her head on his shoulder.

"I'm glad you agreed to do this, Jenda, even though, selfishly, I wish you hadn't. You know I won't rest until you get back and I have my arms around you again."

Arriving at the airport, they looked like just another pair of lovers saying their goodbyes. On her own, as she boarded the plane, Jenda felt frightened. She decided to re-read one of her favorite novels on her digilet. About twenty screens in, she realized how trivial and boring its story was next to the real-life one she was involved in, and she put it away.

The plane arrived on schedule at the Dallas airport and Jenda was surprised to see how crowded the international terminal was. *I wonder what the holdup is?* she asked herself.

And then she almost panicked. What if the international corporate police had caught wind of Recall's plan and were searching bags? *It's okay,* she told herself, *as long as I stay calm and don't attract attention.* As she got nearer the gateways, Jenda saw that they were not inspecting bags, but rather scanning people with an infrared device. She felt relieved, relaxed enough to speak to one of her companions in the slow moving queue. "Do you know what's going on?"

"It's the IHA. That blood disease. Well, I think they're calling it VHA now that they know it's a virus. It's been spreading like wildfire. How long have you been out of the country anyway?"

"I didn't think it was contagious," Jenda said. "Why are they screening us?"

"I'm telling you, now they know it is contagious," the man replied testily, "although they're still a long way from understanding how to deal with it. Lots of cases reported in Mexico and Guatemala this week, so it looks like all passengers from Central America are getting screened."

Jenda thanked her fellow traveler for the information. *Well, here's something else I could worry about,* she said to herself, *but let's say I choose not to.*

When Jenda finally passed through the screening device, she saw that several people had been pulled aside and equipped with facemasks. A gloved and masked physician wearing a Pharmakon uniform was speaking with them. *I'm not going to worry about this,* Jenda told herself again.

On the drive to her habitat, Jenda gave Granny El a call.

"Oh, I'm so glad to hear your voice. I've been worried about you, what with this VHA thing beginning to get all out of hand. At least I was glad you were in Argentina rather than Central America. It's getting pretty bad there." Not worrying about viral hemolytic anemia was becoming harder for Jenda.

"Are you back at work tomorrow?" Granny El asked. "How about we get together for lunch, and you can tell me about your trip. I have no idea what possessed you to suddenly take off to Argentina."

Jenda knew she couldn't do that. The temptation to tell Granny El everything would be too strong, and she had sworn to Montagne that she wouldn't speak to anyone about the plan until afterward, after she had successfully planted the infection via her screen at Your Journal.

"I can't make it tomorrow, Gran," Jenda said. "How about Tuesday? Yes, I promise." Jenda knew she would be back in Costa Rica on Tuesday. In her mind, the promise to meet for lunch morphed into a promise to let Granny El know where she could go for safety as soon as the deed was done on Monday evening.

The autocar stationed itself next to the entryway at Jenda's habitat, popped the trunk, and deposited her bag on the walkway. Upstairs, Jenda heard the lock for her unit click open as she approached. She walked inside and stared at the chaos. She had forgotten how she had left the place, forgotten how she had felt when she left.

Her paintings were still arranged in a semi-circle, propped against the empty boxes and piles of books and mementos. Jenda understood so much more now about what all of this meant, about who the girl was who had made these paintings and composed all these journals. What she was getting ready to do at Your Journal was something that girl would understand. She could almost hear that girl cheering her on. She walked over to the painting that faced the wall, the one of the lady in blue, and turned it around.

Jenda stared at the disassembled screen on her desk. *Whatever did I think that would accomplish?* she thought. But she had felt such perverse pleasure at the time. She wondered if she would feel that way again as the whole system of 'nets began to come apart on Monday evening.

Jenda and Luis had promised one another they would make no contact other than the confirmation of her arrival. So Jenda sat down at one end of the sofa. She uncoiled her digilet, screened up Recall, and navigated to Interloc. "Back home," she said, watching as the syllables came up on the screen. "See you soon." Then she deleted the second part. *He knows,* she said to herself as she snapped the digilet back onto her wrist.

Jenda spent the next several hours going through hers and her mother's things one last time, selecting what she would take with her and what she would have to leave behind. She decided she would be able to fit maybe one or two of her smaller paintings into her large suitcases. She had already decided she would pay the extra fee to take two bags. And when she finally finished packing, she threw a few outfits of clothes into the cases, almost as an afterthought. She removed the baggage tags that read "Jenda Swain" and replaced them with the tags Montagne had given her that bore the same name as her forged passport: Andrea Nelson.

In only four hours Jenda would have to be at work. She considered taking some tabs of Duermata, but instead made a cup of manzanilla tea and sat down on the sofa to read one of her old journals...

Jenda's dreams during her brief sleep that night were a medley of unlikely scenarios. Her mother Tessa was pushing an adult Meli on a beautifully sculpted swing in the garden of the house where Jenda grew up. Meli was cradling a white cat and both of them were laughing and singing a simple children's song. Paloma and Isabel were planting bombs at Your Journal, bombs hidden inside pots of purple chrysanthemums. Luis and Montagne were running a footrace along the road that led from Buenos Aires to San Ramon, while Jenda and her brother cheered them on. Luis was winning. Granny El sat at a little table with the Feldmans, drinking wine. Even Winslow Morris was there; he was trying to sell them something, although Jenda couldn't tell what it was. She thought it might be a picture of her father.

The Resistance

27.

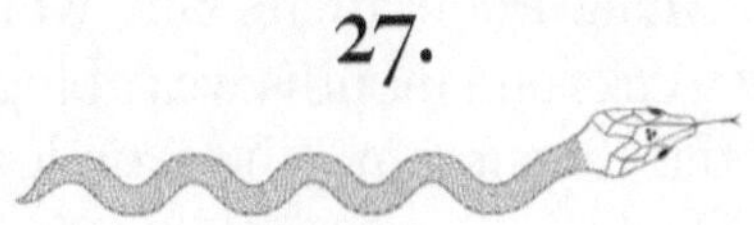

Arriving at Your Journal the next morning, Jenda found her co-workers sympathetic but curious. "We were so sorry to hear. What was your family emergency?" Weldon wanted to know. His expression and tone of voice were redolent with compassion.

Jenda had almost forgotten about her excuse for being absent. "My brother," Jenda replied, looking away. "But I'd rather not talk about it yet." Weldon nodded and went away to share this small bit of new gossip with their workmates.

Jenda unfolded her digiscreen and consulted her calendar. There was a "New Assignment" indicated for the day. She tapped it and was grateful that it was one of those simple transitional assignments. It would keep her occupied during what she knew was going to be a very long day. It would also keep her engaged with her screen, while presenting little risk of distracting her from her primary task. Jenda noted that she had an appointment with the corporate psychiatrist scheduled for first thing Tuesday morning. She confirmed it.

Jenda's mind was racing, and she had to deliberately slow herself down on her simple assignment in order to avoid completing it before lunch. She went to the ladies' room more than usual. She rearranged the few physical items in her work area several times as well.

When her colleagues came by to invite her for lunch, Jenda lied and said she was meeting her grandmother. Then she went to the modest little lunchroom down a side street, the café where the old woman—Malia Poole—had accosted her over a year ago. She ordered the grilled cheese sandwich with fries and a sweet tea. The sandwich contained natural cheese, and the fries were made from fresh potatoes. She thought this might be her favorite café in all of Dallas. She ate slowly, glancing up occasionally at the row of stools by the counter, half expecting to see Malia Poole there. She wondered what life over the next few weeks and months was going to be like for all these people in the lunchroom. She wondered what would happen to Malia Poole.

The afternoon stretched on as if it would never end while Jenda fought back rising waves of anxiety. She wanted to tell her supervisor she was leaving early, but she knew she couldn't introduce the contents of the 2XV insert until the appointed time of 4:50 p.m. Her digilet chimed, indicating she had a message. She glanced at it and didn't recognize the source, so she ignored it and muted the device. She could tend to personal matters later.

At 4:50 Jenda placed the insert into the appropriate receptacle of her desk screen and continued working on her assignment, watching the clock. Montagne's instructions were to leave the insert in place for at least five minutes, but no more than ten. Jenda took a deep breath and waited. A few seconds later, her screen beeped, indicating that she had an urgent message. She touched the message symbol and heard her supervisor's voice: "Hi, Jenda. Glad to see you made it back OK. Could you step into my office for a couple of minutes before you leave for the day? It's important."

A couple of minutes? Jenda thought, wondering whether anything her supervisor could tell her could possibly be important in light of what she was now setting in motion. The clock ticked over 4:52. Should she get up and leave the screen unattended with the insert in place? What if the supervisor kept her for more than a "couple of minutes"? There was no time for indecision. Jenda got up from her desk and headed toward her supervisor's office. It was a long ten meters away. She leaned inside the open door.

"You wanted to see me?" Jenda tried to sound casual.

"Yes, Jenda. Hang on one second while I finish this memo. Gosh, the screens seem even slower than usual for this time of day." He laughed.

Jenda felt perspiration breaking out in her armpits as she strained against the urge to look back at her own desk. She waited, glancing down at her digilet: 4:54... No, 4:55.

"There, that's got it. Yes. Well, I wanted to tell you how sorry we were about your family emergency. No, I won't pry. You can share with the psych office tomorrow. I also wanted to tell you..." He paused and smiled mysteriously. "I want to say, first of all, that your new campaign looks to be your most successful yet. The hierarchy loves it. So much so, in fact..." He stopped and shuffled some images on his desktop as Jenda stole a glimpse of the time again: 4:56. "Well, I guess I could've just sent this right to your own desktop, but I wanted to tell you myself first." His digilet beeped and he paused to check it. "Anyway, what I wanted to tell you is this: You've been promoted! Let me be the first to congratulate you! The details are on your desktop now. What do you think of that?" He grinned expectantly.

Jenda had no idea what to think. She knew she should act surprised, and she certainly was that. *(Zujo! 4:57...)* She knew she should also look pleased and excited, which she wasn't.

"Well," she said finally, "I'm speechless." There, that was true. "I'm overwhelmed. Thank you. I guess I'm eager to go back to my desktop and get a look at the details." She knew this was a feeble attempt to get away, but she didn't care. She hoped her forced smile was convincing.

"Well, I can certainly understand that. Let me just say, I think you'll be pleased with both your new title and your new pay level." Her supervisor rose from his chair. "Let me shake your hand anyway," he said. He walked over to Jenda and shook her hand. Jenda hoped he didn't notice how cold and clammy it was. "Now, go on and we'll talk more tomorrow." Jenda thanked him again. She looked over his shoulder and saw the clock on his screen tick to 4:58. She reined in her desire to run.

She saw Weldon standing at her desk, staring at the screen, and her heart skipped a beat.

"Weldon...what?" Jenda said as she came up behind him.

"Oh, there you are, Jenda," Weldon laughed. "I thought you'd left without screening off and I was about to do it for you."

"Nope, I'm still here, Weldon. Thanks anyway." Jenda pushed him aside as she sat down, her hand reaching for the insert.

"Just trying to be helpful," Weldon sniffed as he walked back toward his own desk.

Jenda extracted the insert just as the clock ticked over 4:59. She exhaled. She saw the message that she knew contained the details of her promotion, a message destined to melt into oblivion in a matter of hours, if not minutes. She felt like laughing. She left the message unopened and screened out, tucking the insert into a front pocket of her handbag. She hoped all the other operatives had been equally successful. Then she picked up her bag and headed out of the building for the last time. And because it was what she always did, she called "See you tomorrow!" to Weldon and her other office mates as she departed.

On the street, Jenda passed a trash bin and dropped the 2XV insert into it, concealed in a wad of tissues from her handbag. Then she headed for an autocar.

Jenda had plenty of time to fetch her suitcases from her habitat and make it to the airport for her return flight to Costa Rica. In fact, she had more than enough time. She loaded her bags into the car and then went back inside and sat on the sofa to drink the last bottle of fizzy fruit drink from the chillbox and check for messages on her digilet. Once she left her habitat, she would stop being Jenda Swain for a while and become Andrea Nelson. She wanted desperately to tell Luis about Jenda Swain's promotion; she knew he would enjoy the irony of it all.

There was a message on the digilet, but it was not for Jenda; it was for Andrea Nelson, and it was marked "URGENT." Jenda tapped the symbol and, as she read the message, her heart sank.

*ALL FLIGHTS TO AND FROM CENTRAL AMERICA
CANCELLED DUE TO HEALTH CONCERNS. PLEASE
CONTACT YOUR AIRLINE FOR INSTRUCTIONS.*

What now? Contacting the airline was probably not a good idea, due to the relatively thin cover Andrea Nelson provided. Montagne had cautioned Jenda that she needed to minimize her interaction as Andrea, because at some point face recognition would kick in or a fingerprint or iris scan would be required. Although they had done their best, they hadn't been able to provide her with all the bells and whistles that would have made all of these things consistently read as "Andrea Nelson." Eventually something would come up "Jenda Swain."

Maybe she could make a reservation to go somewhere else under her own name. No, probably not. Jenda Swain's passport indicated that she had recently returned from Central America and that would raise a red flag. They might even place her in quarantine. In fact, Pharmakon might be looking for her now.

Jenda navigated to Recall on her digilet and pulled up Interloc. There was a pulse from Luis:

```
MURCIELAGO: I heard. Go here. Tell your
grandmother.
```

And there was a list of syllables that Jenda recognized as an EarthSat location phrase. It was good to know Luis had her back but where was he sending her? As much as Jenda wanted to ask, as much as she wanted to have a good long talk with Luis, he and Montagne had been adamant about minimizing communication during what they were calling "the interim".

```
POLILLA: Got it.
```

Jenda paused for a moment as tears welled up in her eyes. She suddenly felt very small and alone.

POLILLA: I love you.

MURCIELAGO: I love you too. Now go.

Jenda fought back the tears and sat down on the sofa to think exactly what she could say to Granny El. She didn't trust herself to have a conversation, so she dictated a pulse: "Hi, Gran. I have to go out of town again. Please meet me here as soon as you can." She added the EarthSat syllables. "If you know where Dad is, please invite him, too." Then she looked up the last pulse she had received from her brother and sent the location phrase to him, as well.

She snapped the digilet back around her wrist and walked out, listening for the lock to click as she walked away. Her bags were waiting in the autocar. She entered the EarthSat syllables into the control panel and sat back. She was glad to be leaving, but anxious about where she might be going. Knowing she was not going to Luis broke her heart.

28.

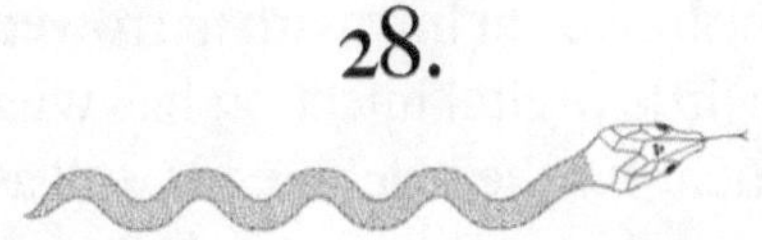

Luis and Montagne monitored developments as best they could from their outpost in Ortega, Costa Rica, growing anxious about the spread of what was now called viral hemolytic anemia in the region. The latest reports indicated that the disease had been identified as a highly contagious and exceptionally virulent form of human parvovirus. Urgent research was ongoing, but with no promising leads as yet for either cure or prevention other than abstaining from Chulel and from contact with sick individuals. Costa Rica was still unaffected, but Mexico and Guatemala reported massive numbers of cases, so it was only a matter of time. There were a handful of cases in Honduras and Panama.

"Are you sure we need to do this?" Luis had asked, as they both examined the statistics on VHA on the Monday afternoon, less than an hour before the digital infection was scheduled to be introduced. "I mean, it looks to me like this disease might decimate humanity pretty thoroughly anyway. Why make it worse?"

Montagne stared out the window and said nothing, his fists shoved deep into his pockets. When he spoke, his voice was heavy with sadness. "I know," he said. "It seems like a lot of people are going to die of this blood disease no matter what else happens. Except maybe for the plutocrats who are rich enough to isolate themselves. Or those who have already stopped using Chulel, like many of the people in the sufficiency communities. I stopped using it several years ago."

Luis confirmed that he had done the same. "But once the disease passes," Montagne continued, "what then? If we did nothing, the plutocrats would be able to go back in and start up again, fabricating a new series of lies about what happened. We have to stop them. And especially with so many people dying."

Luis rubbed his forehead with the heel of his hand and sighed. Montagne looked at him with narrowed eyes and a hard expression. "Our little digital infection has what is essentially a self-destruct element for the machines as well as the scripts. No one will ever use those termini, those digiscreens, any of those machines ever again. Their world will no longer exist. Ever. Their power base will be gone." Montagne's expression softened. "But don't ask me what comes next. That's entirely in the hands of the people who make it through. The one thing I'm sure of is that, with so many people dying, it wouldn't be right for the plutocracy to survive." He paused. "When we worked together, you and I had quite a few discussions about the basic nature of humanity, Luis. Do you remember?"

A faint smile flickered across Luis' face. "As I recall, I was always the more optimistic, the one arguing for the inherent creativity and adaptability of human beings and for our natural drive to look after one another."

"Well, I think you must have convinced me at some point, hermano. I don't think I could have gone through with this takedown if I believed things would turn out worse than what we have now."

Around 4:30 p.m. a message came in on Interloc about the cancellation of flights from Texas to Central America.

"Fuck!" Montagne banged the desk surface with his fist, almost disconnecting the screen.

"Zujo! What do we tell Jenda?" Luis felt an unaccustomed sense of powerlessness. How could they cut him off like this from the woman he loved? "What about the sufficiency community that we were going to send her grandmother to?" Luis asked.

"Right," Montagne said. "It's in New Mexico." He moved over to let Luis send the message to Jenda on Interloc.

Carefully Luis entered the syllables, along with a brief message. "Done," he said, wanting desperately to do more.

"What about Granny El. Do we have her contact phrase?"

Luis shook his head, realizing that Montagne actually knew Granny El and that he didn't. "Sorry. No. But Jenda will pass the location on to her."

They sat back to wait for a response from Jenda. Luis tried to imagine what Jenda was going through as she introduced the virus at YJ. Montagne kept checking his sources, focusing on the bigger picture in which Jenda played one vital part. They scanned a few more stories about VHA.

"I'm beginning to think maybe all of us would be better off in Argentina than here, and the sooner the better," Montagne said. "This disease is looking pretty bad and getting closer to our doorstep all the time. You're the most mobile, Luis, so maybe you should go on back and look after your grandmother and her friends in Buenos Aires. We'll plan to join you as soon as we can. And we'll hope to get Jenda out quickly and send her to Argentina, too." Luis nodded in agreement.

Montagne and Luis knew when each of the operatives—including Jenda—had fulfilled their task. If it hadn't been for the predicament Jenda was in, they might have celebrated. They continued monitoring Recall. Montagne was one of only a few designated reporters being allowed to use Recall. It was a precaution they had taken to avoid imploding the entire zone with people eager to contribute their pieces to the picture of a collapsing society.

Luis began to breathe again when he knew Jenda had received the location. His heart swelled painfully when he received her affirmation of love. He knew she was feeling lonely and a little scared, although she hadn't said anything about it. Luis knew that because he knew Jenda. Montagne, who only knew the old Jenda—the one with sepia-colored hair and badly mended old clothes—assured him that she could handle the situation. Luis hoped he was right.

Luis and Montagne watched as the transport network began to fail and as power outages began to spread in the expected locations. They smiled with satisfaction when Your Journal and LifeBook went dark, followed almost immediately by FlixNews. When the banking network and then the EarthSat system began to fail sooner than expected, both Luis and Montagne became more anxious about Jenda.

29.

The autocar left Dallas heading west on a primary artery. Not many people took autocars on long journeys, preferring instead the comfort and speed of the hyperloops. Jenda didn't know if this was going to be a long journey, but she was pretty sure the hyperloop didn't go wherever it was she was headed. The car breezed along though the continuous inosculation of endurbs which, at some undefined point along the way, became Fort Worth. It occurred to Jenda to be thankful that whatever was beginning to happen out there would find most people at home rather than at work.

By 6:30 the car had entered the suburbs, with their sprawling mansions, each surrounded by its own little world of miniature lakes and forests. Jenda checked the charge meter on the car and realized that, with the overcast skies, the autocar was going to need a recharge. She figured she could use a pit stop, too, and an opportunity to look at a map to figure out where she was going before the medianets started to fail.

At Jenda's request, the autocar pulled into a recharge station in the center of Weatherford, across from an entertainment complex called The Old Courthouse. She connected the car's cable and went inside the café. She bought two sandwiches and a large NutriQuaff and sat down at one of the tables.

Setting the sandwiches aside, Jenda unfurled her digilet and was relieved when NaviGiz screened up with no problem. The location phrase from Luis tagged a destination well off even secondary arteries near nothing in particular in north central New Mexico. Jenda made some handwritten notes on a back page of one of the old notebooks she had stashed in the inside pocket of her bag. This was going to be a long journey.

Jenda needed to think. Fully charging the autocar would take almost twenty minutes, but she thought she needed the full charge. Jenda had never worried about distance driving before and she had to query a mediazone to find out how far a full charge would take her. The answer was five hundred kilometers, give or take. Jenda unwrapped a sandwich. Consulting the map again, she calculated that a five-hundred-kilometer range would be enough to get her safely to Lubbock, even with modest use of the cool air generator. The journey to Lubbock would take about three hours, meaning it would be dark by the time she got there. *Dark and cooler,* she thought. *And surely I'll be able to find a place to spend the night in Lubbock.*

Having an interim destination and a plan in mind, Jenda felt a bit more at ease as the autocar made its way out of Weatherford and back onto the primary artery. The clouds had begun clearing to the west, leaving the sun shining directly into the front window. Jenda turned to look out a side window. The undulating landscape was rising gradually in elevation, but not enough to strain the car's engine. Suburbs gave way to towns separated by stretches of well-watered, genetically engineered crops. There were also a number of meat and egg factories, supplying the needs of the urban areas Jenda had left behind. She saw a string of transport stages stopped on the monorail line between towns. A semaphore by the side of the rail flashed red.

Jenda's route would take her through Abilene, a fact she had tried to ignore as she laid out her plan in the café. Now she let herself think about it and she wondered about Ben. Surely by this time there must be indications of something having gone wrong at Your Journal and, being a high level executive, Ben would know. What would he think if he knew what Jenda had done, if he knew his insignificant little ex-wife had brought mighty Your Journal to its knees? Jenda liked this scenario. She searched the autocar's audio system for some music that would suit her state of mind. Something triumphant but tragic. She finally found an old blues track and settled for that.

Jenda glanced at the road ahead periodically, waiting for the moment when the sun would drop below the horizon and she could enjoy the beauty of an expansive Texas sunset. As she passed by Abilene, the sun's last lingering beams lit up the Your Journal tower, and Jenda saw clearly that the photonic 3-D image at the pinnacle of the building had disappeared. Jenda saw her face reflected in the car window and noted her satisfied smile. As the retiring sun finally spattered the sky with color, Jenda fell asleep.

She awakened disoriented. She stared into the darkened landscape, trying to remember where she was. *Zujo!* she thought. *Have I missed Lubbock?* A quick check of the car's screen showed that Lubbock was just ahead. She quickly entered a command for the car to stop at the next available recharge station. The car still had plenty of charge left—the late sunshine had helped—but Jenda required services. Topping up the car's charge couldn't hurt.

Arriving at the station, Jenda found there would be a wait for charging and she placed the car in the queue. Inside, she found a knot of people around the serving counter.

"It's not just Your Journal and LifeBook," one man said. "Look at this: CorpNet is reporting failures in the air transit control system and FlixNews has gone off the air altogether."

Jenda sat down at a table that gave her a view of the entertainment screen. She was exhausted and the hour was late, but she ordered dinner. She wasn't sure where or when she would be eating again.

She tried to appear neither too interested nor too disinterested in the breaking news being reported by CorpNet. Planes were grounded in all the major continental airports and there were preliminary reports of extensive power outages in Dallas and Washington, D.C.

"Beijing is also reporting a major power outage," the presenter said, "although it is unclear whether there is any connection with the North American outages." Jenda knew these were three of the physical locations where the digital infection had been introduced. There was a connection.

The presenter continued: "We'll get back to you with more details on those outages as soon as we re-establish contact with our affiliates in these areas. In other news, the illness known as Viral Hemolytic Anemia or VHA has claimed its first victims in the US state of Nevada and in Nicaragua. The documented death toll is now approaching the forty million mark."

Jenda wanted desperately to pulse Luis one more time, to check on him and Meli and the rest. But she knew that was forbidden. Before leaving the shop, Jenda bought a large bag of Nutrichips and a bottle of fortified water. The purchase took longer than usual, and the attendant apologized. "We're having to desume a different mediazone," she said. "Ours has gone dead, and connections seem slow all around."

"No problem," Jenda said, fully appreciating the inappropriateness of this stock reply. The inconvenience of a slow mediazone was the leading edge of what was about to be a very big problem. Jenda was grateful the payment system was working at all. She was still a long way from her destination.

When Jenda's car emerged from the queue, she refilled the drinking water dispenser and got back on the road to look for a place to spend the night. She had no intention of being choosy; she was too tired for that. All she asked for was a bed to stretch out on until morning. She stopped at the first roadstead she saw. As the autocar came to a stop, the lighted sign suddenly went dark. Then the lights inside the office flickered and went out. As the autocar door opened, Jenda heard the lock on the front door of the roadstead office click.

Zujo! What now? Jenda looked up and down the artery, hoping to catch sight of another roadstead. She got back in the car and tried to screen up NaviGiz on her digilet, thinking it might find something nearby. It wasn't working.

Now look what you've done, Jenda! She looked out the windows at the mostly empty parking lot. *Well, there's no point in wasting a good charge wandering around in the middle of the night looking for something I'm not likely to find.* Jenda tasked the doors to lock. Then she readjusted the seats. Figuring she shouldn't risk the comfortable oblivion of Duermata, she did her best to stretch out in the tiny vehicle. She finally dropped into a shallow sleep, waking periodically. The night seemed to get progressively darker. All the lights had gone out and as far as Jenda could see, there was only starlight.

Jenda awoke the next morning to brilliant sunshine beaming through the autocar's windows. Although the brightness hurt her sleep deprived eyes, she felt only gratitude and relief. She had slept longer than she would have thought possible. Now she needed a restroom and somewhere to stretch her cramped legs. The roadstead office looked terminally closed.

As she powered up the autocar, a red light flashed and a calm voice announced, "Automatic navigation is not available. Manual controls are engaged."

Jenda's experience with physically managing a car was limited. She took a deep breath and pressed the button confirming manual control, hoping for the best. She set the top speed for five kph below the posted limit and said a quick word of thanks that her contract was permitting the car to keep running even though it clearly was no longer in contact with the autocar corporation. Less than a kilometer up the road, Jenda found another recharge station with a café that seemed to be open. She maneuvered the car into a parking spot and went inside.

The pay point attendant was just positioning a sign that read "Closed". The bathroom facilities, however, were open and that was what Jenda wanted most. After relieving herself, Jenda washed her face and combed her hair. She thought her image in the mirror didn't look much improved.

She went to speak with the clerk, who was still fiddling with the pay point screen. "Why have you closed down?" she asked.

"It's this payment system. It's not accepting charges right now, so we can't sell anything until it's up and running again. Sorry." She didn't sound particularly sorry. She pointed to an open case of fortified water on the next counter, with a sign affixed indicating each customer could take one bottle free of charge. Jenda took one. She wished she had bought more than a bag of Nutrichips at the last station. At least she had bought the large bag. She also wished they still had some kind of physical money in circulation.

Jenda walked around the shop for a bit, telling herself it was for the exercise but looking at all the things she couldn't buy and didn't need. *Although,* she thought, *a pair of sunglasses would've been nice. And maybe a chocolate packet or two. Or a bottle of good Texas cabernet.* She sat down at one of the tables to drink her fortified water and take another look at her notes about where she was going. She found the extra sandwich she had bought in Weatherford.

From Lubbock, Jenda knew she needed to head north on—she squinted at her hasty notes—highway 840. Jenda knew that was not a primary artery. It would take her to the international border near Clovis, New Mexico. Jenda hoped this was not a frontier that required a passport, since the only passports she had access to were a polyplex one reading "Andrea Nelson" and a paper one reading "Jenda Swain" that had expired eighty years ago.

As Jenda ate her stale sandwich, made almost palatable by frequent swigs of fortified water, she mentally mapped out the remainder of her trip. Highway 840 would get her all the way to Albuquerque, New Mexico. There she would turn onto a road numbered NM63. She thought that would probably be well marked. From NM63 there were three more turns and Jenda wasn't at all sure about those. In the age of autocars, road signage had become a low priority, and broken signs were rarely replaced. The signs that still existed were often peeling and faded. She had written down the road numbers for her final three turns but had failed to indicate which direction to turn. She hoped her mental recall of the map would keep her on track.

Back in the autocar, Jenda easily found highway 840. Maybe this wouldn't be as bad as she had feared. Even manual navigation began to feel less intimidating as rolling hills flattened out into open plains and the road became straight as an arrow. Traffic was almost nonexistent.

The landscape stretched out with monotonous sameness in all directions. Fields of ripening crops alternated with fields of humming windmills, all bearing the colors and emblem of the energy behemoth TotExx. Jenda's attention began to wander...

A loud buzzer made her jump to attention. She saw the curve, but for a moment she couldn't think what to do and it was coming up fast. Then her right hand found the turn mechanism and she veered around the curve, tires squealing. The car swung from side to side as she struggled to steady her hand on the velocity control. At last the car slowed and its course straightened. Her heart was pounding as she pulled off at the side of the road. *Okay, calm down,* she told herself. *At least the perimeter warnings are still operating. I have to be more careful. I don't want to end up a mangled heap on the side of the road.* She suddenly flashed on her mother's accident and felt pretty sure she would not have any further trouble concentrating on her task. After a few deep, calming breaths, she pulled back onto the road.

With the bright sun, straight flat road, and slow speed, the car was still registering well over half of a full charge as Jenda approached the international border. A flashing red light signaled her to stop at the crossing booth.

"We wanted to warn you, ma'am," the official said. "There are some power outages and communications problems up the road here. We're offering you a free ten minutes of recharge if you need it. Well, as long as our batteries hold out." He smiled and waved Jenda in.

Jenda pulled into the queue for one of the recharge docks. She didn't know if she would need it or not, but anything that didn't require payment was welcome. There would be mountains ahead. She sat at an outdoor table, shaded by an awning, and munched some Nutrichips while her car worked its way through the short queue.

On the road again, Jenda slowed her speed even more as the terrain became increasingly hilly. The only reasons to stop now were her own personal needs, since the shops and cafés all showed "Closed" signs. A couple of times Jenda pulled off and relieved herself shamelessly in full view of the empty road. Then she cleaned her hands with the sanitary wipes, refilled her water bottle from the onboard supply, and resumed her journey.

As she approached Albuquerque, she watched for her turn onto NM63. She began feeling anxious as she left the central inosculation behind. Then she saw a weather-beaten sign pointing both right and left to NM63. She knew this was a right turn, but the sign's placement was ambiguous, and she didn't relax until she saw another sign confirming her route.

This road led straight up into the mountains. Jenda pulled off momentarily to check her notes. She congratulated herself as she made the next turn with no difficulty. Her cognitive map told her the following turn should be to the left. She found the road, but after a few kilometers decided she should have turned right and had to backtrack. The manual navigation and multiple stops were making for slow progress. The trip was taking longer than Jenda had calculated. Clouds had built up, too, obscuring the sun and causing the autocar's charge to drop rapidly.

Then it started to rain. Big drops splattered across the windows, threatening a downpour. Between the rain and the late hour, it was already getting dark as Jenda searched for her final turn. She passed one turn that she thought might be the one, but she kept driving, wishing she had included more detailed notes about the distance between points and feeling that the turn she was looking for should be a bit further on. It was several kilometers before the next turn came up. Jenda didn't think it looked right. One or two kilometers further on, she thought better of it and turned around. This time she made the turn onto the narrow road—it only went in one direction. But after four kilometers this road suddenly dropped into an old arroyo and the pavement simply ended. As Jenda turned the car around in the darkening landscape, the charge indicator began to blink, meaning that she had only ten kilometers left before the car would come to a halt. She groaned and slumped into the seat.

"I guess I could stay here until morning," she thought, glancing around the empty landscape and hoping that tomorrow would be sunny. Something caught her eye at the edge of the arroyo. She fumbled for the car's headlamps and, after switching the windscreen wipers on and off, she finally grasped the lamp switch. There was a small sign, and it looked fresh rather than old and faded. She pulled up closer to the sign. It contained the location phrase Luis had sent her, and an arrow pointed up the flat bed of the arroyo. There were fresh tire marks along the dirt track.

Jenda took a deep breath and turned the little car in the direction indicated by the arrow and the tracks. The car bounced slowly along the barely discernible path as the last light of the sun was fading. Just as she began to question whether the little sign had been a mirage and to query the state of her sanity in general, she saw what looked like a few houses in the distance. A few moments later she pulled the car into a field alongside no more than a dozen other cars. The little sign had not been a mirage, but Jenda was pretty sure her sanity might still be in question.

30.

Jenda had no idea what to expect as she shouldered her handbag, locked the autocar, and began the short walk toward the line of small buildings. Her last shreds of optimism vanished as she noticed the silhouette of a church steeple with a cross and, a short distance away, a building with a round dome and a crescent moon. "Oh, please tell me he hasn't sent me to one of those Book Communities," Jenda muttered to herself, although it was pretty clear that this was exactly what Luis had done. She had heard about these communities, which had been set up in remote areas by people who became convinced that the use of Chulel went against the will of God, or the will of Allah, depending. She knew there was probably a temple with a Star of David somewhere, too.

Jenda saw a hand lettered sign reading "Welcome" in several languages on one of the houses. There were a few people standing outside, chatting amiably. They smiled and greeted her as she walked up the steps and in through the open door.

She found herself in a brightly lit room painted a pleasing shade of pale green and simply furnished. Behind a table near one wall were two women, one of whom was wearing a brightly flowered headscarf. She greeted Jenda warmly. "We were afraid you weren't going to make it," she said. "But then, you had the longest distance to travel."

"Excuse me?" Jenda said. "You knew I was coming? You know who I am?"

"Well," the other woman spoke up, "unless there is some mistake, you're Jenda Swain. From Dallas, Texas. Am I right?"

Jenda nodded as the woman showed her a paper list that had about a dozen names on it. All of them had been crossed off except hers. The woman laid the paper back on the table and drew a line through Jenda's name with a flourish. "And you're just in time for last supper," she said, as a small bell clanged briefly from another building across the way.

"Let's give her the room assignment first," the woman with the scarf said. She handed Jenda a little paper card with a number on one side and a map of the village on the other. She marked the location of Jenda's assigned dwelling and gave brief instructions, complemented by gestures, on how to get there.

How hard can it be in this tiny place? Jenda wondered, but she thanked the women for their help. The one with no scarf was on the front step, calling to one of the men who was already on his way to wherever it was they were going to have whatever this "last supper" was. He returned, agreeing to help Jenda retrieve her bags from the car and move them to her room.

As they walked toward the car in the darkness, Jenda thanked him for his help. "I think it's you we should be thanking," he replied. "I understand you had a big role to play in what's been happening since yesterday." He smiled knowingly, but Jenda got the distinct feeling he didn't know as much as he was pretending to.

"It wasn't much," Jenda said.

After they deposited her bags in the room, the man said, "Come on, I'll walk you up to the hall for last supper."

"Oh, I don't know," Jenda said, fearful of getting pulled into some kind of religious ritual.

"Don't worry," the man chuckled. "It's only food. Nothing religious about it. We only call it 'last supper' because it's the final meal of the day in our shared dining hall. Visitors sometimes find that a little confusing. There's a first supper, too."

"Ah," Jenda said. "In that case."

The dining hall was as brightly lit as the welcome house, and the serving table was piled high with simple but delicious looking food. Jenda filled her plate and then looked for a place to sit. She suddenly felt very, very tired. There were long tables with benches, but also some smaller tables that seemed to accommodate families. There were children. One of the long tables had some empty spaces, but Jenda didn't feel like talking to anyone. She sat at one of the small tables, facing the wall with her back to the crowd of strangers. She didn't care what they thought of her. She was tired and hungry and wanted to be left alone.

She ate voraciously but soon realized she had taken far more than she could eat. Her stomach began to feel queasy. As she got up from the table, an attendant came by to ask if he could take her plate. Jenda felt an unaccustomed sense of embarrassment for being wasteful. "I'm sorry," she said, but the waiter smiled. "Our chickens just love people like you."

Jenda made her way back to her assigned room without further encounters. It was a modest room, with a single bed, two chairs, two small tables, and a wardrobe. There were curtains on the window and a rug on the floor. It reminded her for a moment of hers and Luis' room at Isabel's apartment. But that was in Buenos Aires. And Luis was in Costa Rica. And here she was someplace that she so far only knew as a set of EarthSat syllables, someplace that was very far from either Buenos Aires or Costa Rica and pretty far from Dallas. She hoped Granny El had acted on her message and would be arriving soon.

A wave of fatigue and loneliness engulfed Jenda and she sat down on the edge of the bed and permitted a few tears to come. More than anything else she wanted to talk with Luis—no, be with Luis. And she had no idea when or even if that was going to happen. She lay back on the little bed and, giving in to mind-numbing exhaustion, she fell asleep.

Jenda had gone to sleep with her back to the east-facing window, so the sun was well up before its brightness penetrated her weary brain. She blinked, trying to remember where she was. When she remembered, she closed her eyes again.

What happens now? she wondered, feeling a bit like someone marooned on a desert island. But here, instead of being surrounded by ocean, she was surrounded by strangers and beyond that a society in a state of universal collapse. She rubbed her crusty eyes and stretched her aching limbs. She looked around for a bathroom. There was none. Then she remembered that the women at the welcome center had told her she would be sharing a bathroom with the other residents of this building.

She got up and tried to smooth the wrinkles out of her crumpled shirt before going out to search for the shared facilities. Her door opened directly onto a long porch and the porch opened onto a vast landscape full of golden and gray-green emptiness, delimited only by a ridge of mountains on the far horizon and a cloudless blue sky. The desert-island feeling receded as Jenda's consciousness embraced and welcomed the vast open landscape. She took several deep breaths, filling her lungs with the clean bright atmosphere. Maybe this place wouldn't be so bad. For a while, anyway.

She found the bathroom and it was basic but clean. She relieved herself and splashed cool water on her face. There was no towel. She remembered seeing towels on a table in her room and made a mental note to bring one with her next time. She dried her face and hands on her blouse.

She walked the ten paces back to her room, closed the door behind her and leaned against it, still feeling stiff and unsteady. She studied the small space that was to be her temporary home. Her two suitcases stood unopened next to the wardrobe. She thought about how few clothes she had packed and how unlikely it was that she could acquire any more. Even if there was a shopping court in this community (and Jenda doubted that there was) how would she pay for anything with the payment system shut down?

Jenda heaved one of her suitcases onto the bed to look for clothes. The effort made her feel a little short of breath and she wondered absently what the altitude of this place was. Opening the case, she discovered that not only had she packed precious few outfits, her selections were somewhat inappropriate for the current setting. She had thought she would be with Luis. She selected the most nondescript pants and blouse of the lot. She had not brought any soaps or shampoo or toiletries of any kind. Not even a toothbrush. Even without soap, the shower would be refreshing. When Jenda picked up the towel, she realized it was one of those real cotton ones, although its plushness had been diminished by use and, she suspected, many laundry events.

After her shower, dressed in plain brown pants and a blue knit blouse, Jenda wandered back out onto the porch. She felt a little hungry. It was probably long past breakfast, but all she had left in her room was a half-bottle of water and some crumbled remnants of Nutrichips.

As she anticipated, the dining hall was empty, except for one attendant, who gestured toward a table in the center of the room. The table held a carafe, a few cups and saucers, and some plates stacked with pastries

The coffee and pastry left Jenda feeling queasy again. As she walked back toward her room for a rest, she spotted a sign on one of the buildings reading "Clinic".

She stopped and reflected for a moment. "Maybe I should let them check me out." She assured herself that she was only suffering from exhaustion and stress. "I could use some kind of boost right now, though, and I'm sure they'll have something to offer."

31.

Luis bought a ticket on what turned out to be the last flight out of Liberia airport for Buenos Aires. He had to sign a waiver indicating his acknowledgment that some of the air traffic regulation systems might not be functioning. As he signed the paper he mentally substituted "all" for "some" and "will not" for "might not". He was grateful that he had bought his ticket on the mediazone the night before, because by the time he reached the airport, all the pay points were down. What had started in North America and East Asia and a few other places was spreading rapidly through every connection possible. There were a lot of connections.

The flight was only half full, occupied mostly by nervous looking people heading home to look after family and businesses. Luis had a whole row of seats to himself, so he stretched out as best he could. Inflight entertainment was not operating, there was no connection to the medianets, and Luis had not brought along any Duermata. He unfurled his digilet and scrolled through some photos, mostly photos of Jenda. He hoped she had found her way to safety and that she wasn't too annoyed about having been deposited in a Book Community. He searched his digilet for something to read and found nothing appealing. He closed his eyes, thinking he would try to sleep. "What I need is a good superhero story," he told himself wryly. So he tried to conjure up one of his Batman comic book tales. He finally dropped off to sleep just as The Penguin was about to be devoured by a shark off the coast of Tierra del Fuego.

Luis woke to the announcement of their approach into the Buenos Aires airport. He looked out the window and was relieved to see it was a clear day with almost unlimited visibility. He closed his eyes again and waited for the plane to touch down, wishing he knew some prayers or at least believed in a power that could guide the plane to a safe landing. He decided to put his faith in the competence of the flight crew, and that proved sufficient.

It seemed odd going through the arrivals area with everything being done by hand. Luis gave the official his plastiflex document, screened on to the identity log. The officer looked at it, looked at Luis, and then wrote some numbers and syllables on a piece of paper, which he attached to Luis' passport. As he handed it back to Luis he smiled and shrugged his shoulders. "Don't lose the piece of paper," he said.

Outside the terminal, Luis found that autocars were not available, but that the tranvía alta was still running on a limited number of routes. One of these would take him close to the Plaza Wanxiang and Galería Picaflor.

The electric powered vehicle slid along quietly above the nearly deserted streets of the city. The few people Luis saw below on the street were walking hurriedly, wrapped in coats and scarves, not speaking. He remembered having read about the alarming levels of noise pollution in Buenos Aires back in the 20th century, an era dominated by internal combustion engines. He pressed his ear against the plexi window and listened to the silence.

Well before the stop where Luis had intended to disembark, the tranvía slid to a jerky halt. The train had run out of power. He grasped a handle and pulled the door open, waiting while the only other passenger got out. Then he stepped onto the walkway. It was going to be a long walk.

Arriving at last at Galería Picaflor, he was grateful to see Isabel behind the desk.

"Ah, Luisito!" she cried. "I'm so glad you made it safely. I got your messages, although I wasn't sure what they meant. I still don't know exactly what's going on. Where's Jenda?"

Luis hugged his grandmother. "One thing at a time, abuelita," he said. "And there are a lot of things."

"Then let's close the shop and go upstairs for some sandwiches and you can start telling me." Isabel went to the front window and turned over a paper sign that said "Open" on one side and "Closed" on the other. As she manually locked the door, Luis realized that there was no power in the gallery; the only light came from the glass storefront.

Upstairs in the apartment, there was even less light, so they dragged a couple of chairs over near the window that overlooked the street. Luis did his best to explain to his grandmother what was happening, taking things step by step.

"So you're saying this isn't going to be just a brief period of the power grid and so on being down?" Isabel said. "Well, then. That changes things."

"Yes," Luis assented, "it changes pretty much everything."

"How do we get Jenda back?"

"As soon as the new 'net is up and running, I'll talk to her and we'll work something out," Luis tried to sound optimistic. "There are supposed to be some small airplanes that will begin to operate, and given Jenda's service, there should be no trouble in getting her onto one of them."

"Good," Isabel said. "You know I've become quite fond of your novia, Luis. I want her back."

"Me too, Abuelita," Luis said.

"And what about Paloma and Ermelinda and Ermelinda's father?"

"Again, we'll all be in touch as soon as the 'net is working. The plan is for them to come here and join us, since we believe this area will be safer from the spread of the VHA."

"That will be wonderful. We'll have our own little—what did you call it? A sufficiency community? Well, under the circumstances, I'd recommend that we close up here and go out to join Max and Emily at their house in San Ramon. I have a fully charged autocar waiting outside. I knew we'd want to go see them." Isabel was already rising from her chair, ready to leave at once.

32.

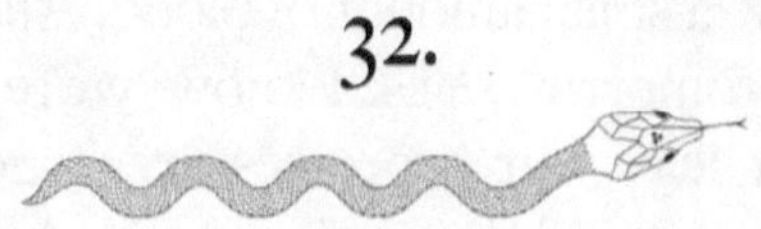

Waiting in the anteroom of the clinic, Jenda recalled her illness during the middle part of her sabbatical in San Miguel and told herself that what she was experiencing now was an episode of the same kind. Her physical harmony was being disrupted by her mental disarray. She looked down at the digilet curled uselessly around her wrist. Luis had said a new 'net—the Novanet—would be coming up after the demise of the old supranet and medianets, and he had scripted her digilet to receive it. There was no indication yet of any activity.

Jenda was called into the examining room by a woman in a white uniform that bore no insignia other than that of the medical community, the Rod of Asclepius. There were no logos of healthcare or pharmaceutical corporations. Jenda sat on the edge of an examining table while the woman took her blood pressure and heart rate and temperature with hand-held instruments that Jenda did not remember having seen before. The woman made notes on paper and then, in a tone of practiced optimism, told Jenda the doctor would be in momentarily.

When the doctor entered, Jenda's first thought was that she was from Gen2. But in this community, where people were aging with the passing years, it was impossible to tell. She could as easily be Gen3 or even Gen4.

"How are you feeling?" the doctor asked, studying the paper on which the assistant had made notes about the state of Jenda's body.

"Tired," Jenda said. "A little breathless at times, probably because of the altitude. Also kind of achy. And a bit nauseous."

"Well, you're running a fever," the doctor said as she pulled back Jenda's eyelids to have a better look at her eyes. "I'm going to order a blood test." She buzzed for the assistant to return.

"This may be unfamiliar to you, but to do blood tests here, we have to withdraw a small amount of blood. And we won't have the results until tomorrow. Yes, I know, we're fairly backward out here, but at least our processes aren't going to fail just because the supranet and the medianets go down." The doctor smiled and patted Jenda's knee. "We'll send someone to your unit tomorrow to let you know when we have the results. Meanwhile, here's something for the dizziness and I recommend that you drink plenty of liquids and try to get some rest. I'm also giving you an analgesic for fever and pain." She paused. "Do you want anything for anxiety?"

Jenda considered it but then said, "No. Thank you." She swallowed the pills the attendant placed in her hand and drained the cup of water.

As she walked back toward her quarters, Jenda told herself that the blood tests would surely reveal nothing more than a slightly elevated white blood cell count. Following doctor's orders, she lay down on the bed for a nap. Later she had a light supper followed by a shower. She started to unpack more of her things and then thought better of it; she didn't intend to be here long. A handful of Duermata guaranteed her a good night's sleep.

The next morning, she woke to the sound of someone knocking on her door. She sat up quickly and the room began to spin. Hoping she hadn't locked the door she called, "Come in!"

Jenda looked up and saw a man with a familiar face.

"Oh, my gosh! Jonathan?"

"Yep, it's me, Jen—your little brother Jonathan. Or maybe your older brother."

It was true. Jonathan looked almost Gen2, while Jenda was indistinguishable from Gen5. It was clear he had not been availing himself of Chulel for some years. Jenda rose unsteadily to give her brother a hug. "God, it's so good to see you, Jonathan. I've been worried, what with the corporate police and all. Have you heard from Granny El?"

"Wait. Corporate police? What do you know about that? And no, I haven't heard from Gran yet. Pulses are neither coming nor going right now. I was lucky to get the message you sent with the location of this place. If you sent it to Gran at the same time, though, I'm sure she got it. Things are getting pretty strange out there now, you know. It sounds like we may have a lot to talk about."

"I know," Jenda replied. "Well, at least I know a little about what's going on. Come sit beside me, little brother, and I'll tell you what I know if you tell me what you know. I've been awfully worried about you."

So Jenda told Jonathan about Recall and about the takedown and about her encounter with Selena, the policewoman from Marvaworld with his picture in her digilet.

"I'd hoped they wouldn't actually try to come after me," Jonathan frowned. "Gosh, Jenda, I'm really sorry you had to get caught up in this." He explained that his flick had been pulled back by Marvaworld because its storyline too closely aligned with real events involving some pretty powerful plutocrats. As a precaution, he had decided to take a leave of absence from his academic job and spend time with a friend in Arizona.

"How did you end up in a Book Community?" he wanted to know.

"I don't think it would have been my first choice, but apparently Montagne knew about the place and thought I'd be safe here."

"You could do worse. You know the people in these communities aren't all religious fanatics. Some are here just because they got fed up and wanted to get away. So you're back in touch with Montagne? And who is Luis?"

Jenda explained things as best she could. "I can't believe what a large chunk of my past was missing, Jonathan. I always thought Mom had gone completely crazy with all her stories about things that, as far as I knew, never happened. But it turns out she was right. It must've been painful for her."

"So you're telling me I have a niece out there?" Jonathan seemed pleased. "I'm not surprised that Paloma took care of her."

"Why do you think Mom remembered about my pregnancy when everybody else forgot?"

"Mom was always a bit moody," Jonathan said. "So she was on a couple of mood medications. Do you think that could have created resistance to the photonic memory process? I think Mom's art was the only thing holding her together after a while."

"I found a few of her sculptures," Jenda said, "and I brought them with me. I'll dig them out and show them to you later. Maybe you remember more about them than I do. About what they meant to Mom. You seem to remember an awful lot about our childhood. Why is that?"

"Just lucky, I guess. You know I'd gotten into meditation in my early teens. So when I first started getting the Chulel process with photonic memory restoration, being in a room all by myself seemed to me like a good opportunity to do some deep meditation." He laughed. "I had no idea it would protect me like it did. Are you feeling okay, Jenda? You look a little pale."

"I haven't been feeling too great. I went to the clinic yesterday and they should be getting back to me soon with some test results. I'm sure I'll be okay. I'm glad you're here. Are you staying? Have they given you a room yet?"

"Definitely staying," Jonathan replied, "for a while, anyway, if they'll let me. I need to go find out about getting a room. Shall I bring you some lunch so you don't have to go out?"

"Room service would be great. Thanks." Jenda gave her brother a smile and a hug.

While Jonathan went to find a room and settle in, Jenda sat on the floor next to her suitcases and rummaged through her things, looking for their mother's sculptures. There were only three. Jenda unwrapped them and set them on the desk in a line. They were all female figures and one of them seemed to have a slightly pregnant belly. *Why hadn't I noticed that before?* Jenda wondered.

She picked up the wrappings that had protected the figures. They were clearly some of her old Vintie attire. She shook out one of the blouses, which seemed to be made of a sturdy cotton, tightly woven and still strong after so many years. It had embroidery around the neckline and sleeves. Jenda held up the blouse to see if it still might fit. The embroidery, she realized, was hand done. As she examined the garment further, she discovered an area along one of the side seams that had been mended long before Vintie Jenda had gotten hold of it. She knew this because the stitches, although clearly executed by hand, were small and regular, the mark of someone who was caring for a garment rather than making a political statement. Jenda suddenly wished she knew where the blouse had come from, who had made it, who had worn it, who had mended it. She felt the blouse had a story and she wanted to be part of it. She took it down to the shared bathroom and washed it carefully in the sink. She squeezed it out and draped it on a towel over the porch railing to dry.

The effort of washing the blouse tired her out. She lay down on the bed for a rest and was about to drift off to sleep when she heard a knock on the door. Thinking it was Jonathan bringing lunch, she called, "Come on in, it's unlocked."

It wasn't Jonathan. It was the doctor.

"Feeling a little unsteady?" she asked Jenda.

"Yes. I'm sorry. I guess I sat up too quickly." Jenda wanted nothing more than to lie back down.

The doctor dragged the desk chair over next to the bed to sit down. "We got the blood test results," she said. "Your white cell count is high."

Jenda looked up quickly, feeling hopeful.

The doctor continued, "Your red cell count is low. Very low. Anemic."

Jenda braced herself on the edge of the bed with both arms as her head and shoulders sagged. She didn't want to look at the doctor. She didn't want to hear what came next.

"I'm truly sorry, but it looks like you've contracted the hemolytic virus," she said. "There isn't a specific test for the virus yet, but you have all the symptoms. And given that you've recently traveled in Central America, well, it seems clear."

Jenda looked up at the doctor. "So what you're saying is that I have something that's going to kill me," she said, surprised that her mind had gone so quickly to this conclusion.

The doctor took a deep breath. "Thus far, to the best of my knowledge, this virus appears to be a hundred percent fatal. So, yes, to be perfectly honest, this is most likely the thing that will end your life." She paused. "Do you have any religious preferences? We have a priest... a rabbi...an imam?"

"No. I've never been a Book person," Jenda said. "More of a Buddhist. Sometimes, anyway." Jenda couldn't think of anything to say. This was not part of the plan she and Luis had worked out.

"I've brought you some more medications that can help with the symptoms," the doctor was saying. She placed the bottles on the table next to Jenda's bed and reviewed instructions for their use. She shook a few tablets into a cup and handed them to Jenda along with a cup of water. "I brought the water jug and cup in case you didn't have anything available to keep you hydrated. The jug can be refilled from the tap. I'll bring in an oxygen apparatus tomorrow. You may not need it yet, but you'll soon find it useful."

Jenda nodded obediently and swallowed the medications.

"Do you have any questions?" the doctor asked.

Jenda slowly raised her gaze to look up at the doctor, her head cocked to one side. She almost smiled as she heard the echo of Malia Poole's voice telling her, "You need to ask more questions." She had so many questions now, but she didn't think the doctor had the answers.

There was another knock on the door and the doctor opened it to let Jonathan inside. They didn't have to tell him anything. He knew by looking at the doctor and at Jenda's stricken face what the diagnosis was. He set down the lunch tray and moved toward his sister.

"Won't he catch it?" Jenda asked the doctor, looking anxious as Jonathan moved toward her.

"No, dear," the doctor said. "All indications are that only regular and especially recent Chulel users are susceptible. He'll be fine. As will most of the people here. We'll warn a few of our newest arrivals about this, and for their sake we'll have to ask you to limit your movements."

Jenda said she understood. Tears had begun flowing down her face, but she didn't collapse into hysterical sobs as she might have done in the past. She felt oddly calm as her brother came and sat beside her on the bed and put his arm around her shoulders. She flashed on a toy she thought she must have had as a child, a tube you looked through toward the light to watch how the colored patterns changed as you turned the tube. She felt like her own pieces had suddenly fallen into a different pattern.

The doctor said she'd return in the evening. She set the chair back in its place and moved toward the door.

"Doctor." Jenda called her back. "I do have one question: How long?"

"Of course," the doctor said. "So far, in most cases...about a week. At most two weeks."

"Okay," Jenda said. "Thank you." She leaned against her brother's shoulder and looked down at her digilet, wishing desperately for it to give her some sign that she would be able to at least talk to Luis while there was still time.

"I brought your lunch, Jen. Do you feel like eating anything?"

Jenda said she didn't but thanked him anyway. "Maybe I'll eat a little bit later," she said, looking up at her brother and trying to smile. She noticed that he had tears in his eyes. "I'm glad you're here, Jon. I don't know what to say right now. I don't even know what to think."

"We don't talk about these things in our world, do we Jen? We did in my Buddhist training in Tibet. But the real thing is always different. We'll find a way through this. I'll be with you."

"I think I may need to lie down for a while now. The meds are making me feel drowsy."

When Jenda woke, her brother was gone, and it was dark. She thought she might be feeling a bit better, so she reached over to turn on the lamp. That made her feel a little dizzy, but it didn't make her want to throw up. The lunch tray was gone, but there was a glass of apple juice and a bowl of fresh Nutrichips on her side table. Jenda arranged her pillows and, sitting cross-legged on the bed, she ate a few chips and drank the juice. Then she picked up the pill bottles, one by one, trying to remember what time it had been when the doctor brought them to her. She swallowed one more of the dizziness pills, one analgesic, and more Duermata. Then she turned off the lamp and lay down. She stared into the darkness, trying to see more clearly this new pattern her life was taking. There were fewer pieces; she knew that. The pieces that stood for Luis-Martín Zenobia shone bright as crystals in the sun, but they seemed small and so far away. By the time she fell asleep, her hair and pillow were wet with tears.

33.

The limitations on Jenda's movements meant she was pretty much confined to her room and its immediate environs. Her meals would be delivered. "As long as you're able," the doctor told her, "you can take walks in the garden next to this building." The clinic put a hand lettered sign at the entrance, warning new arrivals to stay away.

The day after her diagnosis, Jenda and her brother explored the garden. As they approached the first bench, she was beginning to breathe heavily and asked to sit down. One of the oldest community residents was already occupying the bench, but he slid over to make room for them. He introduced himself and offered his sympathy for Jenda's illness.

"You know," he said, in his slightly hoarse old man's voice, "this is what God ordained from the beginning. You remember the story of the Garden of Eden? In the Garden human beings were at one with the Lord, but he chose to give them free will and they chose to disobey Him, to give in to the serpent's temptation and eat the forbidden fruit. From that day to this, human beings have been subject to old age and death. This Chulel thing offended God, you know." He paused. "I don't mean to say... I mean I'm genuinely sorry for your illness, miss." Neither Jenda nor Jonathan said anything, only nodding in acknowledgment of his story. "Well, I must go," the old man said, as he stood up and walked slowly down the path, leaning on his cane.

Jonathan and Jenda exchanged a quick look of mutual understanding. "Gosh, I haven't thought about the whole Garden of Eden thing in a long time," Jonathan said. "I used to wonder if maybe we all wouldn't have been better off if those two had taken a few more bites out of the apple. Seems we're still unclear about the difference between good and evil." He glanced at Jenda, and his eyes held a mischief that she found familiar. "And how come the snake had to be the bad guy? Honestly, I think knowing is always better than living in even the most blissful ignorance."

Jenda smiled in agreement.

It wasn't long before Jenda had to confess she was too tired to continue, and they walked back to her room. She lay down thankfully on her bed and took in a few deep breaths, trying to send more oxygen to her debilitated red cells. She felt as if her head was wrapped in cotton towels. She couldn't think clearly, and she was sure her lungs had shrunk. Only deep breaths pulled in enough air. She sat up slowly and reached again for the collection of medicine bottles on her table. She shook out a few tablets and swallowed them down with gulps of cooling water. Then she felt a sensation on her left wrist. Her digilet had come to life.

Jenda's heart pounded so hard she was afraid she might pass out. She closed her eyes for a second, willing her heart to behave, willing the digilet to produce a message from Luis. Then she unwrapped the digilet and snapped it flat. There was an image on the screen. Jenda tapped it and the familiar symbol of Interloc emerged. She stopped for a moment, her finger poised over the screen as she tried to recall the new access phrase Luis had given her. Then she remembered: "kukulcan&picaflor," the names of Luis' and Isabel's art galleries. She tapped the syllables into the device with trembling hands and waited as the message screen came up. There was nothing for her. Tears came to her eyes. She wanted to shout into the digilet to get Luis' attention. Time was running out. *I need to be rational,* she told herself. *It may take longer in rural Costa Rica for all this to get up and running.* She had no way of knowing that Luis was in Argentina, settling in at Max and Emily's cottage near San Ramon.

Jenda needed to leave a message, but she couldn't think what to say. How would she tell Luis? She decided to start with something easy:

POLILLA: Arrived safely. My brother is
here too. Sad to be away from you. Hope
you are well.

It wasn't much, but the rest would have to wait. Next she sent a message to Meli, and one to her grandmother. Jenda coiled the digilet back around her wrist.

She continued sitting bolt upright, her eyes wide, her heart shattered, her mind in turmoil. *One week,* she told herself. *Maybe two. I may never see Luis again. I will never get to know my daughter.*

Lying down at last, she tried to arrange her aching limbs comfortably. Tears welled up again as she hoped against hope that no one else would be sick. What if Luis caught it, too? What about Meli? And Montagne? Paloma would be okay; she stopped taking Chulel years ago. *I'm glad now I didn't go see Granny El. I wouldn't want her to get this illness. What's wrong with me anyway? Why am I just now thinking about how contagious this thing is?*

And then Jenda thought about all the people she worked with and about all the people in the café where she ate the grilled cheese sandwich and about everyone else she had been in contact with over the three days between leaving Costa Rica and arriving here at... She reminded herself she still needed to ask if this place had a name. As she finally fell into a light sleep, Jenda was also thinking about the infection she had introduced through the YJ screens and remembering having read once about someone called Typhoid Mary.

Jenda woke to the familiar chiming of an Interloc message on her digilet. She picked it up and smiled.

MURCIELAGO: ¡Hola, querida! ¿Qué tal?

Jenda took her time sitting up to avoid the dizziness, positioning a couple of pillows for support. Then she responded.

    POLILLA: Luis! So good to hear from
    you! Are you okay?

There was a pause. Jenda told herself that it was just the slow Novanet. Finally a response came.

    MURCIELAGO: Yes, fine here. So glad
    you made it to Lechuza safely! How are
    you doing?

So that was the name of this place. Jenda filed that bit of information away and tried to think what to say next. She couldn't lie. There was no time for lying.

    POLILLA: You sent me to a good place. But
    I'm ill.

Sitting in the warm sunshine under the vast blue sky outside the Feldmans' little cottage at the San Ramon estancia, Luis felt an icy shiver of dread. He refused it.

    MURCIELAGO: I'm sure you'll be fine in
    no time. Did you see the doctor?

    POLILLA: Yes. She says it's the VHA.

Luis' world shattered. The blue sky went dark, and his heart plunged into a black hole of sadness. In her little room at the Book Community of Lechuza, Jenda's face contorted as she struggled to contain her sorrow.

    POLILLA: Are you sure you're okay, my
    love? Please be okay!

    MURCIELAGO: I'm fine, querida. Except my
    heart is breaking. I haven't had Chulel
    in almost three years now. I'm sure I'll

```
be okay. Are they taking good care of
you? I can't believe this is happening.

POLILLA: What about Meli?

MURCIELAGO: I'm in Argentina now. I came
to see about Isabel. Meli and the rest
will join us here as soon as they can.

POLILLA: And everybody there is okay?
Have you heard from them to know that
they're okay? I don't know where I picked
up this illness and I worry.
```

Their connection was frustratingly slow. Jenda wiped the tears from her eyes and waited.

```
MURCIELAGO: You most likely picked it up
on the airplane. I haven't heard from
Montagne since I left, but everybody was
feeling fine then. Don't worry about us.
Just take care of yourself. How is your
brother?

POLILLA: He's fine and being very kind to
me.
```

Just as Jenda touched the screen to pulse this, a notice came up: "Connection lost. Please repair connection and try again." And then the screen went dark.

Jenda continued staring at the dark screen, trying to maintain her connection with Luis. She knew Luis was doing the same.

He was. And he knew she was.

Both of their faces were tear streaked. They both sat where they were, their hearts torn open.

There was a knock on Jenda's door. She reached for a tissue from the bedside table and dabbed at her face. "Come in," she called.

It was her brother. "You have a visitor," he said. Jenda scowled. This was not a good time for visitors. But as the door opened further, she saw that the visitor was Granny El.

"Granny, no! Jonathan, take her away. Please! No, you'll get the illness, Gran. Don't you understand? Jon, please..." Jenda was becoming hysterical. She pulled the bed sheet up in front of her face.

Granny El stepped forward. "Will you just calm down, Jenda?" she scolded. "I know exactly what I'm doing." Then her voice softened. "This is my choice. You know I wouldn't make a very good old lady. Other people may age gracefully, but I'm pretty sure I never would. No, better to go this way. I've had 165 years, you know. I'm okay with the idea that I'll be coming along right behind you." Her voice was quivering. She sat down on the bed next to Jenda to embrace her.

"Oh, Gran, why are you doing this?" Jenda held back for a moment and then returned her grandmother's hug. "Crazy old woman," she mumbled, as they clung to one another.

Granny El poured a glass of water for Jenda and examined the bottles on her bedside table. Jenda could see that Granny El intended to take charge of her care. Jonathan could see, too, and took his leave, promising to check back later.

Granny El pulled up a chair next to the bed. "So have you heard from that boyfriend of yours?" she asked Jenda.

"How did you know?" Jenda began, trying to remember if she had ever confessed to her grandmother that her affair during this last sabbatical was no mere dalliance.

"Oh, come on, Jen." Granny El's face crinkled into a smile. Jenda loved those crinkles. "I could see it in your eyes that something was different this time. Are you going to tell me his name now?"

Jenda smiled. "Luis," she said softly. "Luis-Martín Zenobia." Jenda even loved his name, and she loved saying it out loud to Granny El.

"Nice name. Now, if you're not too tired, maybe you'd like to tell me a little bit about him." And Jenda spent the next half hour conjuring up the living presence of Luis-Martín Zenobia, aware that her grandmother knew this was the best medicine she could offer.

"Do you know anything about Dad?" Jenda asked her grandmother, thinking maybe she had said enough about Luis for the time being and that perhaps the revelation that Granny El had a great-granddaughter could wait for later. "Do you know where he is?"

Granny El shook her head. "I haven't been in touch with him in years, Jen. Have you asked your brother?"

"I asked him yesterday," Jenda replied. "He said he only has an old contact phrase. He sent the location but hadn't heard anything back."

After her conversation with Granny El, Jenda napped, waking up only when she heard someone rapping on her door with a meal tray. She ate what she could and then went to the desk where she had piled some of the books and papers from her suitcases. She gathered up some of them and sat down on the floor, leaning against the side of the bed, facing the window, its blue curtains pulled back to let in the light.

She was still searching for something, but she hardly knew what it might be. She had brought such an odd assortment of things, such a jumble of puzzle pieces. She wanted desperately to fit more of them together while there was still time. She glanced through a few of her childhood journals. She picked up a sketchbook, one of the last ones her mother had used. It was filled with drawings of the girl depicted in the three statues as well as a mischievous looking boy. Jenda knew they were drawings—memories—of her and Jonathan. She turned the pages slowly, trying to imagine herself and Jonathan as the children in the sketches. She held the book up to the light to get a better view of one of the faded drawings and as she did so, a few pages fell into her lap from the center of the book. She picked them up and knew at once these were not pages of the sketchbook. They were pages written in her own hand, pages from one of her old journals. She looked at the date: April 20,

2030. These were pages from her missing year, from the days just before her journey to Argentina. Her hands shook as she smoothed out the folds and began to read:

These are hard times. Montagne says we must remain firm. We want a better world for our child than the one we live in now. The corporations press us all to destroy the beautiful treasures in our lives—the paintings, the books, the printed photographs of friends and family. They entice us into buying the shoddy goods they know will not last. We resist. Tonight Montagne and I and a few more friends will go to the 3Dec headquarters and put in place the installation I've been creating in Leticia's parents' garage. I'm doing this because I know I must do something. The corporations are killing us, seducing us into serving their needs and forgetting our own. We can't give in. We are the Vintage ones—we must keep sculpting light!

Those were the words she, Jenda Swain, had written more than ninety-five years ago. That was who she had been— a young woman trying to change the world, to shake people into awareness of what was happening, to stop the insidiously expanding control of the corporations.

It didn't work, did it, Jenda? she mused. Or maybe it just took longer than they had anticipated. Maybe it took something more than art installations. And yet... weren't those kinds of things still remembered and honored by the very ones who had brought about this final takedown? Wasn't it all part of the same pattern?

Jenda felt the kaleidoscope of her mind shift once again. The new pattern felt immense and powerful. The pieces fit. She placed the journal pages back inside the sketchbook and held it between her hands, feeling a strange composure, an unaccustomed peace. She felt ashamed for having been so focused on her own personal predicament. *I'm only one piece of the whole,* she thought. *But at least I'm part of it. And an active part.* She felt more certain than ever that what she had done at

YJ was right, that what was happening in the world outside this little community was necessary, despite all the pain and suffering. She suddenly remembered a moment from her past: Grandpa Ned was in the hospital, dying. He was on life support and the family had finally reached the decision to pull the plug.

Maybe that was it. That was what they had done.

She got up and cleared away everything from the desk except her mother's three sculptures and the two paintings of her own. When Jonathan arrived a few minutes later, she directed him to the table.

"I see you found your 'lady in blue,'" Jonathan said, picking up the painting of the Virgin of Lujan. "You told me about how you were haunted by this image when you came back from South America. Gosh, you even got a tattoo of her."

Jenda explained to Jonathan about the Virgin of Lujan and why the image had affected her so profoundly.

"No wonder she haunted you so! I'm glad you finally tracked her down," he said.

He picked up the other painting. "I remember this one, too. The clouds with those strange swirls of syllables are like a watercolor of Grandpa Ned's that used to hang in our hallway." Then he turned his attention to the sculptures, picking up each one and turning it over in his hands with obvious affection.

"What can you tell me about them?" Jenda asked.

"I think these were Mom's favorites of all the pieces she made of you," he said. "You were her dancing girl, dancing like that whenever you felt happy. Sometimes even when you were sad you'd dance this graceful, swaying dance. I'm not sure you ever took lessons, but you always danced. And this one...you were always reading books. Dad used to scold you about carrying around all that paper, all those old-fashioned books instead of using your screen." He picked up the one of the girl with the softly rounded belly. "You know, I wasn't at home around the time of your trip to South America, but I remember once when I visited—not long before Mom's accident—seeing her in her studio, clutching this statue and crying." Jonathan set the pregnant sculpture down and picked up the dancing one again. "Mom had trouble expressing affection," he said. "It was the way she was. She put all her emotion into her art. I think these pieces are how she loved you."

Jenda wiped away a stray tear. "I can't imagine how hard it must have been for Mom when other people's memories started disappearing. And we thought she was the crazy one!"

"I wish I'd been around more. She may have had problems, but she wasn't crazy."

"Can we talk a little about things that you remember from when we were children? Do you remember a classmate named Malia Poole?"

34.

Jenda woke early the following morning to the sound of her digilet telling her Recall was back. She unfurled it without sitting up. There was a message from Luis. She felt dizzy. It had been too many hours since her last medication or else the dizziness was just getting worse. Maybe both. She fumbled for the oxygen apparatus the doctor had brought and took a few nourishing breaths.

Luis' message indicated that he thought a voice connection was now possible and he left instructions. Jenda took her pills and arranged her pillows. Then she followed the instructions Luis indicated. She heard a buzzing. And then she heard Luis' voice.

"Hello? Jenda?"

"Yes, it's me. God it's so good to hear your voice!"

"I've missed your voice too, querida. How are you doing?"

"Okay, I think. Granny El got here yesterday." She explained how Granny El was intentionally exposing herself to the illness and how Jonathan had not been taking Chulel for many years now so he would be safe. "How is everybody there? Have you heard from Meli yet?" Jenda needed to know.

"We're all fine, Jen. Everybody is fine. I talked with Montagne earlier today and he and Meli and Paloma are all in good health. He's got Meli in isolation. Tao-Min is still overseas somewhere. I should tell you, though, Paloma refuses to leave Costa Rica." And then Luis explained to Jenda how Paloma said she could never leave the town with the technical college she had built with the money from Jenda's parents and the street they had named after her, and of course Meli wouldn't leave without Paloma, and so Montagne had decided to stay as well and finish setting up the sufficiency community to ensure that they all made it through.

Jenda said she understood and that she hoped they would all be okay.

"They all said to tell you they send their love. You can call them, too, if you like."

"Yes, I'll definitely do that."

"Are you really okay or are you just saying that. You can tell me, you know."

"I know, Luis. But I do think I'm okay." And she told him about the pages she had found in her mother's sketchbook and how she had felt when she read them. "So, yes, I'm sick," she said finally, "but so are thousands of other people. And our whole society has been sick for decades. This is how it ends for me, Luis, but I refuse to go out feeling sorry for myself."

"Montagne was right about you, Jenda. He told me that back in the day you were one of the strongest and fiercest women he knew."

"Do you remember when I asked you how long you expected to live?" she asked.

"I do. And do you remember what I told you?"

"I do. You said you expected to live to be a very old man. Well, it looks like that will happen. But not me. I'm kind of sorry that I'll never know what it's like to be an old woman. I mean, I may be 112, but I've never been old. And now I never will be. I've lived a lot of years, but I always felt like I was young, with my life still ahead of me. Not much ahead of me now. What do you think comes...you know... After? Can we talk about that?"

"That's one of the great questions of all time, querida. I've read a lot of stories about the things people believe in different cultures, in different religious traditions. But as for me... I guess I used to think it would just be the end. Like shutting your eyes and everything being gone. A natural enough process but not leading anywhere. Now I think I may have some of the same questions you have."

"Remember in my childhood journal when I wrote about my cat Milly? And how she died, and I was hoping that the Buddhists were right and that she would come back again in a new life? I still think I like that idea, only... I don't know if it's true or not. I think I'd like to come back and see what happens after all of this gets sorted out."

"Let's both come back, okay? I'll look for you."

Jenda laughed and agreed.

"I tried to find an airplane to bring me back to North America to be with you. But there's nothing running. Nothing at all, Jenda."

They both fell silent for a moment.

"Well, there is one thing," Luis said finally. "I think they've got things set up where we could do at least a brief session visually. Kind of like what used to be Chat². Shall we try?"

"By all means," Jenda replied. "I'd love to see your face. Although mine isn't going to look so good." She was searching for her hairbrush.

"Okay, just a minute and let me see if I can get this to work. Hang on. You'll need to switch on your camera."

There was silence at the other end and Jenda did as she was asked, combing her hair with her fingers as she waited. And then, suddenly, there was Luis' face on her tiny digilet screen.

"Oh, gosh, look at you. Your beard is getting long," she said. "Can you hear me okay? Is the picture coming through from my end?"

"Clear as a bell, querida. You look good. I can see you're a bit pale, but you're as beautiful as ever. What is that you're wearing?" Luis was smiling.

"Oh, this old thing?" Jenda offered a weak smile in return. "I guess it's one of my old Vintie outfits. It was wrapped around one of Mom's sculptures in the stuff I brought with me, so I washed it out and decided to wear it. Do you like it?"

"It looks beautiful on you. I think it suits you. Abuela Isabel and Max and Emily send their love. The Feldmans have started to have some success in piecing together Abuela Isabel's lost memories. She's remembering a little bit about Abuelo Arturo and about my mother and my uncle Julian. And do you remember she had those two books by a California author in her collection? Well, it turns out that this author, this Martin Jameson, was a professor she met at the college where she was teaching and apparently Isabel and Martin had quite the love affair."

Jenda smiled, imagining a young Isabel experiencing the kind of intense love she had for Luis. "Well, that's a good thing to remember, isn't it? It's always good to remember love."

Luis paused, and Jenda could tell by the rhythmic movements of the image that he was walking.

"You remember when we found the little dove on the sidewalk in San Antonio, querida?"

"I remember. You told me an old story about a bird and a snake."

"That's right. About a contest to see who human beings would be like—the snake that sheds its skin and lives forever or the bird that has to die."

"And the bird won, right?"

"Yes. The bird won."

"I've thought about that, Luis. You know, snakes don't really live forever. Why did those people ever think that?"

He laughed. "Wishful thinking, I guess, querida."

"Yeah, just like us. I think I'd rather be a bird. Or a bird-like human. Knowing."

"That's kind of what the legend meant to the people who told the story. It's the knowing that's important. I think I've begun to feel it since I gave up Chulel. I wish you were going to have more time to experience it. I wish we could experience it together."

Jenda saw his eyes glittering with unshed tears.

"I don't know how long this connection will last, mi amor, so I will say this now: I love you more than I have ever loved anyone in my life." His voice was shaking.

"And I love you, Luis-Martín, more than I ever believed I could love. You've given me my life back, helped me find myself again. If I could, I would be with you for a thousand lifetimes.

Will you look after Meli for me? I know she has Montagne and Paloma, and I know she's a grown woman, but..."

"Of course I'll look after Meli for you. I promise. Listen, our connection is fading. I'll call you back tomorrow, okay?"

"Yes, please," Jenda smiled weakly, feeling suddenly exhausted. "And the tomorrow after that."

And so Luis called Jenda every day until the day she didn't answer.

Luis was able to keep the community in San Ramon abreast of developments via the newly independent Novanet. They watched the story unfold about the collapse of the old order and the emergence all over the world of a variety of new possibilities. They couldn't be fully aware, however, of how the world outside their little community was disintegrating even more completely as people continued to succumb in massive numbers to the lethal blood disease. The fortunate ones were able to choose to do as Luis and his family and friends did—and as Jenda would have done—and resign themselves to eventually dying from old age, giving up Chulel to protect themselves from the fatal illness. Others chose to do what Granny El did and deliberately expose themselves to the illness in order to care for one another or to avoid the uncertainties of old age in a disordered society. Still others took more direct action via drug overdoses or other means.

As the years passed in their little community Luis and his grandmother and their friends Max and Emily—and, after the death of Silvestre, Rosalí as well—would sit around in the evening reading from one or another of Isabel's precious books. Or they would look at the paintings Luis was working on. Many of his paintings were images of a superhero, a dancing female superhero who looked a lot like Jenda and who wore a beautifully embroidered billowing blue superhero cape.

Or they would tell stories. And as one of them would begin to forget, someone else would remind them by telling them a story and then that one would pretend to remember. One of their favorite stories was about when Jenda was a little girl in San Ramon and had a white cat named Milly. They all remembered Jenda's cat, and they would nod and smile, remembering. And then one day the cat had died and Jenda and Paloma and Rosalí had buried it in the back garden, in the shade of the jacarandas and fruit trees that Silvestre and his father had planted.

"But that was after Meli was born, wasn't it?" Emily would ask.

"Oh yes," Rosalí said. "Because the cat was there when Meli was born. It was such a beautiful white cat." Isabel remembered that, too.

After a while even Max and Emily remembered that one, and when he was the only one left it was one of Luis' most treasured memories.

Acknowledgments

Way of the Serpent has its roots in a lifetime of studying humanity and a lengthy career in anthropology, but the story began to take form only around mid-2014. I have been encouraged and assisted (and occasionally chastised) in the process of writing the story by a host of friends and colleagues, including Maria Elena Sandovici, Sangye Teresa O'Mara, Richard Crossland, Patt Brower, Valerie Pheasant, Teresa Roberson, Cheryl Rooke, Catalina Castillon, and Steven Zani. I am deeply grateful to each and every one of them. I also owe a debt of gratitude to Madeline Caldwell, who provided valuable editorial insight on an earlier draft of the book and to Danielle Hartman Acee of Author's Assistant who shepherded me through the revisions for a second printing. None of these people is responsible for the final outcome; I accept that burden fully and happily.

The story referenced in the epigraph is Silvina Ocampo's "Forgotten Journey," recently published in English in *Thus Were Their Faces: Stories*, translated by Daniel Balderston (New York Review Books, 2015). I also refer to a documentary film about the Dani people of New Guinea entitled "Dead Birds." It is by legendary documentary filmmaker Robert Gardner and available from Documentary Educational Resources. I would also like to acknowledge Jason Wilson, author of *Buenos Aires: A Cultural History* (2012: Interlink Publishing). His book helped me greatly in imagining what that city might be like in the 22nd century world I created.

--Donna Dechen Birdwell (2015)

Way of the Serpent was originally published under separate cover in 2015.

THE RESISTANCE

Shadow of the Hare

Before all my teachers
and all my students,
I bow in deepest gratitude.

*The hare offered
its own body
to the hungry Buddha and,
in gratitude for its selfless virtue,
the Buddha traced
its form
upon the
moon.*
– Jataka Tale

Part I
Before

I.

The café was down a couple of side streets, in an area of Dallas I hadn't visited for decades. As soon as I sat down I saw her, and I couldn't help but stare. It had to be Jenda. When I saw her looking at me, I slid down off the barstool and walked over to her table.

"You're Jenda Swain," I said, smiling, hoping she'd say, *And you're Malia Poole!* But she didn't. I hadn't seen her in almost ninety years, and it was clear she'd been taking the age prophylaxis, the miracle drug called Chulel that kept everyone young in our 22nd-century world. Almost everyone. She was giving me that look—that "what-the-zujo-is-an-old-woman-like-you-doing-in-my-world" look—followed by the averted eyes.

"Of course you don't remember," I said. I pulled out a chair and sat down across from her. "Nobody remembers much of anything anymore." I looked down at my wrinkled, age-splotched hands and then up into her smooth, fresh face. It was hard to believe I was two years younger than Jenda. "I idolized you and your boyfriend, you know. Such temerity! The things you did…" I was hoping to elicit some of those things from her or perhaps startle myself into recalling what some of them were.

She said nothing, glancing around the café as if to offer an apology for my presence. For my existence.

A memory suddenly came to me: A full-color portrait of Jenda as she was in high school. Not this business-suited twit, but a passionate firebrand of a girl. An artist?

"Do you still paint?" I wasn't giving up. "You always had your mom's gift for art."

Jenda was clearly embarrassed and growing quietly angry. But I thought I detected the old passion under the surface. *Come on Jenda—show me some of the old spunk.*

She avoided my gaze. "I think you must have made some mistake." Her tone was flat, dismissive. "You may know my name, but you clearly don't know me."

Her face flushed slightly, and I thought I saw a glimmer of recognition in her eyes. Leaning forward, I looked into those eyes. "You need to ask more questions," I said. I pushed my chair back and rose to go; then I looked down at her one last time. "You're the one who doesn't know who Jenda Swain is."

My tears began to fall as soon as I was out on the street. I felt betrayed. *Damn these disconnected memories!* I have more memories than most people these days, but there's that one year from high school—the period when I'm sure I knew Jenda best—that's always been a blank. At least until recently. It's cruelly ironic that now I've reached an age when normal memories start to fade, these submerged ones begin to wash up like shards of sea glass on a beach. I write them down, cataloging them like curios of uncertain provenance.

After I left the café, I couldn't stop thinking about Jenda. She felt like a key to something. I may not remember a lot about her, but I do know that up-tight little prude with the pressed lapels isn't the girl I knew in high school. I'm sure that back then she was a passionate Vintagonist. Something had happened to her; I thought I knew what it might be. In any case, I knew it was something very different from what happened to me.

I still identify with Vintagonists, those people who cherish and preserve old things, not as things in themselves but as links to our past, reminders of shared experiences, repositories of our stories. In the late 2020s and into the '30s, the Vintagonist movement was popular among young people like me and Jenda Swain. While the corporations pushed us toward ever-higher consumption of infinitely recyclable short-cycle goods, Vintagonists celebrated antiques, vintage things, and so-called mementos. To signal our nonconformity, we wore badly mended clothes salvaged from the recycle bins, dyed our hair in shades of sepia, and adorned ourselves with relics like lockets and watch pendants. I still wear one of those, although mine has a more personal significance. We fed one another's rebelliousness in frequent meetings and acts of protest that employed poems and songs and art. The movement dissipated after a while but never went away. Its roots ran deep.

Almost a century later, I feel once again the pull of those old ideas, a riptide tugging at my foundations. I'd found a place where I could have lived out the rest of my days in peace without having to deal with the outside world, but instead here I am, walking around in the corporate fantasyland where everyone is young and cheerful and bright. But it's a flat white brightness—no spark, no color. People stare at me (like Jenda did) but they don't see me at all. I disappear. I don't belong in their world and so they white me out.

I made my way back toward my sister Leticia's habitat. I knew she'd organized an event for the following night at her place. She'd told me that Jenda's high school boyfriend Montagne would be there. I hadn't seen him for decades. Maybe Montagne would have some answers. I'd told Jenda she should ask more questions; maybe it was time for me to ask some questions of my own.

I feel like a refugee here, uncertain about what comes next. Uncertain, too, about some of what went before, during that blank period around the age of fifteen. The past, for me, has generally been constructed from old novels; I adore historical novels. But with these strange memories drifting back, I think it's time to reconstruct my own past, my personal history, and to find out just how much I can recall.

2.

My childhood memories present the usual montage of holidays, birthday parties, sibling quarrels, and endless school days, punctuated by family trips to beaches or amusement parks. I was born in 2015 and was named after one of the daughters of the President of the United States. I always believed—as I suppose most children do—that my family and everything we did was normal and natural. We were neither poor nor privileged, or at least we didn't think we were.

Mine was the last generation to grow to adulthood in the world before the youth miracle of Chulel. We're known as Gen3. Our parents are Gen2, our grandparents Gen1. There are now four more generations and while Gen7 are still identifiable as children and youths, Gen3 through Gen6—the ones who faithfully take Chulel—are indistinguishable from one another. Gen7 is probably the smallest generation of *Homo sapiens* since the Stone Age. The plutocrats decided we had enough people to meet their needs and, with few exceptions, we've complacently capitulated. Mine was also the last generation before the establishment of the corporate-run educational boarding colonies, where people have sent the final few generations of children to be professionally reared.

In early adolescence, I began to wake up to the world outside my family circle. I was an avid reader, and as corporate profitability increasingly pressed us toward digital materials in place of printed paper books, I rebelled. Of course, my fascination with books had begun long before this. My first acquisition was something I'd spotted in a recycling bin while my parents were busy shopping. I was drawn to the colorful picture on the cover and the orderly configurations of lines that I didn't yet recognize as words. I picked up the book and tucked it inside my coat. "Stealing" and "theft" were not part of my vocabulary; I couldn't have been more than three.

Over the years, I surreptitiously collected more and more such treasures, their preciousness increasing once I was initiated into the mysteries of written language. I began purchasing them once I had the resources to do so and knew where to look. I spent increasing hours not only reading but arranging and rearranging my books on the shelves in my bedroom, finding sensual pleasure in the feel and smell and weight of them, the hard squareness of their corners, the colors and images on their covers, the textures of their papers. The occasional, inevitable paper cut was a blood bond. My twin sister Sophia's room, by contrast, was almost empty, bare except for the sleek screen on one wall where she watched endless hours of flicks and read the words of books. For me, books were so much more than words.

It was in one of the secondhand bookshops I frequented that I first encountered Vintagonists. These people—mostly disgruntled youths like me—seemed to love books as much as I did. Through them I broadened my interests to include old garments, antique jewelry, printed photographs, maps, and paintings. My private fetish morphed into public activism. It was sometime during this transformation, I believe, that I met Jenda Swain and her boyfriend, Montagne Williams.

And then there's that gap, around the age of fifteen, for which memories have been not simply elusive, but absent. My therapist said once that it was probably PTSD. Perhaps she was right, but I was convinced there'd been some photonic meddling with my mind, too. She offered to try and help me recover the missing memories, but for some reason the prospect of remembering why I didn't remember sent shivers of terror through every nerve in my body, so we never tried.

I just remember waking up one day in 2031 in my bedroom in Philadelphia, pissed as hell. I didn't remember moving from Dallas to Philly. I was angry because most of my books had been left behind. My twin sister Sophia was gone, too, sent off to boarding school. Shortly after the move, I celebrated my sixteenth birthday. "Sweet Sixteen" they called it, although "sweet" is not one of the words people have generally used to describe me. It was the first birthday I celebrated without Sophia.

I shouldn't have minded so much, since my twin sister and I had already parted ways sometime earlier. As I became passionate about Vintagonism, she and her friends responded by disparaging the entire movement. Sophia embraced cynicism, celebrated nihilism. I later came to suspect that she might have been onto something; believing in nothing conveys a certain immunity to disillusionment. My own passion for worthy causes, on the other hand, has ended mostly in misery, in disappointment that feels like betrayal. I missed Sophia, in spite of our differences. We made an effort to keep in touch, but over the years it became perfunctory and eventually we found it sufficient to pulse one another at holidays and on our shared birthday.

I finished high school in our neighborhood there in Philly at what was called at the time a public school. It was, as I recall, supported by some local governing body. There were still functioning governments in the late 2020s and elections were held for various offices of the state of Pennsylvania as well as the United States of America right up to 2044. I only voted a couple of times after I became eligible in 2033. Hardly anybody voted by that time. We were resigned to the fact that the so-called governing bodies—from city councils right up to the Congress and President of the United States—were all a sham. The turnout for elections kept dwindling and after the 2044 election the plutocracy decided that their wealth would be better spent on less divisive entertainments, so elections were discontinued.

Nothing could obliterate my love of books and in Philadelphia this led me once again into a nest of Vintagonists—"Vinties". My desire to bond more closely with the authors of books had long since prompted me to try my own hand at writing. Now, with a fearlessness born of naiveté and with encouragement from my Vintie friends, I began publishing poems and flash fiction in a couple of underground 'zines. When it came time for me to go to university, choosing a major was easy: I would major in writing and literature.

"Are you sure?" my father asked, looking thoroughly skeptical. "What kind of profession will that prepare you for?"

Trying to ignore the fact that he'd ended a sentence with a preposition, I sat in sullen silence.

"I think she's got her heart set on it, Herbert." My mother tried so hard to understand me, to take what she saw as my part in such conversations.

My older sister Leticia was already attending university in Texas and what she'd told me of her experience was not inspiring. Leti had always dreamed of being a dancer, but Dad had talked her out of pursuing dance as a career. "Nobody makes a living as a dancer anymore," he'd told her. It was true that live performances were dying out, since real dancers could never measure up to the soaring feats of their convincingly realistic digital avatars on screen. So she'd reluctantly decided on a degree in retail management. She hated every minute of her online classes and retail simulations. And then she had to do an internship.

"An internship!" she fumed when we chatted on our screenphones. "In other words, I have to do time as an unpaid shop clerk and submit written reports. Never mind. I'll do the damn degree. And then we'll see."

I knew she was still hanging out with the Vintie crowd. Leticia was always a supporter, an ally of the Vintagonists, but for her there was little of the passion that drove me. Hers was a matter-of-fact, logical association. She was our sensible sister.

I enrolled for my first semester as a writing major and Dad was pleased to learn that my class schedule would include "Suasive Composition" and "Literary Memes in Advertising". I was dismayed. About halfway through the semester I found a job and stopped attending classes. I didn't even bother to check in online, which would have been easy enough. Several people I knew would play the online classes while they did other things and then opt for the test at the end. They said if you were halfway intelligent you could fake your way through the tests. I was too honest to do that. When my report came in at the end of term, my parents demanded an explanation of my uniformly failing grades. I had nothing to say except that I was moving out of the house, into an apartment with a couple of friends in Washington, D.C.

That apartment in D.C. was simultaneously the most dreadful and the most wonderful place I've ever lived. I'd gotten a job at a bookshop and the apartment was above it, two floors up. The only windows opened onto a noisy street. The antiquated heating and cooling systems were inefficient and sometimes declined to work at all. The pipes rattled and whined, and water pressure was unpredictable. But the place had real wooden floors and doors, brass doorknobs and hinges, ceramic fixtures in the bathroom and kitchen, and a vintage chandelier whose crystal pendants were encrusted with the bad habits of those who had dwelt there before us.

I lived with my two best friends, Beatrice and Zelda. It was a two-bedroom apartment and, since I was the youngest and the latest addition, I slept on a cot shoved up against a wall in the dining room. It was an antique army cot, the kind with canvas stretched over a collapsible wooden frame. The canvas had begun to rot, and I was never sure it wasn't going to split and spill me onto the floor. The cot was ugly and smelled of mildew and fermented sweat, but I loved it because it was old. Vintage. I tried to make it presentable by covering it with a turquoise satin comforter, tattered around the edges, that I'd nabbed from a recycling bin. I hadn't noticed the massive stain on one side of the comforter when I'd picked it up. I tried to tell myself it wasn't a bloodstain. I cleaned it as best I could and spread it across my little cot with the stained side down. Occasionally, though, in the middle of the night, I'd think about that stain, think about how it might have gotten there, and I'd turn the comforter over, distancing myself from this unwanted proximity to a stranger's misery.

Beatrice was the eldest of our threesome by a few years. She'd actually completed her university degree and although I told her I admired her for that, I secretly harbored a sense of superiority for having been clever enough to see through the duplicity of university education. Of course, since her degree was in what used to be called computer programming, I thought perhaps her experience had been different from mine. Beatrice was also the only one of the three of us who held a job that paid decent wages.

Zelda, like me, was a college dropout. She'd been a music major and had stuck with it for two years before yielding to exasperation with a curriculum focusing increasingly on technology and marketing. Zelda was a brilliant guitarist and had a voice that could morph from lilting warble to seductive whisper to screaming banshee in a single breath. Her room was full of guitars and electronic equipment, but her favorite instrument was a vintage Martin D45. Zelda had acquired enough skill from her university program to qualify for a low-level job at a music production company, but she also had gigs a few nights a week in pubs and wine bars and coffeehouses. Her acoustic performances always attracted the Vintie crowd.

The bookshop where I worked—Codex2—was, of course, a secondhand shop. The corporate houses had stopped publishing new print books by the early 2030s. Digital books were so much easier to manipulate, so much easier to tweak to fit changing corporate needs. My Vintie friends and I spent hours examining the latest digital issues of books alongside old print copies of the same book and marking all the points where the new version deviated from the original. After they set me up on an underground website, I blogged our findings.

Codex2 was one of the only places to find books in one of the so-called minority languages. There were officially six corporate languages, rapidly being reduced to only two—English and Chinese—which were converging in an odd way with the adoption of syllabic forms of writing both languages digitally. Some of my favorite customers were the ones who came in searching for something to read in a language that embodied their literacy-starved cultural identities. These customers usually arrived in pairs, interlocutors sharing conversation and stories in a dying language. Among my favorites were a couple of sisters who said they were from a country that used to be called Syria. They wore soft scarves around their shoulders and modestly draped them over their heads as they searched out our latest acquisitions in Arabic. They preferred books of poetry, and I would sometimes conceal such a book behind the counter, saving it for the Syrian sisters.

There was also a Vietnamese couple—husband and wife—who invariably pulled every book in Vietnamese off the shelf (there were rarely more than three) and then discussed, volubly and at length, the various merits of each book. At least I assume that's what they were discussing. They always spoke Vietnamese, enjoying the safety of speaking an unsanctioned language in our little shop.

I got to know most of our patrons. In those early years we chatted openly and fervently about literature and the state of our American culture.

"Of course, it's not just America." Zelda's brother Lio mentioned this to me one day at our favorite pub, the Quill & Sheaf, while we were waiting for Zelda's next set to begin. Lio had traveled more than the rest of us had. I'd always loved reading novels about foreign countries, but Lio had been there and could tell stories in first person.

"These plutocrats have no national or cultural identities," Lio continued. "They respect no national boundaries. They're a world unto themselves and they're everywhere. You know they're adopting a lot of the techniques that used to be used only by governments. Totalitarian governments."

"Like what?" I asked.

"For example," he said, slanting his thick dark eyebrows toward his perfectly angled nose, "the Chinese government devised mechanisms for subdividing the internet, controlling most of it for exclusive government use and permitting ordinary people access to only approved zones which were, by the way, invariably slow and prone to conveniently timed breakdowns. Now the plutocrats are doing the same thing here." He tried to explain to me the difference between the supranet, medianets, and something he called the infranet. I wasn't certain I understood the details, but I got his point.

"You realize, Malia, that governments are on the verge of becoming obsolete. Already they work only at the bidding of the plutocracy. And now more and more of those elected to government positions are themselves plutocrats. At some point they'll stop convening the legislatures and parliaments, close the presidents' and prime ministers' and governors' offices, and pay the judges one last time and send them home with fat pensions. And we won't notice the difference, because there won't be any."

"What will happen to people like us?" I asked.

"As long as we behave ourselves like good consumers, we'll just keep doing our part to keep them rich and getting richer."

"That's not what I meant." I scowled at Lio. "I meant people like you and me."

"Time to listen to music," he said, turning toward the stage where Zelda and her band had finished tuning.

3.

As the years went by, it became increasingly difficult to be people like us—Vintagonists, dissidents of all kinds. The story industry was deeply discouraging. The consolidation of publishing houses continued, with emphasis more and more on whether a writer could sell merchandise rather than whether they could write stories worth reading.

Ironically, it was the independent publishing movement that gave the plutocrats their most direct control. Well, not the independent publishing houses. A few of those went underground and continued to turn out books and magazines, both digital and print, that were eminently worth reading. It was the self-publishing movement that proved most vulnerable. Mekong was the biggest self-publishing outlet and also the biggest story merchant. Their takeover of the remaining print retailers in the late 2020s marked the beginning of the end for print books as well as for anything resembling free expression.

In addition to destroying the time-honored traditions of storytelling and generally muddying the notion of truth, the rising plutocracy also managed to subvert an important facet of the environmental movement. Physical books came to be identified with the destruction of forests and people were seduced into submitting old books for recycling, thinking this was a way of saving the world's forests, when really it was a way for the plutocrats to sell more of their digital books and, more importantly, the ever changing devices and platforms for reading them. It was also a convenient way to get rid of evidence that things had ever been any different from the way the plutocrats wanted things to be.

And then there was Chulel.

Up until 2045, this miracle drug that prevented aging had been very expensive and used only by those who could afford it. But everyone could see its effectiveness. Those who had begun using it when it was first introduced in 2025 had not aged at all in twenty years. Then came the announcement that Pharmakon, the drug's manufacturer, was introducing a new and improved and more affordable form of Chulel. People were ecstatic.

This announcement was quickly followed by a firestorm of media reports about consistent Chulel users experiencing devastating memory loss. So Pharmakon partnered with the social media firm Your Journal to offer high-tech photonic memory restoration procedures in conjunction with Chulel treatments. By "partnered", I mean they bought Your Journal.

People were relieved, pacified, content. The low-cost accessibility of the miracle age-defying drug in special clinics dedicated to protecting everyone's precious memories solidified people's convictions that the plutocrats were the ones who truly had our best interests at heart and who had the means to best serve those interests. The willingness of people to entrust their memories and life stories—that is to say, their minds—to Your Journal and to show up obediently at the Chulel clinics for "memory restoration" solidified the plutocrats' control over the populace at large. Ironically, this development had an opposite effect on me. As long as I could get Chulel without the memory restoration, I used it. But when the corporate Chulel spas became the only option, I refused to continue. I had my reasons.

For years after moving to D.C., I still went home to Philadelphia for winter holidays, which most people continued to call Christmas, although they'd long been nothing more than a festival of material consumption and overeating. Leticia joined us when she could. It was a long way from Dallas to Philly and, being a simple shopkeeper, she didn't always have enough credits for the plane or enough days off to come and go by train. Sophia could have come every year, but she didn't. After finishing her advanced training in flickmaking, she'd secured a good job with Marvaworld, the leading entertainments corporation. She had no time for us.

My parents, like most people of their generation, had been thrilled about Chulel and went faithfully every year for their treatments with memory restoration. I eventually concluded that the photonic process wasn't that effective, because as the years went by, they seemed to remember less and less about our shared past. They were, however, always up on the latest gadgets, fads, fashions, and entertainments. Eventually, there wasn't much to talk about and I, too, stopped going home to Philadelphia.

Lio and I became a couple. I can't say we fell in love, because it wasn't like that, or at least not like the stories I'd read about people falling in love. We started hanging out together. Lio became my best friend, which was good, because by that time Beat had a boyfriend and Z a girlfriend and these relationships were taking up more and more of their time, leaving them less time to spend with me. First Beat's boyfriend moved into the apartment and then Z's girlfriend. So I moved out. I went to live with Lio.

"So, are we putting your things in the spare bedroom or are we going to share a bedroom?" Lio asked with a teasing grin as we carried the first of my boxes up the stairs to his place. It was a good question. At that point, we hadn't had sex.

"Can we just put them in the living room for now?" As soon as I said that I felt foolish. Most people assumed we were having sex already. Most people didn't know me like Lio did. They didn't know how weird I was about sex. I was happy enough reading about it. I found it fascinating. But I'd come to realize that other people often experienced some degree of arousal when reading such passages. I felt nothing. I thought for a while I might be lesbian. But no, for all that I resisted Lio, I was not drawn to women at all. Maybe I was asexual, but that didn't feel quite right either. I decided that if we were living together it was time to figure myself out. So I put a few of my things into Lio's room.

I took a long shower that evening, thinking about whether I really wanted to do what I was about to do. *You need to get over this, Malia,* I told myself. *You know you love Lio. It'll be okay. This is what people do.*

I put on my pajamas and stared at myself in the mirror, brushing my hair, putting on a little lip-gloss. Delaying. With a deep sigh, I took off the bottom half of my pajamas. I folded them carefully and laid them on the counter.

When Lio saw me enter the bedroom, clad only in a pajama top, he smiled and swept me into his arms. That felt good. His kiss was good, too. A warm feeling crept right through the core of my body. He guided me over to the bed and I lay there, watching him remove his own clothes. When he turned toward me, I saw his erection and I panicked. I may have screamed, but I know I burst into tears and ran into the bathroom, trembling with a fear I couldn't explain.

"Malia?" Lio stood outside the bathroom door. "I'm sorry, Malia," he said. "I thought this was what you wanted. I don't understand. But we can work this out. You know I love you."

I opened the door. "I love you too, Lio. Will you just hold me? Please?"

And he did. Lio was patient, putting up far longer than he probably should have with my reticence, my unreasonable bouts of crying. We'd been living together for several months before I finally let go, let him come to me completely. After that, I learned to like having sex with Lio. Eventually, I liked it a lot. I never gave myself to any other man but Lio.

Lio—Eliomar Gaston—had learned the craft of repairing and refinishing musical instruments in the Menders' colony of Havana in southern New Mexico near the Rio Grande River. It was where he and Zelda grew up. Menders were people who, like Vintagonists, rejected the rampant, ravenous consumerism foisted on us by the plutocrats. But, unlike Vintagonists, Menders actually knew how to repair, refurbish, and reconfigure things so they would still be useful. Lio specialized in stringed musical instruments—guitars, violins, cellos. He preferred working with the ones made of real wood as opposed to the composite materials characteristic of the vanguard 3D-printed instruments. He could play all of them, although he couldn't play guitar quite like his sister. He'd inherited a cello from a musician who'd had several, and sometimes he'd play it for me. I think the cello is the most beautiful instrument in the world, perfectly matching the register of the human voice, able to bend tones in such a conversational way.

Lio also knew how to fix all kinds of other things, and if he didn't know, he'd figure it out. Fixing things was irregular work and didn't pay terribly well. It was also frowned on by the corporate authorities, who preferred people toss old stuff away into recycling and buy new. Repair work wasn't yet a punishable offense. To earn his livelihood, Lio worked for a retail distribution company, managing delivery drones. I think they liked the fact that when Lio was on duty, the drones never seemed to break down.

Lio got me one of the new communication devices, which were called "digilets." These had all the functions of the best screenphones but were based on a new type of flexible screen with colloidal memory drive that allowed a good-sized screen to coil around your wrist, snapping flat when you took it off. The input surface, instead of being hard, was a bit squishy, so instead of entering a "click" or a "tap", we "cushed". It was a clever device, and since I was someone who was always misplacing a screenphone, the digilet was ideal. Lio had one, too, so we could always be in touch. Beat helped us script the digilets to link up with the infranet, a digital space in the interstices of the internet, somewhere out of range of the plutocrats.

Protest and other dissident activity became increasingly risky around the time of the lost memories panic. Community police were being replaced by corporate police forces that answered only to the plutocrats who employed them. It had all begun with the outsourcing of police functions to private security firms. After a while, it became a simple matter of switching their contracts over from the coterie of plutocrats representing themselves as city governments to the plutocrats representing the plutocracy.

One of the targets of corporate policing was compliance with new ordinances—corporate ordinances—demanding the submission of quotas of paper materials for recycling. That was something Vintagonists—and especially a Vintie book-shop—couldn't do.

Codex2 was raided on July 4, 2045.

The shop was prepared. Most of our books had been sequestered at other locations, leaving the shelves empty of everything but the books we held in multiple copies. We hated to sacrifice even those, but we defiantly insisted we should stay open as long as we could.

If only I'd been so prepared myself. I was minding the shop on my own when the seven police officers entered the shop, guns drawn, shouting at me to come from behind the counter with my hands raised. Seven cops with guns against a handful of books and one lonely bookseller! I couldn't believe it. I was quickly cuffed and guarded by one of the officers while the other six swept all our remaining books into recycle bins, taking perverse pleasure in stepping on the books that fell to the floor, kicking them over to fellow officers while they all laughed.

My Codex2 friends had tried to prepare me. I'd been told that if anything like this ever happened, I was to comply and cooperate. If questioned, I was to say I was only an employee and knew nothing about the business. But when it finally happened I was scared. Scared and angry.

What I was least prepared for was being taken into custody. Somehow, I'd thought that once they had all the books they'd let me go. They didn't. I was locked into a police autocar, all alone, and dispatched to a corporate detention facility, where I was left in the car for nearly an hour before anyone came to get me. Inside the facility I was photographed and documented via handprints and iris scans. Then I was conducted to an interrogation room.

What happened next was not so much an interrogation as it was an indoctrination. It began with a flick that showed sweeping views of majestic forests accompanied by swelling digital symphonic music. Involuntarily, my heart opened to the beauty of it all. If they'd stuck with the flick and the music, they might have had me, but as the images moved to timber-cutting and stacks of books, they started interspersing brilliant light flashes and explosions of white noise. As soon as that began, something in me shut down. My eyes went tight shut as my heart pounded and my muscles tensed. I wanted to run away but that wasn't an option. My head pulsed and tingled. I started to moan, and the sound of my own voice comforted me. I recalled one of Zelda's tunes and hummed it to myself softly, focusing on that, blocking out whatever was going on in that room outside my head.

I don't know how long it went on, but after what seemed like an eternity, the room went dark and silent. I continued humming to myself and didn't open my eyes until I heard the door open. My face was wet with tears, and I guess that pleased them. I was taken to another room where they administered what amounted to a quiz. Although I hadn't watched their presentation, I'd watched enough to know what it was about, so it was easy to give them the answers they wanted. I was rewarded with some free passes to one of the big flicks venues and a new digital reader—latest model, they said—loaded with what they told me were some of the week's bestselling titles. It also contained my pre-loaded identity for access to Your Journal. They gave me passes for the autobus and said I could go home.

I was dizzy, nauseated, exhausted. I needed to gather myself together from whatever disparate places they'd flung me into. I didn't want to get on a bus in that state, so I started to walk, unsure of where I was and with no idea at all where I was trying to go. As I began to feel calmer, I stopped at one of the bus porticos to orient myself. I was only a few blocks from the Quill & Sheaf.

Arriving at the pub, I ordered a beer and began sipping it slowly. The tang and fizz began to bring me back into myself. I looked across the bar into the mirror. *God, I shouldn't be out in public looking like this,* I thought. That made me smile, and my smiling face looked so much better than the scared one that I decided to order a second beer.

I caught sight of Lio in the mirror about the same time he caught sight of me. I knew he'd come; we'd always said that if anything every happened this was where we'd meet.

"Malia! Are you okay?" He hurried over and, after a reassuring hug, took a barstool next to mine. "I heard what happened. They said you were there by yourself."

I started to cry again and Lio put his arm around me and handed me a fistful of paper napkins from the bar. He ordered himself a beer. I managed to pull myself together enough to tell him about my experience at the bookshop and at the corporate police center.

"It's that photonic cognitive procedure," he said. "I'd heard that the corporate cops were starting to use that on detainees. God, Malia, are you sure you're all right? That's pretty powerful stuff. Fiercely invasive."

"I don't think they got to me. I kind of shut down. Shut it out." I turned and grinned at him. "They gave me prizes for passing their stupid quiz."

We laughed.

Somewhere along the line, my digilet had gone missing, so Lio pulsed Z and Beat to let them know I was okay. Before we'd finished our beers, they both showed up and, after hugs and a few more tears, I had to tell my story again. Beat cautioned me about Your Journal, promising to show me how to use it to please the corporate surveillors without betraying myself or my friends. As I listened to myself telling the story, I began to realize that it was one of those stories that you end up telling over and over for a very long time, the kind of story you eventually end up hearing from someone else, barely recognizing it as something that ever happened to you.

4.

Codex2 went underground. Literally. It moved into a basement room under the Quill & Sheaf, behind the old wine racks. I started working the bar while really working for Codex2, taking known friends down to peruse the books.

The whole Chulel thing became more complicated. I'd been avoiding it. I was still young, so it didn't seem important. As a barmaid, however, I was encouraged to preserve my youthful appearance. The promises of memory restoration still put me off. There was something about my blank period that felt like I shouldn't tamper with it and those feelings had been reinforced by my experience with the corporate police. Some of my Vintagonist contacts offered to get me Chulel off-market, so I accepted and started taking it on my own. No memory restoration. I promised myself I would be observant, mindful of any memory lapses that might be attributable to the drug, prepared to stop using it if anything like that showed up. It never did.

I remember the year 2053, the year of the Global Peace Accord that officially put an end to war. Lio and I had gone to watch the celebratory fireworks displays on the mall, sitting in the shadow of one of the big war memorials next to a shallow pool. We lingered, watching the full moon rise, long after the crowd dispersed.

"How do you think they finally got the big weapons manufacturers and military corporations to sign on to the accord?" I asked.

"I've wondered about that. I wish I knew. They'll never make much profit just making explosives for fireworks." He grinned at me. "Although tonight's show was pretty spectacular. And by that I mean over-the-top excessive."

I snuggled closer to Lio as a breeze rose up, rippling the water on the pond where the full moon was reflected. "Of course, weapons aren't just guns and bombs these days," I mused.

"Did you ever see a man in the moon when you were a kid?" Lio asked.

"Yeah. At least I think I did."

"Did you know that in some other parts of the world people see a hare on the face of the moon?"

"I read about that once. I could never see it, though. I guess we see what we're conditioned to see, right? Whatever our culture tells us is there?"

"Probably. And maybe we want it to be a living thing," he suggested, "something with a face and eyes. Something we can relate to."

"Can you still see a face on the moon?" I asked.

"Not really."

"Me either. Though sometimes I wish I could."

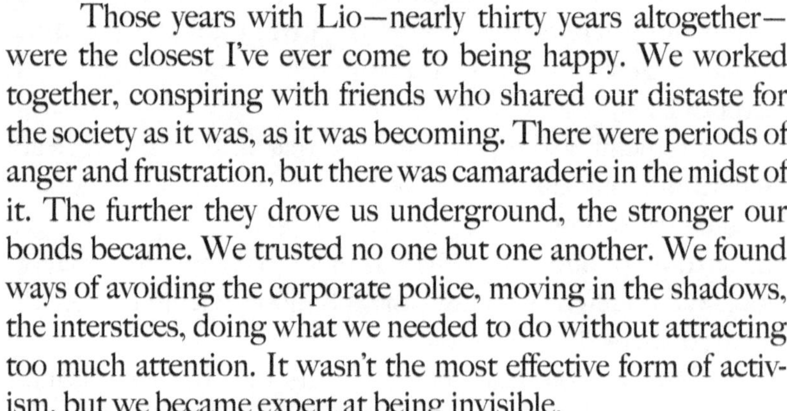

Those years with Lio—nearly thirty years altogether—were the closest I've ever come to being happy. We worked together, conspiring with friends who shared our distaste for the society as it was, as it was becoming. There were periods of anger and frustration, but there was camaraderie in the midst of it. The further they drove us underground, the stronger our bonds became. We trusted no one but one another. We found ways of avoiding the corporate police, moving in the shadows, the interstices, doing what we needed to do without attracting too much attention. It wasn't the most effective form of activism, but we became expert at being invisible.

Vintagonists developed alliances with Menders' communities like the one Lio and Zelda came from. There were also alliances with Simpletons, but these were more problematic. Simpletons looked upon Vinties' attachment to old things with a certain disdain, seeing it as just another form of materialism. I knew very little about Simpletons at that time, but I did understand that their guiding philosophy was simplicity—minimal possessions, minimal consumption, a balanced and earth-based way of life. Arguing that "even a fool can see the wisdom of simplicity," they'd embraced the derisive label of "Simpleton," although they were officially constituted as the Walden Network. They only wanted to be left alone to live their simple lives in isolated places. They never became activists. All three movements—Vintagonists, Menders, Simple-tons—shared a common scorn for the rampant consumerism that we knew fueled the plutocrats' self-indulgent lifestyles and positions of dominance. We got along.

Our alliance was eventually formalized into an umbrella organization known as Recall. That name had started off as kind of a joke, when entry into the infranet was hidden behind a collection of official recall notices of various products. As things developed, the name took on deeper meanings. I found the name "Recall" amusing, as it reminded me of a story I'd read once about an organization that implanted false memories into people's minds to make them believe they'd done something exciting, like making a trip to Mars. This real Recall, by contrast, seemed to be intent on helping people escape just such manipulation.

I was writing more and more. I'd started up my blog again, which was now available on the infranet through the Recall zone. I've looked for some of those old essays and stories recently and they seem to have all disappeared over the years. I should have printed them out on paper.

Zelda's popularity as a musician kept growing in spite of corporate distaste for the kind of acoustic and subtly subversive music she performed. She benefited from Lio's promotional abilities within underground networks.

Lio also had contacts back in his father's native Cuba and he began insisting that Zelda do a tour there. He wanted me to go with them.

"I don't know, Lio," I said. As much as I enjoyed reading novels set in foreign countries and even the occasional travelogue, the idea of traveling somewhere by air, as they intended to do, caused my palms to sweat and my stomach to cramp in protest. Contemplating the possibility of traveling with Lio, however, I almost said "yes."

"It's not that far away," he said. "Cuba is closer than California, you know. In fact, it's hardly any farther than Dallas."

"I didn't know that," I said, giving him my most disarming smile. What I did know was that I wouldn't go. I didn't care how close or far it was. Traveling by air was not something I did.

Lio and Zelda promised to send me lots of photographs and messages from Havana. After I dropped them off at the airport, laden as they were with musical instruments that I knew Lio would keep in top performance condition for the duration, I permitted myself a few second thoughts. It would have been fun to go to Cuba. I'd read some novels about it. One that I remembered in particular was by Wendy Guerra, called *Everyone Leaves*. I asked Lio why his father left Cuba.

"Because of his ridiculous American dream." Lio laughed. "In Cuba, just outside Havana, he was making a decent living repairing old automobiles. But American tourists kept telling him, 'America needs people like you. Nobody knows how to repair cars there anymore.' And so he finally saved up enough money and we came." Lio explained that it hadn't taken long for his father to discover that, although it was true that hardly anybody in America knew how to repair cars, there was also little demand for the service. He ended up befriending some other Cubans who were part of the Menders' movement and settled into the Havana community in New Mexico.

I'd discovered a couple of books from the late 20th century filled with photographs of Old Havana and my Vintie heart was charmed by the decaying buildings and vintage automobiles. When I began getting the photos Lio and Z sent, I was dismayed to see that so many charming old buildings had been replaced by generically ugly modern behemoths.

I complained to Lio about it, and he replied: "Give us credit! Cuba resisted corporate takeover longer than most. But the fact is, most of those old buildings went so long without proper repair and upkeep that there were precious few worth saving. The people had ample skills for repairing them, if only they'd had the resources. I'll keep looking for some old buildings to photograph for you. Wait 'til you see the club where Z is performing tonight!"

When Lio returned from Cuba, he brought me a gift, the pendant that I still wear. It has an old-fashioned clock on one side and a silver moon on the other, a moon with eyes, nose, and smiling mouth. "I looked for one with a hare," Lio said as he fastened it around my neck, "but I probably would've had to go to India or somewhere for one like that."

It wasn't long after this that Lio brought up the subject of marriage. We'd recently attended the simple ceremonies for Beatrice and Robert and the considerably more elaborate event marking Zelda's marriage to Darlene. I think Lio would have liked a formal ceremony in a church with all our friends in attendance, even though none of us was remotely religious. His old-fashioned ideas were part of what I loved about him. Reflecting on our relationship in later years, I've realized that much of his attraction to vintage things was born of authentic nostalgia for a way of life he, and especially his parents, had actually experienced. It was a way of life I'd never known. My passion for the vintage derived from a political aversion to contemporary events and trends.

"I'm not sure what difference getting married would make," I told him. "Would I love you more? Could I be any more devoted to you? I'm happy with our life as it is."

He never pressed the issue. But he did occasionally bring up the possibility of our having a child together.

"Why?" I would ask. Couples without children were becoming the norm.

"Why not?" Lio would respond. "People do still have babies, and most of them aren't nearly as capable as we are of raising another human being."

I knew he would have wanted us to raise the child ourselves; we would never have sent a child to a boarding colony.

"I don't know, Lio," I said. "I'm not sure we ought to bring a child into this world. Do we really know what things might be like by the time they grow to be adults?" I kept using my contraceptives.

My little essays and flash fiction pieces for the blog began to spin out into longer stories. I finished my first novel in 2055 and my second a few years later. They were published under the pseudonym Vlad Carpenter, a name Lio and I devised together, amid general mirth. It probably wasn't that funny, but we were both big Dracula fans. The stories I wrote as Vlad Carpenter were mysteries that leaned toward what used to be called urban fantasy. They had just a hint, a mere suggestion, of the supernatural—maybe a strange animal that kept turning up unexpectedly, mysterious weather patterns, an old woman suspected of being a witch, or an empty building that wasn't really empty at all. And they were invariably laced with subversive political messages. My novels—eventually there were five in all—were published as real printed books by an underground press, although digital versions were also available through the Recall zone on the infranet. Despite our affection for printed books, many people were hesitant about keeping them in their homes. I kept writing, enjoying Vlad Carpenter's increasing clandestine popularity.

Working at the Quill & Sheaf, writing, and selling books, became a pleasant routine. Looking back, I'm not sure why they left us alone for so long. Surely they knew what we were doing. I can only conclude that they thought what we were doing was insignificant.

Those were good years. I was surrounded by good people, people who were deeply concerned about the fate of humankind, people who cared and who refused to allow our disgust with the plutocrats to resolve into bitterness. Isn't bitterness a form of evil?

All that changed in January of 2075.

5.

The Quill & Sheaf was an established music venue and I suppose we thought that as long as we continued to offer top billing to performances by some of the standard corporate-owned groups we were safe. The real music, which included the acoustic stuff, happened downstairs. The wine cellar had been mostly cleared out after the invention of quick-pick wine manufacturing (which didn't require aging) and the space transformed into a second venue, right next to the bookshop.

We'd continued like that for years, nurturing some of the 21st century's finest acoustic musicians. We began getting fervent requests for more acoustic shows, so we decided to offer one upstairs.

We were all terribly nervous the first time we did it, posting guards at all the entrances, banning photography and recording, limiting the night's entertainment to a single set of acoustic music, bookended by more standard fare. The performance was a huge success, so the following month we did it again. We went to monthly performances, on a randomized schedule, announced only via Recall. We began offering all-acoustic performances. We went biweekly, then weekly.

We should have known better. It was the second month of the weekly performances, and everyone was still feeling celebratory after the winter holidays. Lio was minding the front door, and I was behind the bar. If he hadn't sent me that emergency pulse, my life might well have ended that night. The pulse had one word: "RUN". I saw it was from Lio, and I knew he would never mess with me, so I ran.

I ran out from behind the bar, down the stairs, and through the bookshop, locking doors behind me. I exited via a set of outside stairs that we were pretty sure no one knew were connected to Quill & Sheaf. I heard the sirens, the shouts, the tumbled furniture, the screams, and other sounds I couldn't identify or didn't want to. I'd never heard the sound of a laser pistol before. "Lio, Lio," I moaned, standing on the street corner, my hand over my mouth, my heart straining as if it would leap out of my chest, my leaden feet unwilling to carry me away. My brain was exploding with half-formed thoughts and terrors, and I could think of nothing to do. So with tears streaming down my face and my tense body shivering so hard I could barely put one foot in front of the other, I went home, back to Lio's place. I'd wait for him there.

I waited all night and all the next day, startled by every noise, constantly checking my digilet. I pulsed Zelda and got no reply. I pulsed Beat and received a message stating that my pulse was "undeliverable." I tried to check Recall for news, but it was shut down. I knew they did this periodically, when the political situation grew unusually tense. That knowledge only deepened my concern over Lio. Having no other recourse, I accessed some reports on FlixNews and Corporate News Network, hoping for some information. There was nothing. *Of course not,* I thought. *They'll never acknowledge last night even happened.*

Scared and desperate, I finally decided I had to go look for Z and Beat. I had to know what was going on. Maybe I'd read too many old spy novels, but I decided I ought to put on dark glasses and a hat. Since it was cold, I also wore a scarf, which I pulled up to partially cover my face. I went out onto the street, looking exactly like someone with something to hide. I wished Beat and Z were still living in the old apartment, which was only a few blocks south of Lio's and my place. But of course, both of them had long since moved into more comfortable quarters. Beat's place was closer, so I headed there. I knew it would be a long hike, but I thought I could make it before dark, and I didn't want to be shoved in among other people on public transport, under the watchful eye of surveillance cameras.

I was exhausted by the time I arrived, especially after climbing up the two flights of stairs. I knocked on Beat's door. I heard noises from inside and then silence. *Shit!* I thought, looking up at the tiny camera above the door. I removed my scarf, my hat, and my dark glasses. The door opened.

"Oh my god, Malia! You made it out! Where've you been? We've been trying to reach you!" Beat grabbed me in a bear hug. Her husband Robert headed for the kitchen, offering to make tea.

"Make that hot chocolate, Bob," Beat called to him. "With a shot of whiskey. I think this woman needs comfort." She helped me out of my coat and led me to the sofa. I'd begun to tremble, and the tears were starting up again.

"Have you heard from Lio?" My voice shook.

"Not yet. You know the whole Recall zone is on standby right now. That's for protection, of course. Quill & Sheaf may not have been the only place that got raided. This may have been a much broader crackdown. I can't believe Recall would go to such extreme measures over a single raid on a pub."

"And a bookstore," I added. "How do we find Lio?"

"That's going to be a problem. But I promise you, as soon as Recall is back I'll use their portals to do some poking around and see if I can locate him."

I summoned up the last shreds of my severely shaken faith in humankind, wanting desperately to believe that Beat would find Lio for me. I needed to believe that.

"What about Z?" I asked.

"She's gone missing, too."

"But it wasn't her band that was performing. I didn't think she was even there. I didn't see her."

"No, she wasn't there. But I've been in touch with her wife. Darlene says Z had a gig across town. She didn't come home. Darlene hasn't been able to get in touch with her."

I stared at the carpet. "Yeah, maybe this was bigger than Quill & Sheaf."

"You can stay here with us," Beat said after we'd finished our spiked hot chocolate and impromptu sandwiches. "You have to consider the possibility that the corporate cops will go to yours and Lio's place looking for... whatever it is they look for. Although more and more they don't seem too concerned with actually producing evidence of anything. They just do as they please. Anyway, you'll be safe here."

So I stayed with Beat and Robert. I didn't go back to my own place—mine and Lio's—for a week. I didn't do much of anything for a week. I had no job to go to. I was afraid to go back to the Quill & Sheaf even to see what might be left of our inventory of books. It would never be a shop again. I was certain of that. The second day at Beat's I went out and bought some clothes—another pair of pants, a blouse, a sweater, underwear. The third day I went for a walk in a nearby park. Maybe it was my imagination, but it seemed everyone was walking with their heads down, walking quickly, not looking right or left. Everyone seemed focused inward. Sad. Afraid. As I said, maybe it was my imagination. But after that I stayed in Beat's apartment, reading books.

"I'm going back to my place," I announced one morning, as Beat was about to leave for work. Lio had been missing for a week. The Recall zone had come back up two days before and we'd searched repeatedly for information about him, finding nothing.

Beat didn't object to my decision. She was probably grateful to reclaim her privacy, although living with me had probably been more like having a resident ghost than a roommate.

"Be watchful," she said. "And keep in touch."

She'd rescripted my digilet for the new Recall configurations. Configurations that likely did not include Eliomar Gaston. I could sense him beginning to disappear.

I entered the building through a back service entrance and stood in the hallway near our apartment for several minutes. I told myself I was checking for suspicious characters and surveillance devices, although I had no idea what such characters and devices might look like in real life. Finally, I allowed myself to go inside.

Things looked disturbingly untouched. The book I'd been reading was still on the side table next to the sofa, a scrap of paper marking my place. The violin Lio had been repairing lay on the dining table. On the kitchen counter were the remains of our final hasty meal together, painted now in varicolored mold. The last drops of our wine encrusted the bottoms of two glasses with crystalline, blood-red deposits. One glass bore faint traces of lipstick.

Our computers also appeared untouched. I scanned my own first and then Lio's. If anyone had been there, if anyone had gone through our things, I could find no trace. It was unnerving. Everything looked the same, and yet I knew everything had changed. It would never be the same.

I knew I was leaving. I downloaded my latest unfinished manuscript and a few stories and essays onto a portable screen along with some photos of Lio and me. I deleted everything else. I hesitated over Lio's computer and then wiped it, too. I packed a few clothes and too many books. I saw Lio's cello standing in the corner and allowed myself a moment of yearning, wishing I could take it with me. But I knew that was out of the question. Besides, what I really wanted was the music and I couldn't play. I wanted Lio.

I was going back to Texas, to Dallas. Somehow I was going to disappear myself. Maybe there was a space out there for disappeared people. Maybe that was where I'd find Lio.

6.

I could have gone to Dallas by plane, but my irrational aversion to air travel nixed that option. I went by rail. I was hoping to find an empty corner seat somewhere and hide out there with my fears and a good book. I didn't want to think about my predicament in public. I'd think about it later.

I found disappointingly few empty seats and no isolated corners at all. I was surrounded by a couple of dozen nervous people speaking French with an accent I didn't recognize. I asked the woman in the seat beside me where they were from. She shook her head, indicating she didn't understand my question. Another woman, a few rows back, overheard and she approached me, explaining in excellent English that they were climate migrants, being relocated from an area where unfavorable weather had decimated several seasons' crops. They had been processed through a camp outside Washington, D.C. and were being sent to jobs awaiting them in Texas. It sounded like a memorized speech. She told me that she and the other migrants were from Niger and Cameroon. I thanked her for the information.

I continued listening to the conversations going on around me. I made a half-hearted attempt to join in, but my French was so inept that they soon gave up on me. I continued to listen. I may not know much French, but I do know the words *guerre* and *mort* and those words turned up more than I would have expected in any 2075 conversation among climate migrants. *The wars are over*, I told myself. The Global Peace Accord had been negotiated and duly celebrated in 2053. So why were these people chattering so much about war and death? They seemed more like refugees than migrants.

My intention was to visit my older sister Leticia at her boutique in Dallas, but I'd given her no forewarning of my arrival. I was still dubious about the current political situation and fearful that I might pose a threat to her. I located her shop and watched for a while from across the street. Her place was small but pleasant. The clients I saw through the window appeared to be middle level professionals with good taste. I watched Leticia laughing and talking with her customers. She looked happy. I decided she didn't need me in her life.

Uncertain about what to do next, I wandered. I tried to remember where Vintagonists had hung out during my high school years. This was difficult, since it required reaching back across my blank period. I seemed to recall some side street off Greenville Avenue where there had been a coffee shop. I decided to look for it, although I had little hope it would still be there. Our high school days were more than forty years gone.

I boarded a bus heading north on Greenville, away from downtown. I thought the street I was looking for might begin with an M. We passed Marquita, Monticello, Merrimac. None of those sounded right. Nothing looked right. The Greenville Avenue I remembered had been lined with small shops, cafés, bars, a couple of entertainments venues. Now it was all office buildings and habitat towers. Mercedes, Morningside. I got off at McCommas, where I saw a squat brick building that looked old. Feeling thoroughly disoriented, I began walking east. I found nothing but more habitat towers. It occurred to me that all of this—all of the side streets—had always been residential. Maybe the old place wasn't on a side street, but rather at the rear of a building that faced Greenville. Or McCommas. I turned down an alley and looked to my right, examining the backs of the buildings. I saw a door, halfway down the block, with a drab, threadbare awning. I felt a tickle of memory.

The door beneath the awning wasn't locked, so I opened it and stepped inside. I was greeted by the warm fragrance of fresh brewed coffee. There were tables and chairs and very few patrons. I felt another twinge of memory, but I cautioned myself: *Just because this is a coffee shop, doesn't mean it's still a Vintagonist hangout. Or ever was. Take it easy.*

I still had a little money in my pocket. There was still physical money in circulation in 2075, although fewer and fewer establishments accepted it. I had a feeling this was one establishment that would. I walked up to the counter and ordered an Americano.

"This place looks like it's been here a while," I said, watching the barista work, watching for any reaction.

"So I hear," she said, noncommittal. "They tell me it's come and gone several times."

I decided to be bold. "I remember going to a coffee shop somewhere around here when I was in high school. I don't know if this is it, though. I don't..." I paused, looking directly at the barista. "Recall."

She looked down at her work, then up at me. "That's not the pass phrase," she said softly, offering me a smile. "But I guess it'll do. I take it you're from out of town now?"

"Just passing through," I said, taking the steaming mug, cupping it in my cold hands. "Kind of looking for a place I could stay for a while."

"Here in town?"

"I don't think so. I think I'd prefer something out in the country."

"How far out?"

I laughed and gave her a sidewise look. "The farther the better."

She nodded and scribbled something down on a paper napkin. "Did you ever go to Marfa?" she asked, handing me the napkin.

"No, but I always heard about it."

"Well this is out in West Texas, not too far from Marfa. I think they'd give you a place to stay. For a while."

I folded the napkin and placed it in my bag. "Thanks."

I finished my coffee and caught the next bus going back to where I'd come from. At the train station again, I checked first to make sure my stored baggage was secure, then I sat down to study a map on my digilet, to determine where I needed to go to reach this place near Marfa. I asked if the train went to Fort Stockton.

"Yes'm," the ticket seller said. "Train leaving in about an hour, but it's the overnight. Kinda long layby near Big Spring, waiting for another train to pass. You can come back tomorrow morning and catch the ten o'clock express. Lots more scenic."

"The overnight will do," I said, thinking it was ideal, precluding any need for a hotel room in overpriced Dallas. In view of the money I was saving on a room, I sprang for a compartment with a bed.

I slept better that night than I'd slept since before the raid on Quill & Sheaf. I woke once and looked out the window to the south, toward distant mountains outlined against starlit sky. The gentle swaying of the train quickly lulled me back to sleep. When I woke again, it was almost sunrise, and the train was slowing for Fort Stockton. The end of this particular line was El Paso, another 400 kilometers away.

I wasn't sure what came next for my own journey. I needed coffee. The little café inside the terminal was just opening for business, so I dragged up my two bags and sat at a table. I ordered coffee and a doughnut and settled down to study the map again. It looked like Marfa was still at least two and a half hours away, accessible only by bus or autocar. I hadn't used autocars much, since all of my life I'd lived in cities with plenty of public transportation. I checked my funds and decided I could afford the autocar. It would carry me all the way to my destination, which, according to the scribbled address on the napkin, was a place called Walden 27. I knew it would be a Simpleton community.

As the autocar made its way across the broad expanse of West Texas, I felt myself and the city girl I'd always been beginning to disappear into the emptiness.

Part II
Absence

7.

It was mid-morning on January 17, 2075, when I arrived at Walden 27. It was the first day of my next half-century.

I was directed to the intake office, where I told them I only needed a place to stay for a short while. I didn't mean to stay. They told me the paperwork was the same either way. Regardless of how long I intended to remain, I had to agree to abide by all the rules and regulations of Walden communities. I signed the papers. I was tired and I told myself it didn't matter what was in the documents. This was temporary. They could run the town however they liked; it was their town. It wasn't mine.

They gave me a room for the night in a hostel, promising to have a cottage prepared for me to move into the following day. After lunch, I unpacked a few things and read for an hour or two, feeling relieved to be in a place where I could feel safe, but unwilling yet to dwell on my reasons for being there. I ate supper and intended to spend the rest of the evening reading, too.

As I sat in that disconcertingly immaculate room with its sparse furnishings, as I looked out across the rows of tidy houses, the fields of carefully tended crops, and the empty expanse beyond, the full weight of my circumstances hit me. Or rather, it climbed up my tired legs, sunk its claws into every vertebra of my spine, and coiled itself heavily about my neck and shoulders. I tasted the tears clogging my throat and I knew I wasn't finished running away. I walked back down the stairs and outside and found a path leading away from the village. Energized by anger, I began to run.

The path grew steeper as it reached the hills surrounding Walden 27. I slowed to a walk, staring fixedly at the ground, watching one foot fall in front of the other. I climbed. The path became rougher, and I wasn't certain it was a path anymore.

I stopped. Off to one side I saw some tall rocks—huge, jagged boulders—standing in a tight semblance of a circle with a small opening, an opening just about my size. I squeezed inside and looked up into the sky and there, directly overhead, was the pale disk of the nearly full moon. I fell to my knees and let the tears empty my heart. I cried for all that I'd lost—for Lio, for Beat and Z. I cried for the Quill & Sheaf and Codex2 and everything we'd tried to do there. I cried for all the books I'd left behind and all the lovers of books who I'd probably never see again. I cried for Lio's beautiful cello and its music.

When the tears finally ran out, I looked up again into the twilight sky and saw that the moon had drifted beyond the limited window of my enclosure. I sat for a while longer, holding hands with my loneliness, watching my fear recede, trying to see what would come in its stead. The sharp stones under my knees and ankles and the cold descending with the night finally told me I should get moving. I exited the circle and turned toward Walden 27. There was barely enough light to find the path, but it was open country, and I could see the town. I thought it looked pretty as lights began to flicker on in the houses and buildings. I still wasn't sure how long I'd stay in this odd community, but I knew it was where I needed to be for now. As I began my slow, deliberate trek back to Walden 27, I looked up once more at the moon, round and bright.

My second night at Walden 27, as they'd promised, I spent in my own cottage. It was a tiny thing, newly built on a quiet street at the farthest edge of the town. It had a surprisingly spacious sitting room, which I thought could also serve as a study. There was a small, fixed screen on one wall above a table. There was no kitchen, only a sink, a small chillbox, and a heating device. I was told that I would take my meals with other singletons in a neighborhood dining room. My sleeping space was in a loft over the sitting room, and it had a big window that opened away from the town, out toward the mountains.

I lay in the unfamiliar bed, looking out over the darkened landscape, reflecting again on all the circumstances, the decisions, that had brought me to this point in my life and to this place. As I pondered, my eyes gradually focused on something that made the hairs stand up on my neck and arms. I was sure it was a mountain lion. A cougar. I stared at it where it crouched on the hillside, silent and staring, its tail swishing, moving the grasses side to side. I couldn't take my eyes off it. My hand covered my mouth as I wondered if I should raise an alarm of some kind. Then the clouds parted, and the brilliance of the full moon showed me that my mountain lion was really only a lion-sized boulder, the grasses stirred by the wind. I laughed at my foolishness, but I also shed a tear or two.

Everything familiar was gone now. This was a whole new world.

I didn't know a lot about Simpletons, officially known as the Walden Network. I knew it was their commitment to simplicity and self-sufficiency that had earned them their moniker, which was initially intended as a slur. I knew that Simpleton communities were reputed to be masters of the art of communal sufficiency.

In Walden 27, I quickly learned that everyone worked, everyone ate, everyone had a place to live and people to look after them if they fell ill. They respected fine crafted things meant to last, which made for good relations with Menders, who also had developed a number of sufficiency communities scattered about the country. In my own experience of dissident movements, only Vintagonists insisted on living in the midst of the cities, maintaining clandestine structures within the purview of the corporations' own sovereign territory.

The appearance of Walden 27 was pleasant enough. The streets were well kept and lay, insofar as possible, at precise right angles to one another. There were a few old stone buildings at the town's center and even some of the newer structures utilized the ample local supply of varicolored stone. The setting was another matter. It felt like we were a million kilometers from civilization. But I guess that was the point. I reminded myself that this isolation was why I had come here.

There was something about my first desperate run out into that vast countryside that eventually drew me back for another visit and then another. At first I told myself I merely needed to get away from the Simpletons, just like I did that first day, only not so urgently. But then I began to think I was out there not to get away from things, but because I was looking for something. But what was there for a city girl like me to find? It was just a massive expanse of monotonous rocks and weeds and bushes and sky. A lot of sky. And a lot of bugs. It was boring. Boring and itchy.

But I kept going for walks anyway. And then one day I noticed how the dry grasses swayed and danced in the breeze, some topped with slender white plumes, others dotted with delicate seedpods that glinted like soap bubbles. I began to see the different shades of greens and golds and grays. I saw a small bush beside the path with stems that were almost blue. I saw how the boulders in the valley had once been part of the hills above and how some of the boulders—the ones with the gently rounded corners—had fallen long before the ones with sharper edges. I saw a pattern in the bright green mold clinging to a veined stone.

I could see. And what I saw was a world more subtle, more intricate than I had ever realized and, within its own generous time and space, more enduring and reliable than anything built by human hands or ingenuity, bigger than anything built by plutocrats. I sat down on the ground—right there among the sharp stones and crushed leaves and rabbit poop—and I laughed until I cried, my eyes wide open.

I started taking longer walks, hungry for this new perspective, eager to discover what new things I could see. I didn't care what the names of things were, although I gave some of them my own names. I came up with a lot of questions that I could have asked someone. Instead, I made up stories, my own whimsical explanations. My excursion into nature gradually became a retreat into my own fanciful world. I never quite reclaimed my singular epiphany.

At least once a week I revisited the rock shelter I'd discovered that first day. I'd sit within its fastness in silence, eyes closed, listening. I became familiar with the voices of different birds and insects. And sometimes, when the wind was just right, I'd hear a sound that was something between a hum and a sigh. There was a lower tone and a higher one and I recognized the interval as something Lio had demonstrated to me once by swinging a long plastic tube in rapid circles. I never discovered exactly where this sound was coming from, but I called it the voice of the mountains, and I listened intently whenever it manifested. On one particularly windy day, I thought I detected a third tone, higher still, but it quickly disappeared and I never heard it again.

When I first arrived at Walden 27, I still felt the need to know the exact time of day or night and I positioned my little digital clock on my table like some deity in a shrine. I learned that Walden 27 was at the far western extreme of the Eastern Time zone. There were only two North American time zones by this time; I remembered having read that, before the original four time zones were established for the convenience of railways in the 19th century, every town kept its own time, keyed to its own subjective experience of the sun's movements. I came to realize that time zones and clocks meant little to the community of Walden 27.

As my stay extended into weeks and then months, I, too, stopped keeping track of time. *It's all relative anyway,* I told myself. We mark our distance from some event in the past or from some planned, imagined future, organizing our activities within the diurnal/nocturnal cycle, across the flow of seasons. In Walden 27, residents rose with the sun, broke for lunch when the sun approached its zenith, or when the temperature rose to a point making a break desirable.

Tracking the cyclic phases of the moon became more important to me than the name of the month or the count of days on a calendar. I noticed how the moon phase tracked with my menstrual cycle. I began to observe the stars and how they shifted position in the sky as we moved toward spring. They don't actually shift, of course; it's we who shift our position relative to them. I'd never seen so many stars before coming to Walden 27.

When spring came, the yard around my cottage was planted with a variety of fruits and vegetables. Every square meter of fertile land in the whole of Walden 27 was planted with something edible or useful and it was all worked cooperatively, which meant that I was always encountering people in my garden, working the ground, tending the plants. I had to remind myself it wasn't "my" garden, though I soon began to do a little weeding there and, later on, I did claim some of the produce for myself.

The lack of regimentation was seductive. In Walden 27, we kept our own time. I relegated my little clock to a dresser drawer.

8.

I settled into Walden 27. I never overtly committed in my own mind to the idea of staying. I simply stayed.

I had jobs. Here at Walden 27, they were called *tareas*, a Spanish term that seemed to convey a sense of responsibility more than obligation. Tareas were tasks that needed to be done. Most people had at least two regular tareas, as well as periodic assignments that I think would have been considered volunteer work in the past. Here it was all tarea.

I had few practical skills. I'd never done any gardening or tended any livestock or built any barns or chicken coops or done any sewing or baking. One thing I'd learned from Lio was the skill of restoring and maintaining wood finishes, so that became one of my regular tareas: I worked two mornings a week at the wood shop.

My other tarea was at the community library. As an assistant librarian I was able to spend time with books—handling them, inhaling their intelligent scent, recommending them to patrons, discussing them with other bibliophiles. The library was open four afternoons a week, though we often stayed open well into the evening for the benefit of discussion groups or when we got behind with reshelving and repairing the books. We did what was needed. I was disappointed to see that Vlad Carpenter's books were not checked out very frequently, sometimes languishing on the shelves for a year or more, sometimes being returned by a patron after only a day or two. Apparently Vintagonists and Simpletons had different tastes in literature.

During that first year at Walden 27, I often wrestled with the idea of contacting someone—Beatrice, Zelda, one of my sisters—to let them know where I was. But each time I thought I would, I didn't. Hadn't my intention been to disappear myself? As the months passed, I became more resigned to my self-imposed solitude and I began to find the remoteness of Walden 27 reassuring, comforting.

I wasn't alone, of course. I had a whole Simpleton community surrounding me, supporting me. The focus of the energy of Walden 27 was a protective, communal turning inward. The old Vintie Malia had been concerned with activist engagement with the world, with society, but that had become increasingly difficult over the years. Here at Walden 27, I was going to have to let it go altogether.

Eventually I was motivated to look back over the contract I'd signed, curious about exactly what it was I'd agreed to as a member of the Walden Network. I learned that there were certain sanctions against antisocial behavior: first, there was exclusion from social life—something like shunning. Second, there was exclusion from the community, which was similar to the old European custom of outlawry. I found it somewhat ironic that the shunning seemed to be considered the harsher punishment, apparently because it was carried out under the watchful eyes of fellow Waldeners. It was applied numerous times during my residence at Walden 27, and I was surprised at how effective it was. Exclusion from the community—always declared to be temporary—was seen as more of a test of character, an opportunity to reestablish in the transgressor's own mind the full value of Walden life.

I found that I'd promised not to use my digilet or the commercial medianets for outside contact. Waldeners had their own internal network that connected us with one another and with other Walden settlements via fixed screens in our respective residences. Anything more than that required going to the community center to use a wired screen. I had unwittingly violated these rules a few times by logging in to Recall on my digilet. But when Recall revised personal protocols again, I'd given up. Being unable to access the 'nets was one thing; knowing it was forbidden annoyed me.

I observed that there were very few youths and children at Walden 27. When I asked about it, I was told that the community had reached the carrying capacity of the tract of land it controlled and that residents, naturally, had no desire to upset the balance. Their equilibrium was achieved not through any Shaker-like devotion to celibacy but rather through diligent use of contraception. Abortion was available, too, should anyone request it, but I only knew of one abortion in the entire time I lived there.

Although most Waldeners didn't use Chulel, I didn't stop taking it right away. Chulel was available in Walden 27, but it was used primarily by people whose own parents or grandparents had suffered excessively in old age from conditions such as crippling arthritis, Parkinson's disease, or personality-devouring dementia. I'd brought two doses with me, so I knew I could continue for a couple of years without attending the clinic. I studied the Waldeners around me. Some of them were clearly old and I wasn't sure how I felt about that. It seemed so unnecessary. I heard a few former Vintagonists joking with one another about having become "Vintage," just like those books and objects we cherished. "Should we cherish ourselves and one another any less?" they asked.

In late summer of my second year at Walden 27, there was a minor crisis that turned into an unexpected opportunity for me. It was an unusually hot August even by West Texas standards, so when our power distribution network went down, I assumed that we'd overtaxed it due to the heat. There were backup systems, but some of those hadn't been used in so long that they failed as well.

"What will they do about it?" I asked Frances, the head librarian, as I entered the darkened and only slightly cooler building for my regular tarea. I was referring to the supervisory council of Walden 27, an elected body of leading citizens.

"Probably call in a Mender," she said, picking up a stack of books to move to a table nearer a window. "That's what we usually do. With something this big, they'll probably have to get someone from over at Havana, which may take a little longer."

"Havana?" I was stunned to hear that name. "How far is that from here?" Why hadn't I thought about far West Texas being next to New Mexico, along the Rio Grande, maybe near Lio and Zelda's home community?

"Well, it's not the one in Cuba, you know," Frances laughed. "This one's in New Mexico. I'd guess it's about three hours away, maybe a little more. They'll get us up and running in a few days, I'm sure. Is the backup system working in your neighborhood?"

"Yes, although it's been kind of fading in and out." My mind was already busy, trying to figure out how to contact this Mender from Havana when they arrived. I needed to ask about Lio and Z. "Do they know where the problem seems to be with our network?" I asked.

"I'm not sure but, if I had to guess, I'd say it's likely at the transfer node over between the produce market and the bakery. Looks like some birds have been nesting in the equipment. That might have something to do with it."

I walked past the produce market and the bakery on my way home. Sure enough, there were several people there, cleaning out some brush and removing debris that might have been bird nests. I didn't ask any questions. One of the things I'd learned about Walden 27 was that every tarea had its minders and that we were expected to mind our own tareas and let other people mind theirs.

The next morning, before reporting to the wood shop, I went back to the market. I carried a shopping bag, thinking I could acquire a few pieces of fresh fruit. While I waited in line, I watched the people working on the equipment. There was a stranger among them. I knew that if I wanted to speak with him, I was going to have to be brazen. I left my place in line and went over to the fence.

"Hello!" I called. "Could I speak with someone for a minute?"

One of our local workers looked up, scowling. She walked over to where I stood. "Do you have business here? What is it you want?"

"I'd like to speak to the Mender from Havana."

"Yes? What business might you have with him?"

"I know some people from there. I thought he might have some news about them. Or maybe he'd take them a message."

She frowned at me. I was pretty sure that what I was requesting wasn't against any particular rule. It was just considered bad form. She shrugged. "We're due a break. I'll see if he wants to talk to you."

A minute later the stranger stopped working and came toward the fence. He walked around through the gate, and as he approached me, he held out his hand. "You wanted to talk with me?" He was smiling.

"Yes," I said. His handshake was firm but gentle. "I know some people—used to know some people—from Havana. Their names are Eliomar and Zelda Gaston. Do you know them?"

The man glanced toward the other workers and folded his arms across his chest. "Where did you know them?" he asked.

"In Washington, D.C. They were two of my best friends, but then something happened, and we lost touch."

He looked down, scuffing at a crack in the sidewalk. "Your friend Zelda is in Havana. But Eliomar..."

"Yes? What happened to Lio?"

"I was told that they have him in prison somewhere. Look, that's all I know. I have to get back to work."

I didn't know whether to laugh or cry. I was shaken to the core, but I managed to mumble some kind of "thank you." Lio was alive! Well, probably. But prison? Would it be better if he were dead? I started toward my house and then remembered I'd been going to work and turned around. I needed to think. I needed time to think of a way to get in touch with Zelda. I decided to call in sick for my shift and turned around once more toward home.

By mid-afternoon, I'd made up my mind. I went to the office of the supervisory council to enter a formal request to visit Havana. Again, it wasn't something that was proscribed, only something vigorously discouraged. I was grudgingly issued an overnight pass and told that I would have to ride with the Mender. Their disapproving attitude didn't faze me. I was excited about my journey, although fearful about what I might discover.

I left Walden 27 that evening with the Mender, whose name was Jason Cruz. I settled in for a three-hour ride, but after a few minutes on the road, I had a feeling it wouldn't take that long.

"Isn't the maximum speed on this road 110 kph?"

"Not if you know how to reconfigure the controls on your autocar." He grinned at me. "We'll be there in a little under two hours."

Curious, I checked the time on the car's clock. An hour and forty-seven minutes later, he was dropping me off at Zelda's house. "I'll be by just after first light tomorrow morning to pick you up," he said. "If you need a place to stay, you can pulse me. My wife and I would be happy to have you stay with us."

I thanked him for his hospitality and promised to be ready on time the next morning. He drove away and I stood for a moment on the walkway in front of the house. It was a simple house, well built, considerably bigger than my cottage in Walden 27. I sensed I was at a threshold, and I was apprehensive about what I might find on the other side. I walked up to the house and knocked on the door.

As soon as I saw Zelda, I knew there was something very wrong, but I couldn't have told you what it was. She looked out of sync, as if she were trying to move in two directions at once. At first she didn't recognize me, but when I told her who I was she gave me a big smile and a hug. I sat on the sofa with her wife Darlene, while Zelda went to the kitchen. She came back with open bottles of lemonade and a plate of homemade cookies.

"We've been so worried about you, haven't we Darlene?" Zelda looked at her partner as if she were searching for verification.

Darlene nodded. "I heard from Beatrice that you'd left D.C., but nobody seemed to know where you'd gone. We feared the worst," Darlene said. "I can't believe you've been living so close by for more than a year." Then she told me that Zelda had indeed been detained on the same day as the raid on the Quill & Sheaf. "They took her to a large facility in Maryland, and she was there for... I guess a couple of weeks. Maybe more. Then they set her up with a new identity and a job at a food distribution center in Cleveland."

I was shocked. But it was what wasn't being said that hurt my heart most. What wasn't being said was that Zelda herself had no recollection of these events. I could tell she barely remembered me. I watched her watching Darlene, her brow furrowed as she tried to identify with the woman who was the subject of this story.

"How did you find her?" I asked.

Darlene laughed and put her arm around Zelda's shoulders. "The corporate cops didn't realize how many fans my girl had. Someone in Cleveland recognized her and posted on Recall, on the Returns page, so I went and got her."

"I was lucky, right Darlene?" Zelda smiled.

"Really lucky," Darlene assured her, although I was certain "lucky" didn't apply to what had happened to her before Darlene located her in Cleveland.

"What's Returns?" I asked. "Has anyone posted anything about Lio?"

"No, unfortunately," Darlene replied. "We keep checking, but we haven't seen anything about anyone who meets Lio's description. We kind of assume he must still be in custody somewhere. Recall people are very good about posting pictures and information about anyone who shows up seeming disoriented or unable to answer questions about their past." Darlene looked at Zelda, who seemed unaware of how well this description had fit her.

"So they let you access Recall here in Havana?"

"Oh, gosh, yes. People here are all about Recall. We have a community-wide shield that protects us from surveillance from outside."

I felt a wave of jealousy. It would be nice to live somewhere a little less restrictive than Walden 27. Would they have any use for my modest skills in wood refinishing and book repair here in Havana?

"I'm lucky to have my Darlene." Zelda's eyes filled with tears. "She's all I have now. Now that my music is gone."

"She can't play guitar anymore," Darlene said, in response to my bewildered expression.

I looked at Zelda's hands and saw no evidence of injury.

"It's not her hands. She has no sense of pitch anymore, no rhythm. She can't stay on key even to sing. I don't know how they managed to do it, but they killed her music." Darlene pulled Zelda toward her, kissing her gently, stroking her hair.

I remembered the sound of Zelda's singing, the crazy riffs she played on her guitar, and my heart ached for what the corporations had taken from her, from all of us.

"What about Beat?" I asked.

"We were in touch for a while. But the last I heard, she was getting pressure from her employer to sign up with the Chulel spas—you know, the places that give you the memory adjustments. Apparently her husband Bob had begun going to the spas already and was encouraging her to do it, too."

"I see." I felt disappointment. Beat should know better. "Were they still living in D.C.?"

"Yes, but she mentioned Bob had been offered a position somewhere in Florida and that they might be moving."

I felt Beatrice disappearing and I shuddered inwardly. It seemed like everyone was being taken from me, one by one, piece by piece.

We talked a little more about life in Havana. It turned out that the community had quite a waiting list and rarely accepted unrelated people from outside. My nascent hopes were dashed. If Lio and I had married, I might have stood a chance. We ate supper at a local café that served good Cuban food. Zelda did her best to participate in the conversation, but she was slow, and her contributions often veered off track. I was increasingly certain that the music wasn't all the plutocrats' agents had killed.

I rode back to Walden 27 the next morning with Jason. "Did you find what you were looking for?" he asked.

I couldn't answer.

9.

For several weeks after my visit with Zelda and Darlene, I was despondent. The story of what Zelda had endured, my imagined scenarios of what Lio might still be going through, the loss of Beatrice—all of this unhinged me. I caught myself staring at walls. I'd get teary-eyed at the least little thing. I thought about leaving, going out to search for Lio. But what could I do? How would I even begin such a search? I used to imagine that I'd eventually contact Beatrice or Zelda and that one of them would know something about Lio. Now I was sure that would never happen. I felt angry and powerless.

At first I went every few days to the wired screens in the community center to contact Darlene and see if there was any word of Lio. I received disapproving scowls. I slipped back to once a week and then to a couple of times a month. And then I stopped going.

I also stopped going for walks. The countryside no longer spoke to me. What did I really know about our natural environment anyway? The stories I'd made up to amuse myself had lost their appeal. Stones didn't really transform into bears or mountain lions under the dark of the moon. Jackrabbits couldn't really speed along so swiftly that they could take off into the air, flying with their great ears as wings. Hawks and owls didn't consume fallen stars; they ate mice and baby rabbits.

I had to stop grasping after a future that would never be. I would simply remember Lio as he had been. *Lio is dead*, I told myself. I took a silk scarf he'd given me and tied it to a nail on the wall near my bed where I could see it, touch it. I would remember Lio. But I'd let him rest in peace.

Still, sometimes in the summer evenings, when I sat outside on my back steps, eating a handful of berries or tiny tomatoes I'd plucked from the garden, I'd watch the sun go down and wonder if somehow maybe Lio still existed and, if he did, where he might be watching that same sunset.

And then I did the only thing I'd ever known to do in difficult circumstances: I started writing. I didn't have any ideas for stories, so I wrote a few poems and essays. They weren't very good, but at least I was getting back into the habit of writing. I'd become curious about the Walden Network, and I decided to do some research for a short history of the movement. Frances recommended that I ask permission from the council in order to access records. After a brief interrogation, in which I strove to emphasize my admiration for Walden Network and the Way of Simplicity, I had my permission.

I'd already begun my research by checking out Henry David Thoreau's *Walden* from the library. At first, I was surprised at the fact there was only one copy of the book, and a vintage one at that. Simpletons ran their own publishing house, so I knew they could have reprinted it if they'd wanted to. After I started reading the book, I began to understand.

I felt an immediate mismatch between the poetic meanderings of the solitary philosopher and the thoroughly businesslike, community-centric contract I'd signed upon joining Walden 27. At first his worldview reminded me of the naïve spirituality I'd nurtured in my early days here, during those long walks in the hills. Thoreau's veneration of nature was more absolute than mine had ever been, merging as it did into a disdain for any human contrivance. In the great outdoors, I'd only been a storyteller, spinning my little fables about the natural world that hosted my physical and mental excursions.

Then there was the fact that Mr. Thoreau had lived alone with no responsibility to anyone. His only tareas were the ones he set for himself. He wrote, "It would be better if there were but one inhabitant to a square mile." I thought he would have loved West Texas. But then I also noticed that his cabin was within earshot of a regular rail line and only an hour's walk from town. He sometimes went to the town or had guests from there at his cabin. Or visitors who were travelers from the road. We of Walden 27 never went anywhere and visitors from the outside were a rarity. There were no incidental travelers; Walden 27 wasn't on the road to anywhere.

The more I read of Mr. Thoreau, the less I liked him, and the more I wondered how this entire network had come to bear the name of his little pond. I did like his pond—we had far too little visible water out here—and I did wonder what a forest would be like, remembering something I'd read once about the social sentience of trees. There were no forests around Walden 27. There were trees, yes, but most of them were loners. Like Mr. Thoreau. And me.

I began having doubts about my stubbornly solitary lifestyle. Was it a reasonable way of life? Mr. Thoreau thought so, even though he never seemed to achieve it. I allowed myself to recall the more convivial life I'd had in D.C. I'd been surrounded by friends there and the loss of them still hurt. I missed having friends.

I began getting to know my fellow Waldeners, in particular a man by the name of Walter Acosta who showed up frequently at the library and participated in one of our reading groups. Walter was a local man, born and raised not more than a hundred kilometers from Walden 27 (which was not a great distance by West Texas standards). He told me his father had been the sheriff of one of the big West Texas counties in the early 21st century. His father's family had been cattle ranchers here since before the first Republic of Texas, back when the region was still part of Mexico. His mother claimed to be part Cherokee and had joined a reorganized tribal fragment centered on a now extinct village with the charming name of Valentine. Listening to Walter's stories, I began to develop a fondness for the peculiarities of West Texas.

"Daddy wanted me to be a businessman and get a job with one of the corporations like TotExx or Mekong," Walter explained. "Mekong had bought up near half the county and put in that spaceport up in the north sector. They weren't really hiring many people there, but Daddy had his hopes."

"Mekong had a spaceport? I thought they were all about books. Well, digital books," I said. "But of course they sold anything you wanted. Anything they wanted you to buy."

"Spaceport's still there."

"Is that where those rocket trails come from that we see sometimes?"

Walter nodded, glancing at the sky. There were no rocket trails in sight.

"I understand about the parents," I said. "With mine, too, it was all about getting a job with the corporations."

"In my case, my grandpa had got me into raising animals as a kid and Mama—God bless her little New Age heart—had got me interested in plant-based medicines and remedies, so I thought I could major in biology and do something with all that. Turned out I wasn't much of a scientist. But I got through, just by the skin of my teeth, and even got a job with Mekong. They hired me as kind of a corporate park ranger. My job was to keep the critters out of the spaceport facilities."

"That sounds okay."

"Yeah, I kind of liked it for a time. I got to work outdoors and it wasn't too demanding. I kept working up there until after Mama passed. Then Daddy got so taken in with the entertainments and the gambling that pretty soon we had nothing to talk about anymore. And then things started to get weird up at Mekong and so I quit and came down here instead. Looks like this is where I stay."

Walter lived with his partner Jess in one of the larger family homes that Walden 27 offered as an option to its residents. The people in such homes weren't necessarily related by kinship. Waldeners referred to them as "house families." He invited me to have dinner with them a few times and then one day he invited me to move in.

"You fit in with our family so perfectly, Malia," he assured me, offering his most charming smile. "We always have such great talk around the table whenever you come to take a meal with us. Everybody wants you to come."

I was tempted, but I declined. I'd become accustomed to my tiny cottage, and I thought sharing the occasional meal with Walter and Jess and the three other members of their house family would be enough to satisfy my need for social interaction without threatening my equally critical need for solitude.

I continued my research on Walden Network. One day, as I was going through a stack of books at the library that were awaiting repairs, I ran across a volume that I'm sure I would have found in the book catalogue if it had been catalogued. The book was called *Walden Two* and was written by a behavioral psychologist called B. F. Skinner in the mid-20th century. I took it home with me and began reading.

I quickly realized that the fictional town Skinner called Walden Two had little in common with Thoreau's vision. The original *Walden* described a philosopher's contemplative personal retreat in the woods. *Walden Two* was about a carefully engineered and managed community. I knew it was fictional, but the book read almost like a manifesto for an intentional community designed according to the author's particular set of propositions and scientific conclusions about human nature and human behavior. It wasn't a very good novel.

There was a lot to like about the imagined town called Walden Two. It was very sensible. But certain things struck me as odd—for example, Skinner's obsession with hours of labor. At Walden 27, all people really seemed to take account of was completion of tareas. Some people finished quickly and moved on to their own activities. Others worked long hours. (I had a feeling Mr. Thoreau would have been one of those.) Dr. Skinner's fictional psychologist, who was the guiding force of Walden Two, didn't seem to do much work of any kind other than planning. He struck me as behaving rather like a privileged plutocrat.

One passage in Skinner's book almost made me laugh out loud: "A wealthy class to provide leisure for the artist is characteristic of a great age." He obviously had never met anyone from the 21st century's "wealthy class." Our own "great age" had reached the conclusion that any art worth having must be the kind that not only earned a living for the artist, but profit for the plutocrats as well. Art had to be marketable. Artists should produce what the market demanded. In Dr. Skinner's designed community, on the other hand, artists were nurtured and given ample time to pursue their arts—music, painting, writing. I liked that part.

I found a few more things to like, but mostly I found Dr. Skinner's supposedly utopian vision unattractive. It struck me as too authoritarian, although the fictional founder kept insisting it wasn't. I also didn't like Skinner's dismissive attitude toward history, and I couldn't miss the irony of reading those words of disdain nearly a century and a half after they were written, as I engaged in my own little piece of historical research. More than anything else, I think I resented his belittling of a library as nothing more than a shoddy secondhand bookstore. I happened to have a personal fondness for both of those things.

I skipped through Skinner's long passages on the rearing of children. I was afraid it would be too much like the educational boarding colonies established by the plutocrats. Besides, as I've mentioned, children were a rarity in Walden 27; they were not something I knew much about nor found particularly interesting.

At this point I was still taking Chulel. After using the two annual doses I'd brought with me, I'd acquired more from the Walden 27 apothecary. As I dug into my research, I began wondering why Waldeners in general eschewed Chulel. I wondered what Mr. Thoreau and Dr. Skinner would have thought about it. I'm pretty sure Mr. Thoreau would have turned up his nose at the unnaturalness of Chulel. I was uncertain about Dr. Skinner, until I tracked down another book he'd written. It was called *Enjoy Old Age: A Practical Guide*. It was intended to aid the aging in accommodating to the physical and mental disabilities incumbent to their stage of life and claimed to offer "uplifting advice." It terrified me and I vowed to continue taking Chulel.

10.

"I have to make a run up to Palmyra day after tomorrow," Walter told me one Thursday evening when I'd joined him and his house family for supper. "Do you reckon you'd want to come along?"

Because of Walter's familiarity with the region, he was occasionally set tarea of running errands such as this one to the Book Community known as Palmyra, with which Walden 27 maintained an arrangement of mutual support. He'd told me that Palmyra lay to the southwest and was predominately Muslim, although it included Christians of several denominations and a small group of Jews. Like Walden 27, they operated as a sufficiency community.

"Would they let me?" I couldn't believe I was asking such a question. How much of myself had I signed over to the Walden Network, anyway?

"Most of what I'm taking are hygiene supplies for their women, so you'd be my assistant on this particular run."

I knew what he was talking about. We had a workshop in Walden 27 that manufactured products that women could use during their menstrual periods. No one here seemed to have much discomfiture about discussing such things across gender lines, but maybe some of the people in Palmyra were more reticent. Walter was offering me my first opportunity to take a trip outside Walden 27 since my sad journey to Havana, New Mexico. I agreed to go and quickly received the necessary approval.

I was happy to be going somewhere outside Walden 27. I sometimes grew annoyed with the easy contentment I felt there most days. I was still a Vintagonist at heart, wasn't I? And didn't we hold fervently to the belief that engagement with the world was important? I reminded myself that we were only going to Palmyra, a Book Community that perhaps constituted its own self-contained world even more completely than Walden 27 did. Regardless, it was a beautiful spring day, and I intended to enjoy the outing.

"I hope it doesn't rain," I remarked as I stared out the truck window. There were clouds overhead and darker ones gathering on the horizon.

"Don't say that," Walter replied. "You know we need all the rain we can get around here."

"Oh, right. Has there always been such a water shortage in West Texas?"

"No, I don't think so. I hear the Apaches managed to make a good living in these parts back in the day, but then they had full access to the springs up at Balmorhea that used to run more than fifty-six million liters a day. There's never been a lot of rain, though, as far as I know. We have to conserve every drop of water we can."

The clouds dissipated as the day heated up. It didn't rain.

Walter was eager to show me some attractions of his beloved West Texas. "I think we have enough time to drop by the old Chinati Foundation in Marfa," he said. "Well, I guess it's now the 'Chinati Art Experience.'" He explained that the Experience was housed in several large modern buildings where tourists and sabbaticos could watch 3-D projections of some huge concrete geometric forms built back in the 20th century by an artist called Donald Judd. "They're classic minimalist abstract art," Walter explained. "That's what the advertising says. Anyway, at the theaters, you can select what time of day and what time of year you want to experience the sculptures. The light interacts with the forms in different ways depending on these variations. Personally, I like early fall, just before sunset. They have music to go with it, and the sculptures move and dance along with the tunes."

"That could be nice," I said, struggling to visualize dancing geometric forms. "Is that what we're going to see?"

"Hardly. Those shows are pricey. They're mainly for plutocrats and for any professionals who earn enough credits to pay their way. There's a fancy hotel up in there, too."

After a brief silence I asked, "So where are we going?"

Walter smiled. "We're going to see the real thing."

I was puzzled.

"The actual sculptures are still there," Walter laughed, "right outside the theaters that show the simulated ones."

We pulled off the road and walked about five hundred meters to a large open field where I could see some huge rectangular concrete blocks, square in cross section, that were maybe five meters long and about half that high. They were arranged in geometrically varied groupings. All the blocks were weathered, with moss growing along their eroded edges. Some had large cracks with grasses growing through. A few of the less solid blocks had collapsed in the center. A few more had tilted on their foundations and I saw why when a ground squirrel darted into a hole underneath the one nearest to us.

Even in their deteriorated state, the sculptures were impressive. I liked how they were now a collaborative work of both artist and nature. Walter set down his bag inside one of the more intact structures and began laying out a picnic.

"This set of sculptures was what saved Marfa from the fate of a dozen other small towns in these parts that faded off the map long ago," he said. "Instead of dying out, Marfa got to be a tourist destination. But that's also what finally handed it over to the plutocrats. Ordinary folk like my family couldn't afford what Marfa had to offer. Certain times of year, this place is just lousy with sabbaticos. But I kind of like that we've reclaimed these sculptures as a people's park." He handed me a plate laden with sandwiches and fresh fruit.

"Tell me more about this place we're headed to," I said as we ate. "Palmyra. All I know so far is that it's a Book Community. Where exactly is it located?"

"Technically, it's in Mexico."

"What? You didn't tell me we'd have to cross an international border. Won't I need documents for that?"

"Relax." Walter chuckled. "Not all borders are the same. Besides, Mexico doesn't really claim Palmyra anymore. It's kind of a no-man's-land. No worries."

"I don't understand."

"Palmyra is down near Presidio, just north of Ojinaga. Real pretty area, where the Rio Conchos joins up with the Rio Grande. Daddy told me that the town started off around maybe 2017 as a detention center for Muslim immigrants, mostly from Syria. There were also some native-born Americans who happened to be Muslim who got thrown into the mix for reasons that most people don't seem to remember. Anyway, when Texas went independent in 2020, they kind of forgot about this particular detention center—some people say it was on purpose—and it got left in the hands of its corporate managers. And then the rivers changed course in the big floods a few years later and the corporation folks just up and left. Abandoned it. The upshot is that what started off a detention center became an independent community. The original Muslim residents took in some dissident Catholics from Central America and then, a little later, some Jewish refugees from Israel. It was one of the earliest Book Communities, making peace among all the children of Abraham, as they say. Population's around four thousand or thereabouts now."

We remained in the shade of our chosen sculpture for a while longer. Walter poured more tea, and I pulled a book out of my bag.

"Why are books so important to you, Malia?" Walter asked. "I mean, I like a good story as much as anybody, but I'm happy enough reading on my screen. With you it's always a printed paper book."

I was taken aback. Books—physical books—had been an integral part of my personal world for as long as I could remember. "You know I've been a life-long Vintagonist," I said, not at all certain how much that explained, feeling somehow I was confusing cause and effect.

"But Walden Network publishes new books, too," Walter countered. "Why should we bother with print copies of new books?"

"Because," I said, groping for something that would make sense to Walter, something true, "once it's in black-and-white, on paper, between covers, it can't be changed. It can be discussed, argued over, disagreed with, and challenged, but what you've written is there for anyone to see." I had a fleeting thought about the print-on-demand paperbacks that had become popular in the waning days of print books, but I decided not to challenge my own argument. I knew my love of books was in large part irrational, and that was something I was still reluctant to share with Walter.

After we got back on the road, I watched the landscape growing drier and more barren the farther we traveled.

"How do these people in Palmyra make a living? This doesn't look very promising," I said.

"You'll see." Walter winked at me.

And I did. As we came up over a low hill, I stared open-mouthed at a verdant valley where two rivers met. As the community of Palmyra came into view, I saw the minaret, the church steeple, and the dome topped by a Star of David.

We concluded our business in Palmyra with no difficulties. I supervised the delivery of our merchandise to a very business-like contingent of women while Walter went off to negotiate for return cargo. We were each provided with a room for the night and supper in our respective gendered areas of the communal dining hall. I observed that families ate together, and I was surprised to see that some of the families included two or even three children. Single or otherwise unaccompanied men and women ate at separate tables. The custom seemed a bit anachronistic and clearly unnecessary to me, but it was not my place to criticize. My tablemates chattered about their work, as well as about who was seeing whom and what they each would be wearing to the community festival next week. I didn't ask, but my conclusion was that these women didn't simply look young. They were young.

Walter and I departed immediately after breakfast the next morning. The truck was loaded with fresh produce, boxes of dishes from Palmyra's ceramics atelier, and a couple of crates of cheeping chicks. As we made our way back toward Walden 27, I finally asked Walter the question that had been gnawing at me.

"Why do the plutocrats tolerate these sufficiency communities? Palmyra. Walden 27."

Walter's gaze swept across the landscape before turning back to me. "I'm not altogether for certain," he said, "but I'll tell you what I think. I think it's because we're people they don't have to concern themselves with. As long as we keep to ourselves, they can kind of ignore our existence. We're not part of their world. And that, Malia, is as much their choice as it is ours. Maybe more so."

I'd never thought about it that way, but I had to admit there was a certain compelling logic in what he said. It implied that members of sufficiency communities—Simpletons, Menders, Book followers—weren't so much renegades from society as we were its outcasts.

"So as long as we pose no threat to them they just let us go our way? And really, with the kind of power and control the plutocrats wield, how could we ever pose a threat?" I sighed.

"Exactly." Walter paused. "Although...Did you ever hear about those seed warehouses they set up a hundred or so years back? Somewhere in Scandinavia, I think it was."

His change of topic caught me by surprise. "Oh. Yeah, I think I read about that somewhere. Do you suppose they're still there?"

"That's not my point," Walter said. "My point is that Walden Network, Menders' colonies, Book Communities—all of us are kind of like those seed warehouses, preserving the seeds of different ways of life."

"Ah," I said. "I suppose we are in a way. Do you think we'll ever get to plant those seeds in wider fields?"

Walter tilted his head, and I detected a small shrug of his shoulders. I had a sudden vague recollection about Dr. Skinner's fictional behavioral scientist and his highly managed social laboratory. Was it possible we were somebody else's laboratory and not simply our own experiment?

We rode on in silence. Except for the cheeping of the chicks.

II.

The more I accommodated to life in Walden 27, the more I found myself resenting change, so when a new member joined our singleton dining community, I wasn't particularly pleased. She introduced herself as Mandy Pequot. I was mystified why anyone as young as she appeared to be was eating with the singletons. Before the meal was over, I had to ask.

"How old are you, Mandy?"

She gave me a look that took me back to my own days of sullen adolescence. She shrugged her shoulders and may have rolled her eyes. "I'm seventeen," she said, with a touch of petulance. "Eighteen soon." In fact, she'd only recently turned sixteen, but I didn't learn that until later.

In time, she and I both relaxed a bit, and we became what I would call friends. I'm not sure she would have agreed to that terminology. Not at first, anyway. We sat together at meals and always seemed to find something to talk about. I learned that she was working in the produce-processing center, washing and sorting fruits and vegetables. She began to supply me with information about what was coming in at the market.

"Pequot is an unusual last name," I remarked one day, as Mandy and I lingered over an especially nice dessert. Everyone else had left the table.

She gave me a sidewise look. "It's not really my last name," she said. "It's just the name of a place near a lake."

"Is that where you're from?"

"Never even been there. I think it's in Minnesota. I thought it sounded pretty." She gave me a crooked grin, which failed to mask her apprehension about sharing such personal information.

"You know that makes me even more curious about who you are and where you're from." I laughed. "I won't ask, but please know you can trust me with whatever you feel like telling me."

She played with the last bit of cobbler in her bowl, pushing it with her spoon from one side to the other. "It's no big deal, really," she said at last. "I was at one of those educational boarding colonies. And I decided to leave. And I met somebody from Walden 27 in town. And, well, here I am." She shrugged.

"You met someone in Alpine, you mean?"

"No, Fort Stockton."

"What were you studying in school? Do you miss it?"

"It wasn't really school. It was more like... I don't even know a word to describe it. It was like they were turning off our minds and writing stuff inside our heads. Anyway, I'd finished the basics and they were training me to work in one of the hunting resorts. You know, those places where rich people go to shoot tame animals so they can feel like bigshot hunters. They were expecting that's what I'd be doing the rest of my life. And the way things are going, even I could see that might be a really long time. So I left."

I was taken aback. I'd heard stories about the cognitive photonic programming that supposedly went on in the children's boarding colonies. I remembered my own brief experience after that first raid on Codex2. I thought Mandy must be an unusually strong-minded, strong-willed individual to have walked away from it. I was impressed. "What about your family?"

"My family?" She shook her head. "When they sent me off to the boarding colony they never expected to see me again. We were just poor goat ranchers." Mandy smiled. "Have you ever seen angora goats? They're pretty little things. Dumb, but pretty. And we just sheared them, never hurt them. Anyway, my folks were guaranteed I'd end up with a good job if I went to the colony. They thought I'd be better off."

I wasn't sure what I thought about that. I recalled my estrangement from my own parents. "Do you find your work here more to your liking?"

Her face clouded. "I guess so," she said. "At least there's no killing. Fruits and vegetables don't bleed."

Her claim of satisfaction wasn't convincing. There was something she wasn't telling me, but I figured it could wait. I didn't want to push too hard and have her clam up on me. I remembered being young. So we switched the conversation to books. She'd told me that she never had the opportunity to do much reading. I encouraged her to come by the library sometime, offering to help her locate something she'd like.

She did come to the library, and I offered her a book about a young wizard called Harry Potter. There was a whole series of these books, and I recalled that they'd been fairly popular among some of our customers at Codex2. A week later she returned for another and then another. She wanted to talk with me about the stories and our friendship grew.

And then one day Mandy was absent from our evening meal. I decided to go in search of her. Like me, she had her own cottage, despite her youth. When she came to the door, I could see she'd been crying.

"Sorry I missed dinner, Malia," she said, as if I'd come to scold her. "I wasn't hungry."

"Well, I've brought you some food anyway. You'd just as well put it in your chillbox. You might want it later."

As she opened the door wider to take the food, she looked up into my face and began to sob. I went inside, closing the door behind me.

"What is it, Mandy?" She'd turned away from me, but I could see her shoulders convulsing with silent pain. "Please tell me. Maybe I can help." I wanted so much to put my arms around her, but I didn't want to overstep. I took her arm and gently guided her toward the sofa.

Between sobs, in bits and pieces, her story came together. I learned that the person she'd met in town, the one who'd brought her to Walden 27, was the man who was her direct supervisor at the produce center. She'd been living on the street in Fort Stockton for several days when he ran across her.

"He seemed kind," Mandy said. "He gave me some fresh fruit. And then he offered me a job."

I knew the job wasn't his to offer, but I began to see the direction her story was taking. This man who had initially seemed like her savior had ended up trying to convince her that she owed him something for rescuing her from the road and a life as a fugitive student.

"He started coming to my cottage at night." Mandy hesitated, closing her eyes. "He said I needed to show him some gratitude. He wanted..." She opened her eyes and looked up at me, shyly pleading for understanding. "He wanted sex." Her hands balled up into fists and she pounded them on her slender thighs as the tears welled up again.

"Oh, Mandy, that's so wrong!" I looked at her small, fragile frame and saw the despair shrouding her face. *She's barely more than a child*, I thought. "That's abuse. There's no other word for it." I knew there was another word for it, but it was a word I couldn't bring myself to utter aloud.

I took a deep breath and reached over, taking one of her hands in mine. "This is going to stop," I said, my voice trembling with rage against this man I didn't even know. "Here and now. We'll take it to the supervisory council and put an end to it once and for all."

She looked up at me with terror-stricken eyes. "But he said if I told I'd have to leave. I've got nowhere to go, Malia." She began to sob again.

"No, little girl," I said, fighting the surge of anger that was now pounding in my heart and resonating in my temples. "You won't have to leave. If anyone does any leaving, it'll be him."

"But he can't leave. He's married. He has a daughter."

"Oh, lord." *Bastard!* I thought. My anger threatened to boil over and I struggled for some semblance of calm, for Mandy's sake. "Look, Mandy." I reached over and took her other hand, turning to face her, gently turning her to face me. "Look at me, little girl, and listen to what I'm saying. You are not to blame for any of this. He's an adult and he has abused you in the worst way. He must accept the consequences. I'll go with you to file the report. Tell me his name. Name him."

"Donald," she said quietly. "Donald Bruce." Her eyes were oceans of pain, overflowing. She pulled away. "I haven't told you everything yet." She clasped her hands together, squeezing them between her knees as her shoulders arched forward more tightly. "I'm pretty sure I'm pregnant."

What wanted to be a scream of anguish for this child's dismal fate collapsed into a soft moan as my own tears began to flow. I reached for Mandy and drew her in protectively, inside the bubble of a fierce anger that raged outward against this evil man and all the evils of this evil world. She clung to me, trembling. We sat there a long while, two women crying together.

When I was finally able to speak, I murmured softly, "We can handle this, too, Mandy. We can do this."

Mandy sat up. She nodded and inhaled sharply.

"First thing tomorrow morning, we go to the supervisory council," I said. "Then we go to the doctor. I'll be with you. It'll be okay. But I'm not leaving you alone tonight. Shall I stay here, or would you rather come to my cottage?"

She agreed to come to my cottage and, although she didn't say it, I knew it was out of fear that her abuser would come looking for her at her own place later that evening. How often had he done that? Again my anger seethed.

As soon as we reached my cottage, Mandy began to relax. We drank tea and then I settled her onto my sofa with plenty of blankets, even though it wasn't cold. The sofa was narrow and barely long enough even for her small body, but she insisted she'd be fine.

In my own bed in the loft, I stared into the darkness, trying to understand the full import of the anger that overwhelmed my futile efforts to pacify myself into sleep. I didn't even know this Donald Bruce and yet I despised him and everything about him. He was a monster who had taken this child's innocence and destroyed it. I was eager for morning to come, impatient to deal with this tragedy so that we could put it behind us, so that it could be forgotten and life could go on. Why did I think that was possible? How could something so heinous ever be forgotten? At last I fell into a troubled sleep, waking the next morning with the urgent sense that my dreams had been trying to tell me something. I closed my eyes again, trying to call up the elusive images. There was a man and a young girl sprawled on the floor as he attacked her. I was sure I was the girl, but the man's face was unclear. He looked too young to be Donald Bruce. The image faded and I got up to check on Mandy.

The two of us shared a light breakfast at my cottage—coffee and some fruit and a muffin from the bakery. We didn't want to join the others in the dining room; we only wanted to get on with the business of the day. Our own business. We used my fixed screen to tag ourselves "sick" on the Walden 27 boards and to make an appointment for Mandy at the clinic. Then we set off to make our report to the council.

I didn't know what to expect. I'd had infrequent dealings with the council and in truth didn't fully understand how they functioned. My research had produced no clue as to how they'd handle a situation like this one. But I knew where the office was and soon we were seated on a wooden bench, awaiting the arrival of the council member who was in charge of the office for the day. A disturbing thought arose in my mind. *What if Donald Bruce is on the council? What if he's the one in charge today?* But when the door opened and the expression on the receptionist's face told me this was the person we were waiting for, I sighed with relief. The council member in charge was my friend Frances, the librarian.

"Hi, Malia," she said brightly. "I thought I saw that you were calling in sick for your afternoon tarea."

"More like a personal day, I guess. Anyway, we need to talk to you."

She ushered us into the office and closed the door. I introduced her to Mandy. "My young friend has something she needs to tell you. Something you need to know about." I took

Mandy's hand in mine and tried to give her an encouraging look. Her hand was ice cold and trembling.

"I would like to report..." She faltered, her voice choked with tension. And then the words began to tumble out. "My supervisor, Mr. Bruce. He abused me. He said I'd be sent away if I didn't have sex with him. I'm barely seventeen. I didn't know what to do. And now I'm pregnant."

Frances' eyes grew wider with every word. "Donald Bruce?" she said. "Good lord! I'm so sorry about this. But, my dear, I have to say I'm grateful that somebody's finally found the gumption to report him. Up to now it's just been gossip. You've not been his only victim, child." She took a deep breath, turning to her desk screen, tapping it aggressively. I felt Mandy's hand relax a bit. I thought it felt warmer.

"He's the one who sponsored you, isn't he? Someone should have warned you about that man." She sat back in her chair, drumming with her fingers on the desk. Then she pushed a portable screen toward Mandy. "You can write up your report here. Then the clinic will have to do a DNA match. That's all we'll need from you. We'll deal with Mr. Bruce. We'll also provide whatever medical and psychological and even social services you need, should you desire to continue the pregnancy." She looked inquiringly at us.

I felt Mandy shudder. "No way," she said. "I want everything about this man cleaned out of me."

Frances nodded. "We'll also assign you to different tarea. We're short one worker at the library, so maybe there?"

"She knows a lot about raising goats," I said.

Mandy gave me a surprised look, and I saw one corner of her mouth curve up into a hint of a smile.

Frances nodded and added a note into her screen. "I'll send you a list of choices, Mandy, but I'm officially giving you a week off. Let me know if you need more." She patted the portable screen, looking at Mandy. "Just write what happened, dear. Intimate details aren't necessary. Only the pertinent facts. Now. I'm going to go get a cup of coffee. You and Malia can leave the screen on the desk and go when you're finished. And Mandy... Thank you again for your courage. I'm sure you're saving other women from abuse. You're doing the right thing."

As I watched Mandy entering her story into the screen, I kept having these strange sensations that I later described to myself as a sort of mental nausea. Like trying to regurgitate poison. Or lies. I held it in check with measured breathing, concentrating on a couple of hens scratching for breakfast in the yard outside the window.

"Done," Mandy said at last. She picked up the screen and held it out toward me. "Would you mind reading it over to see that it makes sense?" I must have betrayed my dismay at the request because she followed up: "Please?"

"Sure," I said. My mind had finally calmed, but now it was turning all topsy-turvy again. I'd do this for Mandy. I struggled to distance myself from the events she described, focusing on the words, the grammar, the sense, the logic. It was hard to do; the events she was describing defied logic and were utterly senseless. It was rape; the word itself seared my mind like a hot iron. By the time I finished reading, tears were escaping from my unwilling eyes. I nodded without looking up and handed the screen back to Mandy. "I think that covers it. I'm sure this will do fine."

We left the council offices, making our way toward the clinic. "Have you thought about what you're going to do?" I asked.

"Nothing to think about. Like I said, I want to be shed of this man, every part of him."

We walked the rest of the way to the clinic in silence.

It didn't take long for the physician to confirm her pregnancy, which she said was around eight weeks along.

"How do you wish to proceed?" she asked, looking first at Mandy and then at me.

"Abortion," Mandy said simply. "No question. I need an abortion."

"She has good reasons," I added.

"Yes, I received the order for DNA testing from the council. I understand. Well, then," the doctor continued, "there are several procedures available. Most women prefer the pharmaceutical method, since it's non-invasive, relatively painless, and permits you to take care of everything at home."

"No." Mandy spoke firmly. "I want it done now. Here. I don't want to walk out of here still pregnant." Her pleading look and the tears collecting in her eyes made her case.

The doctor explained the procedure in some detail, as Mandy and I both gave her our undivided attention. "Do you want your mother to stay with you?" she asked Mandy.

We both smiled at that.

"I'm her friend," I said. "Her mother doesn't live here."

"And, yes, I want my friend to stay with me."

I watched as Mandy was prepped for the procedure and then stood next to her, holding her hand as the doctor inserted first the speculum and then a device to dilate her cervix sufficiently to permit insertion of the tube that would evacuate her young womb. The little machine hummed for a few minutes. Mandy winced a couple of times as her uterus cramped, doing its part to squeeze itself empty.

And then it was over. The devices were removed, and the doctor began poking at the tissue that the vacuum tube had removed. I'm not sure what came over me, but I heard myself asking, "May I have a look, too?"

"Certainly," she said. "Do you want to see, Mandy?"

Mandy closed her eyes and shook her head "no".

I looked. The bloody fluid contained coagulated lumps and several fragments that a few minutes before had been an embryo, a potential human being. I went back to Mandy and placed my arm around her slumped shoulders. Tears flowed down Mandy's cheeks and somehow I knew they were tears not only of relief but also of grief, a grief that her body felt in its loss. Her body couldn't understand why this had to be done, why it had to submit to her mind and will. Hormones are complicated.

I knew I'd stay with Mandy that night, sleeping on her sofa as she'd slept on mine the night before. I wanted to keep an eye on her, care for her, bring her food and drink and let her experience fully what she'd been through. I wanted to help her move forward to an understanding that she was free now, free from the abuse and oppression of a man who had thought of nothing but his own physical desires. It would take time for Mandy to recover. She needed a friend.

The next morning Mandy insisted I go to my tarea at the wood shop. "I'm going to be okay, Malia," she said with a gentle smile. "Can you bring me lunch when you finish work? And maybe a book?"

My fellow workers at the shop were all agog talking about how Donald Bruce in produce-processing had been brought before the supervisory council last evening on charges of rape and how he had been sentenced to nine months of shunning, during which he would reside in a cell at the very center of town, away from wife and child and in plain view of the whole community of Walden 27.

"Nine months!" one of my companions said. "That's harsh, but I'm sure he deserves it. There's been talk before."

I was shocked at the rapidity of the Walden 27 judicial process, although I couldn't quarrel with its verdict. I kind of wished they would have banished him from the community forever, but I knew they felt prolonged shunning was more appropriate. Their intent was not simply to punish the man, but to change him. For reasons that I still find hard to comprehend, it was about this time that I stopped taking Chulel.

12.

At the calendar age of eighty-seven I completed my first new novel in nearly thirty years. And for the first time I published under my own name. It wasn't quite up to Vlad Carpenter's standards. It was a simpler story, loosely based on the life history of one of the early founders of the Walden Network, a woman named Madeline Ellis. Madeline had known Kat Kincade at Twin Oaks Community, which had been modeled on the fictional town in B. F. Skinner's *Walden Two*. My initial suspicions that the founders of the Walden Network had been aware of Dr. Skinner's book had been well founded. My novel was in limited distribution, but it was received with warm appreciation.

"How did you learn so much about books, Malia?" Frances asked me one evening as we labored over some much needed book repairs.

"I told you, I've been a book addict most of my life," I laughed. "Plus, I worked at that bookstore in D.C. before I came here." I'd never told her much about that period of my life. "You know, there aren't really libraries out there anymore. Well, there are. Only they don't have any books. Not real books like these." I held up the volume I'd just saved from disintegration, inspecting my handiwork.

"Do you think there are still very many books out there? Maybe books that people have stashed away somehow?"

"That's hard to say. The corporate authorities were rounding them up pretty vigorously for recycling."

"I've heard stories about that," Frances said, "about how sometimes they would raid bookshops and even take booksellers into custody."

I thought about the raid on Codex2 in 2045. That may have been one of the stories she'd heard, but, if so, she hadn't heard it from me. That was ancient history now and hadn't we managed to rebuild our inventory and keep Codex2 open for another thirty years?

"I'd guess there are still a lot of books around," I said, "but you'd have to know where to look."

"Would you know?"

"I might know who to ask."

That was the beginning of my new—and ultimately rather brief—assignment as acquisitions clerk for the library. They let me use the wired screens to communicate with some people I'd known back in D.C. One of these was Alicia Urbanek, who I discovered was now living in Austin. She said she still had some books and that she'd be delighted to have them housed in an actual library, even if it was a library off in the middle of nowhere.

I began making preparations to travel to Austin to meet with Alicia, hoping to return to Walden 27 with a couple of boxes full of books for our library. It was almost 700 km to Austin, and I calculated that the trip would take approximately five hours.

Of course I was nervous, even though the woman I was going to meet was someone I'd known ever since my earliest days working at Codex2. As I sat in the autocar that Walden 27 had assigned me for the trip, I kept thinking back to conversations Alicia and I had shared at the bookshop in D.C. She wasn't a passionate Vintagonist like me, just a woman who loved reading and who was aware of the changes that were being made in the corporate-issued digital versions of books. She preferred the printed ones. I wondered how she'd ended up in Austin. I wondered what kinds of books she'd have for us. I hoped there would be no difficulties with the payment device I'd brought to compensate her for the books. *Stop worrying,* I told myself. *It'll be nice to see an old friend,* I told myself. *Enjoy the scenery.*

I was meeting Alicia at a coffee shop on Guadalupe Street, a few blocks north of the Ex University campus. I arrived early, ordered a coffee, and sat at a table off in the corner, where I immediately began to feel self-conscious. First of all, everyone else had their digilets. I'd left mine in Walden 27; I hadn't used it in ages and had serious doubts about whether it was still functional. I could see that it would have looked old and clunky alongside these newer models. I almost laughed, thinking about my "vintage" digilet. Second, there was the way I was dressed. It wasn't that everyone else looked so great. It was only that nobody else was wearing the iconic trousers and tunic of the Simpletons of Walden Network.

I made a mental note to ask for permission to wear something different next time I came into town. *If there is a next time*, I mused. But what would I wear? I decided I should go shopping before I headed back. I'd buy myself one outfit. I'd use the payment device and tell the supervisors at Walden 27 that it was an essential business expense. I started scripting that conversation.

Then I saw Alicia. I'd have known her anywhere; she looked exactly as she had thirty years ago in D.C., thanks, of course, to Chulel. Her eyes passed over me as she searched the tables, eventually coming back to me, offering an uncertain smile. I knew that I'd put on a little weight since I'd stopped taking Chulel and that my hair was a little gray, but I didn't think I'd changed that much. Apparently I had.

I smiled up at Alicia as she bent to give me a quick hug. "It's so good to see you," she enthused as she took a chair that put her back to the room, her face to a wall.

"However did you end up in Austin?" I asked. "I thought you were from the Northwest. Portland was it? Or Seattle?"

"Seattle," she said. "But you know how it is these days. Ties with family and friends seem to evaporate the more people avail themselves of those memory adjustments." Her jovial tone couldn't mask the sadness in her eyes. "Anyway, after so many of my friends left D.C., I started looking to leave, too. Then I was offered a job here in Austin, curating exhibits at one of the interactive museums."

"You don't look any different than you did in D.C.," I said, "and yet you remember..." I didn't have to complete the thought. Alicia knew what I was alluding to.

She leaned forward, speaking more softly. "Thank goodness for Recall, right?"

We talked a while about things we remembered from D.C., speaking quietly, not wanting to attract attention.

"Are you sure you're okay with letting go of your books?" I asked.

She waved a hand dismissively. "I've read all of them, Malia," she said. "Most of them many times over. I'll keep a few of my favorites, of course. I can keep a half dozen or so hidden away. But I need to get rid of the rest and I can't think of anything better than having them go to your library." She leaned forward and touched my hand gently. "It's the best thing. I don't know who to trust anymore," she said, "except for you, of course." She patted my hand. "I've always been able to trust you. But other people... Sometimes someone you thought you could trust turns out to be a corporate police lieutenant or something." The look in her eyes told me this was not hypothetical.

"I understand," I said.

We dawdled over our coffee, finding plenty of shared memories to talk about.

"Look, I know you need to get back to West Texas," Alicia said, as our conversation began to lag.

"It's a long drive, but the autocar will do all the work," I responded with a smile.

We went out to Alicia's autocar, which she repositioned alongside mine. Before we got out of her car, I pulled out the payment device I'd brought from Walden 27. As soon as she saw it, Alicia held up a hand, shaking her head vigorously.

"Put that away. You're doing me a favor, Malia. Really. If anything, I should be offering to pay you." She smiled, but I thought it was a sad little smile. We made a quick transfer of the two heavy boxes, moving them from her autocar to mine.

Before we parted ways, she placed a small bundle into my hands. "This is for you, Malia," she said. "Just something you might find useful." And without even giving me time to say "thank you" she got back into her car and drove away.

I did stop by a boutique nearby on Guadalupe Street, intending to buy that new outfit to wear next time I left Walden 27. But as I sat in the car, watching the stylishly dressed and unfalteringly young women coming and going, I lost heart and drove away without even going inside.

As the car began its journey back to Walden 27, I opened the packet Alicia had given me. It contained a digilet and a portable screen. I was uncertain what I would do with them; my agreement with Walden 27 forbade use of such things. By the time I reached my cottage, I'd decided what to do; I hid them away in a bottom drawer of my dresser.

Some of these Waldener rules continued to rankle my latent Vintagonist sensibilities. I'd recently come across an essay by Thoreau called "On the Duty of Civil Disobedience," which advocated flouting the laws of governments that were engaged in unconscionable actions. At the time Thoreau was writing, the worst of these "unconscionable actions" was slavery. I was reminded of how Vintagonists and our allies had used measures such as boycotts, forced divestiture, and demonstrations to protest against the "unconscionable actions" of the plutocrats. And now, here I was, submitting to rules I disagreed with, offering up no protest whatsoever.

Frances was thrilled with the books I'd acquired. Alicia was a discerning reader and her collection was impressive. I smiled when I saw the Codex2 stamp inside the back cover of almost every book. Of course, it didn't say "Codex2". We were never as blatant as that. I smiled again when I realized that she'd sent no Vlad Carpenter books. I knew Alicia had some. They had to be among the ones she was keeping for herself.

13.

Less than a month after my trip to Austin, a message arrived for me on the wired screens in the office telling me that Alicia had more books for me. According to her message, one of our other D.C. bibliophile friends had passed through Austin recently and left a few dozen books with her, requesting that she search out a decent resting place for them. I should have paid attention to that twinge of suspicion that wanted to know why Alicia would have accepted more books when she'd been so eager to get rid of her own. But Frances was thrilled at the prospect of more acquisitions, and I couldn't refuse.

I was to meet Alicia at the same coffee shop where we'd met before. The closer I got to Austin the more doubts gnawed their way into my conscious mind. I remembered only too clearly Alicia's expression of relief when she'd delivered those boxes of books to me the month before. *Why in heaven's name would she have accepted more books?* It didn't make sense, but I refused to permit myself to begin conjuring up explanations. I didn't want to frighten myself.

I did decide I should wait in the car outside the coffee shop. I would wait until after I'd seen Alicia go in. I felt a little foolish doing this, but I did it anyway. It was hot inside the car, and I had to let all the windows down to get fresh air. The breeze was hot, too.

A car came to a stop nearby, just out of sight of the customers inside the coffee shop. It wasn't an ordinary autocar, but rather one of those big corporate vehicles, the kind with attendants. I was surprised to see Alicia get out of the back seat. A man inside the car spoke to her and she nodded. The car pulled away, stopping around the corner. Alicia didn't go inside immediately. Instead, she took a minute to look around. She saw me. I know she saw me. Our eyes met, but she gave no sign of recognition. Instead, she looked down and slowly shook her head "no" as she adjusted her handbag. Then she walked into the coffee shop.

My heart was thumping like tabla drums by this time. What was going on? I wanted to go inside, talk to Alicia, ask questions. But she'd sent me a message. Her "no" wasn't my imagination, was it? I waited, my mind a jumble of potential explanations, possible courses of action—the storyteller's curse. The storyline that appealed to me most was the one where I waited until she came out and then followed her home where I could talk with her out of sight and hearing of whoever was in the big car.

So I waited, sweating in the midday heat. After about twenty minutes, Alicia emerged from the café. She didn't even look in my direction this time, instead walking purposefully around the corner toward the parked car in which she'd arrived. As she approached the car, a large man emerged from the front seat. He stood staring at her, feet planted, his face red and distorted, his arms crossed over his broad chest.

I heard him say, "You failed, Alicia." His voice sounded tense. "Explain yourself!"

I couldn't hear Alicia's response. She cowered, and I thought she looked like she was on the verge of tears. The man grabbed her by the shoulder with his left hand. She turned her face away just as he raised his right hand and struck her across the cheek. She stifled a scream and covered her face with her hands. The man gave her a vicious shove, and she fell back heavily against the car, lost her balance, and landed seat-first on the ground. He grabbed her arm and jerked her to her feet as he opened the car's door and thrust her inside.

All this played out in slow motion as I watched, spellbound and speechless. Despite the intense heat, I began to shiver. I couldn't catch my breath. I felt weak and queasy. I heard a sudden noise, and I thought *Gunshots!* I covered my ears and cowered lower in the seat. But it couldn't be gunshots. Other cars continued driving slowly past. Customers inside the café kept on drinking and chatting, unperturbed.

I sat up and looked toward the car that was carrying Alicia away. Should I follow? That had been my plan. My trembling hand pressed a button. It was the one that instructed my car to return to its point of origin. As the car started up and pulled onto the road, I broke into helpless sobs, quaking with a fear I couldn't explain. It was as if I were the one who'd been attacked.

I knew I should help Alicia. I should report the attack. But to whom? What if the man who attacked her was the corporate police lieutenant she'd told me about? Angry and helpless, I let the car take me away, farther and farther away. The anger and terror traveled with me, refusing to dissipate. I felt as if someone were shaking me, trying to bring me to my senses. Should I go back to Austin? There was something I was missing here, and I groped for answers.

By the time I was forced to stop the car to use the bathroom, I'd begun to feel a little calmer, though I was still dazed, shaky, fearful. It was getting late, and the day had become overcast, so I purchased a full recharge for the car and bought myself some cookies, a bottle of NutriQuaff, and some pills called Duermata, which let me sleep for the rest of the journey. I woke up about ten kilometers outside Walden 27.

"Do you need me to help you unload the books, Malia?" the attendant asked when I returned the autocar to the community lot.

"There aren't any books," I told him. I didn't explain. I just headed for my cottage, walking quickly, head down, hoping I wouldn't encounter anyone on the path. At my doorway, I paused, looking in the direction that I thought was toward Austin. And then I went inside. I couldn't bear thinking about the day's events. I ate a quick snack and took some more Duermata.

The next morning, I headed for the library to find Frances. We'd made arrangements for me to go to the library instead of the wood shop on this particular Thursday morning.

We'd been counting on spending time together sorting and cataloguing the new shipment of books.

As soon as Frances saw me, she knew there was something wrong. "Malia?" she said. "What happened?"

I'd hoped to be able to tell Alicia's story to Frances without tears, but that didn't happen. She tried to reassure me.

"Don't worry about the books," she said.

The books were the farthest thing from my mind. In fact, I was pretty sure there hadn't been any books this time. "I'm worried about my friend Alicia. Why were they treating her like that? What was the point of this whole meeting? I don't get it."

"I shouldn't have let you go alone. Maybe I shouldn't have let you go at all. There have been reports about intensified efforts to search out underground book hoarders. I thought since you were meeting with a friend, it would be okay. You'd managed to pull it off last time with no problem. I'm really sorry."

"Is there no one to take our part? No one to stand up for Alicia and protect her?"

"I'm afraid not." Frances had her back to me as she stared out the window. "I'm afraid this is the way the world is now. Just be thankful for Walden 27."

14.

Any thoughts I might still have harbored about leaving Walden 27 were gone, and I lost myself in my work. I fell into a routine that left little time for questioning or contemplation.

On Monday and Thursday mornings I worked at the wood shop. My workmates were a pleasant lot, for the most part, and since we worked with hand tools these were quiet hours, conducive to quiet conversation. These were also the days I went to Walter's to have supper with his house family. On Tuesdays, Wednesdays, Fridays, and Saturdays, I worked at the library from after lunch until we were finished. I got on well with Frances and got to know more of our patrons. Mandy worked the same shift as me on two of my days.

Most of the remainder of my time I spent writing. I'd abandoned my research into Walden Network in favor of pure fiction. My new stories weren't as thematically weighty as Vlad Carpenter's had been. There were no political subtexts. These new novels were mysteries—cozy little mysteries in which bad things only happened to bad people, and everything worked out in the end. I even injected a little romance. My readers seemed to like that, which reminded me yet again that my intentionally solitary lifestyle might be lacking something.

I sent a message to Darlene to see if she and Zelda had found anything about Lio on the Returns page of Recall. They hadn't. There was also no word about Beatrice.

Mandy and I continued to enjoy each other's company. In addition to taking all our meals together, we sometimes went for long walks in the hills surrounding Walden 27. I was surprised at how much she knew about the plants and animals in our environment—real information, scientifically factual and often practical and useful. It embarrassed me to think about the childish stories I'd made up about these things in my early months at Walden 27.

Mandy had reached that age when most young people in the outside world would have begun taking Chulel and I was curious how she felt about it.

"Do you think you'll ever take Chulel?" I asked her one evening as we engaged in our ritual of dawdling over dessert.

"I doubt it. I don't think my parents ever did." She paused with her fork in midair.

"I've been thinking, Malia." She put down her fork and wiped some *dulce de leche* from her lips with the cotton napkin. "My parents would be in their sixties by now. I've been wondering if they're still able to do all the work around our little ranch, wondering if maybe they might need some help."

"Are you thinking of going back?"

"Maybe," she said. "Maybe just to visit, to see how they're getting on. I know the council doesn't look kindly on such requests, but maybe they'd let me go. Just for a visit." She paused and then looked up into my face. "Or I could do something to get myself expelled for a few weeks." She grinned.

"Well, I think you should try asking first." I liked the way this girl thought. She had spirit.

Mandy asked for the permission, and we were both a little surprised when it was granted with no pushback. When she came to tell me she was leaving, I knew I wouldn't see her again, but we both pretended that she was only going away for a few days. I hoped she'd be able to be a help to her parents. I knew she'd be a competent ranch manager herself. I knew I'd miss her.

Another person I cared about had gone away.

15.

Over the next two decades I wrote seven more novels. I held occasional readings at the library but after a while attendance at these events began to dwindle. My stories were becoming too repetitive, too predictable. Unexciting. I needed to write something new, something better, but I was uninspired.

I'd begun to experience some of those symptoms Dr. Skinner had dealt with in his book on aging. Some things were obvious: I had more gray hair and lines had appeared around my eyes and mouth. Physical activity became more taxing. Other changes were less visible.

When my menstrual periods became shorter and less intense, I was initially grateful. I wasn't even too concerned when they started to become irregular, although the unpredictability was sometimes inconvenient. But then one cool fall day, as I sat at our communal supper table with the windows open, the breeze stirring the tablecloth, I suddenly I felt as if my whole body was on fire. That was when I knew I could no longer deny it: this was menopause, the "change of life".

I took my changing body to the clinic, where they prescribed some herbal supplements and offered apologies for the fact that, ever since the advent of Chulel, medical research had abandoned things like symptomatic relief for menopausal women. There were meds to prevent conception, meds to enhance female sexual response, but nothing for the no-longer-normal symptoms of menopause. I took what they gave me, and it got me through the worst of it. Eventually the symptoms evened out and I was able to stop taking the supplements.

"Did you hear?" Frances asked in a stage whisper as I arrived for my regular afternoon library tarea.

"Hear what?"

Her eyebrows shot up and she motioned for me to join her in the break room where we could talk. As soon as the door was closed behind us, she answered.

"I can't believe you haven't heard about the man they found. He was unconscious and just lying out there in the mountains. Who knows how long he'd been there! Where could he have come from?"

I hadn't heard about this, but my curiosity was immediately piqued. "Don't we know anything about him? Has he regained consciousness?"

"I haven't heard. We don't even know his name. They say he had no digilet, no identification at all. They just found him this morning, so that's really all I've heard so far."

My mind went immediately into story mode, fabricating a half-dozen different possibilities. The only one I utterly refused was the one that began, *It's Lio...*

That evening at supper, the mystery man was the topic of animated conversation around our singletons' table. Everybody had something to say, but nobody seemed to have much information.

"The people who brought him in said his clothes and hair were all caked with mud. Do you suppose he'd been in the river?"

"Maybe he crossed over from Mexico. People used to do that all the time. Back and forth where there were no guards."

"One of my tarea partners was just leaving their shift at the hospital this morning when he was brought in. Apparently he was badly dehydrated but not malnourished. They think he probably hadn't been out there more than a couple of days."

"Yes, but who is he?" I wanted to know.

"He won't say. Or doesn't know."

I was deeply disturbed by all this talk of the person who wouldn't say who he was or maybe didn't know. It reminded me of Zelda.

I decided to put my name on the tarea list for hospital duty. I wanted to know more about this man who'd landed in our remote town. I didn't want to hear just gossip, what other people thought, what they'd heard someone say about what another person thought. I wanted to see, to know for myself.

Meanwhile, I asked around, trying to determine if he'd been found upriver, closer to New Mexico and maybe the community of Havana, but no one seemed to know. *Of course it's not Lio*, I told myself. But that night I dreamed about people who kept disappearing and reappearing in random places. One of them was Lio. Another one was me.

The following morning I was tapped for hospital duty. There were never very many people in our hospital at once, so I knew my round of delivering midday meals and refilling water dispensers wouldn't take long. Soon I'd know if the mystery man was still here. I'd be able to have a good look at him and maybe speak with him.

I examined each name sign on the door facings as I went about my tarea. There was Oscar Branson, who'd fallen trying to do tricks on his bicycle, leading to a chorus of comments (mostly behind his back) about how he probably should have given up such pursuits at least two decades ago. He told me he'd be going home tomorrow and asked if I knew anyone who had anything to trade in exchange for a slightly damaged bicycle.

There was old Mrs. Leverman, who'd had a heart attack. She wasn't looking well, but she smiled and thanked me for the lunch. There were also three people with a virus who were being kept as a precaution to prevent the illness from spreading through the whole community. I had to mask myself before entering their shared room and scrub my hands when I left.

And then I found a door sign that read, "Sally Who". I scrutinized the date of admission, the notes about the patient's condition, and realized that this was the person I'd been searching for. Our mystery man was apparently a mystery woman. I felt relief and disappointment in equal measure.

"Hi, Sally," I called brightly as I entered her room with the lunch tray.

She was sitting up in bed, staring out the window. She didn't respond. She didn't even react.

"It's a beautiful day, isn't it?" I offered, continuing with more meaningless pleasantries while she continued to ignore me. She was a pretty woman with short, wavy brown hair and a pale, slender face. It was impossible to tell how old she was. She looked young.

I walked to her bedside and gently touched her arm. She startled and slowly turned her face to look at my hand, then up into my face. When she looked at me, I thought her eyes looked very old.

"I've brought your lunch. It's on the table. I'll sit with you a while."

She was like a dreamwalker, moving in slow motion as she approached the table, took her seat, picked up her napkin, and spread it across her lap. I watched, saying nothing.

"It was... I..." She looked out the window again, squinting at the brilliance of the sun. Then she looked back at the plate of food, blinking as her eyes adjusted. She shook her head. Sadly, I thought.

"Not supposed to be here," she mumbled.

"Where were you going?"

She looked into my face with blank, expressionless eyes. "Not here." Tears seeped into those eyes. "It didn't work," she said, as she picked up her fork.

I reported all of this to the shift supervisor.

"Yeah," he said, "that's about all we've been able to get out of her. Still no name, no details."

It was well past lunchtime when I finished my tarea, too late to eat at the singletons' dining room, so I headed for Walter's house. He welcomed me and put together a plate of cheese and fruit and buttered bread. He poured us each a glass of cold cider and sat with me. I told him about Sally Who.

"You know," he said, "the folks over at Palmyra told me a year or so back about something similar. Some fella showed up lost, talking crazy. They finally figured out he'd come from this place up in the mountains called Final Answers. The good Christian from Palmyra said the Final Answers folks had some cockamamie ideas about how to release your spirit into the great bliss beyond, peeling off the material world like... like a banana or something." Walter shook his head, smiling slightly.

"Final Answers? What kind of place was that?"

Walter took a sip of his cider and gave me one of his looks as he set it down. "I guess you could say it was a suicide resort," he said. "Yeah, that's what I'd call it. Rich folks who decided they didn't want to live forever after all. Crazy plutocrats."

As I lay in bed that night, thinking about Sally Who, I couldn't help but wonder just how bad things had gotten out there in the world beyond Walden 27. My storylines about our mystery person had taken a different turn. They were no longer built around questions of *Who is he?* or *Where did she come from?* or *How did she get here?* My big question now was simply— *Why?*

16.

Sally Who became part of our community. She never was able—or willing—to say who she really was and so we stopped asking. To us, she was just Sally. It turned out that she was an accomplished artist and before long, blank walls all over Walden 27 were adorned with graceful murals depicting scenes of Planet Earth as if seen from outer space.

As my post-menopausal years wore on, the little lines on my face deepened into wrinkles. And then I started to become forgetful. It wasn't so bad at first—just misplacing my glasses (I needed glasses by then) or finding I'd put the box of tea on the wrong shelf. Since I lived alone, I decided it was nothing I couldn't live with. The only really aggravating part was when I knew there was a word for something I wanted to write, and I couldn't quite put my finger on it. Eventually, though, my absent-mindedness began affecting my work at the library: I started mis-shelving books.

Frances took me aside. "You're making a lot of mistakes, Malia. Are you okay? Can you tell me about this?"

Her kindness made me uncomfortable. Frances was one of the Walden 27 residents who still took Chulel. She'd told me about how she'd tended her own mother through a long and painful descent into dementia, and I couldn't help wondering if she thought that was what was happening to me.

"I'm sorry, Frances. I'll try to be more careful. I guess maybe I'm becoming a little forgetful. I'll try harder to concentrate on my work."

"Look, Malia. This isn't a big thing. Our apothecary can give you a remedy that can help."

Remembering my reticence to access the memory restoration processes associated with Chulel, I hesitated. "I don't know," I said. "I'm not sure."

"I'm told it's a very mild remedy. Lots of our older residents take it. You could at least try it and see if it helps."

I tried it. The apothecary assured me it was safe, an herbal remedy that had been used for centuries. After a couple of weeks, taking two pills a day, I could tell it was helping. It was a relief. I thought maybe this might have been why I'd been unable to write that ninth novel. Maybe now that my mind was clearer, more nimble, I'd be able to think of something. Maybe the words would begin to flow again.

The ninth novel never took off, so I went back to the unfinished story Vlad Carpenter had been working on before my life in Washington, D.C., had ended. I'd picked it up several times over the years, gaining encouragement from reading the pages I'd written as a younger woman, a free woman. A rebel. This time I felt only depression and despair.

The Simpleton way of life had worn me down and I was afraid it was too late now to make any other choices. I reminded myself how much I enjoyed working at the library here, dealing with the books. *But nobody ever sees these books except the people in this small town.* I reminded myself that the world outside Walden 27 was treacherous. *But isn't that the real world? Why am I hiding from it?* I reminded myself that out there, I would be alone.

In the midst of this growing malaise, I began remembering things. Odd things. It was amusing at first. I'd wake up in the morning thinking about a high school history teacher. Or a cup of coffee would suddenly take me back to a Vintagonist meeting with friends in Dallas. I remembered the colors of a hand-loomed scarf I'd snitched from a recycle box. I remembered some scraps of a poem I'd written for an English class.

And then one day it hit me: all of these memories were from my blank period, from sometime between 2029 and 2031. Was it possible that the pills I was taking to support my short-term memory were prying loose some things in my long-term memory as well?

Once the memories started coming back, there was no stopping them. It was a Pandora's Box. I started having nightmares. Violent nightmares. I thought I should stop taking the pills, but I didn't. Instead, I began writing all these fragments of memory down in a notebook. One of the memories that had returned was the memory of being curious.

I went back to the research I'd been working on when the ideas for my mystery novels started coming and I realized that I'd been running away from what I was about to discover. I suppose I never really had any illusions about Walden 27, but I'd so wanted to believe it was a benign sort of place. It wasn't. The Walden Network had been superimposed on a movement that had started out being purely about simplicity, minimalism, and a gentle, earth-based way of life. The Walden Network had more in common with Dr. Skinner's *Walden Two* than with Mr. Thoreau's poetic vision of the simple life.

17.

It was in early spring of 2125, when Walden 27 was abuzz with talk of gardening and animal husbandry, that I decided to break the rules. I dug out the screen and digilet that Alicia had given me and placed them near a window to see if they would recharge. *Just to see,* I told myself.

By the time I got home from the library that evening, I'd convinced myself not to be optimistic. I picked up the digilet first and saw that it was fully charged. I stared at it for a moment, hesitating. Then I opened its little screen, hardly daring to think it would connect me with the outside world but hoping nonetheless. There was a symbol indicating that I needed to update my operator. I figured Recall would be beyond my reach, but my curiosity was piqued. I chuckled to myself. *Well, let's see if we can do that.* I cushed the symbol. It began to gyrate and then the screen went dark. I laid the digilet on the side table with a sigh. *Foolish,* I said to myself. *Foolish, foolish old woman. The past is gone. Give it up. You're too old to be breaking rules.*

When I returned from supper, I saw the digilet and the screen lying where I'd left them and an involuntary sigh escaped my lips. I picked up the devices, intending to relegate them once again to the dresser drawer, but as I jostled the digilet, its screen lit up again. I examined it eagerly. "Your access phrase has expired. Touch here to request a new phrase." I stared, my finger poised over the symbol. Did I want to do this?

Of course I did. I cushed the symbol. I followed instructions. There were unfamiliar things moving about on the screen and then a brightly colored burst of images resolving into a message: "Welcome to the medianets!" Below the message were several choices. I could access FlixNews or Corporate News Network. I could access Your Journal or LifeBook. Or I could shop. I was uncertain about establishing a verifiable presence beyond Walden 27, so I avoided Your Journal and LifeBook. I was hungry for news, so I cushed the symbol for FlixNews.

After reading a few stories in FlixNews and a few more in CorpNet, I reached the inevitable conclusion that everything was hunky-dory in the outside world. It only made me hungrier for real news.

I decided to shop. First I searched for my sister Leticia's business in Dallas and found that it was still in existence. It was called Leti's Avant, and it now had a slick little entry featuring some very odd-looking garments and accessories. I'd become so accustomed to the non-fashion of Simpleton life that I almost laughed out loud at the oddities on display. I saw that Leticia had added a dance studio to her business. I remembered her childhood fondness for dance and my heart knew this was making her happy.

On a whim, I input the term "recall" to the shopping search box. I knew this had once been part of a clandestine pathway into the Recall zone of the infranet. What came up was a page detailing several products that had recently been recalled for various reputed malfunctions. One of them was a digital reader. I cushed that. I read the brief explanation of why the item was being recalled. I saw the FAQ: "frequently asked questions." *Why can't they let us ask our own questions?* I thought. I cushed the FAQ. At the bottom of the list was this question: "Do you have other concerns? Contact us." I cushed again. And for the briefest moment, I glimpsed a page that looked disturbingly like the old entry page for Recall. It was like an electric shock, this glance at an almost forgotten past. The page was gone before I could fully register its contents. Instead, there was an error indicator, telling me that the page I was looking for did not exist. Did Recall still exist? And then I was back on the opening screen for the medianets—FlixNews, CorpNet, shopping. I sat in stunned silence, my appetite for connection, for knowledge, whetted by this brief glimpse.

I was hooked. I updated the screen as well as the digilet and every night for the next week I spent an hour or more perusing the medianets, trying to read between the lines of the news stories, trying to figure out how to reconnect with Recall, hoping it was still there somewhere. I'd been using the search box on the product recall page, searching for all kinds of products that I thought might reveal that secret gateway into the infranet, delving further and further, many levels deep into the various zones.

It was nearly midnight on the seventh night, when yet another search box popped up and it occurred to me to input a name: Vlad Carpenter. The screen lit up almost immediately: "Welcome, Vlad. Please input your access phrase." What was it? Did I have it written somewhere? Would it still work?

There was a knock at the door.

It took the second knock for me to convince myself that there really was someone there and that I should respond. I shoved the screen under a cushion and went to open the door.

"Hi, Carl," I said. "What brings you and Eric out this late at night?" My heart sank, but I convinced my lips to smile. Carl and Eric were influential members of the supervisory council of Walden 27. This was not going to be a social call.

"May we come in?" Carl was looking over my shoulder into the sitting room. I was thankful I'd hidden the screen.

"Of course. Please." I stepped aside and ushered them into my tiny space. "Please, sit down anywhere." There weren't that many options. Eric sat in my only upholstered chair. Carl took one end of the sofa. I sat on the other end. The screen rested underneath the cushion between us.

"May I offer you a cup of tea?"

"No, thank you, Malia. It's late, so we'll get right to the point." Carl cleared his throat. "It's come to our attention that you've been breaking the rule about not accessing the medianets."

I must have looked confused and that was genuine. I'd expected questions, but they weren't here to ask questions. They already knew what I'd been doing. My expression quickly resolved into what felt more like the rebellious expression of a teenage Malia. *So what if I have?* I thought.

"As you know," Carl was continuing, "as it's written in the contract you signed when you joined our community, there is a prescribed sanction for this breach."

I knew there was a sanction, but I was having a hard time remembering exactly what it was. I reminded myself that there were limited options in Walden 27.

"The sanction, as you well know, is for you to be expelled from the community for a period of not less than two months, after which you may petition for reinstatement under a new contract."

A good Waldener would have been stricken, crestfallen, reduced to tearful remorse by this pronouncement. I was exhilarated. This was the motivation I needed to finally get back out into the
world and find out for myself what was going on. I made no attempt to defend myself against their charges.

I couldn't wait to go.

Part III
Return

18.

I headed for Dallas, traveling light. After fifty years in Walden 27, I had precious few possessions: my old digilet and portable screen, as well as the newer ones from Alicia; my Vlad Carpenter novels; a few basic toiletries; the watch pendant Lio had given me; a worn leather handbag, also a gift from Lio; and the silk scarf—now threadbare—that had hung by my bedside for so many years, my symbolic contact with a life I'd left behind. Now I was leaving again.

I'd also brought a couple of changes of clothes. I liked the loose trousers and tunics—they were comfortable, made of sturdy fabric and impeccably tailored—but I knew they would mark me clearly as a Simpleton—a Simpleton turned out into the world because of some transgression. That could be a problem. I wished I'd had the courage to buy something at that boutique on Guadalupe Street in Austin.

The supervisory council provided an autocar to drive me to Fort Stockton, where I picked up a prepaid train ticket to Dallas. They'd also given me a payment device that they said would provide me with necessary food and lodging until I found work. Waldeners were not ungenerous in their imposition of punishments. I knew I should have felt chastened and fearful, but instead I felt exceptionally alive. My only real regret was in leaving my friend Walter and his family; I'd left a handwritten note for him on the table in my cottage and sent a message via the fixed screen to let him know to look for it. I'd also left one of my books as a parting gift for Frances.

I was amazed to see that the old ground-level train had been replaced by a shiny new monorail, which was powered by solar cells in both the body of the cars (they called them "stages" now) and in the elevated tracks. I was also amazed at the timetable, which claimed I would arrive in Dallas in barely over two hours. I was going to be amazed a lot over the next few weeks.

We sped along quietly above vast industrial farms and past factory buildings whose purposes were impossible to ascertain. The signs and symbols on the buildings were unfamiliar to me. Some of the buildings had no signs at all. I turned my attention to my fellow passengers. Their screens and digilets made mine—even the newer ones from Alicia—look like antiques, so I left them packed away in my bag. Everyone seemed relaxed, placid. I couldn't tell what they were reading or watching, but whatever it was, they appeared to find it satisfying.

My only plan was to go to my sister Leticia's shop, the address of which I'd verified during my unsanctioned adventures in the medianets at Walden 27. I was uncertain what kind of welcome I might get from her, but I had to go somewhere. I hoped she'd at least put me up for a night or two until I figured out what to do next. I thought about my other sister, my twin Sophia. Should I try to get in touch with her? Maybe Leticia would have a contact phrase. The last I'd heard, Sophia had been putting her degree in flickmaking to good use at Marvaworld. I remembered those distant family holidays in Philadelphia after she'd begun taking the Chulel treatments with memory "restoration"; it was possible—likely, in fact—that she wouldn't remember me at all by now.

I looked out the window, telling myself I shouldn't keep staring at my traveling companions like some deranged *voyeuse.* I focused on their reflections in the glass. They all looked so young. Young, well-dressed, well-groomed, content, absorbed in their devices. I looked at the reflection of my own face, a face deprived of Chulel for more than four decades. By the calendar, I was now 110. But since I'd taken Chulel for more than forty of those years, I calculated that I was effectively somewhere in my late sixties.

You're old. I spoke silently, firmly to the woman in the glass, watching her scowl back at me. I'd never thought of myself as old in Walden 27; there had been others far older than me. Now I forced myself to take stock of the woman in the glass—her gray hair, her collapsing face, skin sliding away from what was still good bone structure, skin irreparably marred by sun and wind and sorrow. Okay, and smiles; smiles were etched into that face as well. And I still had clear eyes. The sun damage only meant I'd spent unguarded hours in the out-of-doors. I couldn't say I regretted that. It's the price I paid for foolhardy days of youthful abandon. I knew the state of my skin was only going to get worse and would never get any better. *You're old,* I told myself again, *but you may have more gumption left in you than the rest of this crowd put together.* I didn't look quite so old when I smiled.

I thought about Beat and Z. *I should let Z's wife know where I'm going,* I thought. Did I know where I was going? Should I try to track down Beat?

And what about Lio? Back in Walden 27, I'd convinced myself he was dead. Now, out here in the world again, maybe I had the opportunity to find out for certain. Except I wasn't sure I wanted to know. These were concerns I hadn't permitted myself to voice for years and I found some sensitivity still remained in the scar tissue of my heart.

Arriving in Dallas, I had to ask someone how to use the payment device Carl had given me. It looked the same as the one I'd taken to Austin to buy the books from Alicia, but of course I'd never used that one. It was a remarkable device, but I saw other people using their digilets to pay for things and realized that this device itself set me apart as much as my odd clothing, my gray hair, and my wrinkled face. I was getting fairly competent with autocars, so I accessed one and gave it the address of Leticia's shop. The autocar didn't care what I looked like or how I was dressed. It simply did as it was directed.

Leticia was busy with a customer when I arrived, so I kept my back to her, examining a display of jewelry made out of some kind of plastic, which I thought was ugly. Leticia looked plumper than I remembered, and I'd forgotten she was so much shorter than me. Growing up, she was always my older sister, my "big" sister. We'd spent little time together as adults. She approached me after the customer left.

"May I help you?"

I turned and looked squarely into her eyes. I smiled. There was not even a glimmer of recognition on Leticia's face. "So you don't even know your own sister now?" I said it in a teasing voice, but my heart was wounded.

"Sophia?" she said.

"No, silly. It's Malia." I'd forgotten about these identical twin dilemmas, but Leticia's confusion told me she hadn't seen our sister Sophia lately.

"Oh my god, Mali! Where? How?" She grabbed me in a fierce hug and began to cry.

She closed up the shop and the two of us walked the few blocks to her apartment. She called it a "habitat." Leticia had always been the most grounded of the three of us, the sensible sister. Now I found her taking me under her wing without question. She insisted on pulling my bag for me. She fed me and made up the bed in her guest room, insisting I stay.

"Just until I decide what I'm going to do," I said. "Thanks, Leti."

We talked well into the night. Leticia, it turned out, was still affiliated with the Recall movement. Her dance studio was on the rotation of meeting places for a local group of old Vintagonists and a few allies. "You remember Montagne Williams?" she asked. "He's still active. He still comes to gatherings."

I was grateful to attach a name to a face that I'd been seeing glimpses of lately in my fragmented returning memories.

Leticia and I finally said goodnight. Before turning out the light, I picked up my screen and navigated uncertainly to the page that I'd dared to believe might give me entry into Recall. Again I input the name "Vlad Carpenter" to the search protocol. This time when the welcome message came up, I noted that it was for something called "Interloc." I wasn't sure what that was, but I tried several access phrases that I thought I might have used in the past. Of course, nothing worked. After more tries than I would have thought I'd be entitled to, the page locked on a blank screen. Defeated, I turned out the light and settled down to sleep. *Tomorrow.* Leti would help me figure out how to get back into Recall tomorrow.

That night I dreamed about Vinties. Montagne Williams was giving a speech, but I couldn't catch the words. I cheered and applauded. There was a blonde girl with him. I thought her name was Jenda Swain.

19.

I woke early and went into Leti's kitchen, intent on making myself a cup of tea or coffee. I searched the cupboards, trying not to make noise.

"You're up already?" Leticia stood in the kitchen door, smiling, trying to smooth her excessively curly hair with her hand. "I thought you'd probably want to sleep late this morning."

"There's a whole world out there for me to discover," I said, grinning at my older sister who looked about half my age. "No point wasting time sleeping. Now, where do you keep your coffee?"

After breakfast, Leti took me with her to the boutique. "We need to get you some clothes that will help you blend in a little better," she said.

"You mean something that won't make me look like an escaped transgressor?" We laughed.

She showed me some things in bright floral patterns and clingy fabrics. "These are the latest style," she insisted.

"I know nothing about style," I replied, "but I know I'd prefer something more subdued. And not so... body-hugging." I selected a loose style in a soft blue and brown geometric-patterned fabric that draped, but didn't cling.

Leticia scowled, but after projecting it on me in the fitting booth, she grudgingly approved. Then the machine scanned my body, and my dress began to emerge from the 3-D printer like something from an old photocopy machine. We also selected a couple of ready-print blouses that Leti assured me could easily be paired with my Simpleton trousers. She wouldn't even let me talk about paying for anything.

"This evening we'll go to a shop I know where we can get you a new digilet. And tomorrow night there'll be a dance at the studio that you might find interesting,"

"I don't dance. Not anymore, anyway." I remembered nights at the Quill & Sheaf when they'd bring in a dance band and Lio would take me in his arms.

"This one isn't about the dancing." She said, giving me a sly look.

"Oh? Oh! Yes, I'd love to join you. Do you think maybe Montagne will be there?"

"He rarely misses."

I spent the rest of the day exploring. Leti had explained that her habitat and shop were located in what was now called an "endurb"—a region where people could live and work and shop without the necessity of long commutes. "Of course," she told me, "some of the people who work for one of the big corporations in the city center still commute." She showed me where I could catch the monorail to go downtown if I wished to go.

Of course I had to go. I put on one of my new blouses and caught the train.

The streets in the city center were even quieter than the ones in Leticia's endurb. Autocars were the only traffic, and they barely whispered as they ferried their passengers from place to place. People on the street walked alone or in pairs, mostly absorbed in personal screens or digilets. Walden 27 had been quiet, but it had been a different kind of quiet, undergirded by a communal conviviality. The calm of Walden 27 had been reassuring; the quiet of downtown Dallas felt ominous.

The buildings presented a solid front, broken only by the streets, which didn't seem to intervene as frequently as they once had. I'm not sure what kind of material the buildings were made of, but it was neither rough like old brick and stone nor shiny like metal or glass. It made me think of deflated balloons stretched over a frame. There were no windows that I could see. At street level there were panels that were actually oversized digital screens, showing mediacasts and advertisements. Nobody stopped to watch, although I saw some of them glance at the screens, reacting occasionally to something they must have been hearing through their earpieces. I was able to identify several buildings as pertaining to Pharmakon, LifeBook, and Your Journal. I was curious about what might be going on inside these monolithic structures, but their entrances looked so forbidding that I walked on by.

It was nearly noon, and I was getting hungry, so I thought I'd try a side street. I wasn't optimistic about the food I might encounter. My sister had done her best to cook a nice breakfast, but the eggs had tasted funny to me, and the mushrooms were like cardboard. One thing I was sure I was going to miss about Walden 27 was the fresh food.

On the side street, I began to see a few more people. A woman smiled at me. There were discernible storefronts. And then I caught the aroma of something frying and I thought it smelled like real potatoes in fresh oil. I sniffed out the source. It was the café where, as I've said, I ran across Jenda Swain.

She was definitely the girl I'd seen in my dream last night. I watched her for a while before speaking. I sensed a serious mismatch between the Jenda I thought I remembered and this prim businesswoman sitting there eating her greasy sandwich. It hurt my heart. I spoke to her in the hope that she'd say something that would resolve the dissonance or help me remember some of those things that still flitted in and out of the edges of my memory. But she didn't. How did a passionate Vintagonist become so utterly transformed? Unfortunately, I knew one possible answer to that. I knew Zelda.

Seeing Jenda pried open even more windows into my blank period. The rest of the day, as I made my way back to Leticia's endurb, back to her habitat, disconnected images and sensations kept pressing upward into my consciousness.

One of those sensations was fear.

I told Leticia about my encounter with Jenda. "She seemed so different," I said. "At least I think she did. I have trouble remembering her."

Leticia turned away, but I could see the little furrows between her eyebrows deepen. "Jenda recently started coming to a weekly dance class at my studio. She has no idea I'm anyone she ever knew, so I'm not surprised she didn't remember you, either. You and she were friends once, even though she was two years older. You were pretty upset when she went away after graduation. And then the folks took you off to Philly and you probably never saw her again. I was getting ready to go to university myself and probably didn't pay as much attention to you as I should have. It was a tough time for you." She looked at me then, searching, as if she expected some kind of response or reaction. I felt only confusion.

Later that evening Leticia took me to the Device Mart, where she said we'd be able to exchange my antiquated digilet and screen for newer, more useful models. I took along my devices from D.C. as well as the ones that were a gift from Alicia. Leti introduced me to the shop manager, Gordon Eskwith. When I put my two digilets and two screens in front of him, he began to chuckle.

"Zujo, old girl," he said, picking up the devices I'd had with me when I arrived in Walden 27 back in 2075. "Where the fuck did you stash these away for the past... what? Fifty years?"

"Same place I stashed myself," I said, quietly amused.

"Do any of these have trade-in value?" Leticia asked.

"Probably more than I can offer you," he said, looking serious. "A lot of what's in these older models was probably supposed to have been expunged by updates years ago. Someone with more knowledge than I have might be able to make use of that. You should get these into more capable hands."

"But she needs something she can actually use. Can you update the newer ones?" my sensible sister asked.

Gordon scratched the back of his head and stared off toward a distant corner of the store. "She'd be better off with something even newer than these. You know how fast things change. I'll tell you what. I've got some items that were brought in for repair and never picked up. I could give you a special discount on those."

I pulled out my payment device, uncertain how much I could pay or how much he'd be asking. As soon as Gordon saw the device, he scowled, giving Leticia a questioning look.

"She's okay. She's my sister. She's been away. But she's with us."

He nodded thoughtfully. I wondered where he thought I'd been. Prison? A mental hospital? He didn't seem to mind.

"How much?" I asked.

"How does free sound?" He smiled up at me and gave Leticia a wink.

"What? Really?"

"Pukka," Leticia said. I wasn't sure what that meant, but she was smiling, so it had to be good. "Can you help us transfer her stuff from the oldest devices to the new?"

Gordon hesitated. "It would be easier from the newer screen."

"Unfortunately, the only things I care about are on the older screen," I said.

"Okay. Well, I think I can do that, depending on what it is. But as for the digilet, I'm afraid it won't be possible. You'll have to input everything by hand. If you leave your screen with me, I can do the transfers this evening and you can pick it up tomorrow."

Leticia was nodding agreement, but I laid my hand on top of the screen. "Sorry," I said, "but I'm not letting this out of my sight. How long will it actually take?"

"Well, there are several steps. It may take an hour or more to get everything done. I didn't want you to have to wait that long. What's on it?"

"I'll wait," I said. "And the only thing on it that I care about are the documents and photographs."

"I'll get us some supper," Leticia offered. "What kind of pizza do you like?"

By the time Leti returned with the food, Gordon's transcription device was whirring away, copying and translating and rewriting the files from my old screen. While it worked, we ate the pizza, which was good, and drank the beers Gordon brought out from the rear of the shop. As I watched him interact with Leti, I began to think maybe they were more than good friends. The transfer process ended up taking under an hour.

"I didn't mean to pry," Gordon said as he handed me the two screens, "but I couldn't avoid noticing that you have a document in there that appears to be an unfinished manuscript of a Vlad Carpenter novel. Do you actually know Vlad Carpenter?"

"We're acquainted," I said.

"Wow," he replied. "The Recall world would love to see another Vlad Carpenter novel. Is he still alive? Do you think he intends to finish it?"

"I don't know," I said. "We've been out of touch for a while."

Before we left, Gordon set up both my new screen and new digilet to permit standard pulses as well as pulses via Recall's communication facility, which is called Interloc. He and Leti tried to teach me how to input text using the new syllabic keyboard.

"And what do I cush after that?" I asked, scowling at the unfamiliar arrangement of characters.

"'Cush'?" Gordon chuckled. "Nobody says 'cush' anymore."

The new procedure seemed awfully complicated, but they assured me it would be a lot faster than the old keyboard, once I got the hang of it. Then they showed me how to get the digilet to transform spoken messages to text and I decided I liked that a lot better. We thanked him and said goodnight.

I was grateful to have working devices again. A writer needs good devices. I'd made up my mind that I wanted to write a memoir—not for publication, just for my own edification. I thought it would help me make sense of these fragments of memories that have been plaguing me.

20.

One disturbing thing I've observed since leaving Walden 27 is the mirrors. They're everywhere. And they're huge. In Walden 27 mirrors were rare and small, so my self-image was compiled mostly from memories, bodily sensations, and more than a little imagination. I have a very creative imagination.

Leticia has a full-length mirror in her hallway, right outside the bathroom. Curiosity led me to engage in a thorough inspection of my body this morning after Leti went to work and it has resulted in a soul-crushing revision of my self-image: I'm not so much sturdy as I am fat. There's a fold just below my startlingly pendulous breasts that I hadn't noticed before. My upper arms, although strong enough to carry large stacks of books, look as if gravity is trying to draw all the flesh downward, creating patterns of lines that I'm fairly sure no one would consider pretty. My pubic hair has thinned out more than I'd realized and my buttocks, which now slump where I'm sure they used to curve, are dimpled all over.

I've read that women used to pay huge sums of money to have their faces and breasts and other body parts reconstructed to emulate more youthful models. We've always longed for eternal youth, I suppose, clinging to the freshest flower of our threshold of maturity. Chulel is merely our latest effort.

Leticia has recommended that I start using makeup "to blend in." She's also remarked on what a beautiful shade of golden brown my hair used to be, a thinly veiled way of suggesting that I color it. I'm considering the makeup. My face does look awfully pale and splotchy and my eyes—which Leti says have always been my best feature—have begun to recede behind little drooping folds. Makeup can't fix that, nor can it hide the pouches and circles below my eyes. I refuse to consider hair color. Resuming Chulel is out of the question.

"There's really no harm in using it," Leticia argued, "as long as you don't go to the spas where they do that so-called memory restoration. I've been able to get Chulel off-and-on over the years, using it whenever I could get it. But I've recently located a solid supplier who can get it for me on a regular basis. I had a fresh treatment last month." Leti is clearly committed to maintaining her youthful appearance. I suppose it's part of her business plan.

As for me, beyond a few touches of makeup, I've decided to make peace with my appearance. I'm old. I'm old in a society in which being old is not only anomalous, but something suspicious, even subversive. Maybe that's something I can make peace with.

I wore my new dress to the dance at Leticia's studio at which I didn't expect to do any dancing. She asked me to mind the sign-in table, a benevolent gesture that I knew was intended to help me identify people I might be supposed to know.

I recognized Montagne Williams as soon as he came in. He was the same darkly handsome man I'd seen in my recent dream, only a little older. Maturity looked good on him. I smiled as he approached the table, extending his hand.

"You're new here," he said. "I'm Montagne Williams. Welcome."

"I know who you are," I said. "And I'm not new. Just been away for a while." I put out my hand to grasp his. "Malia," I said. "Malia Poole."

"Zujo! Zujo! We gave up on you years ago, Malia! Where have you been keeping yourself?"

Leticia saw that he'd arrived and came over to the table to relieve me so Montagne and I could wander off and chat.

I gave him a synopsis of my life story. "What about you?" I said. "I see that you're still involved with Recall."

"Yes," he said. "We exist mainly on the infranet now and in local gatherings like this one. Not much in the way of public activism anymore. Not like the old days. We work close to the chest. It's safer that way."

"I saw Jenda yesterday," I said.

Montagne scowled. "I run across her from time to time. She doesn't remember me, you know. Ever since that episode in Argentina. I'm kind of surprised that you remember me."

"Why?" I said. I knew he was part of my blank period, although I'd known him long before it. Him and Jenda. I was curious to hear what he'd have to say. What was it about what he'd already said that seemed to have caused a small explosion somewhere in my brain?

"I thought your intention was to forget all about what happened."

"What happened'? What do you mean? What happened?" There was a buzzing in my head, accompanied by a loss of peripheral vision. Things were whiting out, like in a snowstorm. I took a deep breath, and the sensations backed off.

"God, I'm sorry. I've said the wrong thing, Malia."

"No, you've probably said exactly the right thing. I've been remembering things lately. Fragments and pieces of things. I'm not sure I'm ready to remember everything yet. Whatever that 'everything' might be. But..." I forced a smile because I really wanted to smile at Montagne, "it's good to know that whatever those memories are, someone else is holding them for me. Just in case I do want to remember. Everything."

"I think I get that," Montagne said. "Someday we can talk if you want to. When you're ready. But tonight, let me introduce you to some of our other network members. I'm leaving town in a few days for a business trip. How long are you going to stay in Dallas?"

I had no answer. So far I'd given no thought at all to how long I'd be staying. As Montagne introduced me to the other Recall members, a sense of belonging began to arise in me, something more profound than anything I'd felt in Walden 27, even after fifty years of living there.

21.

"I think I need a job," I said to Leticia the next day. I almost said "tarea," but I knew that what existed out here in the real world were jobs. Jobs entailed working under formal contract as an employee, something that now felt to me like being owned by someone. I didn't like it, but I needed to support myself. I knew it was what was expected.

"Of course," she said. "You can work at the boutique. I'm always in need of assistance. I don't pay particularly well, but since you'll be living with me it should be enough."

It sounded tempting, but I had to laugh. "You're very kind, sister, but really, I don't think having an old crone like me minding your shop would be good for business."

"It's only for—what? Two months?" I noticed that she hadn't disagreed with me. "And then if you decide to stay longer, maybe we could talk about something else."

"I'm not going back to Walden 27."

"Oh. Well, then. Remind me again what work it was that you did there."

"I was an assistant librarian and a wood finisher. I don't suppose there's much demand for either of those things around here."

"No," Leticia said, "there's not. But how about this: you know that recycle box that's at the front of my shop? I know some people at the recycling company. I can call and ask if there are any job openings at the clothing recycling center."

I smiled, remembering the pleasures of pilfering through recycle boxes in my youth, looking for clothes to wear. "That could work," I said. "I might like that."

I started my job at the recycling center the following week. Leticia showed me how to set the alarm on my digilet, and I resigned myself to the idea that, once again, my life would be regulated by the clock.

The job was easy enough. I monitored the machines that sorted the garments according to fiber types. I had a switch that could pause the machine if it started to get clogged or if I thought it had made an error. The latter usually happened when the machine encountered a garment of mixed materials. I enjoyed stopping for those. Sometimes it was an evening gown covered in sequins. Sometimes a jacket with real fur trim. Or a wool tuxedo coat with silk lapels. Yesterday it was this diaphanous ivory tulle thing with seed pearls stitched by hand all along the edges. These were the kinds of things I would once have considered treasures to be removed from recycling and taken home to refashion into something wearable without obscuring their integrity, their history. Their stories. I wasn't sure how long I'd be able to fend off the reemergence of those old habits.

Taking the monorail to work each day, going in the opposite direction from downtown, turned out to be one of my favorite parts of the job. I became a shameless people-watcher. I wasn't afraid of looking at people anymore. It seemed illogical, but my oddity—the fact that I was an old person in an ocean of youth—made me invisible. It wasn't simply that I was old. I was intentionally old. I'd rejected the Chulel that they valued so highly. I was a political as well as a social anomaly. People couldn't help but see me, but they didn't want to see me, so they didn't. They refused to acknowledge my existence. Does that make sense? No? I said it was illogical. But I admit to enjoying the bizarre anonymity.

It gave me a certain boldness. I started going for a beer on my way back from work, stopping at a place called Semper Bellum. The patrons at this establishment seemed like a convivial lot who didn't mind a stranger in their midst. After a few visits, I concluded that most of them were participating in some kind of game, something like our old online computer games. It had to be a type of war game, based on the vigorous debates I overheard about infantry movements, covert ops, drone ordnance delivery, and so on.

One day, after drinking an unaccustomed second beer, I finally worked up the nerve to ask one of the patrons a few questions. He said his name was Marcus and from him I learned a little about the teams that battled one another, about how they assembled their teams, and about the heavy bets that he told me were invariably placed on outcomes.

"We've got a major op scheduled for Friday night," he said. "We always put the big ones up on the wall screens. You should come watch."

I'd never been terribly interested in war games, but curiosity got the better of me. I decided to take him up on his invitation.

On Friday night there was a larger crowd than usual, and people were clustered around individuals who seemed to be the main players. Some of them were equipped with audio gear so they could communicate with one another over the general hubbub and give direct verbal orders to their onscreen characters. Some players controlled drones, some of which provided surveillance, while others carried bombs. I sat down next to Marcus, and he tried to explain a little more about what was going on.

"Are you playing against a computer program?" I asked. "Or whatever you call that these days."

"No," he said. "We play against other teams. Somewhere in another bar across town, or maybe in some other city, other players are controlling the enemy."

"Why are the enemy all dark-skinned?"

"Are they?" he asked. "I guess just because they are."

"So why are they the enemy?" I asked.

Marcus laughed. "It's a game. We couldn't keep playing without enemies. There always have to be enemies."

I watched a while longer, amazed at the realistic quality of the onscreen images, the interaction between players in the bar and the dark-skinned fighters on the ground. It was unnerving. I decided to go home. I haven't gone back.

I did run into Marcus in a grocery shop one day and he told me that our conversation had started him thinking. "I'd noticed that a few of the fighters had something written on the backs of their uniforms that looked like contact phrases, so I copied down a couple of them and sent pulses."

"Really? Did you get any response?"

"Yeah." Marcus frowned and scanned up and down the aisle where we were standing. No one else seemed to be buying pickles and jam that day. "I don't know if it's just another part of the game—you know, something to make it seem more realistic—or if..." He laughed and shook his head.

I was too stunned to speak.

"Anyway," Marcus continued. "I don't go to Semper Bellum anymore. I owe them a lot of money. Bad bets. But I'll figure out some other way to pay them off."

I returned to Leti's place without the groceries I'd intended to buy. I didn't know whether I ought to mention all of this to her or not. Maybe I'd just wait and talk to Montagne about it the next time he was in town. It would be one more thing I could ask him about.

After my third pay receipt from my new job, I told Leticia I was going to look for my own place.

"Why?" She gave me a perplexed look. "I've got plenty of room here for both of us. We've been apart for so long. Besides, what can you afford on your pay?"

"I enjoy your company, Leti. And I promise we'll get together often. But we're both used to having our own space. And as for what I can afford, whatever it is will be enough. Remember, I lived the Simpleton life for fifty years. I don't require much."

Through my employer, I got a unit in a habitat complex close to my work. It was even smaller than my cottage in Walden 27. The proximity to work was convenient, but it meant I had to give up my daily rail ride. I'd need to find other opportunities for people watching. The new place wasn't in a nice endurb like Leticia's place, but rather in an area designed for lower level workers, of which I, apparently, am one.

The line of shops across the front of the building gave us access to each thing they thought we'd need. There was a grocery store with a limited variety of foods as well as beer, wine, and several psychoactive beverages. I tried some of the latter and quickly decided they were not to my liking. There was a clothing store that even I could see was an outlet for the things that hadn't sold at the endurban boutiques. The household goods shop sold defective or otherwise rejected merchandise from 3Dec, where more prosperous consumers ordered up custom goods from the 3-D printers. There was a pharmaceuticals dispensary that always seemed busy. There were no entertainments venues or restaurants or pubs or coffee shops; it was as if they aimed to discourage social interaction.

Each habitat unit was equipped with a huge wall screen offering an immense range of uniformly mindless entertainments. I kept mine turned off until the habitat monitor came around to inquire if it was out of order. "We noticed that you haven't been using your wall screen," they said. After that, I kept it turned on whenever I was at home, but with the sound muted and the screen tuned so dark that all I could see were a few flickering shadows. I tried to remember to switch the channels from time to time.

At first I was uncertain about whether it was safe to access the Recall zone and Interloc from my new place, so I pulsed the question to Montagne. He assured me that, as long as I accessed Recall according to his instructions, there would be no problem.

Everybody in Interloc seemed to have a pseudonym—a "persona"—and if you didn't know someone's persona, it was unlikely you were going to be able to contact them. I wanted to use my real name, thinking then people would be able to find me even if I couldn't find them, but the system wouldn't let me do that. So in Interloc I became "Crone-1". Montagne Williams, I discovered, was "HillBill". I thought I might have found

Beatrice: the persona was "rhythME", which I thought might have been a play on her nickname, but I received no response to the message I sent, so I was forced to conclude that wasn't her. Or if it was, that she didn't remember me.

As Crone-1, I made some subtle inquiries through Recall and determined that there would be considerable interest in publishing Vlad Carpenter's next book, so I began working diligently on finishing it. It had become clear to me how the story was going to end, and I decided it was closer to finished than I'd realized. Montagne recommended an editor to me, though I didn't tell him why I needed one. I still wasn't ready for anyone to know I was Vlad Carpenter.

Crone-1 began to collect a following of witnesses in Interloc. I thought I knew why, and it disturbed me: Growing old was an experience most of these people would never have and they were curious. Put another way, I was a curiosity, a relic from another time and place. Another reality. I would have been okay with being an advance scout for a stage of life they expected to experience one day. But instead I represented something they had consciously rejected. It was as if I'd volunteered for some bizarre experiment, some journey to a forbidden planet they would never visit. I didn't yet know that stopping Chulel was becoming increasingly commonplace among participants in the Recall network.

22.

One night as I was eating my solitary supper, I turned up the sound on my screen to block out the infrasonic groaning of some road surfacing machines on the street below. I was thinking that a few potholes would be preferable to the deafening noise of the machines, which was interfering with my work on a key scene in my novel that still twanged a bit.

I was feeling increasingly annoyed when something from the screen caught my attention. They were talking about the release of a new flick. I backtracked the cast and brightened the picture to see if I could pick up what had grabbed me.

"Critics are acclaiming Jampel Jenkins' flick, *The Nagas and the Garuda*, as a masterpiece of visual storytelling, but he insists on giving credit to his co-writer on the screenplay, Sophia Poole."

Sophi! I gave my full attention to the wall screen and there she was. She looked so young. It was hard to believe we were identical twins. I pulsed Leticia and she followed up with an audio pulse.

"Shall we go see it?" she asked. "It's opening this weekend at the entertainments complex near the shop. I'm sure I can get us tickets."

We went. I wore a new dress that I'd pilfered from work. I'd known I wouldn't be able to resist. The cut of the dress was flattering and it was expertly tailored from a soft purple blended silk and linen fabric that had confused the machine. The dress only required minimal alteration to make it a perfect fit. I hoped the previous owner wouldn't be at the screening.

The flick was surprising. I wondered if the political implications were real or only my imagination. Sophia was our nihilist sister. Would she have written anything like this?

"I don't think you were imagining it at all," Leticia said as we departed the theater, heading for a late supper at a neighborhood restaurant. "Surely the naga characters were avatars for the plutocracy."

"So who did the garuda represent?"

Leticia raised her eyebrows and gestured first toward herself, then toward me. We laughed and linked arms.

"We should send Sophi congratulations," Leticia said later as we toasted our sister's success with glasses of wine while waiting for our food to be served.

I offered my best skeptical frown. "Do you think she'll remember who we are?"

Leticia spread her digilet out on the table. "I don't know, Mali. But it can't hurt to reach out, can it? Let's put together a flick-message."

We composed the message on Leticia's digilet, putting our heads close together, grinning like a couple of silly schoolgirls, and saying nothing of any real importance. Surely Sophia would enjoy a congratulatory message. And if she did remember her sisters, she'd know we'd seen her flick. Someday maybe we'd even be able to talk about what had finally led her to take a political stance on something.

Before we'd finished our meal, Leticia received an audio pulse. It was from Sophia. She adjusted her digilet so I could be part of the conversation.

"I'm swamped with calls right now," Sophia said after the initial greetings, "but I had to call you girls back. I know you probably thought I'd forgotten you long ago, but I've seen to it that that won't happen. We should get together!"

I said something about being busy working and writing.

"So you're writing? Good for you. I'd love to see something you've done. You always wanted to be a writer, didn't you? Let me know if I can help out when you're ready to publish."

I couldn't tell her that I'd already published five novels as someone called Vlad Carpenter. I didn't want her to know about the eight I'd published in Walden 27. I wasn't particularly proud of those.

"I'll keep in touch, twister," I said, using the term we'd used as kids as a contraction of "twin sister."

"Sisters should always keep in touch. I love your dress, Malia. You'll never believe it, but I used to have a dress exactly like it that I absolutely loved. I finally dropped it off to recycle no more than a week ago." She smiled and I hoped she couldn't see me blushing. Part of me wanted desperately to share the joke with her, but another part of me was ashamed of my theft, my poverty, so I said nothing.

"Well, that was unexpectedly nice," Leticia said after we'd concluded our conversation with Sophia.

"I'm shocked that she remembered us. The last time we were together in Philly it was like she'd already forgotten. What do you suppose she meant about seeing to it that she won't forget us?"

Leticia was frowning, still staring at her digilet. "I'm not sure," she said. "I'd be curious to know just how much she really does remember."

"She didn't react when I called her twister," I said. She also didn't seem to remember that I'd shown her some of my published poems and essays back in Philadelphia.

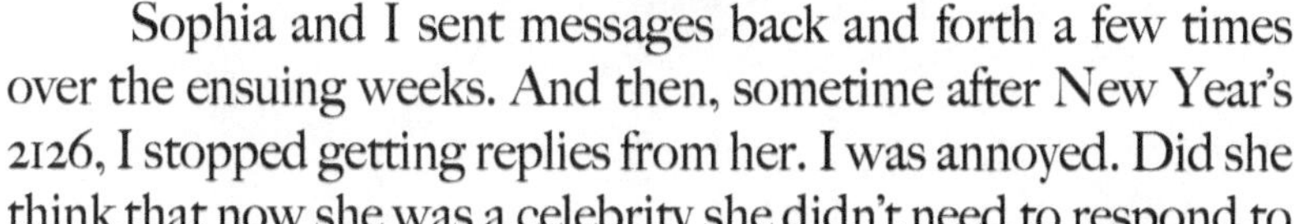

Sophia and I sent messages back and forth a few times over the ensuing weeks. And then, sometime after New Year's 2126, I stopped getting replies from her. I was annoyed. Did she think that now she was a celebrity she didn't need to respond to me?

"What have you heard from Sophi?" I asked Leticia when we met at her dance studio in mid-February. I was helping her set up the studio for another Recall get-together that evening. They were calling it a Valentine's Dance.

"Nothing," she said. "I was going to ask you the same thing. Haven't you heard from her?"

"No. Maybe she's had enough of me and decided to shut me out." As soon as I said that I wished I hadn't. I had no right to complain. I'd ignored Sophia for far longer than this.

"Maybe she's just busy working on her next project," Leti said. "Let's give her time."

"Sure, that could be the reason." I wasn't convinced.

"Did I tell you Montagne is back in town? He should be at the meeting tonight."

I shivered, even though it was warm in the studio, especially with the sun streaming in through the clearstory windows.

"Oh good," I said. "It'll be nice to see him again."

I wasn't sure if I meant that. I wasn't sure if I wanted to find out what he knew about me, about my blank period. Last week I'd decided that I did want to know. At that moment, though, knowing that Montagne would be there in a couple of hours, I wasn't so sure.

23.

Leticia waylaid Montagne as soon as he arrived at the event. I thought he looked tired. Haggard. A grayness seemed to drain the vibrancy from his face. Leticia didn't seem to notice.

"Malia and I are worried about Sophi," she said. "We've been trying to get in touch with her and can't seem to rouse a response."

Montagne took a glass of wine from the table and took a big gulp before responding. "It could have something to do with that flick."

"*The Nagas and the Garuda*? Why do you say that?"

"Didn't you know?" Montagne took another sip of wine. "That flick has been withdrawn."

"What? Why?" Leticia asked. She exchanged a look with me as I joined their conversation.

"Marvaworld never made a statement about it of course, but the consensus among Recall is that it was considered politically offensive. I've heard that the director has gone into hiding. He's someone else you know. You remember Jonathan Swain, don't you? Jenda's brother? He uses the name Jampel Jenkins professionally."

That was something I hadn't known. "Do you think Sophia's gone into hiding, too?" I asked.

"Let's hope so," Montagne said.

I was remembering my own unpleasant encounter with the corporate police back in Washington. I thought about what had happened to Zelda, what might have happened to Lio. I fervently hoped that my sister had found safety somewhere.

Leticia excused herself to go and tend to a minor crisis at the hors d'oeuvres table, leaving me alone with Montagne. He set down his empty wine glass and looked for a full one.

"You seemed a bit tense when you came in," I said. "Is everything okay with Recall? With you?"

"I wish I could talk about it, but I'm afraid I'd say something I shouldn't." Montagne shoved his fists into his pockets and looked away. "So I'd rather not say anything. Not unless..."

"This has something to do with me, doesn't it?" It wasn't really a question. I knew it was true. And I knew it was time. "Shall we go somewhere more private?"

Montagne tilted his head and narrowed his eyes, probing my soul. "Are you sure, Malia?" There was a gravity in his voice that I hadn't heard before.

I nodded. I opened a door that I knew led to a room Leticia used for storage. Inside it was quiet, sounds muffled by the racks of costumes along the walls. There were no chairs, so we stood.

Montagne studied my face for a minute more and then, taking a deep breath, he began. "Since we spoke last time, I've tried to think what I'd say to you if you came to me ready to retrieve the memories you've lost. There's no easy way, so I'll start by telling you a story. The story takes place in a coffee shop where Vintagonists used to gather."

"The one behind the storefronts on McCommas?"

"Not that one." He smiled, relaxing a little. "That was a good one, though. Lots of good memories there." He took a deep breath.

"One night," he said, "a group of young Vinties gathered at this coffee shop, mainly to socialize, though there was also talk of organizing another protest against 3Dec. People were laughing and happy, drinking too much coffee, knowing it would make them stay up way too late and fall asleep in class the next day. They hardly noticed when a stranger entered the coffee shop." He continued, explaining that the stranger was a young man, wearing a loose coat that hung heavy on his small frame. He stood in the shadows near the bar for a while, watching. Then with a shout like the cry of an enraged beast, he leapt up on the bar, brandishing a gun. Not just any kind of gun. An assault rifle. Still shouting, swearing, spewing hate, he began firing. There was blood and exploded flesh everywhere, people screaming, trying to hide from the monstrousness of what was happening.

I'm not sure this is exactly the way Montagne told the story to me or if it was the way I began telling it to myself as I began to remember in painful detail the events he was recounting.

I tried to hide. I was under a table. More shots. I covered my head, trembling, biting my lips to keep from screaming. Something fell in front of me. My friend, part of her skull shot away, her eyes finding mine as she exited. I closed my eyes then. I couldn't bear to see any more. The shooting stopped.

But it wasn't over. I heard the man jump down from the counter. I heard his heavy tread. I heard bodies being moved. Another shot. He was checking to make sure we were all dead. This was it. I was dead.

But I wasn't dead. I opened my eyes and saw his boots, blood-spattered, measured steps, coming closer. With the butt of his rifle, he shoved aside the body of my friend, my friend who had hidden me, protected me. He peered under the table and our eyes met. Now he would shoot me.

But he didn't shoot me. "Well, well, well. What have we here?" He laughed. "This is my lucky night," he said. He grabbed my arm and dragged me out. My head hit the edge of the table and blood began flowing warm and wet from the sharp pain on the side of my head. He laid the gun aside and threw me to the floor, grabbing my trousers with one hand, his own zipper with the other. I tried to roll away. He struck my face. His penis was erect, hostile. He ripped away my clothes, forced my thighs apart, and plunged into me. Again and again, lifting my whole body, my head hitting against a wall with every vicious thrust.

"They say the girl passed out, which would certainly have been a mercy. She was pretty messed up by the time the emergency team arrived. There was one other survivor, but he never walked again." Montagne looked at me with a pained expression. "I'm sorry."

"It's okay," I said hoarsely. "I remember." And I began to sob. Montagne tried to put his arms around me, to comfort me, but the brutal memories were fresh wounds, and I pushed him away.

"I'm so sorry, Malia," he said, after allowing me a few moments with my grief. I battled for composure and my tears began to subside. "You said you wanted to know. I had to respect that."

"It's okay," I said again. "It's okay. But why did I forget so completely? Why did I forget everything about that whole part of my life? It doesn't make sense."

"Well, that's the part that links up with what's been troubling me." He looked at me as I wiped my eyes on my sleeve.

I inhaled deeply and nodded to reassure him it was okay to go on. *I'd just as well get the whole thing over with.*

"You know Jenda and I were a couple back then."

I nodded again.

"What you may not remember is that we got pregnant. Well, not many people knew about that, but you figured it out. You were like Jenda's shadow."

"I was a nuisance."

"You could say that. Anyway, Jenda's parents were furious. It was bad enough that she was so embroiled in all our Vintagonist nonsense, but now she'd gone and gotten herself pregnant right when she ought to be getting ready for college and a career. So they sent her away for what was supposed to be a gap year trip—that's what we were all told, anyway. But when she came back she wasn't pregnant anymore. Nor was she a Vintagonist. I was never sure exactly what had happened until recently. I assumed she'd had an abortion, but I didn't know why she suddenly didn't remember me or any of her other Vintie friends."

"Poor Jenda," I said.

Montagne continued. "I learned recently that where she went was a place in Argentina called Instituto Nueva Vida, a place whose advertised services included abortion and cult deprogramming."

"That sounds awful," I said, "but I don't see how that explains why I don't remember things."

Montagne held up his hand. "Shortly after Jenda returned, and not long after the incident we were just talking about, you came to me wondering if I could tell you where Jenda had gotten her abortion."

I took a deep breath. My eyelids clamped down and my hands closed into protective fists. Anger burned through the heavy sorrow in my breast as I comprehended the import of what he'd said. "So I was pregnant? By a rapist?"

"I'm sorry," Montagne said.

"Will you stop apologizing? As if any of this is your fault or as if your regret can make it anything other than what it was? Just go on. Tell me the rest. I need to know. I need to know everything."

"You seemed as much drawn to Jenda's forgetfulness as to the abortion, which you could've gotten anywhere. You said you wanted to obliterate the whole evil incident, and I had no trouble understanding that. Well, I didn't know at the time where Jenda had gotten her abortion, but I figured since her personal maid, Paloma, had been traveling with her, she'd know. So I sent you to Paloma. I'm not sure what happened after that, but I do know you were gone for a while and after you came back your family moved away to Philadelphia."

"I'm not sure I made the best decision," I said, fighting the tightening in my chest with deep breathing. "The abortion was right. There's no question about that. But there would've been other ways of handling the trauma. Better, perhaps, than living all these years with this blankness." I was feeling a bit better, but I could see Montagne was still scowling. He looked uneasy. "Is there more?"

"Actually, yes. There's more information about the clinic Jenda went to in Argentina, the Instituto Nueva Vida. I assume it's where you went, too."

"Go on."

"I've been in touch with someone who used to work there, and he told me that Jenda never actually had an abortion. I have a daughter. I found out last week that she's been living all these years with Paloma in Costa Rica."

"I need to sit down," I said, leaning into a rack of very unsupportive tutus.

Montagne went out and returned with a wooden stool and a cup of water. I sat down and took a few slow sips.

"Give me a minute to catch my breath," I said. "My old heart wasn't ready for all of this, I'm afraid." *Everything* was turning out to be quite a lot.

"Can I get you something? I'm sorry. I forget. You know I've finally stopped taking Chulel now, too, but only for the past ten years or so."

"I'm okay. Thanks for the seat." I took another deep breath and another sip of water. "Do you think my abortion was phony, too?"

"Jenda's situation was unusual. She was removed from the clinic before her treatment was completed. I didn't ask for your records, so I can't tell you what happened to you. But I can give you the contact information where you can find out."

"Yes. Please."

"Actually, it might be better if we did this together. Maybe I could come by your place tomorrow or Saturday? I'm going to Costa Rica next week. To meet my daughter. So we need to do it right away."

I gave him my address, and he agreed to come around in the evening on Saturday after I got off work. We were ready to go back out and join the group. Montagne opened the door and then closed it again, turning to face me.

"There's one more thing I probably ought to tell you about the Instituto Nueva Vida."

I sat down again.

"According to my source, they never really intended to perform abortions. Mostly they placed babies with plutocrat families. The only reason Jenda's and my daughter is with Paloma is because they took Jenda out of the Institute before her daughter was born."

"Oh," I said. I'd already begun convincing myself that, unlike Jenda's, my abortion had been performed as planned. "So they were selling babies? Maybe mine?" A shiver of dread went through me. What kind of child might I have given birth to? Why would they have preserved the offspring of a monster like...? It occurred to me that I didn't know my rapist's name. Was that something else I wanted to know?

I told Leticia that I was tired and needed to go home. She knew I'd been talking with Montagne and offered to let me stay overnight with her, but I refused. She offered to summon an autocar and I accepted. As she gave me a sisterly farewell hug, my body went rigid, resisting the physical contact. I returned the hug as best I could.

As the car carried me toward my habitat, I thought about Mandy. I thought about how her experience had affected me back in Walden 27. Maybe now I understood why. I contained my tears until I was safely inside my habitat. And then the dam burst. There was no loud sobbing this time. I sat quietly, slumped into the sofa, letting the grief sweep through me like a monsoon flood. It was a force of nature, something that had to happen, had to be endured. My mind was devoid of thoughts, emptied of images and sounds, brimming with pure burning anguish. There was no escaping this, nowhere to take refuge. So I gave myself to the sorrow until it was finished with me.

I don't know how long I sat there. One thing I've learned in my pathetic life is that everything changes. Finally I began to come to myself. My body ached from fatigue and tension. My eyes were swollen from the surfeit of tears. My throat was clogged with phlegm. I coughed. I peed my underwear a little. I laughed.

Old woman, I said to myself as I pushed my unwilling body up off the sofa, *you've got some shit to deal with.* I was not clear exactly what I meant by that, so I decided to make a cup of tea. I added two spoons of sugar, although I normally took only one. I sat down to think about what I'd learned tonight. *Last night.* I could see the sky outside my window beginning to glow with the prospect of dawn.

I was raped as a teenager. I was brutally raped by a murderer. A mass murderer. I was impregnated by a rapist mass murderer. Perhaps I bore his child. My child. That was the part I still didn't know about. Did I want to know? I wasn't sure. At one point in my life, I'd been desperately sure I did not want to know about any of this. I had a chance now to completely reverse that decision. I was already most of the way there.

I finished my tea and dictated a pulse to my employer saying I was sick and wouldn't be in today. I found a bottle of Duermata and calculated how many tabs I needed to take in order to get five hours of sleep. Then I swallowed the whole handful and went to bed.

I was not accustomed to so many hours of uninterrupted sleep. I didn't even dream. But as soon as I woke, I remembered the nightmare that wasn't a dream, the one that actually happened to me all those years ago. I remembered that I didn't have to go to work, so I lay in bed, thinking.

I let myself imagine what it might have been like, giving birth alone in a foreign country and having both the child and the knowledge of the child taken from me. These were not memories. This was a scenario laid out by a writer, a spinner of tales. I went further. The child—was it a boy or a girl?—was given away. No, sold. The child was sold to a wealthy couple, a couple so desirous of a child that they would pay any price to acquire one. Any price, perhaps, but the loss of the wife's lovely figure. As I thought this, I pressed my hands against my own generously rounded belly and squeezed my upper arms against my deflated breasts. I wondered if my child had been permitted to suckle at those breasts.

A wealthy couple, desperate for a child. Surely they would have cherished him and raised him well. Or her. Would the child have pleased them? Would she have shown any predilection for violent outbursts like her father? But if the parents were gentle, surely her early tantrums would have been dealt with lovingly and the child would have grown up healthy and happy. Did she love books?

I grew weary of my exercise. These characters had no names, no faces. I remembered a flick I'd watched with Sophia one day—I was never a great fan of flicks myself. It was about a woman who insisted that she had a son even though no one else remembered him. In the end she was able to reclaim him by remembering being pregnant. I didn't remember being pregnant. Whoever this child of mine was—son or daughter—I had no memories of them. No memories at all. But wasn't that flick also about some kind of special tie between mother and child? Did such a tie exist even though I had no recollection of my child? I wasn't sure.

I needed to pee. I wanted coffee.

I should go somewhere today, let myself take a holiday, I thought. If I'd still been in Walden 27, I would have taken the path that led out into the hills and walked until I was done walking. Walking and thinking. Maybe I would have visited my little rock shelter. Where could I go in Dallas? Walking around my own neighborhood held no appeal, so I caught the monorail downtown. Then, without getting off, I rode it back again. I rode downtown and back seven times. Since you only pass a pay point when you get on and when you get off, it was cheap entertainment for the day and it gave me ample time to think.

Before returning to my habitat, I stopped at the grocery and bought a few things I needed. When I'd put everything away in the cupboards and chillbox, I pulsed Montagne: "I won't be able to meet with you. I wish you well on your journey to meet your daughter."

The next day I went to work as if nothing had happened.

24.

Vlad Carpenter's latest novel proved to be quite a hit with the Recall community and, in the wake of its popularity, sales of his previous five books took off, too. The editor Montagne recommended finally convinced me to come out of the closet, as it were, and I held a book signing at a Recall meeting at Leticia's dance studio. Some of our network members arrived with three or four Vlad Carpenter novels stashed in a backpack and insisted that I sign all of them.

"I had a feeling," Leticia's friend Gordon from the Device Mart grinned, shaking his finger teasingly. I wrote a special note inside his copy of my new book.

It's odd, being an underground celebrity and still a nobody as I walk down the streets. At least now I'm a nobody with a good deal more self-confidence.

When I'd canceled my meeting with Montagne, negating my opportunity to know the details of what happened to me at the Institute in Argentina, my thinking had been this: what good would it possibly do to know if I'd had an abortion or a child? If the abortion had been performed—or maybe if the child had been stillborn—I had to admit, it would be a relief to know that. To be certain. It would be sad, but it would be a relief. However, asking the questions would also invite knowledge of a more threatening nature, knowledge that there was a person out there who was equally of my flesh and the flesh of their monstrous father.

I'd decided it was better not to know, so even when Leticia queried me about what Montagne and I had talked about, I'd refused to answer. I figured she must have known about the rape, but maybe not about the abortion. I didn't want to talk about it. I didn't want to burden her sisterly love with these tales from the distant past. It was all behind us now, wasn't it?

As the weeks went by, I began to second-guess my decision. Everyone I saw, male or female of any age except Gen1 or Gen7, had to be scrutinized as I wondered, *Could that be my daughter? Could he be my son?* For better or worse, I needed to know. I needed to know everything.

Montagne sent a message of congratulations on my new book. He seemed overjoyed to finally be in the company of his daughter. Her name is Meli and she's a teacher at a technical college in rural Costa Rica. Montagne told me he plans to move to Costa Rica permanently. He said he'd be back in Dallas before the end of May to collect his belongings. I made an appointment with him to carry through with our unfinished business.

I don't get visitors, so when the knock came I knew it was Montagne. I welcomed him and offered the cookies and fruit punch I'd prepared.

"Are you absolutely certain about this, Malia?"

"It's what has to be." I set down my glass of punch, which had begun to splash in my trembling hand. "Let's do it."

"Do you want me to include you in the conversation?"

"No, I don't think so. You can tell me what I need to know afterward."

Montagne entered a contact phrase on his digilet and waited for the recipient to pick up. "Hello? Dr. Winfield?"

I took a deep breath. I listened as Montagne explained that he was making another inquiry about the Institute.

"Yes, of course," he said. "I'm transferring the payment now." And he began coding in a funds transfer on his digilet.

"Montagne, wait! Tell me how much this is costing me. I may not be able to afford it." How could I have been such an idiot! Of course the information would come at a price.

Montagne waved his hand. "Don't worry," he whispered. "It isn't much. I'll cover it. A gift for an old friend." He winked.

"Received?" He spoke into the digilet. "Good. Yes, the client in question is Malia Poole." He spelled out my name.

We waited. Montagne listened, making acknowledging noises and scribbling on a pad of paper. "And you'll pulse all of that information to me? Good. Is there anything else you can tell me about her experience there? I believe she received some photonic treatments as well. Yes." He scribbled some more. "Okay, please include that in the report you're sending. Very good. Yes. Thank you again, Dr. Winfield." He snapped the digilet around his wrist.

"Well?" I said.

Montagne picked up the paper and took a deep breath, staring at his notes and then looking up at me, as if to give me one more opportunity to tell him I didn't want to know, to tell him to rip up the piece of paper, throw it away, burn it. But I did want to know. Finally he began.

"According to the data Dr. Winfield retrieved from the Institute, you were admitted on August 12, 2030 and gave birth to a healthy son on October 17. The child was placed with a couple in Jaipur, India. The adoptive father's name is Ayush Kalyani. His wife is Lakshmi. You were given targeted photonic treatments over a period of thirty days and released from the Institute on October 23. He's sending us the details, as you heard, but that's most of it right there."

"I have a host of questions," I said. "First of all, how the zujo did I give birth to a viable child after only a five-month pregnancy?"

"I should've said something about that earlier. Dr. Winfield told me they were using growth hormones on the fetuses, encouraging rapid maturation so that patients could return home sooner. I know, it sounds crazy, but apparently the process had been used in animal husbandry for long enough that they thought it was worth the risk. Dr. Winfield said all the babies he saw seemed to be normal and healthy."

"Seemed to be? It sounds totally insane. And dangerous. So my son is in India?"

"Well, they don't maintain contact after the placement, so there's no way of knowing if he's still there. Well, actually there is, but I don't know if that's what you want to do."

"Lord, I've come this far, Montagne. And you know I have to be concerned. You know, about the integrity of the boy's genome. His father wasn't exactly first class stuff. Did the Indian couple have any notion of that I wonder? My god, I put myself in this institute's hands willingly." I felt that tightness in my chest again and I knew I needed to calm down. I picked up the glass of fruit punch, using both hands to steady it. "Would you like a little rum in that punch?" I asked. "I think I'm going to put some in mine."

"Sure. Thanks. Now, let me see what I can find." He took his portable screen out of the bag he'd placed on the floor. He reached for another cookie.

"Here's an Ayush Kalyani in Jaipur, Rajasthan. He owns a string of factories assembling all kinds of screens, digilets, game devices. Wayee! A high-level plutocrat for sure! He seems to be the right generation. No information on the wife. But here are some pictures of him with his son. Yes, the son is the right age. His name is Jai. There are wedding pictures from a few years back. He's a good looking man, Malia."

I went over to the sofa to sit next to Montagne and look at the photos. Jai Kalyani was indeed a good-looking man. He just didn't look like his father. Ayush Kalyani had brown skin and black hair. The son, on the other hand, had fair skin and golden brown hair. I couldn't see his eyes, but I guessed they would be a soft brown. In the photo, he was smiling broadly, his arm around his new wife, a stunning woman with flowing black hair, gleaming dark eyes and skin like caramel mousse. She was beautiful, but I couldn't take my eyes off my son. My son did not look like a violent lunatic. I took a deep breath and exhaled slowly.

"Are there any other pictures? Any other information about Jai?"

Montagne worked with his screen some more. "He's a scientist."

"Really?" I was surprised.

"It says here he's a cognitive scientist working in something called artificial intelligence bio-interface projects and holding joint appointments at the Jaipur National Institute of Technology and Jaipur National University. He's won some awards."

"Montagne, I think I need to know something about Jai's father."

"I told you. He's a digital technology tycoon. Oh." He stopped and looked up at me. "You mean his biological father. Are you sure, Malia?"

"I'd kind of like all the characters in my story to have names," I said. "And maybe I'd like to know if this particular character had any interest in science. I know I never did." *Except when I was researching something for a novel*, I reminded myself.

"Let me see what I can find. I used to know his name, but I don't want to say anything without verifying it first." He explained that he was accessing a Recall zone that maintained historical data on violent crimes of the past century. "Crimes are so much more civilized these days," he remarked. "Not much need for old-style guns anymore."

Knowing that I was drinking rum calmed me. Montagne was taking his time. He was a careful man. I respected that.

"The boy's name was Roland. Roland Roxahrza. He was a college freshman who had declared a major in chemistry. When the police arrived on the scene of his crimes, he rushed them and was shot dead, even though he had no weapon in his hands at the time. His parents... Do you want more?"

"Yes," I said. "Everything."

"His parents were found dead in their home of multiple gunshot wounds. The weapon used in all the shootings belonged to the father, who was a manager at a local restaurant.

It doesn't mention the mother's employment. Roland was their only child."

"Another drink, Montagne? I'm having one."

"Of course. I'll join you."

I poured the drinks and tipped a few more cookies onto the plate. "If I wanted to go see this Jai Kalyani, how would I go about that? You found your daughter in Costa Rica. Maybe I should go find my son in India."

"I don't know, Malia. Well, I mean I do know. I just don't know if it's something you should do. Maybe you should think about it."

"I don't want to think about it. I want to do it. I've been thinking too much lately. I've built up some credits from my book sales and I can't think of a better use for them."

"Well, let me do some investigating for you. I know someone who's traveling at the moment. Maybe you could link up with her. I really don't think you should be traveling such distances on your own."

"Worried about this old heart?" I laughed, tapping my chest with a fist. "This heart has been stomped and trampled a thousand times over and it's still beating. But I guess I wouldn't mind a companion for the trip. I've never traveled outside North America before. Well, once I suppose. Will I need a passport?" This was all beginning to feel real.

Montagne leaned back on the sofa. "They don't issue paper passport books like they used to, you know. People who travel a lot can get a digital passport to keep track of their travel records, but in your case, they'll just scan your DNA with a contact sensor and input travel records directly into your digilet."

"My DNA? Will they have mine? I've been out of circulation for a long time." I was worried about what else accessing my records might reveal.

"The database they use was set up in 2070. Anything much before that probably won't be included. When did you enter the Walden Network?"

"In 2075." I did a mental check. My arrest in 2045 shouldn't be a problem. Once again, I felt grateful for Lio's warning that had saved me from being arrested in 2075. "Will my time at Walden 27 be a problem?"

"Hmm. Mostly that kind of thing is ignored, but when people leave one of the communities they might take more of an interest in that. If they ask any questions, you'll need to clearly disavow them."

"I can do that. No problem." I drained the last of my drink. "There was one more thing I meant to ask you about, Montagne." I set my glass down and wiped a trace of lip-balm off the edge of it with my thumb. Then I began telling Montagne about my experiences at the Semper Bellum pub and about what Marcus had told me about the contact phrases. As I spoke, I saw Montagne's face growing tense, his hands gripping his thighs.

"I wish I could tell you there was nothing to worry about," he said. "That it's all just part of a game devised by scripters somewhere. But I have to tell you, you're not the only one with questions about those games. I do know they're big business, generating enormous profits for Coronet Games and other plutocrats. What you said about your friend Marcus motivates me to maybe begin to ask more questions. Maybe we can get some of the Recall scripters involved in an investigation. Although most of them are busy on another project right now."

A couple of days later, I received an audio pulse from Montagne. "How would you like to travel to India with my daughter's wife?"

"That sounds wonderful," I said. "Tell me about her."

"Her name is Xi Tao-Min and she's a behavioral scientist. Once I told her about Jai Kalyani's research, she jumped at the chance to extend her journey. When do you think you might be ready to travel, Malia?"

"Tomorrow would be good," I said.

Montagne laughed. "I don't think we can arrange it that quickly. Tao-Min won't be finished with her project in Nigeria for another few weeks. Right now she's off in the countryside somewhere, but she'll be in Lagos the last week of July. I think she plans to remain in Lagos for several days."

"Can I meet her there? I've never been to Nigeria." I'd never been much of anywhere, but Nigeria sounded particularly intriguing. I couldn't believe I was saying these things. For most of my life I'd adamantly refused to even consider flying. Hadn't I refused to go with Lio and Zelda to Cuba? Hadn't I taken the train when I fled Washington back in 2075?

I felt different this time. I understood now why I'd been so afraid to travel for so many years: It was that trip to Argentina when I was just a scared teenager. I found it hard to believe I'd made that journey all by myself. I was nervous about flying to Nigeria—I'd be crossing the entire Atlantic Ocean, for heaven's sake! But I was going to do it. I was definitely going to do it.

Part IV
After

25.

Montagne made the travel arrangements and put me in touch with Xi Tao-Min. She and I sent pulses back and forth a few times and I thought she seemed like a lively and intelligent woman, the kind of person who'd make an excellent traveling companion.

I studied a map of Nigeria to see where Lagos is and to see how far it was from Tao-Min's research site in Taraba state, which is on Nigeria's eastern border with Cameroon. I also drew down a map of India and located Jaipur, in the state of Rajasthan. I'd forgotten that India was such an immense country. It isn't as big as the United States of America, even after Texas and California went independent, but certainly a lot more culturally diverse. Or at least it used to be. Diversity, of course, has been increasingly submerged beneath the pluto-crats' thick overburden of servile conformity. I located some commercial books on India and a few more through the Recall zone and I drew them down into my portable screen. I also searched out a few novels by Indian authors and drew down those, too.

I did all these things to keep from dwelling on the real rea-sons I was making this journey. Pretending I was just a tourist precluded my fretting too much about outcomes, about whether or not I'd find Jai Kalyani, about what kind of man he'd turn out to be if I did find him. It kept me from building up expectations. Hopes. Fears.

Leticia bought me a new travel case and tried to get me to buy some new clothes, but I insisted the clothes I had were perfectly fine. I didn't tell her about the clothes I'd pilfered at my job during my final week of work. I figured they wouldn't fire me once I'd handed in my resignation. What I did tell her was the reason for my sudden travel plans.

"I never knew you were pregnant," she said, tears coming into her eyes. "I felt so bad for you, for what happened, but now I see that I never knew how bad it really was. I should've been a better sister."

"I could've told you," I said, "but I didn't. It's not your fault that you didn't know. And then, of course, I forgot the whole thing and I didn't know either." We hugged. She wished me well on my journey.

"Place your right hand flat on the scanner," the airport security guard instructed.

I complied, trying to keep calm as I adjusted my position to observe the information on his screen: "Malia Poole. No travel history. Formerly associated with Walden Network. Voluntarily severed association March 24, 2125."

That was kind of them, I thought. A few moments later, I was seated in a departure lounge, waiting to board the plane, excited, uncertain about what lay ahead, reassuring myself that I was doing the right thing.

As the flight took off and soared into the air above Dallas, there was something about the sensations that felt strangely familiar. I'd told myself that I wanted to stay awake and watch out my little window for the entire flight, so as not to miss anything, but as the world receded beneath a monotonous cloudscape with only occasional glimpses of land, I unfurled my digilet and commenced reading one of the books I'd drawn down. A real book would have been far more satisfying. The trip was scheduled to take eighteen hours, with one stop in Madrid. I had books and I had Duermata.

Tao-Min and I had exchanged photos of ourselves so that we'd be able to find one another at the airport. I searched for her face as I exited into the unfamiliar space of the Lagos arrivals terminal. It was filled with people speaking English or French in strange accents or speaking minority languages I couldn't identify. Tao-Min recognized me before I recognized her. She was a good deal taller than I'd imagined.

"Malia?" She wanted to be sure.

"Tao-Min!" Seeing her smiling face was a relief. She gave me a quick hug and took charge of my case.

"How was the flight?" she asked. "Montagne told me you hadn't traveled much."

"It was fine. A little boring. Traveling over such a great distance should be more impressive." It was hard for me to believe I'd crossed a vast ocean and landed on another continent. I felt a bit disoriented, uncertain what time it was or even what day it was. Should I be hungry?

The guesthouse where we'd be staying until Tao-Min finished up some final business in Lagos was small, but with all the vanguard amenities. I was glad we weren't staying in one of those massive hotels favored by sabbaticos. Since I'd never had anything but what our society considered lower level jobs, I'd never experienced the luxury of the sabbatical, the one-year vacation every ten years. You had to work for one of the corporations to get those. Somehow, I didn't think I'd missed much.

Tao-Min offered me the option of going out for lunch or having something brought to the room. I opted for the latter. If we'd only been staying the one night, I'm sure I would have insisted on going out. But I was tired. Granted, I'd slept a good eight hours on the flight, but my joints ached, and my feet were swollen.

"Are you ready to try some Nigerian food?" Tao-Min asked, uncoiling her digilet in preparation for placing an order. "Most of it's kind of spicy."

"I'm from Texas," I laughed. "Spicy is good. But I'm getting old, so not too spicy."

"Medium. I think I know exactly what you need."

While we waited, we chatted, asking those awkward questions that people ask when they know they're about to spend a lot of time with a virtual stranger.

"Where are you from, Tao-Min?" I asked.

She laughed. "I'm not from China, if that's what you're thinking, although I can speak a little Mandarin. I was born in

Indiana. My parents were scientists—college professors—and we lived in one of those small college towns where it was okay to be a nerd, even a girl nerd. I guess the term these days is 'wirebrain.' Anyway, I definitely fit the description. I suspect that at the age when you were probably writing stories, I was writing computer programs and trying to train my kitten to go through a maze. Have you ever tried to train a kitten?"

We both laughed. I began to realize that she probably wasn't much younger than I was. Chulel creates such confusion! She followed up with a few questions about my background and I could feel the two of us settling into a pleasant sort of "getting-to-know-you" space.

The lunch was delicious. I can't tell you what it was called, but it included some unusual preparations involving beans, greens, and plantains. Tao-Min insisted I take a second helping of the greens.

"The iron will do you good," she said. After we finished, she recommended that I sit in the only upholstered chair with my feet up. She offered to massage my ankles to relieve the swelling. I wasn't accustomed to having anyone look after me like that. I wasn't sure how I felt about it. The massage was nice.

"Tell me about your work here," I said. "Montagne wasn't entirely clear about what it is you're doing. I just know you're a behavioral scientist of some kind." The only behavioral scientist I knew anything about was the author of *Walden Two*. I hoped Tao-Min wasn't like him.

Tao-Min handed me another glass of herbal tea. She explained that she'd come to Nigeria to aid in the investigation of a group of primates—bonobos, *Pan paniscus*—that had escaped some twenty years ago from a laboratory in the state of Taraba, along the eastern border of Nigeria with Cameroon.

"It was presumed that they'd all perished," she said, "that they'd been killed by predators or died of diseases or starved because of being outside their natural eco-niche. They belong in the central African rain forests. But then we started getting reports from people who'd seen them. Well, actually, a lot of the reports were of small hairy people living in the bush. You know what bonobos look like, right?"

"I've seen pictures. They do look more humanlike than chimps or gorillas."

"Exactly. Mainly it's their more upright posture and more slender build that cause us to see them that way. Well, in this case, it wasn't simply the appearance of the bonobos that contributed to the reports. They were building camps."

"What?" She had my full attention at this point. "What do you mean?"

"Rough shelters. Campfires."

"No! Building houses and making fires? How the hell is that even possible?"

"That's what we wanted to know. Before I got involved, there'd been attempts to requisition data from the corporate lab they'd escaped from. It was one of the big pharmaceutical corporations—part of Pharmakon now, of course. All they offered were memos reassuring us that the animals carried no infectious diseases. 'No threat at all,' they said. Then recently they offered bounties for return of the bonobos, dead or alive. That's when we decided to come look for them ourselves. Not in hopes of collecting any rewards but to find the poor creatures before the bounty hunters did."

"And did you find them?"

Tao-Min got up and walked over to the window then turned to look at me. "We did," she said. "We counted twenty-two of them. We identified five of them as from the original group of seven that escaped. It was uncanny, Malia. They were walking around on two legs and actually seemed to be communicating with one another in something resembling a vocal language."

"Wow." I was fascinated.

"We're pretty sure they were research subjects in some kind of genetic modification project. You know scientists have been messing with genomes for more than a century now—adding and subtracting and multiplying and dividing genetic sequences *ad infinitum*. Splicing a bit from this species into that species. Some of the results have been extremely useful. Profitable, too. Others, of course, have been disastrous. But this! I always believed scientists had enough moral fiber left to draw the line at manipulating human genes this way."

Tao-Min paced, her hands clasped behind her back. "Bonobos are so similar to us genetically, I guess I can understand the curiosity as to exactly which genes account for the obvious behavioral gulf between them and us. But this is inexcusable. This was a total breach of professional ethics. And now some of the scientists seem intent on eradicating the whole experiment, which I think is even worse. I sided with a group advocating a 'wait-and-see' attitude and we've prevailed, at least for now. We set up a protection zone but I'm not sure it will be respected."

I tried to think of something intelligent to say. "Sounds like they're doing a good job of raising their little bonobo children out there," I said, thinking it sounded like a rather mundane observation.

"That's one of the most interesting aspects." Tao-Min was frowning again, but her eyes sparkled. "It looked like there were three new generations, maybe four. In twenty years! My thinking is that the researchers had also altered something about maturation cycles."

I remembered what Montagne had told me about how the Institute in Argentina had been accelerating fetal growth in order to shorten pregnancies and move babies onto the market more quickly. My mind reeled. Was there nothing about our lives that was beyond being revised in the laboratories?

Tao-Min checked the time on her digilet and announced that she was due at a meeting with some of her colleagues. "Will you be okay here?" she asked.

"Fine," I replied. "I'm thinking I'll go out for a little stroll." I felt stronger after my healthy lunch and the swelling in my feet had gone down. I accompanied Tao-Min to the lobby and then set out on my own to explore the neighborhood.

26.

We'd passed through downtown Lagos on our way from the airport and I thought the central area looked an awful lot like Dallas. It had the same forbidding façades of buildings with uninviting entrances and no windows, the same digital skins with colorful, moving images. I had no desire to go back there. The environs of our guesthouse would be more interesting as well as more accessible.

The neighborhood was not unlike Leticia's endurb, although it had a different cultural veneer. Most of the buildings here were only a few stories tall, with freshly plastered walls and lots of big windows and broad balconies. I thought Dallas could use more of those. At street level, the shops offered the usual inventory of clothing and household goods and entertainment devices, all recyclable. But different smells wafted from the cafés. Some of them had music that overflowed into the street as well and, although it was synthesized music, it was in a different style, more rhythmically complex than what I might have heard in the cafés of Dallas. The people on the street had that placid, disconnected look that was becoming familiar to me. They had their digilets and their listening devices.

I heard a commotion from inside one of the cafés and, as I passed the door, I was nearly knocked down by a man who was being summarily and vociferously ejected from the premises. I didn't understand the language, but when the man saw me, he began shouting in English, with a distinctive French accent.

"Nobody wants to say it, but I say it! There are wars, terrible wars. They want us to go on fighting, so they send weapons. More and more weapons. Terrible weapons! We blow each other up but we don't die. They put us back together and put us back in the field. Are you listening to me old woman? Do you hear what I tell you? They play their evil games, and we have no escape. They take our children. Our children!"

I was transfixed, staring, trying to comprehend what this person was saying. It wasn't the unfamiliar accent that was hampering my understanding. I understood the words well enough. But what did he mean? Two uniformed men emerged from a nearby building and forcefully escorted the man away. He continued to shout as they conducted him down the street and into a doorway. I looked around, expecting to see a crowd of curious onlookers, but I was the only one on the street. A woman emerged from the café and peered off in the direction where the screaming man had disappeared.

"What was he talking about?" I whispered.

The woman waved her hand dismissively. "He's crazy," she said loudly. "Completely deranged. Pay him no mind." She went back inside the café.

Shaken by this encounter, I made my way back to the guesthouse to wait for Tao-Min. I kept thinking about what the man had said. *But the wars are over,* I told myself. *There have been no wars since the Global Accord of 2053.* Then I remembered the immigrants who had been my traveling companions on my train journey from Washington, D.C. to Dallas. Hadn't they been from this part of Africa? But that journey had been fifty years ago. Even if there had been a few remaining wars then, surely they would have ended long since. I took a couple of tabs of Duermata and lay down for a nap.

Tao-Min returned about the time I woke up. She was eager to take me to one of her favorite restaurants for dinner.

"Before we go," I said. "There's something I want to tell you. Something I want to ask you about." Over the years I'd learned to be careful about discussing sensitive topics in unfamiliar places. I told her about my encounter outside the café and what the man had said.

Tao-Min looked troubled. "There are rumors," she said. "And some of the local people we worked with in Taraba talked about the wars. At first I thought they were referring to historical conflicts, but the more I listened, the more it sounded like something ongoing, something current. Finally I asked one of our aides, a woman I particularly trusted. She didn't want to talk to me about it. But she did confirm that there were persistent rumors of chronic conflicts in several areas of central Africa."

"What if they aren't just rumors?" I asked.

"I wondered that myself," Tao-Min responded, "so I kept asking questions. Probably more than I should have. It was hard to find people who would talk to me. And hardly any of them claimed to believe the stories themselves, though they said they knew other people who were convinced they were true. But I was able to gather a lot of stories. They kept saying the wars are managed like games. They told me about whole groups of soldiers being airlifted from one region to another and given a target, but no explanation of who they were attacking or why. Or suddenly they're given generous supplies of some entirely new weapons and no explanation of where they came from. Bombs would be dropped from drones, and they had no idea where the drones had come from or who they belonged to. Sometimes, on the streets of the Taraba capitol, Jalinga, I saw people—women as well as men—with awful scars and artificial limbs."

"If this kind of thing is actually happening, why don't we ever hear about it?"

Tao-Min shook her head. "Some of the people I talked with had the same question. They'd been told that there were always crowds of reporters following the fighting in the field with all the most vanguard cameras and recording equipment."

My mind had suddenly called up images of the men in the Semper Bellum pub, placing their bets on war games. I recalled images of the fighters on the all-too-realistic screens on the pub's walls. Maybe Marcus really had been in communication with someone, with a real person somewhere in Central Africa. The possibility was chilling. I told myself that such a connection was unthinkable. So why was I thinking it? I couldn't bring myself to mention it to Tao-Min.

"What about the children?" I asked. "The man outside the café said they were taking away the children."

Tao-Min nodded. "I did hear a few people mention periodic sweeps to round up children. They're told the children have to be evacuated for their safety. I have no way of knowing how much truth there might be to any of this. These are just things I was told."

All during dinner and all the next day my mind wove backward and forward through all this information. My doubts, my suspicions about the connections—the man on the street, the people Tao-Min talked with, the refugees on the train from D.C., the gamers at Semper Bellum—weighed on me more and more. Montagne had seemed to take the possibilities seriously. *Talk to Tao-Min about it,* I told myself. But I didn't. It was as if I believed that saying these things out loud would give them the power of truth and I didn't want them to be true. What possible motivation would drive the plutocrats to pursue such insanity? I knew their usual motivation for anything would be profit, but how could there be profit in such pointless consumption of resources.

That night I dreamed of a huge casino in which the currency was human lives and plutocrats sat in their luxury boxes enjoying the games.

For the next several days, as I waited for Tao-Min to finish up her work in Lagos, I mostly stayed in our room reading my books. I sent a couple of pulses to Leti, telling her pleasant things about Lagos. Once or twice I accessed the Returns page on Recall to see if there was any information about Sophia. I found nothing. There wasn't anything about Lio either.

I had time to reflect on exactly why I'd come here, on the goal of my journey. I still hadn't sorted out whether I wanted to actually meet my son or only see him, lay eyes on him. Maybe just laying eyes on my long-lost son might be enough, maybe even letting him lay eyes on me. I was almost certain I didn't want to reveal my relationship to him. I told myself it had been too long, and I was too old. *He has his life.*

On the evening before we were due to leave Lagos, Tao-Min returned looking worried. "Have you heard anything about this new virus?" she asked.

"Virus? Human or computer?" I smiled.

"Human." She didn't look amused. "My biologist colleague at the university was telling me about it today. She's very concerned."

I pressed for more information.

"They started off calling it 'Idiopathic Hemolytic Anemia', which only meant they didn't know what the zujo was causing it. But she says they know now it's actually a virus, a highly contagious and deadly virus. She told me that the death toll in affected areas of China is appalling."

"Do you think there's danger of it spreading to India?"

"From what she told me, I'd say there's danger of it spreading everywhere. She believes it has to be an airborne virus to spread the way it does. We'll be pretty far from known areas of infection in Rajasthan state so we should be safe for the time being. But I think we ought to keep an eye on this."

Epidemiology was not something I'd ever researched for any of my novels, so I had to rely on Tao-Min's expertise to calibrate the extent of my concern. I decided this ranked pretty far down on my list of worries.

27.

On the day of our departure for New Delhi, India, we arrived at the airport early and found it swarming with children.

"Your tickets have been changed to the forward compartment, no extra charge," the airline agent informed us.

"Why is that?" I wanted to know.

"The entire rear compartment was purchased as a block by one of our corporate humanitarian organizations and they've subsidized your upgrade. They're taking a group of children to India as part of a cultural exchange program. I'm sure you'll be quite comfortable."

The forward compartment boarded first, so we were able to watch the whole parade of children that boarded after us. I hadn't seen that many children in one place since I was a schoolgirl myself and that was a very long time ago. There must have been almost a hundred children, more girls than boys and some of them so young they had to be carried. The eldest looked no older than eleven or twelve and there were fewer of them. Adult caretakers herded them about in groups of no more than a dozen. The children were surprisingly quiet, and I found their expressions impossible to read. I'd never before seen such stone-faced children.

Our flight time was expected to be just over ten hours, nonstop. I remarked to Tao-Min that the seating in the forward compartment was a lot more comfortable than what I'd experienced on my previous flight.

"I understand that it used to be even more accommodating," she replied, "but now that the plutocrat class fly on separate aircraft, this is just for mid- to high-level professionals." I tried to imagine what the plutocrats' aircraft might be like, experiencing something like envy in spite of my decades of practiced contempt for such things.

Occupants of the forward compartment also disembarked first when we landed in New Delhi. But I was urgently in need of a bathroom, so by the time we got to the area where we'd be registered and documented, we found ourselves waiting in line behind the throng of children.

"Where are they going?" I asked the woman in front of me. She was one of the caregivers.

She gave me a look of tired exasperation and shifted the toddler she was carrying from one hip to the other. "Different places," she said.

"Are any of them headed to Jaipur?" I offered my most disarming smile.

"A few," she said.

"And what exciting cultural experiences will be waiting for them there?" I tried not to sound sarcastic.

The woman suddenly looked as if she were on the verge of tears. "I'm very tired," she said. "It's been a long journey, and it isn't over yet. I really need to concentrate on dealing with the children." She turned her back to me, our conversation clearly at an end.

I looked up at Tao-Min. She had a worried expression but said nothing. We didn't talk to one another again until we'd left the arrivals terminal and were safely enclosed in the autocar that would take us to the hotel where we were spending the night.

"I don't like this," Tao-Min said. "I've got a bad feeling about those children. Cultural exchange? What the zujo? Are you craicking me? Some of them are toddlers, for god's sake."

"What do you think is going on?"

"Well, I didn't want to say anything before, because I didn't want to worry you unnecessarily."

"Yes?"

"It's said that there are some corporate research facilities that use children as subjects. Montagne told me that, according to Dr. Winfield, that's where some of the children from your

Argentine institute ended up. You're lucky your son didn't get caught up in that. You're lucky you had a son. A white son."

"What are you suggesting?" I was taken aback. "I thought we'd gotten past all those ignorant gender and racial prejudices long ago. Surely they don't drive decisions anymore. Not in the 22nd century."

"I have no idea." Tao-Min sighed. "Just remember, though: A lot of the most powerful plutocrats came of age in the late 20th or early 21st centuries when racism and misogyny were still significant forces. They would have the power to impose their own prejudices. They would be able to construct and maintain the world the way they wanted it to be, the way they believed it ought to be. You know, when I was in graduate school there were some of the students—the ones from plutocrat families—who just had this aura of privilege about things, as if they deserved to get the grants and the positions because of who they were. And, yes, they were all white."

On the train to Jaipur the next day, Tao-Min told me about her contact at the university who she thought might be able to help us locate Jai. I told her how much I looked forward to seeing some of the Jaipur tourist attractions I'd read about, like the famed 18th-century palace called Hawa Mahal and the architectural astronomical instruments of the Jantar Mantar. I knew I was deliberately avoiding talking about why I was here.

Our first morning in Jaipur was devoted to being tourists. "It'll help us get oriented to the city," Tao-Min said. I thought she probably also was accommodating me and my trepidations.

"I was expecting everything to be more crowded," I remarked as we strolled along the street after breakfast, keeping to the shade as the heat rose in the morning air. "The books I've read always talked about the masses of humanity on the streets of Indian cities, but even in Delhi yesterday—the little we saw of it—things just didn't seem that crowded. And I thought there would be cows. Where are the cows?"

"Don't you remember what happened in the bovine flu epidemic?"

"When was that? If it was while I was hidden away at Walden 27, I'm probably unaware, so tell me what happened."

Tao-Min paused and looked up and down the street. It wasn't an empty street by any means. There were people moving to and fro, most of them absorbed in their devices just like in every other city I'd been in recently. Many of them were clearly tourists or sabbaticos. There were no cows.

"Bovine flu originated in India," Tao-Min said. "It wiped out hundreds of thousands of cows and even more people before they finally developed the vaccine. The worst hit areas in terms of human mortality were Indian cities. After the epidemic, they established rural sanctuaries for the cows, since they were fearful of keeping them inside the cities anymore."

We resumed our walk as I tried to imagine these streets as they once were. I thought again about the new epidemic Tao-Min had told me about and wondered what its consequences might be. *We humans think we're masters of every-thing until one of these little viruses comes along to remind us just how vulnerable we really are.*

"Didn't there used to be problems with stray dogs, too?" I asked.

Tao-Min smiled. "Fertility control programs took care of that one. I'm sure there are still dogs here in India. Probably cats, too. And surely rats and mice." She grinned at me. "Indians have always maintained a cultural space for animals."

Even without the cows and dogs and even with fewer people, the streets of Jaipur had a palpable intensity. There was something about the August heat that seemed to ignite and exaggerate the brilliant colors of the clothing and of the products for sale. It drained my energy but produced a dizzy intoxication that was not entirely unpleasant. In fact, I think I would have found the city thoroughly enjoyable if I'd truly been there as a tourist. But I wasn't a tourist. I was a woman with a mission. I was also a woman haunted by the specters of a man on the street in Lagos and a planeload of children whose destinations and destinies I still questioned.

We visited the Hawa Mahal and explored a bazaar. I found the palace delightful, although tiring. The bazaar was a disappointment. Only a few stalls offered handcrafted goods. Most of the wares were shoddy 3-D prints of handcrafted models. The crowds of tourists and sabbaticos didn't seem to notice or care. I found a charming hand-carved wooden box with a depiction of the full moon on its lid, a moon clearly bearing the image of a hare. It reminded me of Lio, so I bought it. I immediately felt guilty for having purchased an item that had no clear purpose, so I followed up by purchasing a string of prayer beads to put inside it. I'd never used prayer beads, but it muddled my Simpleton logic and left me feeling defiant and satisfied.

On our second day in Jaipur, Tao-Min went to meet with her colleague, leaving me on my own. I didn't do much other than take a morning walk around the neighborhood of our guesthouse. I followed the flow of pedestrians, thinking they must know where they were going. They led me to an entertainments complex catering to tourists and sabbaticos. In addition to the usual games and gambling, there was a large park where you could purchase rides on elephants and camels. I watched, mesmerized by the lumbering gait of the elephants, the awkward grace of the camels. I felt a bit sorry for the poor creatures. I knew they'd traditionally been used as work animals. Now it was clear they were just a diversion and a way of extracting value from tourists. I thought they looked bored.

By midday, the heat and gathering rain clouds drove me back to the cooled air of the guesthouse. I'd been well acclimated to the hot summers of West Texas, but this was different. There it had been dry heat. Here the air was soggy with monsoon humidity, making it difficult to breathe.

I hadn't been back at the room more than half an hour when the sky exploded in a thunderstorm that put the ones I'd experienced in West Texas to shame. At Walden 27, our storms had been mostly about the lightning and thunder. This Jaipur storm had plenty of that, but it also had rain—intense rain, a roaring shroud of rain that obscured the city and turned the streets briefly into rivers. I pulled a chair up next to the window and watched. It was quite a spectacle.

Tao-Min returned around midafternoon, tired and wet but smiling. "I think I'm making progress," she said. "I'm told that Jai is out of the country at the moment, but I've met an associate of his who's agreed to take me to tour his research facility tomorrow. Do you want to come along?"

I didn't answer.

"Well, you can think about it," she said.

I decided that I wouldn't go. "I don't want to get in your way," I said.

She insisted I wouldn't be in the way, but finally acquiesced, promising to take diligent notes and, if possible, some photographs so she could give me a full report.

28.

During the hours when I knew Tao-Min would be touring Jai's facility, I went out on a quest of my own. I'd easily determined where Jai's father, Ayush Kalyani, worked. I was curious about the man who had raised my son as his own and I'd decided that I wanted to lay eyes on him as well. The guesthouse summoned an autocar for me and I gave it the address of the office building that was headquarters for the Kalyanis' assorted enterprises. There was a brief shower of rain that graciously subsided just before I arrived at the complex, leaving everything steamy clean.

It was an impressive building, standing on its own in a landscaped park well away from central Jaipur. I wasn't certain what I'd do while I waited to see if I could get a glimpse of my son's adoptive father, but I'd brought my screen, thinking perhaps I could sit down somewhere and read a book, or at least pretend to read. I was relieved to see that the park included a couple of kiosks selling tea and snacks. There was also a scattering of benches where people could sit and enjoy their food and beverages. I purchased a cup of chai and found a spot that afforded an oblique but unimpeded view of the main entrance to the office building. I dried off the bench as best I could with the napkin that came with my chai and settled down to watch and wait.

I screened up one of my books on India. The day was mild and cloudy, but I knew unbearable heat lay just behind those clouds. I saw it emanating, too, in the steam that hovered on the pavements. I waited, paying more attention to the birds searching for damp crumbs than to the words of my book.

After a while, a large attended autocar pulled up in front of the entrance to the building. A uniformed man stepped out of the car and stood at attention while a second door opened and a handsome, well-dressed, bearded gentleman emerged. I recognized him from the photos Montagne had shown me. It was Ayush Kalyani. I caught my breath and stared. He moved with grace and confidence. *Such a man must have been a good father,* I thought.

The autocar door hadn't closed. A second man emerged, and my heart lost all semblance of rhythm as I realized that this fair-skinned man had to be Jai. As he turned his face in my direction, I was certain it was he. *Had he seen me? Had he looked at me? No, of course not.* But he was stepping away from his father, coming in my direction. I wanted to flee, but I held my seat. This was incomprehensible. He was almost in front of me. I caught his fragrance as he passed, an aroma of incense and fine cologne. He walked briskly and seemed a little out of breath by the time he stopped at the tea kiosk.

"Welcome back, Mr. Jai," the tea seller beamed. "We weren't expecting you until tomorrow."

"Thank you, Deepak. The usual. Yes, I came back early from China because of that infernal disease that seems to be taking down so many people. They'll get hold of it soon, I'm sure. We've got all our best scientists working on it. No need for us to worry here in Rajasthan, in any case." He smiled, radiating confidence.

"You sure you're okay, Mr. Jai? You're looking a little pale."

Jai laughed. "Maybe you forgot, Deepak, but I always look a little pale. Perhaps I'm a bit jetlagged. Anyway, off to work now! See you soon, Deepak."

Jai turned and saw me staring at him. I looked down quickly at my screen, but not before I saw that beautiful smile of his one more time. I knew this one was for me and my heart sang. This is what I'd wanted to know. My son was okay. He was a kind man with a gentle manner. In that moment I could finally acknowledge how deeply troubled I'd been that he might have turned out to be some kind of monster, some genetically flawed subhuman being prone to violence, devoid of feeling. I'd been so afraid he'd be like his natural father.

I knew I was going to burst into tears at any moment, so I quickly put my screen inside my handbag and made my way back to where I'd left the autocar. I walked with my head down, keeping a tight rein on myself, repeating like a mantra, *It's okay, Malia. The boy is okay.*

I gave myself over to the tears all the way back to the guesthouse, while there was no one to see me cry. They were gentle tears of joy. By the time the autocar's door opened to let me out, I was more or less composed. I was still smiling. Arriving at the room, I was surprised to see that Tao-Min had already returned.

"There you are," she said with evident relief as I opened the door. "I need to talk with you, Malia. I've been trying to think how to tell you this, but there's really no way other than straight and honest." She wasn't looking at me.

I was mystified. I was dying to tell her about my encounter with Jai and his father, but I would listen to what she had to say first.

"I toured Jai's research lab this morning," she said.

"Yes, I know. Is that what you need to tell me about?"

As succinctly as she could manage, Tao-Min told me what she'd learned, what she'd seen. "His research basically focuses on an applied interface between artificial intelligence and photonic cognitive structuring. Malia, he's embedding digital devices into his research subjects to make them more easily controlled by photonic means. They're calling his new company PedagogiTech and they're intending to market the devices to all the children's boarding colonies around the world as a new form of pedagogy."

"That sounds awful." I was desperately trying to reconcile this with the image of the kindly man I'd watched buying tea. "What kind of subjects is he using? I can't believe he'd use live animals..."

"Oh, he's not using animals. He's using children."

"What? How...?"

"What I was told was that people volunteer their children for these projects in exchange for a promise to educate each child for high-level employment. But I don't believe them." She paused, finally turning to look into my face. Her eyes narrowed, her severe tone softened. "Malia, I saw some of the children who were on the plane with us from Lagos. One of them recognized me so I know I didn't imagine it."

I began to cry. "There has to be some mistake, Tao-Min. That can't be Jai's research. Jai isn't like that. I saw him this morning. He's kind and gentle. He has soft eyes."

"Wait. What? You saw him? I thought he was out of the country."

"He just got back. I went out to Ayush Kalyani's office complex today because I wanted to get a look at the man who raised Jai. I never expected Jai to be with him. But he was. He's not someone who would do the kinds of things you're talking about. I'm sure of it. Really, Tao-Min, you mustn't say these things about Jai. Someone is lying to you."

"But I saw the labs. I saw the children. They even showed me some of the official reports of their results."

"Then it's someone else's research. It's not Jai's."

"So why was his name on the door? Why was his name listed first on all the reports?"

"I have no idea!" I shouted. "That's not my problem! My problem is you and the fact that you're lying to me, and I don't know why!" I felt an ominous tightness in my chest. I saw Tao-Min taking deep breaths, watching my outburst with studied calm. That made me even angrier.

"Look, Malia," she said. "I'm going to walk down to the lobby for a few minutes and maybe pick us up a couple of bottles of juice. I'll be back soon. Then we'll talk some more."

She walked out, closing the door quietly, firmly. As soon as she was gone I picked up the closest object at hand and hurled it at the closed door. I began to cry again. The object I'd thrown was the wooden box I'd bought at the bazaar, the box that reminded me of Lio. I bent over to retrieve it, remembering what Lio had said about our cultural predilections for seeing what we wanted to on the face of the moon. The discomfort in my chest was escalating into pain and I was short of breath. My heart alternated between fluttering and exploding. I needed to sit down.

With the box clutched against my chest, I sat on the edge of the nearest bed. *Breathe*, I told myself. I remembered reading somewhere that when you're having a heart attack and you're all alone you should cough. I coughed. Again. The discomfort began to subside and my heartbeat took on a steadier rhythm. Why had I said such unkind things to Tao-Min? I didn't want to believe what she was telling me, but I knew she wouldn't lie. I'd called her a liar. Tears fell silently as my shoulders slumped, and my head fell forward.

I was still sitting like that, still clinging to my wooden box, when the door opened again and Tao-Min came in, holding two bottles of fruit juice and a packet of some kind of snacks. I looked up at her with guilty eyes.

"I'm sorry," I said. "I shouldn't have lost my temper."

She came and sat beside me. She opened the juice and handed it to me. "It's okay," she said. "This has got to be hard for you and the only way I'll know how you feel is if you tell me. Or show me. So, really, it's okay."

"What kind of juice is this?" I asked. "It tastes nice."

Tao-Min smiled. "It's lychee fruit. It's always been one of my favorites."

"It doesn't make sense," I said as I drank my juice. "How could someone look so kind and yet be conducting such heartless research?"

"I don't know. The people who guided me around today seemed to see nothing wrong with what they're doing. They were proud of the advances they're making and optimistic about the future benefits of their research. I wanted to ask how they coped with what they're doing to the children, but I think they really believe the children were sent there voluntarily. I don't think they know where they're coming from."

"And you only know because we saw them on the plane from Lagos. Maybe their parents were sending them voluntarily. We don't have any proof that they were being abducted, you know." I thought about Mandy Pequot. Hadn't her parents willingly sent her off to a boarding colony in exchange for a promise of future employment? Or maybe they'd been driven to it by poverty.

"That's true," Tao-Min said. "But if they were being sent by their families, why that ridiculous story about a humanitarian cultural exchange? That part is clearly a fabrication."

We talked a while longer. My writerly rationalizations coupled with Tao-Min's more scientific analysis enabled us to work through most of the possibilities. I gradually resigned myself to the idea that although my son's demeanor in interacting with a tea seller was above reproach, his professional research was another matter. Sometimes people are complicated.

29.

When I woke from my Duermata-induced sleep the next morning, Tao-Min was already standing at the window, digilet in hand. She turned when she heard me stir.

"We've got a pulse from Montagne," she said. "He won't say why, but he says we need to come home right away. He says we have to arrive no later than Sunday afternoon."

I sat up in bed, rubbing the crust from my eyes and trying to claw through the fog in my brain. I nodded, barely comprehending.

Tao-Min snapped the digilet around her wrist. "Sorry," she said. "I should give you a chance to wake up. I've brought us some tea." She poured a cup for me, putting in two sugars and just enough milk.

"I'm awake now," I said after a few sips. "Mostly awake anyway. Tell me again about the message from Montagne."

"There's not much to it. He says to come home right away and apologizes for not being able to tell us why."

"What day is today?"

"Thursday."

"Do you think it'll be possible for us to get home so quickly? Do you think this has anything to do with that sickness you were telling me about?"

"The VHA? That's possible. But I think he would have told us if that were the case. It's all over the news now."

"Is it? What are they saying?"

She picked up her portable screen and shifted through some items. "They're saying that it's definitely a virus, of course. An airborne virus. They've also concluded that only people who are long-term and recent Chulel users are susceptible."

"That's just about everybody, isn't it? Except me, of course. What about you?"

Tao-Min tilted her head side-to-side in that funny way they do here in India. "It looks like I've gotten lucky. The clinic I went to in Costa Rica for my last two Chulel infusions turns out to have been using something that wasn't really Chulel. They were shut down a few months ago and we were all notified and issued vouchers for free visits to a spa in a different city. I hadn't decided if I'd go or not. So, you see? I got lucky."

I thought about my sisters. I knew Sophia had always been a committed Chulel user. And Leticia had been so pleased about finally finding a reliable supplier of off-market Chulel. Not so lucky for her.

Tao-Min continued, "According to this report, VHA has an incubation period of only twenty-four hours before symptoms begin to appear." Her eyes widened and she took a deep breath. "Death occurs within one to two weeks of the onset of symptoms."

"How are they treating it? There has to be some kind of treatment, right?"

"Palliative care only. They're accelerating research but haven't discovered anything yet that affects the progress of the disease. None of the antivirals work."

Tao-Min laid the screen on the table. "I've heard something else about the illness from my colleagues here. They told me the disease has been tracked back to its source in China."

"Didn't we already know that's where it started?"

"Well, yes, but this is more specific. Apparently it originated in a laboratory that was involved in producing an early form of Chulel. You probably wouldn't remember that; it was sold on the streets under the name Fontana."

"No," I said. "That doesn't sound familiar."

"Anyway, after Chulel went on the market, the primary researcher left China, but his associate kept working on the formula. Apparently he thought that if he could discover a weakness in Chulel—some kind of side effect or something—he might be able to market his own drug to combat that weakness. What he found was a progressive deterioration in the Beta chain of hemoglobin. And he realized that this might make Chulel users vulnerable to human parvovirus."

"What's that?"

"It's a disease that primarily affected children and had been almost eradicated. He revived it, strengthened it..."

"Wait. You're telling me he deliberately developed this virus in order to market his own drug?" I silently cursed whoever had done this, cursed his selfishness and greed.

"I was told that his plan was to have targeted antiviral and vaccine at the ready, but that part of the plan didn't work out. He'd made very little progress toward the antiviral when the virus escaped his safety precautions. After that there was nothing he or anyone else could do. I don't know if all of this is true or not. I was told that the researcher was one of the first victims."

I was stunned. "Why would someone deliberately work to develop such a horrendous disease?" I asked.

"There were a lot of diseases that were developed in the 20th century to serve as weapons of war," Tao-Min said. "Eventually international treaties put a stop to that. This was different, of course. This was being done for profit."

I couldn't think of anything to say. Human beings were selfish brutes. Why did I always try so hard to convince myself otherwise?

"This is not going to turn out well," I said.

"No, it isn't."

"How far has it spread?"

"Look, I think I need to start making our departure plans. If we're going to make it back by Montagne's deadline, we'll need to leave very soon. I'm going to go downstairs and see if the concierge can help me with getting us to... Are you okay with coming to Costa Rica with me? Then we'll get you to Dallas from there. Will that be okay?"

"Sure. Wherever we go, we ought to go together."

Tao-Min turned toward the door and then back toward me. "Are you okay with leaving the situation like this with Jai?"

She didn't wait for me to answer. "Think about it. We'll talk when I get back. If there's anything else you feel we need to do on that score, we'll have to do it right away."

How did I feel about Jai? I'd seen him. He looked happy. If it hadn't been for what Tao-Min had told me about his research, I might have wanted to get to know him. I'd be this nice old auntie who liked making friends with strange men. Strange plutocrats. No, I was done here. Jai had his life and, regardless of how I felt about his research, he'd be okay.

Suddenly I caught my breath. *China*, I thought. *Chulel.* Jai was clearly a Chulel user, and hadn't he just returned from China? And hadn't the tea seller told him he looked unwell? Jai was not going to be okay. Jai was ill and he was going to die. My heart tumbled into an echoing well of sadness. I walked to the window and looked down onto the busy street below, breathing in the burning anguish that pushed me beyond tears. My heart was torn open, my fragile hopes shattered. There was nothing left to do but go home, apparently by way of Costa Rica. I started packing.

Tao-Min returned with bad news. "The New Delhi airport is on a minimal schedule because of the disease," she said. "They've canceled all flights to and from known hot spots and are screening every passenger to everywhere else. Most of Central America is now being considered a hot spot, so I tried to get us flights to Dallas. The only available flights would put us through Moscow and Quebec City. But they can't get us on a flight until early Saturday morning. With total flight time plus layovers amounting to nearly forty-eight hours, that puts us past Montagne's target. And yes, I factored in the time zone differences. I'm going to pulse him for advice. What have you decided about Jai?"

She looked up from her digilet, where she'd already begun to compose the pulse for Montagne, and saw my suitcase on the bed, almost fully packed. "Oh," she said. "That helps." She gave me a tense smile, which I returned.

I sat down on the bed. My distress and the flurry of activity had increased my heart rate again and I was breathing heavily. I still hadn't mentioned anything to Tao-Min about my episode yesterday that I tried to convince myself had not been a heart attack. She had enough to worry about. I watched while she sent the pulse.

"There," she said, coiling the digilet once more around her wrist. "Let's hope he gets back to us quickly, because things seem to be changing by the minute. Shall we have some breakfast?"

She insisted on ordering an ample meal comprised of dahl with spicy potatoes, naan, and ice-cold glasses of a sweet yogurt beverage. "We need to keep our strength up," she said. Sometimes she reminded me of my sister Leti.

As we ate, Tao-Min kept glancing nervously at her digilet, which she had laid next to her plate, ready to respond as soon as anything came through. We were almost finished with our meal when it finally chimed. As she read the message, she looked surprised, then distressed. She laid the digilet down.

"Well, what did he say? Are we okay to go?"

"It wasn't from Montagne. It was from my colleague at the university. She wanted to let me know that we have a confirmed case of VHA here in the city." She paused, looking again at the digilet as if searching for some escape from what she needed to say next.

"It's Jai, isn't it?" I said, forcing the words past the burning lump in my throat.

"Yes. It's Jai. He was apparently already symptomatic when he returned from China, but there was no screening in place at the airport. Besides, he's a high level plutocrat. He probably came in on a private jet. No telling how many people he's infected with the disease."

Tao-Min was clearly disgusted at Jai's irresponsible behavior. I only felt sadness for the man himself. For his parents. For his wife. For the tea seller.

"The disease would've come here anyway, Tao-Min, if it's as contagious as you say. No point blaming Jai for this."

"You're right," she said. "I'm being selfish. I was only thinking about how this is going to complicate our departure. It will, you know."

I knew she was also thinking about Meli, wanting more than anything to be with the woman she loved. Her concerns were different from mine.

The digilet signaled the arrival of another pulse and Tao-Min grabbed it eagerly. As she read the message, I could see the tears beginning to fill her eyes. She lay the digilet down gently and then picked it up again.

"I'll read you exactly what Montagne says. He says, 'Sit tight. I promise we'll get you out as soon as possible, but it will be at least a couple of weeks. You'll understand soon. You should Chat² with Meli while you still can.' That's it. Well, there's also something about digilet settings that he says I should copy down and then wipe. I'm not sure I get what's happening and I know Meli won't be able to tell me anything more, but I think I need to talk to her."

"Yes. Definitely. I'm going down to the café to get a cup of tea."

I left Tao-Min alone to converse with Meli. I knew she was worried about the fact that Meli was still a Chulel user. I thought she must be heartbroken that she wouldn't be rejoining her as soon as we'd thought.

As I drank my tea, I watched the people hurrying by on the street with their umbrellas. I tried to think what might be happening that would cause Montagne to advise us to stay in Rajasthan for another two weeks. Maybe more. My ordinarily hyper-imaginative mind failed me; I came up with nothing. Then I thought about the illness. This city was going to be filled with sick people in a matter of days. Not just sick people— terminally ill people. Dying people. What would it be like in two weeks? From what Tao-Min had told me, I felt sure she and I would be safe. Her two years without Chulel were not quite my forty-plus years of abstinence, but hopefully enough to resist this VHA.

I thought about Jai, about how he must feel, knowing he'd brought this illness into Jaipur. *He shouldn't blame himself,* I thought. And then I thought, *Does he blame himself? Does he feel anything for the children in his research project?* With a sigh, I acknowledged that I really had no idea how this man felt about anything. As far as I knew, he'd never murdered anyone. Maybe that would have to be enough.

My thoughts turned to my sisters, and I sent a quick pulse to Leticia, urging her to try and protect herself from this VHA, adding that Tao-Min and I had decided to stay in India a few more weeks. No explanation. Then I opened the Returns page on Recall to look for Sophia. There was nothing about her, nothing about anyone I knew.

I wasn't sure how long I ought to allow Tao-Min with her personal conversation before returning to our room, so I ordered another cup of tea and a plate of deep-fried pastries dusted with sugar. I'd eaten only one of the pastries when I looked up and saw Tao-Min approaching. Her confident stride didn't match the evidence of recent tears on her face. She sat down and reached for a pastry.

"Meli's okay," she said, absolving me of the need to ask. "Montagne has put her in quarantine already, which she finds irritating, because at this point they have no idea how long her isolation might have to last. But she said...." There was a catch in Tao-Min's voice, and she paused to compose herself. "She said that she'll do it because she knows I'll be safe from the illness, and she wants to be there for me when I get home." She quickly whisked away a stray tear before looking around for the waiter, who was already on his way to our table. "Chai, please," she said.

"What will we do for the next two weeks? Do you think we should stay here?" I asked.

"I think staying in Jaipur is probably better than trying to go to Delhi or one of the other cities with major international airports. We kind of know our way around here, at least. And as for what to do while we wait... Maybe we could make ourselves useful. Since both of us are safe from the disease due to our Chulel status, perhaps we could volunteer to help out at one of the hospitals. What do you think?"

"You know, in Walden 27, everybody had to do first aid training and take occasional shifts as assistants in our hospital. I'd like to do something useful. No point in sitting around the guesthouse doing nothing."

"I haven't had any particular training or experience, but I'm strong and a quick learner. I could assist with moving patients, helping to keep them comfortable. I'll contact my colleague and see if he can get us an assignment."

30.

Tao-Min's colleague got us in at a hospital affiliated with the university's medical research facility and on Monday we reported for work. The medical staff were grateful for our help and immediately assigned us to the VHA wards. We had no need for the elaborate protective gear most of the staff were forced to wear around VHA patients.

I was surprised at how many patients were already there, until I reminded myself of what Tao-Min had told me about the 24-hour incubation period. There were only a handful of Chulel-free people who could work without the encumbering suits and hoods and we were issued badges indicating our approved status. Most of the other badge-wearers came from the ranks of lower-level workers who tended to sweeping, cleaning and trash removal. My heart sank, realizing that in another week or so they'd also be removing bodies.

My tarea was bedside care. I gave people water and helped them with their meals and their palliative medications—analgesics, anti-nausea pills, sleep aids. I held their hands and looked into their faces. They seemed grateful to be able to see mine. Tao-Min assisted with medical procedures that were awkward for personnel wearing the protective gear; she also helped patients to the bathrooms and showers.

Returning to the guesthouse after our second day of work, we encountered a knot of people clustered around the wall screen in the lobby. We joined them. I could barely see the screen over the heads of the gathered crowd, but I could hear, and I watched Tao-Min's face as she watched the images.

The news wasn't good. Reports were coming in about multiple crises around the world—disruptions in communication and banking systems, power failures, transportation breakdowns. Planes were grounded at major airports all across North America and Europe. "Beijing is also reporting a major power outage," the presenter said, "although it is unclear whether there is any connection with the extensive North American outages reported around Dallas, Texas, and Washington, D.C."

Once we'd reached our room, I asked Tao-Min, "Do you think this is what Montagne was warning us about? The timing is right. But how would he have known?"

"He wouldn't have known unless it was something deliberate. If this is what I think it is, it means Recall finally decided to go through with the takedown."

"Takedown? I'd heard occasional rumors that there might be something coming, but I had no idea it could be anything this big. What do you think happens now?"

"I think it all comes apart. This is going to get a lot worse before it begins to get better. Montagne told me once that Recall had put together plans for disaster recovery. I don't know what they are. And I never thought the disaster would be self-induced." She turned around and looked at me. "We wait, I guess, and go about our business."

"I'm glad we have some business to go about," I said, but inside I felt the nudge of doubts and resentments. What gave Recall the right to do this? What did they foresee that would be any better? Yes, our society was a mess. It had engaged in some very nasty business. I thought about what the plutocrats' agents had done to Zelda. I thought about all my beloved books at Codex2. I thought about the bonobo experiments, the war games, Jai's highly questionable project. But then I thought about what had happened to me. Nobody made Roland Roxahrza rape and kill. Where was human nature in all of this? Would this turn out to be like the experiment in China that led to the escape of a virus that had no cure? Maybe a better way would emerge, maybe the seeds planted by sufficiency communities like Walden 27 and Palmyra would finally take root. But there were no guarantees. At this point, nothing seemed certain. *Anything is possible*, I told myself.

Before the end of the week, the power grid and communication networks across India had failed and the shops were being emptied, with no guarantee of new supplies coming in. There was backup power at the hospital as well as emergency food supplies from somewhere, so Tao-Min and I got one meal a day there.

Most of the residents of our little guesthouse had quickly made their way elsewhere, leaving only Tao-Min and me and two young students from France—Paul and Simone. Most of the guesthouse staff were too afraid of the disease, too baffled by the disintegration of their normal life to come to work. When the café closed, Tao-Min and I began eating breakfast and supper in the kitchen with one old man and the two French teenagers. The old man, Shankar, took over the kitchen in addition to his regular job of cleaning floors and removing the trash and recyclables.

"Are you sure you don't mind?" he'd asked. "I come from street sweepers. Some people even now would refuse food from my hands."

We assured him that we harbored no such disapprobation and were in fact deeply grateful for his willingness to provide food for us. The fact that he somehow managed to come up with something for us to eat every day seemed like a small miracle. He also kept a minimal level of power going, via solar panels on the roof and an array of batteries. This enabled us to cook, preserve food in a chillbox, and run a few fans and lights. It wasn't enough to run the cooling equipment for the building, and I soon felt the loss of it. When the public water supply grew unreliable, Shankar rigged up rain barrels. There was plenty of rain. He also brought in drinking water in large jugs. I don't know what we'd have done if we hadn't had Shankar with us.

After Paul and Simone learned what Tao-Min and I were doing, they volunteered to assist Shankar in exchange for a place to stay. "Until things improve," Simone said. Paul had been training as an engineer and proved to have excellent problem-solving skills, tested repeatedly when first one thing and then another broke down. Simone had been training to go into media production; she took on general cleaning and laundry. People were beginning to do laundry again. The five of us quickly became a tight community.

The wards at the hospital continued to fill up rapidly and by the beginning of the second week we were tending patients in the hallways and lobbies in addition to the regular rooms and wards. When my break period came up on the Sunday, I decided to take a walk through some of the other areas of the hospital. I told myself I was only curious to know whether they were as full as the one where I was working. Most of them were. I even saw surgical suites that had been converted to patient care.

When I walked out of the stairwell on Level 4, two floors above the level where Tao-Min and I worked, I was surprised by the relative calm, the silence. A fully garbed and hooded desk clerk rose and began to gesture for me to stop until they saw my badge. Then they sat back down and continued working.

I walked down the hall and around a corner. I studied the tags on the doors: "Patient 7 from 1," and a name. I saw numbers up to fifteen, all indicating "from 1." I wasn't sure what that meant until I came to the tag that read "Patient 1." The name was "Jai Kalyani."

I stood motionless by the door for a moment and then, feeling sudden resolve, I pushed it open. I took a deep breath. "How are you doing today, Mr. Kalyani?" I asked with a smile.

Removing the oxygen mask from his face, he smiled back. "I'm okay. But why are you in here without your protective gear?"

"Can't you see? Don't all these wrinkles and gray hair answer your question?"

He laughed weakly. "Oh, I see," he said. "Yours is the first face I've seen in almost a week. It's nice. I think I like your gray hair and wrinkles."

I offered him a drink of water. We talked. That first day we didn't talk about much, but I knew I'd go back. I didn't tell Tao-Min. This was too precious to share.

On the second day, he wanted to know where I was from. Tao-Min says people always want to know where you're from if your appearance or accent is different from what they expect. She says this gets tedious. I wouldn't know; I've never traveled to places where I was a foreigner. Not that I recall.

"Dallas," I said. "Dallas, Texas."

Then he began to talk to me about his work. He had to take frequent breaths of oxygen to converse, but I didn't try to make him stop. He told me that he worked with cutting-edge educational research, working with groups of child volunteers.

"And where do you get your volunteers?" I asked, hoping I sounded only casually curious.

He took another breath of oxygen. "Well, we call them volunteers. At first I think they were. But now they're mostly refugees. From various countries. Some of my staff objected to this. But I convinced them that what we're doing is for the good. These children have no one. We take them in. We feed and clothe them. We give them something significant. A way to be of benefit to humanity."

I think he believed what he said. He spoke persuasively. I could almost understand how his staff might have come around to his way of seeing things. I wanted to believe that he didn't know the children had in fact been abducted and sent to him by people whose motivations I still could not fathom. I wanted to ask more questions, but I felt no inclination to disturb his peace of mind. Better to let him die with his self-conceived benevolence unchallenged.

A day later I asked him about his family. He was growing weaker, so he didn't say much. He told me his mother had died some twenty years ago. I could tell he idolized his father.

"I was a good son," he said. "I treated my parents well. I made them proud. They were proud of me."

"Are you married?" I asked, seeing in my mind's eye the wedding picture Montagne had shown me.

Jai rallied a bit, offering me a sad smile, breathing in deep gasps. "Yes," he said. "My wife is at home. Our old family home. In Ramgarh. I love my Sarah. So much. Someone will have to tell her. About me. She'll be worried. We have a baby. My son. My son." He drifted away, his eyes closed. He didn't see the tears that had begun coursing down my cheeks.

The next day, Jai was barely there. I knew we were losing him. I wiped his face with cooling cloths and massaged his hands and feet. He opened his eyes and saw me there. "You have kind eyes," he whispered. "My mother had eyes like that."

I was due back on my floor, but I couldn't leave. Jai lost consciousness again. His breath came in irregular gulps that I knew provided no relief for his oxygen-starved organs. I stroked his forehead and took his hand in both of mine, weeping quietly. "Oh, my son, my son," I murmured, looking into his face.

Suddenly his eyelids flickered open, and our eyes met. Something passed between us in that brief moment. Then his eyes closed, his chest grew still. I continued holding his hand for some minutes more as it grew cold. I was unwilling to turn his body, this flesh of my own flesh, over to the corpse tenders. My heart fluttered uncertainly in my chest. I had a distinct feeling that I'd be following him soon into whatever space he'd disappeared into. Soon, but not yet.

I wiped away my tears and arranged Jai's body into a dignified posture, his legs straight, his chin slightly up-tilted, his hands folded across his chest in a mudra I'd seen on some statues. Satisfied, I dried my tears and walked out into the hallway toward the floor clerk.

"Jai Kalyani has passed," I said.

The clerk nodded and I heard her speak into her communication device: "We've lost Patient One," she said. "Please send the collection team."

"Did you know him before?" she asked me.

"Not really," I said. "We had some connections."

"He was an important man in Rajasthan, you know. There were rumors sometimes about his research and I guess maybe he did some bad things. But he wasn't a bad man. He wanted to help people. He and his father built this hospital for the sick. He made sure that Chulel was available to all our people, so they wouldn't have to suffer old age. He paid his workers well, even the lowest, so they wouldn't suffer poverty. And on those rare occasions when someone died, he always contributed to the funeral expenses. He saw all these things and he tried to change them. But they didn't change him. He embraced his privilege. He was no Buddha."

31.

On the day that Jai died, I didn't want to join the little group in the kitchen for supper, so I said I was tired and went straight up to the room. A short while later, Tao-Min came in, bearing a plate of food from the kitchen.

"You know you need to eat," she said.

Her kindness was more than I could bear, and I collapsed into helpless sobs.

"Malia, what's wrong?" She set the plate down and embraced me gently. She led me over to the bed and sat me down. "Something's happened," she said. "Maybe you should tell me what it is."

And so I told her. I told her about discovering Jai on the fourth floor, about my visits with him, about everything he'd said. And then I told her about what the desk clerk had said.

"I was so afraid he'd be a monster. He tried so hard to be a hero. But it turns out he was just a man."

I didn't object when Tao-Min took my hand in both of hers, stroking it gently the way I'd stroked Jai's hand. We sat for a while longer and then she insisted I eat at least a little of my supper. It was thoroughly cold at this point, but our cook seemed to have an unlimited source of spices for seasoning, so even cold the dahl and rice tasted nice. I thought briefly how a dish of yogurt would have made it even better, but there was no yogurt anymore. Somewhere out there cows and goats were going unmilked. Things were in quite a state.

"Where was it he said his wife and baby were living?" Tao-Min had pulled out her screen again as she did every day, to see if she could access anything. She laid it down and pushed it away.

"Ramgarh," I said. I'd repeated that name over and over to myself so I wouldn't forget. "He said that their family home was in Ramgarh."

"Let's ask Shankar tomorrow if he knows where that is. If it's not too far, maybe we could take a day off and go visit."

Shankar knew and he told us it wasn't far at all, easy enough for a day trip in the solar powered car we'd been using to go to work each day. "Ask anyone there," he said. "They'll probably know the Kalyani house." He didn't ask why we wanted to go there. He did say he knew where to get a full charge for the car from a recharge station that was still functioning. We were grateful for that, since the car's solar panels couldn't provide much on a rainy day. We were having a lot of rainy days.

There was no way to notify the hospital that we weren't coming in, so after we charged up the car we stopped by before setting out on our journey. I sat in the car while Tao-Min dashed through the light rain and went inside to speak with the clerk of our floor. While I waited, I watched some workers at a side door of the complex. They'd just finished loading a truck, which now headed off down a road I hadn't noticed before. I looked toward the horizon in the direction it was going. When I saw the cloud of steamy smoke, I knew what was on the truck. It was taking the bodies of the most recently deceased victims off to be burned. I wondered if Jai's body was among them. I looked away, choosing to watch instead for Tao-Min to return.

"What did they say?" I asked as she re-entered the little vehicle, shaking her wet umbrella outside before placing it in the back seat.

"What could they say? It's not like we're paid to do this job." She started up the car. "Sorry," she said. "I suppose I'm feeling guilty. What they actually said was that it was a good idea for us to take a day off. They said, 'Have a nice day.' And, you know, 'Namaste.'"

We found the route exactly as Shankar had described it and were soon emerging from the city into the countryside of Rajasthan. The light rain continued to fall, softening the tawny golds and greens of the landscape. The sparse, scrubby vegetation reminded me of West Texas, but of course all the plants were different. I did see some flowering shrubs that looked a lot like Texas lantana.

The rain rose and fell in intensity as we headed farther north toward the town of Chomu. The tollbooths along the highway were empty and silent, the recharge stations abandoned. We passed through a village and at first it seemed to be empty, too. But there was a cloud of damp smoke rising from behind the almost-new habitat complexes and we saw a child in a front garden, staring at us as we passed.

"Probably cooking fires," I said, not wanting to entertain the alternate possibility. "There's no power, so they'd have to resort to that, wouldn't they?"

"You know a lot of people have started tending to the sick in their own homes. They see no point in taking them to hospitals where they're certain to die anyway. God, this is so frustrating!" Tao-Min stared out across the landscape, where smoke from another distant fire mingled with the monsoon moisture. "Why can't someone figure out what's going on and put a stop to it? We've had epidemics in the past—Ebola and COVID in the last century and of course bovine flu just a couple of decades back. We've always managed to fight them off. This one seems unstoppable."

"There will be survivors," I reminded her. "People like us. And the children. Anyone who hasn't been taking Chulel."

We were silent for a while. Tao-Min looked thoughtful. "I've been thinking about what Recall did," she said at last, "taking down the system like this. I keep trying to figure out how I feel about it. Do you think they did the right thing?"

"I don't know," I said. "It seems extreme, especially in light of the sickness." I was quiet for a moment, staring out at the mostly empty landscape. "Yesterday I was remembering something my friend Walter told me about how the sufficiency communities were conserving the seeds of alternative ways of life for the future. There's also something the farmers at Walden 27 told me: they said that sometimes they had to plow under a failed crop in order to make ready for the next planting. Maybe that's what Recall has done. Of course, who's to say whether the next crop will be any more successful?"

"I guess that will be up to us, won't it?"

I wasn't sure. We settled into thoughtful silence, enveloped in the murmur and plash of the gentle rain, washing and soaking the earth, collecting into puddles and rivulets along the roadside. As we passed through the town of Chomu, we saw a hospital with all its windows open and with beds set up on a broad veranda, sheltered from the rain by plastiflex sheeting.

"Why aren't the attendants wearing protective gear?" I asked.

"Because it doesn't work," Tao-Min answered. "Haven't you noticed how we have fewer doctors and nurses at our hospital every day?"

From Chomu we turned west, following the course of a stream. Because it was the monsoon season, there was a shallow flow of water. We saw a young boy, huddled under a torn umbrella, attempting to fish in a deeper eddy.

"What if we can't find anyone to ask about the Kalyanis?" I asked. "Everything looks so empty."

"I'm sure we'll find someone. People are just staying indoors. Either they're sick in bed or else they're trying to avoid contact. Besides," she smiled, "it's raining. I've been trying to imagine what people in these towns must be going through. We're just lucky to be immune to this and to have some knowledge of what's going on."

"I'm not sure the knowledge helps," I said. But her remark set me thinking about what it must be like for people who didn't know, how they must be searching for answers, groping for explanations. *Future generations will tell stories about this,* I thought. I wondered what kind of stories they would be. I hoped there would be future generations.

By the time we reached Ramgarh, the rain had ceased and there were hints of sunshine between the clouds. The town was a fascinating mix of old and new. The streets were in excellent repair and there were vanguard habitat complexes and office buildings all along the main road. And then suddenly there was a structure that reminded me of a tiered plate of cupcakes, with peaked domes and matching archways.

"Where do you think we should inquire?" I hadn't seen anything that looked promising.

"How about here?" Tao-Min stopped the car in front of a building with a sign whose English version read, "Visitors Registry."

I got out of the car and was greeted by a warm breeze that smelled faintly of smoke. I was reminded of family barbecues in my childhood, and I put my hand over my mouth and nose as I realized why. The door to the Visitors Registry was locked. Tao-Min knocked but no one answered.

"What now?" I decided my efforts to avoid breathing were pointless.

We looked up and down the street. We walked to a corner and surveyed the cross street. There was an open window on one of the buildings, where a curtain moved languidly, in and out, as if the room itself were breathing. We walked toward it.

Tao-Min knocked on the door closest to the open window and we waited, watching. The curtain looked worn, its tiny clusters of pale blue flowers fading into the graying white fabric. She knocked again. We heard shuffling sounds and both of us glanced up as a face disappeared behind the curtain.

"Hello," Tao-Min called out. "Namaste. We want to ask you a question. Is there someone here we can speak with?" The figure reappeared at the window and slammed it shut.

"There's our answer," I said.

We walked to the next intersection. A block away on a side street, we saw a man sitting in a chair beside an entryway and we headed toward him, walking quickly, fearful that he might disappear, too, before we could speak with him.

"Namaste," Tao-Min said, as we both made the appropriate gesture. We'd stopped at a respectful distance.

As the man turned toward us, returning the gesture silently, we could see that he was old. Not a Chulel user.

"We're looking for the Kalyani house," Tao-Min said. "Can you tell us where it is?"

The old man seemed to stare at the pavement and then he looked up, but not at us. His gaze appeared to be directed far off into the distance. I realized then that he was blind.

"The Kalyanis. Yes, yes. I know the Kalyani house. Such a beautiful place, with gardens and peacocks. So much color."

"Can you tell us where it is? How to get there?"

He squinted and lifted his chin, studying something we couldn't see. "There will be only sick people there. Everybody's sick and dying. I don't know why." His head tilted downward, his chin nearly meeting his chest. Gesturing with a gnarled hand, he began to give us instructions. "Take this road. Go downhill until you see the little park where the children play after school. Turn left there, past the Parvati shrine, the one where the young wives come every morning to offer garlands of marigolds and pray for sons. Keep going until you see the entrance to the great Siva temple on your right. Turn there, on the far side of the temple. From there you'll see the entrance to the Kalyani place on the hillside."

Tao-Min thanked the man, and we headed back the way we'd come, back toward the car. I had my doubts as to whether we'd be able to follow these instructions, but it was all we had. Tao-Min seemed more confident.

"It's obvious he hasn't always been blind," she said. "His descriptions were vivid."

We stood for a moment surveying the lay of the land, and finally agreed on which direction was "downhill." It was the direction toward the rising cloud of smoke.

Back in the car, we began our search. We saw no park, no place where children might play. As we continued downhill, the smoke hung heavier, penetrating even the tightly enclosed space of the car. I wished for more rain.

"What about that corner where we saw the new building under construction?" Tao-Min suggested. "Do you think that could be where the park was?"

The idea seemed reasonable, and at least it would take us away from the smoke that invaded my lungs and caked my heart with sadness. We reversed course. Turning at the new building, we spotted a decrepit shrine across the street. A few blocks farther on we saw the temple, the turning, and the entrance to an estate. There was a road winding uphill, but the gate across the road was closed.

Tao-Min got out to see if she could open it, but found it securely fastened. She knocked on the door of the guardhouse. When there was no answer, she tried the door. It opened.

"There's no one here," she called to me. "We can go right through."

I got out of the car and joined her.

"Will you be okay walking up to the house?" Tao-Min asked.

"I think so," I said. "Just don't go too fast."

It wasn't a particularly high hill. A footpath wound alongside the road, sloping gently upward. In a few places stone steps provided for more rapid ascent. I found them more useful as a place to sit down and rest. Sweat was oozing from all my pores and refusing to evaporate, leaving me feeling sticky and uncomfortable.

At last we reached the house. It wasn't like the old buildings we'd seen in the town. This was a country house in the British style and looked as if it might have been plucked out of an 18th-century landscape painting.

We walked across the brick driveway and stood on the doorstep, looking around for some sign of life. A large spider skittered into a crack between some stones. I began to get a bad feeling about the place, but I said nothing, choosing to rely on Tao-Min's confidence.

She knocked firmly on the door. It was a thick wooden slab of a door, and it absorbed the sound like a pillow. I looked around for a buzzer or bell of some sort. There was a button. I pressed it and we waited. Then I saw the old pull rope. I tried to reach it, but its frayed cord was beyond my grasp. Tao-Min grabbed it and gave it a good pull. From somewhere inside the house came the discordant clatter of a sluggish bell. There was no movement, no other sound.

"It looks like we climbed all the way up here for nothing." I was feeling disappointed and a bit wretched, tired, despondent. I knew a lot of words for how I felt. Then from deep within the house, we heard the faint cry of an infant, and I was instantly alight with optimism.

"They're here," I whispered.

Tao-Min pulled the bell rope again. The bell clattered more loudly this time, more insistently; there was still no response. "I'm going to look for another entrance. Wait here."

I didn't argue. I sat down on the narrow stone porch and stretched my legs out in front of me. I looked up, scanning the three rows of windows for movement, straining my ears for sounds. There was nothing. *Of course they're afraid,* I thought. *These are fearful times. If we could only get them to understand that we mean them no harm.*

Suddenly I heard the report of a firearm and a scream.

32.

"Tao-Min!" I headed off at an ill-advised trot in the direction she'd taken. Before I reached the corner of the house, I saw her. She was clutching her left shoulder. There was blood. The man following her held a rifle and it was pointed at her head.

"Now go on your way and don't come back," the man growled.

"No! You don't understand. Damn it all!" I shouted, ignoring the discomfort in my chest. "That child up there is my grandson. I have a right to see him!"

The man lowered his rifle a bit and stared at me, looking, I thought, for some resemblance to his employer. Then he raised the weapon again, this time pointing it off toward the horizon. "You have to leave," he wheezed. "I have my orders."

It was my turn to stare at him. "You're sick," I said. "I'm sorry. Will there be someone to take care of the baby? Can you at least tell me my grandson's name?"

Again he lowered the rifle a few degrees. "Samant," he said. "He's called Samant." Perhaps I imagined it, but I swear I saw a smile flicker across his face, a twinkle of fondness light up his eyes.

I joined my hands in the prayer gesture. "Thank you," I said. "Namaste." I would have stayed and argued. I would have told him I was with Jai when he died. I would have told him how concerned Jai was about his beloved wife and child. I think he might have relented in the end. But Tao-Min clearly required medical attention, and I wasn't sure where we'd find it. We needed to leave.

"How bad is it?" I asked as we began our descent.

"I think it's just a flesh wound. It hurts like hell, but I think I'll be fine. Just take it slow."

I could see the dark, wet stain on her blouse. It was spreading. We needed to move slowly to keep her heart rate down, to minimize the bleeding. We needed to move fast to get her to a doctor right away. I knew we couldn't do both. Going down was easier than the ascent, but when Tao-Min stumbled for the second time, I insisted we stop for a moment. My heart and knees were grateful for the rest.

By the time we arrived at the car, Tao-Min's blouse was soaked through, and the blood was oozing through her fingers as she continued to press against the wound.

"Let me sit here for a minute," she said, leaning back in the car's seat. She didn't look good.

I heard a noise and looked up at the path. There was a girl running nimbly down the final set of steps toward us. She carried a small bag, but nothing that looked like a weapon. She approached the car, motioning for me to open the window.

"Your friend is hurt," she said. "I came to help. She needs to get out of the car and sit where I can fix her wound."

The girl worked expertly, injecting an anesthetic, cleansing the wound, applying medicines, and finally painting on a layer of binding material to stanch the bleeding. She covered it all in clean white gauze secured with medical tape.

"There," she said. "Now some pills for pain." She rummaged in her bag once more and drew out a small silver packet, which she opened and handed to Tao-Min. "Get her some water."

It felt odd taking orders from one so young, but I quickly fetched a water bottle from the vehicle. After Tao-Min took the pills, we helped her walk back to the car and settled her into the rear seat.

"Thank you," I said to the girl. "Can you tell me your name? My name is Malia Poole."

"I heard what you said to Chiranjeet back there. Is it true? Are you the baby's grandmother? Is Mr. Jai your son?"

"Yes," I said. "It's true. I didn't know until recently. It's a long story." I really hadn't meant to tell anyone this, but now I'd told two people, the man with the gun and now this girl.

She smiled. "I always knew Jai's real parents had to be European. Or American."

"Texan, actually." I said. "I should tell you, Jai passed yesterday. I work at the hospital, and I was with him. You can tell Sarah that he spoke of her and the baby with great love."

"I will," she said, smiling. "Namaste." And she was gone, bounding up the hillside like a young goat.

"You didn't tell me your name!" I shouted after her. I heard her laugh as she disappeared behind a thick hedge.

"Are you going to be able to manage the car on your own?" Tao-Min asked as I entered the car on the side with the driving controls.

"Of course. Just show me which buttons to push and I'll be fine."

"You've never done this before, have you?" she said. "You've never managed an autocar on manual."

"It can't be that hard," I said. I knew I had to do it, so there was no point in being afraid. Tao-Min explained all the buttons and levers to me. "Got it," I said as we lurched onto the road, narrowly missing a small tree. "Relax," I said.

"I have no choice," Tao-Min replied. "That's some potent medicine she gave me." Her words were beginning to slur and by the time we were out of Ramgarh and headed back toward Jaipur she was asleep.

My stomach began to churn, and I decided to attribute it to hunger rather than nerves. We'd packed a lunch, but I'd have to stop in order to retrieve it, and I thought reaching the city before sundown was more important. So I kept driving, grateful for the sunshine, hoping it would keep the car charged. I was grateful, too, for the dearth of traffic, as the car swerved alarmingly every time I had to negotiate a curve.

I began to wish I'd paid more attention to our route on the trip out. I watched for signs and landmarks. I slowed when

I saw a sign pointing off to a place called Chomu. Wasn't that the town we'd passed through this morning? But it couldn't be. Another sign clearly indicated that Jaipur was straight ahead. I continued without turning. The farther I went, the more unfamiliar the road became. My hunger was nothing compared to my desperate bladder, so I finally pulled into an abandoned recharge station, stopping so abruptly that it woke Tao-Min.

"Are we there?" she asked sleepily.

"No, I'm stopping to go to the toilet. Do you need to go?"

"No, I'm fine. Just resting." Her eyes closed again.

The toilets were unusable so I went behind the building and crouched on the ground. From the smell of things, I wasn't the first to do so. I wished for toilet paper and maybe some running water and scented soap. Back at the car, I poured some water from one of the bottles into my hands and then dried them on my blouse. I retrieved the lunch basket from the back of the car and devoured a few crackers. I wasn't sure if I should keep going ahead or reverse direction and take the turn to Chomu. I removed Tao-Min's digilet and opened it up, searching for the directions she'd entered. There it was: Chomu.

Look, I told myself. *This road may well go to Jaipur, but if I take it I'll enter the city on an unfamiliar road, maybe even after dark.* I decided to go back. I wasn't sure how many kilometers I'd brought us out of the way, but the last thing I wanted to do was to get us lost.

It seemed like forever before I found the turning for Chomu, probably because I was creeping along like a drowsy tortoise for fear of missing it. I made the turn and immediately began to recognize small things that reassured me I was on the right track. I looked over at Tao-Min and stared at the red stain beginning to form on the bandage covering her wound.

Dammit! I thought. *She's still bleeding.* I needed to drive faster. I was beginning to feel more confident managing the vehicle and I had to get Tao-Min to town. She needed to see a real doctor. I increased the car's speed by five kph and after a few minutes added on another five. I was sitting bolt upright in the seat, my hands gripping the control levers. I tried to remember how long it had taken us to drive from Jaipur to Ramgarh. I was well aware the return trip was taking much longer.

As I approached Chomu, I remembered the hospital we'd seen there. Should I stop and let them attend to Tao-Min? What if they wanted to keep her overnight? No, I should press on. I didn't even slow down passing through the town. I was ready for this journey to be over.

When I finally saw the city of Jaipur on the horizon, I released a sigh, feeling as if I'd been holding my breath for the past hour, at least. I began to see streets and landmarks that I recognized. I made my way to the hospital and pulled into the emergency entrance, bringing the car to a halt more smoothly this time.

I thought someone should have come out, but when no one did, I went inside. There was no one at the desk, no one in the hallway. "Hello?" I called, my voice echoing in the empty space. I called again and began knocking on doors. Finally I saw someone in medical garb—although not the protective gear—coming toward me.

"We're not accepting any more patients," the man said. "There's really nothing we can do for them. You'll have to take them home."

"You don't understand," I said. "It's a gunshot wound."

"What? Well, yes, of course. Let's have a look."

He accompanied me out to the car and together we managed to get Tao-Min inside and onto a gurney. "It looks like someone's already attended to this," he said. "Looks like a professional job."

"But she's still bleeding."

"Yes, I can see that. Well, we'll have a look." He removed the bandage. Underneath it there was more blood. "I'll have to put in a few sutures," he said. "Why don't you sit down while I tend to this?" He gestured toward a line of chairs by the window.

I sat, but I could still feel the road moving under my feet. My neck and shoulders ached. Why had I led Tao-Min into this? It was all my fault. Trying to do the right thing never seemed to work out for me. *And crying won't help*, I told myself, even though that was exactly what I felt like doing. I sat still with my eyes closed, taking deep breaths, telling myself to relax. It helped a little.

"Missus?" It was the doctor. Or nurse. I didn't know and didn't really care as long as he took good care of Tao-Min.

"Yes? Is she okay?"

"Yes, missus. It's a fairly deep wound and it tore up the flesh pretty badly. Missed the artery, thankfully. But I've stitched her up and injected some more anesthetic at the wound site. What medication did she take for pain?"

"I don't know," I said. "The girl took away the packet after my friend took the pills."

"Well, I'll give you some more pills for her, but don't let her take any of them until this has worn off. I'd give it at least another hour. The local should keep her comfortable in the meantime. And these pills won't make her quite so groggy as whatever she's already had." He wrote some instructions on a piece of paper and then handed me the paper and the bottle of pills.

"Don't I recognize you?" he asked. "Haven't you been working upstairs?"

"Yes," I said. "We both work here."

"That's what I thought. How the devil did she manage to get herself shot? No, don't answer that. It's none of my business. Just glad it wasn't any worse. Are you okay? Do you need anything to help you relax and get some sleep?"

"I've got some Duermata," I shrugged. "That should be enough."

"Well, take it easy," he said, smiling. "And take the day off tomorrow. Doctor's orders."

33.

Shankar was waiting for us when we finally reached the guesthouse and he helped me get my woozy patient up to our room. A few minutes later he knocked on the door with a plate of food. I ate it out of gratitude, since I was too tired by that time to know whether I was hungry or not. I managed to stay awake long enough to give Tao-Min the new pain pills. Then I took a few Duermata and lay down for some much needed sleep.

I'd thought I would wake after the Duermata wore off. I'd intended to check on Tao-Min. But instead I slept until morning. When I opened my eyes, I saw her standing by the window, holding the bottle of pain pills and studying the handwritten instructions.

I coaxed my stiff body into a sitting position. Looking at Tao-Min's bandaged shoulder, I realized that yesterday's unlikely events had actually happened.

"How are you feeling?" I asked, throwing back the covers.

"Like I've been shot and drugged." She attempted a smile but winced with the effort of turning her head in my direction. "Thanks for getting me back safely."

"No thanks, please." I said. "I'm the one to blame for putting you in harm's way to begin with. I should be asking your forgiveness, not accepting your thanks."

"I was a willing participant. I wish I could thank that girl who bound up my injury. It had already occurred to me that there probably wouldn't be any blood available to replace mine if I bled too much. Healthy blood is a rare commodity these days."

"The doctor at the hospital said she did a good job."

"Hospital? You took me to the hospital? I don't remember that at all."

"Yeah, the doctor recognized us. He said we should take today off."

"Can you help me figure out what the instructions are for these pain pills? I'm assuming that's what's written on this piece of paper."

I got up and helped Tao-Min with the pills and then insisted she get back into bed. I arranged pillows so she could sit up, just as I'd been doing for so many patients at the hospital the past two weeks. It felt good knowing that this patient would get well.

"Do you want your screen?" I asked. "Maybe you'd like to read a book."

"Sure. And would you please lay my digilet over there in the sun? I've been trying to keep it fully charged. Just in case."

I did as she asked and then went downstairs to the kitchen to make tea and search for something that might serve as breakfast. It was still early; Shankar wouldn't be in until later. I put some water on to boil, grateful for the hours of sunshine that had permitted the solar collectors to function yesterday afternoon.

Yesterday. I saw in my mind's eye the beautiful house on the hillside, sunlight glinting off its windows, the cry of an infant emanating from its cloistered depths. I needed to figure out how to get back to Ramgarh. I needed to see my grandson. *There has to be a way,* I thought.

Searching the cupboards, I was dismayed to see how scanty our supplies were. Shankar always seemed to have something to prepare every day and never talked about how much remained. There was one more packet of tea and a little sugar. The container that had held the fortified powdered milk was empty. We had some noodles, a small bag of rice, something that looked like dried mushrooms, and a sack of beans infested with bugs. Dead bugs. I think I'd have been less concerned if they'd been alive. I found a small packet of cookies and decided that would have to be breakfast. I resolved to talk with Shankar when he got in to find out what we could do to get more food.

Tao-Min was not in bed when I arrived at the room with our breakfast tray and I was preparing to scold her when I noticed she was holding up her digilet and grinning at me.

"A pulse! We got a pulse! While I was sitting there feeling sorry for myself, I suddenly remembered the instructions Montagne gave us earlier about new digilet settings. So I found the notes I'd written down and entered the new settings and, voila! A message."

She read it to me: "Hoping to hear you've made it through okay. If you're reading this, you've successfully configured for Novanet. Things will be slow for a while. Please reply."

It wasn't a lot of information, but knowing we were back in touch, that we once again had the means of contacting people outside our immediate locale, was heartening. She dictated a return pulse and sent it. We stared expectantly at her digilet.

"Tea?" I offered. "He said things would be slow. We shouldn't expect immediate response."

"Of course," Tao-Min replied, accepting the cup of tea and reaching for the stale cookies, which I'd attempted to arrange invitingly on a china plate. "Give me your digilet and I'll get it set up, too." Mine was in urgent need of recharging, so after she'd entered the new settings, I laid it on the windowsill. It looked like there would be at least intermittent sun for a while.

After we finished our meager breakfast, I carried the tray down to the kitchen. Shankar and Paul and Simone all wanted to know about Tao-Min, and I assured them she was doing well. Shankar offered me another cup of tea, which I refused. I didn't want to be greedy or wasteful.

"Our supplies seem a bit depleted," I said. "Is there anything I can do to help us get more food?"

"You could steal food from the hospital," he said. "No, no. That's a joke. Well, maybe not. Many people steal now. But how can it be stealing if there's no one to sell you things, no way to buy things? We're lucky to have contacts. They promised to have lentils today and maybe some flour. I don't ask where it comes from. I'm trying to find where we can get a few chickens. For eggs. Eggs would be good. We could keep the chickens in the lobby." He was smiling, but I knew this wasn't a joke. I tried to visualize chickens in the lobby.

I hoped Montagne would have a plan for us soon, some means to get away. But wouldn't it be the same everywhere? Things were never again going to be the way they were before this collapse, before the VHA. My little grandson Samant would never know what the world had been like once upon a time. *I need to find a way back to Ramgarh.* These were the things I was thinking about as I made my way slowly up the stairs to our room. I also wondered why we hadn't moved down to the ground floor. If we had to stay much longer, maybe we should.

"Any news?" I asked.

Tao-Min was holding her screen. "Nothing from Montagne," she said, "but this Novanet thing has some news pages. Recall nodes in almost all parts of the world are back in touch. The only place escaping the pandemic so far seems to be New Zealand. There've been some outbreaks of violence in Dubai and New York. Also trouble in Tokyo and Johannesburg. A couple of the reports talk about youth gangs. This is crazy. I guess I didn't understand that Recall was a worldwide organization."

"I'm surprised, too," I said. "I've been affiliated with them in one way or another most of my life, but it always felt like just a small group of like-minded people trying to survive, trying to make a difference." They'd certainly made a difference now. Was I part of that?

In the evening, we finally received a message from Montagne: "We're trying to get some airplanes up and flying, but it may take another couple of weeks to get one to India, most likely Mumbai. We'll let you know."

Tao-Min also had a message from Meli. As she finished reading it and began to replace the digilet around her wrist, she turned toward me with a mystified expression. "Meli says to tell you that her mother was one of the operatives in the takedown."

"Jenda? Jenda Swain?" I couldn't believe it. Something had clearly happened to her since I saw her at that little café in Dallas. The Jenda I saw then would never have done something like this. I wasn't sure how I felt about it.

"I keep forgetting that you know my mother-in-law. I haven't met her myself, since I was out of the country when she visited Meli. She says Montagne's trying to figure out how to get Jenda to Costa Rica."

"I guess we're all having difficulty getting where we want to go these days. Do you think we could move to a downstairs room tomorrow?" I asked. "I could do without all this climbing."

I tried to insist that Tao-Min stay home another day, but she was having none of that, so we returned to the hospital the next morning. She even insisted on managing the car.

After only two days' absence, we were shocked by the changes at the hospital. I knew they'd stopped taking new patients, but I hadn't expected the place to be so empty. The few doctors and nurses still on duty were clearly working in spite of their own sickness. Tao-Min and I walked outside again and sat on a bench in an alcove, out of the rain.

"I don't think they require our services anymore," Tao-Min said, looking dejected. "With my injury, I doubt I'd be much use anyway."

We sat in silence for a few minutes, watching the workers loading another truck with corpses to carry to the funeral pyres. Tao-Min was almost in tears.

"I've been wondering something," I said. "What do you suppose has happened to the children at Jai's lab?"

Tao-Min looked startled. "Why hadn't I thought about them?" she said. "We could go see."

We weren't sure where the children were housed, so Tao-Min drove us to the lab facility she'd visited earlier. Was it only a couple of weeks go? She drove slowly through the complex. It had stopped raining. The place looked deserted, but we thought we heard voices.

We turned a corner, and it was like entering a different dimension. There was a field full of boys and girls playing soccer, running and laughing and splashing. Tao-Min stopped the vehicle, and we got out to watch. After a few minutes, one of the older children separated himself from the game and loped toward us.

"What are you doing here?" He sounded petulant. "This is our ground. You should go back where you live."

"We just wanted to see if you were okay, if you needed anything. My name is Tao-Min." She put out her hand for the boy to shake, but he looked away, ignoring the gesture.

"We need nothing. Only to be left alone," he said. He had his hands on his hips, his shoulders back, his chest out. He spoke with authority, even though he couldn't have been more than twelve years old.

"Who's looking after you?" Tao-Min asked.

"All the grown-ups got sick and went away. Some died here and we buried them right. Now we look after each other."

"But don't you need food? What do you have to eat?"

The boy looked impatiently out toward the field where the game continued. "We have food. Some of these buildings were like farms with lots of animals. Mostly rabbits, but some dogs and fat rats, too, and a few monkeys. We eat what we find."

At first I recoiled in horror, but then I reminded myself that these children likely came from rural places where the killing and butchering of animals for food was commonplace. They were merely being resourceful, doing what they knew how to do.

"That will run out," Tao-Min said. "And then what will you do?"

The boy looked up at the sky for a minute and then into Tao-Min's face. "Then we go to the bush and find food there. This place is good," he said. "Where we come from there was war and killing and everybody angry. We like it here. And we like it best without grownups. My name is Joseph," he said. He put out his hand then and Tao-Min shook it gravely. He gave me a nod, acknowledging my silent presence before turning back to Tao-Min. "You seem like a kind person. I'm sorry you're hurt. To visit is okay. But, please, don't send anyone to help." He ran back onto the field and was quickly swallowed up in his game.

We got into the car and rode away in dazed silence.

"That," I said, "is not what I expected."

That night we talked with Shankar about the children. He listened thoughtfully as he chopped up the single carrot he'd been able to acquire to add to the pot of lentils. "Did you say there are some open fields out there at the research complex? Maybe we could plant some things that they'd be able to use. The monsoons are ending now. It's time for planting."

The next day Tao-Min and I, along with Shankar and Paul and Simone, crowded into the autocar, our laps full of tools. All that day we worked digging up useless grass, digging deep into the soil. Shankar said it was good soil. Tao-Min could use only one arm, and I had to work seated on a low stool, but we made progress.

As I dug, I thought about my grandson and about his mother, Sarah. I'd begun to think that if I went back, maybe they'd let me help care for them. The caretaker had already been ill. Was Sarah ill too? Surely there were other servants there with her. The girl who helped Tao-Min seemed capable enough, but she was so young. Surely, by now, the girl would have told Sarah who I was, told her I'd been by Jai's side when he died. This time she'd let me in, let me lay eyes on my grandson. Would that be enough?

The next day we cleared more ground while Shankar began planting beans and vegetables. We didn't know where he got the seeds; he didn't say. Occasionally, we saw one or more of the children watching us. We didn't approach them, and they kept their distance.

Watching the children, I thought again of Samant. It seemed I thought of little else these days. I kept thinking about him all the way back to the guesthouse. It had been a sunny day, producing enough energy for hot running water and as I enjoyed my shower, I worked on the plot of the story I was composing, the one called "Malia Returns to Ramgarh." I refused to put Tao-Min in danger again. I'd go on my own this time. I knew the way to Ramgarh now and I knew how to manage the autocar. I also knew Tao-Min would never let me go alone if she knew, so I'd have to sneak away. Should I leave a note?

My heart began beating faster as I envisioned all of this. Too fast. My ears rang and I felt light-headed. I looked up into the steam-shrouded mirror and the old woman staring back at me from behind the mist said, *No. You can't do this Malia. You can't do this alone.* She tried to tell me it was impossible. I refused to listen. "This will take time," I said aloud. My story only needed a little revision.

On the third day of our digging and planting, Joseph came striding across the field. He stood at the edge of our plot and watched for a few minutes.

"I like your farm," he said. "It looks good."

Shankar introduced himself. He and Joseph shook hands and then stood side-by-side, arms folded across their chests, discussing agriculture like a couple of old farmers.

"You know," Shankar said, "some of these people working with me will have to go away soon. I might need someone to help with this farm, someone to help eat the food when it comes to that."

Joseph nodded. "I think we might come to an agreement," he said.

The following day, we had more help than we knew what to do with. The children were diligent workers. I sat at the edge of the field on my little stool, watching. Two of the younger girls sidled up to me shyly. They asked my name. They asked if they could touch my hair. They asked why it was that color. The girls told me their names were Beulah and Abigail. They said they were sisters.

"What is that bandage on the back of your neck?" I asked Abigail.

She put her hand up and touched it gently. "This?" she asked. "Joseph said we needed to take out the thing-a-jigs the teachers put in us. He made a cut. It hurt but he put medicine on, and it feels better now. Do you know any songs?"

That night I told Tao-Min about Abigail's wound. "I can't believe they're taking it upon themselves to remove those digital implants. Can't we offer them some help with that?"

"We can offer," Tao-Min replied. "But I've never seen such adamantly self-sufficient youngsters. I wouldn't count on them letting us help even with that. And I wouldn't want to jeopardize what we've got going so far."

The next day Tao-Min made it a point to work alongside Joseph. After a while, she broached the subject of the digital implants. "Did you understand what those were?" she asked.

"I did," he answered. "The little ones probably didn't notice, but I could tell how I felt different when they gave us the lessons, the ones with the lights. I didn't like it."

"I can understand why you'd want the devices taken out," she continued, "but are you sure you can do it safely?"

"I do it in the same room where they put them in. I wash my hands like they did. I use the same knife, same medicine."

Tao-Min and I exchanged glances. We were impressed.

"One problem," Joseph continued. "I can't take out the one in me."

"Would you like some help with it?" Tao-Min asked.

He smiled shyly and stood up. "Come with me."

Joseph and Tao-Min walked off toward one of the buildings in the complex. When they returned barely an hour later, Joseph was smiling broadly, and he had a clean white bandage on the back of his neck.

Every day I watched the children, imagining what Samant would be like as a boisterous five-year-old or as a shy preadolescent. I wondered if he'd be as captivated by stories as Beulah and Abigail were, as captivated as I'd been when I was a child.

I was surprised at how many childhood songs and stories I remembered once I put my mind to it. I'd run out of the memory supplements I'd been taking ever since Walden 27, and I was becoming a bit forgetful again. But these memories from my distant past came up fresh and clear. I knew some of the children spoke French, so I asked Simone if she could share some songs or stories that she knew. Singing and storytelling became a regular part of our day.

It still rained occasionally, but most days we were able to work at least a few hours in the fields. We also tended to the chickens Shankar had managed to locate. I was grateful that we hadn't needed to keep them in the guesthouse lobby. Shankar also found us a goat and he promised that if he could find another one, eventually we'd have milk. He had to keep reminding Joseph of that, as the boy eyed the goat, talking about how tasty it would be roasted over a fire.

Joseph had told us about a classroom in the building where they were living and on days when it rained we gathered there. Shankar and Paul got some solar panels and batteries working again and Tao-Min reconfigured the classroom screens for Novanet. The screens were equipped with instructional materials, some of which we deleted, realizing they were part of the experiments that were being run on these children. After I read through some of the history lessons, we deleted those, too. Basic materials on math and science we left intact. We didn't insist that the children attend class. We didn't really have classes as such. We just let them use the materials for learning; we only helped them find answers to their questions.

I decided that the desks in the classroom should be arranged in small circles rather than in rows facing one direction, so one day I took it upon myself to move them. It was a sunny morning, and all of the children were still outdoors, tending to the tasks that they easily understood would keep them fed. I should have had better sense. As I shoved the third desk into position I was already short of breath. Then I began to feel a tightness in my chest. That was familiar, but I thought maybe I should stop for a minute and take a little break. The tightness escalated into pain. Dizzy and nauseous, I sat down, on the verge of panic. My mind sparkled and I thought I heard Lio's voice.

34.

I don't remember what happened after that. Tao-Min told me later I'd had a heart attack. I guess I did know that much. She said one of the children discovered me lying on the floor of the classroom and ran for help. I was gasping for air and turning a bit gray, so they put me in the car and rushed me to the hospital, hoping there would be someone there who'd be able to help.

"Lucky" hasn't generally been a good description of my life, but that day I was definitely lucky. One of the few remaining aides at the facility turned out to be someone with real medical training. He gave me oxygen and some pills that he said would help. I guess it worked, because I'm still alive, awake and aware and beginning to wonder what comes next. I have few doubts anymore about how it will all end.

The aide promised to put me in touch with a doctor who apparently has been living in the Indian equivalent of a Menders' community. "I'm almost certain you need to have surgery," the aide told me. "This doctor can do it for you."

"I'm not sure about all that," I told Tao-Min as I began to take my place again in the world of the living. "Maybe I should make peace with dying and not pursue this surgery."

"Talk to the surgeon, Malia. Let him examine you. Get an authoritative diagnosis. This may not be as bad as you think. You mustn't give up so easily. The children have been asking about you. They want you back, you know."

That warmed my heart. And by "heart" I don't mean that unreliable lump of palpitating muscle, but rather that inner source of whatever it is we call love. "Tell them I want very much to be back with them, too," I said. "I'm feeling stronger now. And I have my little pills. Perhaps tomorrow I'll go out with you."

"Don't push it," Tao-Min said. "We want you back, but we want you well."

"What have you heard from Montagne?" I hadn't thought to ask about that since my incident.

Tao-Min removed her digilet and then put it on again. "He says there'll be a plane through Mumbai soon. But before we make plans, I think we should consult with this doctor to see when you'll be well enough to travel. If we don't take this plane, I'm sure there'll be another."

"What does Montagne mean by 'soon?'"

She fiddled with her digilet some more. "Next Tuesday. I can tell him we won't make it. I really don't think you ought to risk it yet."

"That's for me to decide," I said.

"Well, we can talk about it this evening. Shankar and Paul are ready to go out to the farm. Simone is staying with you again today."

"She doesn't need to do that. I'd rather she go work with the children instead. Really. That's what would make me feel happier. I can take care of myself here."

"Are you sure?"

"Yes, I'm sure. Now, go. All of you." I gave her what I hoped was a reassuring smile. "Just leave me a little lunch in the kitchen."

Alone for the first time since my incident, I wasn't sure what to do with myself. Simone could have kept me occupied, working out more activities for the children, helping me reclaim the French I'd studied in school. I liked Simone. But now I'd sent her away and I found myself questioning whether that had been a good decision.

I read for a while, struggling through a short story in French that Simone had shared with me. It was about a little blind girl whose parents, with collusion from the village priest, had conjured a beautiful and perfect world for her, never letting her encounter anything ugly or sad. She was so angry when she discovered what they'd done, what the world was really like. "*Je ne veux pas etre heureuse,"* she cried. *"Je veux savoir!"* I liked that. *I don't want to be happy—I want to know.* I made a cup of tea and read the story again.

I went to the room and pulled out my digilet, intending to send a pulse to Leticia. There was a message from Montagne: "I received a pulse from Jenda's brother. He said she's passed away from VHA. I thought you'd want to know."

Poor Jenda, I thought. I felt sorry for Meli, who had only met Jenda recently, and for Tao-Min who now never would meet her. I wondered how Jenda had felt about what she'd done for Recall. That was something I'd never know. I sent Montagne a brief pulse, thanking him for the information. I didn't say anything about my heart attack. I was sure Tao-Min would have mentioned it to him already. I also dictated a pulse to my sister Leticia, although I wasn't feeling at all optimistic about receiving a reply.

I set out the lunch Shankar had left and took my time eating it. There was one small cookie. I placed it on a saucer and walked outside to enjoy it with my tea.

I hadn't been outdoors for days. Someone had placed a little wooden stool next to the guesthouse entrance, and I sat down. The stillness of the city was unnerving. I tried imagining it as it was that first day when Tao-Min and I arrived. I'd thought it was quiet then, but by comparison it had been alive, vibrant, and colorful. The silence of the new reality kept imposing on my awareness. I strained to listen and all I heard was the intermittent flapping of a piece of cloth somewhere. I thought maybe it was a curtain at an open window, like the one we'd seen in Ramgarh. Or some laundry hung outside and forgotten. Maybe the flapping was a length of sari someone had draped out an upstairs window to dry. I visualized the sari wafting red and golden in the breeze.

I sipped my tea and was surprised at the noise I made. The cup clattered as I set it into the saucer. I shifted my weight to lean forward, to get a better view up and down the street and the old wooden stool creaked. There was nothing to see.

I'd finished my tea and was about to go back indoors, when I thought I heard something else. I stilled myself and listened. Could that be footsteps? I heard nothing for a moment and then I found it again. It definitely sounded like footsteps. There was no clump of a heavy heel. These were soft shoes, the kind a woman wore. But not the kind of woman who favored fancy shoes. Soft, simple shoes on the feet of a simple woman. I listened, transfixed by my own storyline, as the footfalls grew louder, more distinct. Closer.

I saw her as she turned a corner, far down the street. She was wearing a sari, but not the red one with gold embroidery I'd seen in my mental meanderings. Hers was made of a faded green cotton cloth with a printed border. She carried a large basket. I thought my mind must still be blurry from my incident or the medicine, because I felt no inclination to avoid this woman. She seemed as familiar as a character in one of my novels.

As she approached, I put my hands together in greeting. "Namaste," I said.

She looked at me curiously, then returned the gesture with one hand, maintaining her grip on the basket with the other.

"Namaste," she replied. "I think you are the woman who came one day to Ramgarh. Yes?"

I stared. It wasn't my imagination after all. This face was familiar. "Are you the girl who fixed up my friend's injured shoulder?"

She smiled, set down the basket, and joined both hands in front of her heart, bowing slightly. "I come looking for you," she said.

I invited her in and offered tea. I put the kettle on to boil. "Tell me about the Kalyanis," I said. "How are things at the big house in Ramgarh?"

"All dead, missus," she said simply. "Only me and the boy who takes care of the gardens and goats."

"But what about the baby?" I was seized with fright. "Surely the baby didn't get sick!"

"No, no. Baby Samant is fine. That's why I come. I'm bringing him to you."

I stared at her. "What? Where? Oh, the basket."

She reached for the basket then and moved aside the blanket. Samant was sleeping, long dark lashes resting against pudgy, ruddy cheeks. He was exquisite.

"You will take care of him," she said, with the same confidence I'd observed in her capable treatment of Tao-Min. "You said he's your grandson. He belongs to you."

"Well, of course." I heard myself say this. I watched myself begin to shed tears and mumble foolish nonsense words as she took the sleeping child from the basket and placed him in my arms. She said something about a bottle of milk and packets of formula, and I think she said she'd come back tomorrow and bring a goat. And then she was gone.

I don't know how long I sat there, holding the baby awkwardly as if I were afraid I might break him, my mind a swirl of strange thoughts and sensations and memories and the odd notion that I ought to unbutton my blouse and offer my breast to my son. No, my grandson. I felt something warm spread across my skirt, and it took me a moment to realize that my grandson had peed.

I had never in my century plus a decade of living been entrusted with the care of an infant, but I remembered reading something about diapers, which are sometimes called nappies, and I reached for the basket and found a folded piece of white cloth that I thought met the description.

I laid the baby on the table and unwrapped the blanket from around him as he began to wail. I tried to say calming things, all of which sounded utterly silly, but which seemed to have the desired effect. He stopped wailing and fastened his eyes on my face as I unlatched the device that held his diaper in place. I removed the wet cloth and stared for a moment at his tiny genitals and then at his little fists that flailed wildly as he kicked his legs and emitted noises that I thought sounded wonderfully happy. How could this oddly proportioned being ever transform into a full sized human? I laughed at the idea and baby Samant squealed and smiled. I dried off his little bottom as best I could and then tried to figure out how to attach the clean, dry diaper. My first effort was unsatisfactory, leaving a gap along one leg where I could clearly see his miniature penis poking through. I swear he laughed at me. My second effort was a little better and I thought it would have to do.

I picked him up and spread the damp blanket over the back of a chair to dry. He was heavy. I hadn't thought to ask how old he was, what date he'd been born, or if he had any names other than Samant. And Kalyani, of course. I could ask the girl when she returned with the goat. Had she really said she was going to bring a goat? I still didn't know her name.

I sat down and laid the baby in my lap with his head on my knees, his feet kicking my belly and breasts. I drank in his every movement, mesmerized by his odd squeals and burbles. I placed one hand next to his and he grabbed my finger.

"You're a strong fellow, aren't you?" I said. "You're going to be fine, Samant. Nana Mali will take care of you." And suddenly I burst into tears. As I cried, the baby began to whimper, his lower lip quivering pitifully. I clasped him to my breast, and we cried together, grandmother and grandson.

You're an old woman, Malia. How could you possibly raise this baby? What are you thinking? You're not even a healthy old woman. This was a problem. I needed to think.

My tears ceased, but the baby's didn't. I thought he might be hungry, so I found the bottle of milk and offered it to him, cradling him against my heart. He sucked hungrily and before the bottle was empty, he was asleep again.

I was still sitting there, holding baby Samant, when Tao-Min and the others returned from their day's work. They were talking and laughing, but as soon as they caught sight of us they fell silent.

"Malia?" Tao-Min spoke first. "Is that...?"

"Yes," I said. "It's Samant. The girl who fixed your shoulder came and brought him to me. What are we going to do?"

The baby woke but he didn't cry. Tao-Min explained to Shankar and Paul and Simone who this child was and how he came to be in our guesthouse. Everyone wanted to see him, to hold him. Tao-Min and I were both on the verge of tears.

Shankar, fortunately, claimed to have had some experience with babies. He searched through the contents of the basket, coming up with more clean diapers, an empty bottle, and some packets of dried milk, which he explained were a special variety prepared for babies. He pulled out some small soft cloths and a couple of containers of preparations that he described as baby cleanser and skin conditioner. There was also a bundle wrapped in a piece of red silk, which he handed to me. Simone took charge of the soiled diaper and blanket, taking them away to be laundered.

Tao-Min took Samant and she and Shankar watched as I undid the silk-wrapped bundle. It contained several documents. The first was Samant's birth certificate, which was written in both Hindi and English. According to the English version, my grandson's full name was Samant Lalit Mansukh Kalyani and, based on the date of his birth, he was now almost three months old. The remaining documents were only in Hindi, and I handed them over to Shankar for interpretation.

"This one," he said, "is the baby's horoscope. This is a very old tradition here, to record all the details of a child's moment of birth. Samant was born under the sign of Mithuna. I think you call that Twins? His birth was June 2."

Gemini, I thought. And then I thought about my twin sister Sophia. "What else?" I asked.

"His lunar mansion is Rohini, ruled by Chandra, the moon. The deity of that mansion is Pajapati."

"What are these other papers?" I wasn't much interested in horoscopes, but it was nice to have the information. I could tell by the length of the document that there was a great deal more.

Shankar examined one of the remaining pages. "This one is the baby's genealogy, but only on the mother's side."

I nodded, understanding. "And the last page?"

Shankar's eyes softened as he read it. "It's a letter," he said finally, "a letter to Samant from his mother."

"That's a lovely thing," I said, the words sounding awkward to me even as I spoke them. "But I don't think I could bear hearing it right now." I thought maybe he could translate it for me some other time. But then it wasn't for me, was it?

After supper, Tao-Min and I pulled out a drawer from the dresser in our room and placed it on a table between our two beds. It wasn't much but it was a place for Samant to sleep until we could come up with something better. We didn't talk. I think we were both overwhelmed by this sudden change in our lives, uncertain as to exactly what that change meant.

35.

Even if we'd had any Duermata left, I wouldn't have taken it. I wanted to be able to awaken immediately if Samant needed me. He slept remarkably well, while I lay awake most of the night thinking. By morning I was still uncertain about what needed to be done, but I'd narrowed down my options.

Samant began to fuss, so I picked him up and went to the kitchen to heat up the milk preparation Shankar had left in the chillbox. I went back to the room to feed him. As soon as Tao-Min opened her eyes, she smiled and reached out for the baby. I let her finish feeding him. There was a sudden noise, accompanied by a pungent odor.

"Oh," I said. "I think that means we need to look for a clean diaper."

"Let me do it this time," Tao-Min said.

I collected all the necessary paraphernalia and handed it over. I watched while Tao-Min cooed over Samant as she cleaned him. When she'd finished attaching the clean diaper, she picked the child up and turned triumphantly toward me.

"I think you're getting the hang of that," I said as she handed me the wriggling bundle.

"I'll stay here with you today," Tao-Min said. "They'll manage out at the farm without me."

I felt an unexpected surge of resentment. I knew it would be sensible for me to have help looking after the baby and the look on Tao-Min's face as she gazed at Samant told me her offer was not entirely selfless. But I also knew I needed to spend time alone with my grandson. I needed time to think.

"I'd rather you go to the farm, Tao-Min," I said, trying not to sound harsh. "This is just one child, and they are many. Really, I can manage here."

After everyone had left for the farm, I took baby Samant for a walk outside. I paced up and down in front of the guesthouse, not going far, watching my grandson's face as he reacted to the breeze ruffling his downy hair, the call of a bird, the changing rhythm of my gait as I reversed directions. I felt how connected I was to this child and thought again about my options, about how this was going to play out.

The dilemma felt intractable. I thought about where it had all begun, in a coffee shop back in Dallas with one man's unconscionable assault on a frightened girl. Or had it begun with that girl's desire to eradicate the incident, or with her subsequent desire to remember? All of these happenings and many more, small and large, had brought me to this moment, and what I decided to do next would be no less portentous.

Samant fell asleep and I took him back to the room, laying him gently in his makeshift crib. He stirred as if he were about to awaken, so I patted his back and hummed a tune to him until he settled. It was one of Zelda's tunes.

I found my digilet—I never wore it anymore—and screened up the Recall zone page called Returns. I felt the need to check one more time and this time I knew it was Lio I was looking for. I shifted through the photographs. There were a lot of photos. My mind was about to wander off when I saw him. I caught my breath and stared.

Yes, clearly it was Lio. It was Lio looking as young and handsome as he'd been that day in D.C. when he pulsed me the one word, "RUN," right before the corporate cops stormed the Quill & Sheaf. It was Lio with his arm around a woman, a beautiful, youthful-looking woman, who gazed up at him with eyes full of the kind of devotion and love I'd once felt. What was left of my heart—my poor sick, broken, trampled heart—fell into pieces. Through my tears, I read the information panel that accompanied the photograph: "This is Eliomar Gaston. He now goes by the name Edward Barton. He manages a 3Dec outlet in Phoenix, Arizona, where he lives with his wife Brianna. I knew Lio in Washington. He remembers nothing."

I'd been right. Lio was dead. They'd killed him just as surely as they'd killed Zelda's music. I knew now what I would do, and my tears fell in copious, cleansing streams of acceptance.

When Samant woke, I picked him up and I didn't put him down again for the whole afternoon. I babbled on and on to him, telling him all sorts of silly things I suddenly remembered from my childhood, telling him how I thought his father was a decent man, only misguided, although not nearly so misguided as his disaster of a grandfather. I told him that I prayed he would never, ever encounter anyone as viciously misguided as his grandfather. I told him about his two aunties, Leticia and Sophia. "You'll call them Auntie Leti and Auntie Sophi, and they will spoil you with stories and candy." And then my tears started again. I wasn't sure that part would ever happen.

I was still crying when Tao-Min came in, entering our room quietly, I knew, in case the baby might be asleep, which he was. "Malia, whatever is wrong? Is Samant okay?"

"He's fine, Tao-Min. We're both fine. But I need to talk to you about something. Come sit next to me and hold him while we talk."

I explained to her then what I'd decided. "When that plane leaves Mumbai on Tuesday," I said, "I want you to be on it. And I want Samant to be with you. No, don't say anything yet. Let me finish. I'll stay here and I'll meet with the doctor, the one who knows about cardiac problems. If he says I should have surgery, then I'll do it. And when I'm better, whenever he says I'm healthy enough, I'll come and join you in Costa Rica. But in the meantime, I want you and Meli to care for Samant as if he were your own son. Will you do that for me?"

Tao-Min was in tears. I saw her holding the baby closer, as if she were already one of his mothers, even as she tried to argue against my plan.

"I'll wait here with you, Malia. I couldn't leave you."

"Yes you can. You know you need to go to Meli. She's been waiting too long for you."

"But who will look after you here while you have the surgery, while you recover?"

"Paul and Simone have said they intend to stay here and keep working with the children now that they know they've lost all their family in France. Simone will take care of me."

"But..." Tao-Min was running out of arguments.

"Once the doctor fixes me up, I'll come." I couldn't look at my grandson, so I looked up at Tao-Min. "It will be okay," I said. "This is the best way."

It was almost evening when the girl came back with the goat. She'd brought two. "Two goats are required," she said. I didn't tell her Samant was leaving. I knew the children at the farm would benefit from the milk. Sometimes deception is a good thing.

That was Friday. On Saturday Tao-Min spent a half-day at the farm, using the rest of the time to make preparations for traveling to Mumbai with little Samant. Shankar had somehow come up with some cans of milk to send with them.

On Sunday, they set off for Mumbai. Paul went with them to manage the car and to bring it back. They were allowing two days to get there, even though we'd determined that the trip should only take about eighteen hours on the road. "You never know what might happen," I said.

Meli had sent me a pulse, telling me that she hoped to be out of her protective isolation in another week and how much she looked forward to taking care of little Samant for me. Tao-Min confessed that she and Meli had often talked about the possibility of having a child of their own.

Tao-Min and I cried, of course, as we said goodbye in front of the guesthouse. "Don't worry," I said to her one last time. "I'll come and join you as soon as I recover from the surgery."

After they left, I went to our room and cried the rest of the day, my tears blending with the rain that fell gently, incessantly on the street outside. I let Simone in to bring me some supper. She wanted to talk about some plans for the children, but I sent her away. "We'll talk about it tomorrow," I said.

I hadn't wanted to lie to Tao-Min like that, but it seemed the only way to convince her to take my grandson with her. I knew she and Meli would be excellent mothers for him, and he'd have Montagne as his grandfather, Paloma as his grandmother.

I had no intention of contacting the cardiac surgeon, no desire to go through a painful and uncertain operation. I'd take care of my health as best I could and continue taking the pills, which actually seemed to be helping. I'd live out whatever remained of my life here in Jaipur, doing the work that had come to me, taking care of my son's other orphans.

That night, after Shankar left and Paul and Simone had gone off to sleep, I went out on the street. Nights were so dark these days. Tonight seemed brighter. I looked up and saw the full moon. *It's just craters,* I thought. *Craters and shadows. No face, no hare. Why can't we see things as they are instead of as we wish them to be?*

Some people seem happy enough sharing stories that don't square with reality. I knew now I was not one of those people. To surrender to pretty stories, to pretend to see what isn't there—this was something I could no longer do. How much of my life I had spent in the worlds created by stories! I'd created my own stories, too, hadn't I? And I'd put them out there for others to read and experience. Were my stories the kind that lured people into unrealistic delusions? I hoped not. I hoped they were, instead, the kind of stories that opened windows onto the true nature of things, shedding light, inviting fresh thinking, dispelling confusion.

This world has changed, I thought. Humanity, I knew, remained as vexed and vexing as ever. Breathing deeply, I exhaled a wish for the future. The future belonged to Samant and to all the rest of the children—a new generation. My generation was done.

The next day Shankar brought a little truck to take us to the farm, and I assured him I was well enough to join them. I felt useful there. It was astonishing how much I missed Samant, when I'd spent so little time with him. About midday we received a pulse from Paul, saying he'd seen Tao-Min and the baby safely onto the airplane. On Wednesday, Paul returned with the car.

Early Friday morning I received a pulse from Tao-Min: "Arrived in Costa Rica. Samant is fussy but well. Everyone sends love."

I slept unexpectedly well that night.

I rose before dawn, feeling a need to go outdoors. Before going out, I opened the carved wooden box I'd bought at the bazaar and took out the prayer beads. With the beads clasped in my hand, I walked along the street, watching the moon grow larger as it dropped toward the horizon, watching it change from silver to gold. Turning, I saw the first faint traces of dawn in the east and I thought about how this precious blue-green planet turns, always moving toward morning. I didn't know any prayers, but I held the beads close and gave all my heart to the wish for Samant to be happy.

Acknowledgments

I knew there would be more stories to tell about the world I'd created in *Way of the Serpent*. Malia wanted me to tell her story first, but you'll soon be able to read Jonathan Swain's story, too, in *Flight of the Owl*. After that... Let's just say that there are reasons why I refused to call this a trilogy!

I extend special thanks to those who have graciously offered their support and assistance in this continuing endeavor—Elena Sandovici, Steven Zani, Felicia Pheasant, Teresa Roberson, Bonnie Arnett, and Linda Dugger. And I couldn't have done any of this without the expert support of Danielle Hartman Acee of Authors' Assistant.

–Donna Dechen Birdwell, 2016

Shadow of the Hare was originally published under separate cover in 2016.